I0629660

SEL

SEL

SEXY EROTIC LINGERIE

A WILL CHISHOLM MYSTERY

B. C. HOWARD

SEL is a work of fiction. All of the names, characters, places, organizations, incidents, and events are the product of the author's imagination or are used fictitiously. Any resemblance to actual incidents, events, organizations, locales, or persons, living or dead, is entirely coincidental.

SEL. Copyright © 2023 by B. C. Howard. All rights reserved.

No part of this publication may be reproduced, distributed, transmitted, or used in any form or by any means without the express written permission of the author or publisher, except in the case of brief quotations embodied in critical review and certain other noncommercial uses permitted by copyright law.

Hardcover ISBN: 979-8-9878158-2-3
Paperback ISBN: 979-8-9878158-1-6
eBook ISBN: 979-8-9878158-0-9

Book design: Danna Mathias Steele
Cover images: © Chaoss / Adobe Stock

To Columbus

*S*he looked at me like she knew me. Smiled like she knew what I was thinking.

"You're making my nipples hard, staring at me like that, Tom," she said.

Calling me Tom sounded fake. The stiff pressure pushing from inside my black shorts—the only thing I had on—started to ease. But I had picked it. Because every guy I'd known named Tom was boring, nondescript, someone you would never remember. And I didn't want to be remembered.

I stared at her face—a flawless diamond dipped in smooth tanned skin, swathed in waves of silky brunette hair. Her eyes were large hazel gems nestled in settings of long feathery lashes. With a slight upturned nose and full moist lips, she was as erotic as I remembered.

I started to breathe faster.

"I love this open-cup, sheer teddy you picked for me to wear," she said and stepped closer. "It's Allura, my favorite. And black is my favorite color."

She cupped her right breast in her hand, lifted it to her slightly parted lips, slipped her tongue out and caressed her nipple slowly. She moaned softly, then stopped, gazed at me and smiled.

The stiff pressure in my shorts rushed back. I realized I was holding my breath. I let it go.

She slinked closer and said, "I know you're getting hard, Tom."

Calling me Tom didn't matter anymore. I reached down to my shorts, my eyes riveted on her, my mouth open, barely breathing.

She took another step towards me. She lifted her right leg and planted her black stiletto heel on the seat of a metal chair. Then she slid her right hand down to her crotch where a small black satin bow held the slit in her teddy closed. She undid the bow.

"Allura is the most exclusive lingerie in the world," she said. "Exclusive, just like—"

A shrill ring suddenly screamed in my left ear.

I jerked back in my chair and her voice went silent. A faint sound floated from the earphone now resting on my right shoulder. I looked back at the screen. The video continued.

Another piercing ring sounded.

It startled me again. But I kept watching her. She glided her left hand down to the slit in her teddy. Her eyes widened. She mouthed something I couldn't hear.

My cellphone whined at me one more time.

I sighed and paused the video on my laptop just as it zoomed in, freezing the image of her legs spread wide, her fingers opening the slit in her teddy, her lips moaning what seemed like Tom.

I grabbed my cell and looked at the number. I didn't recognize it.

One last obnoxious ring . . .

"Yeah?" I snapped into my cell.

"Oh, I'm sorry for calling so late," a woman's voice said timidly. "Is this Will Chisholm?"

"Who's this?" I demanded.

"I'm, I'm Peggy Grant. I'm trying to reach Will Chisholm of Chisholm Investigative Services. I'm so sorry. I must have the wrong—"

"No, it's okay. I'm Will Chisholm. Sorry, I thought you were a crank caller."

"Oh, Mr. Chisholm," she said and cleared her throat. "Thank you. I know it's late. What time is it? Oh, I'm really sorry. I just couldn't wait."

Her voice was hoarse, like she had been crying.

"That's okay. How can I help you, Ms. Grant?"

"Thank you. I'm sorry—"

"It's okay, Ms. Grant, but it's—"

"You can call me Peggy. Thank you again."

"Okay, Peggy. It's late. Can you tell me why you're calling?"

"I'm shorry—sorry. It's my daughter . . ."

Jesus, she's drunk.

Then I heard her start to weep.

"Give me a second," I said.

I pulled a notebook from the clutter of folders on the table, then tossed the airphones on the keyboard. I glanced at the frozen image on the screen, her sensual lips calling Tom, calling me. I sighed, grabbed a pen, and wrote the date and time at the top of a blank page.

"Alright, Ms. Grant—Peggy, tell me about your daughter."

"She's, she's dead . . ."

I felt like a jerk. Then I remembered she was drunk. Maybe it really was a crank call. Or a joke. But I didn't know any women who wanted to joke around with me anymore, never mind talk to me. Especially at one in the morning.

"Did you say she's dead?" I asked.

She started to cry harder. I felt like a jerk again.

This better not be a joke.

"Ms. Grant—Peggy, is your daughter really dead?"

"Yes. She was murdered," she said and started sobbing hysterically. "My Alyssa was murdered."

A surge of panic raced through me. I stood up and stared at my laptop—the frozen image, the erotic face, the perfect breasts, the sensual legs . . .

This better not be a fucking joke.

"How did you get my name?"

She took a few seconds. It sounded like she was trying to compose herself.

Then she said, "Your business card was in Alyssa's bag. I, I thought you might be able to help. I'm sorry for calling so late, but I need to do something."

Her voice quavered. She seemed close to losing it again.

"Peggy," I said firmly, "calm down and start from the beginning."

The sound of ice cubes rolling down a glass came through the phone, followed by a gulp.

Unbelievable.

She sniffled and said, "My daughter was murdered. I . . ."

I waited a few seconds, then said, "That's okay. Just take your time."

I bent down and wrote some notes: "Alyssa—murdered daughter—last name Grant? / description / when / where / Peggy Grant—mother—drinking problem? / why me? / NYPD?"

She took a deep breath and said, "I don't know where to begin."

"Don't worry, Peggy, I'll walk you through it."

I'd done it a thousand times during my five years with the Boston Police Department. Calm her down. Call her by her first name. Start with simple factual questions. Then let her run with the story and fill in the details after she finished.

But I sensed this time would be different.

"How old was your daughter?" I asked.

"Uh . . . Alyssa is twenty-two."

"Was her last name Grant?"

"Yes. She isn't married."

"Can you tell me what she looked like?"

"She is—I mean, she was . . ."

She choked on a cry and stopped to catch her breath.

I let her recover, then said, "That's okay. How did you learn about Alyssa?"

"Um, the police called me Saturday night. Around three, I think." She started to whimper. "They told me she was dead—murdered . . . behind a strip club . . . all cut up . . . My baby's dead."

I stopped writing.

"What strip club?"

She sniffled loudly.

"Peggy, what strip club?"

"It's in Manhattan. On the West Side, I think. A place called Champagne."

"Champagne?"

"Yes. My baby was a good—"

"Did you say Saturday night?"

"I, I guess it was really Sunday morning. That's what the police said."

I straightened up and turned away from the table. I walked to the middle of my apartment. Five slow steps. The only light came from the small lamp on the table. It made a long shadow of my body that stretched across my bed into blackness and silence. I stared down at the faded, brown-speckled carpet. Maybe stained. I was never sure. There was no more stiff pressure. Just the rapid pounding of blood racing from my heart to my limbs, preparing my body.

"Why did you call me?"

"I, I told you. Your card was in Alyssa's bag. She left it here in my apartment Friday night when she stayed over. That was the last time I saw her."

"The police are working on it. Why call me?"

"You're a private investigator, aren't you?"

"Yeah."

"Alyssa had your card for a reason. Was something wrong? Please, I have to know."

"I don't know why she had my card."

"I need your help, Mr. Chisholm. They said she was strangled with a teddy. And all cut up. They showed me pictures. She was naked. Oh *God*, my Alyssa's dead . . ."

I heard her start bawling again. I closed my eyes and squeezed them as tight as I could. I tried to block out the image of her daughter. My head started to pound. I took several quick breaths. The pain faded.

"Mr. Chisholm . . . Mr. Chisholm . . ."

"What?" I snapped and opened my eyes.

Black and white dots flashed in front of me. The room swirled. I turned and nearly lost my balance. I stepped towards the table, towards my laptop, towards the frozen image—towards her.

"My daughter was a good girl," she cried. "She was a model. She was going to be an actress."

She went back to sobbing. But it was just noise now, bleeding into the silence and blackness around me. I hung my head and closed my eyes again. I clenched my fist.

"Please," she whimpered, "can you help me?"

"I can't. I'm sorry."

"But I think Alyssa knew who killed her."

My eyes shot open. I saw my laptop, her legs spread apart, her breasts reaching out, her lips calling—calling me.

"Why do you think that?"

"Your card."

"What about it?"

"Alyssa wrote a man's name on the back. I think it was to tell you. I think it could be who killed her."

"What name?"

"Tom."

2

"*A*llura Alyssa," I said and gulped down the rest of the pink champagne in my glass.

I had drunk nearly a bottle. It still tasted cheap. But it had some alcohol in it because my head was spinning with the multicolored strobe lights. I suppressed a burp.

"Allura Alyssa," she said. "I like that. Now you have to tell me *your* real name."

She leaned her bare left breast towards my mouth and brushed her nipple along my lower lip.

"I told you," I said. "Tom."

I looked in her big hazel eyes and gave her a sly grin.

"What if I do this," she said and started to rock on my lap. "Will you tell me now?"

The pressure inside my pants grew. I lifted my groin up between her legs, then bit her nipple gently. It was firm and smooth.

"Oohhh, that feels so good," she said.

She stopped rocking and leaned back so her breasts were out of reach. Then she furrowed her brow, pursed her lips, and tapped me on the nose lightly in mock reprimand.

"You're so naughty. You know there's no touching." She giggled, then said, "Come on, I told you my name is Alyssa."

"Only because I said I don't like Brittany."

"I can be anyone you want."

"I like Alyssa."

"What if I don't like Tom?"

"What does it matter?"

I reached to my right and grabbed the bottle of champagne. Poured the last of it into my glass and put the bottle back in the bucket of ice. I raised my glass, winked at her, and took a long gulp.

"It matters," she said, "because I've never told a partner my *real* name before."

"Never?"

"Well, once."

"Hah, so I'm not special," I said and took another swig of champagne.

"It was a cop."

I looked up at the strobe lights. They were mesmerizing. The dark room swayed with the loud music. I suppressed another burp. I had definitely underestimated the champagne. It was starting to taste pretty good.

I turned my eyes back to her. Gazed at her face, her shoulders, her breasts. She was more mesmerizing than the strobe lights. She must have felt me getting harder because she pressed down firmer on my lap and slowly rolled over my groin. The music drowned out my weak gasp, but my eyes widened, bringing a knowing seductive smile to her lips.

"Wait, did you say you gave a cop a lap dance?" I said.

She bit her lip and nodded. I lifted my pelvis slightly so she would rub even harder against the growing bulge in my pants.

"Was he in uniform?" I asked wryly.

The corner of her lips turned up and formed a coy smile.

"What makes you think it was a *he*?"

I laughed, shook my head, and stopped pressing my groin into her. She continued to roll along my lap.

"Okay, so how did you know he *or she* was a cop?"

"I didn't. I thought he was just another dance partner. But then he threatened to arrest me."

"Really? For what?"

"Solicitation."

"What happened?"

"He asked me some questions, finger fucked me until he came, and then left."

"Did he ever come back?"

"I don't want to talk about him anymore."

She leaned towards me, lifted her breasts to my face and cuddled my cheeks between them. Then she sat back, raised her arms, and moved her hands behind her head. She lifted her hair up and tilted her head to the side.

"I *wanted* to tell you my real name," she said. "Don't you *want* to tell me yours?"

"Yeah. It's Tom."

She let go of her hair, placed her hands on my chest and slid them up to my neck, then to the sides of my head. She spread her fingers wide and combed through my hair until they were behind my head, her breasts squeezed together a few inches from my face, her nipples dark and swollen.

I looked up at her eyes. The strobe lights danced behind her on the ceiling. I moved my head towards her right breast.

She leaned back out of reach and shot me a teasing smile.

I grinned and said, "Is Alyssa really your name?"

"It is. Do you like it?"

"I do."

"I like that you like it."

"Why?"

"Because I like you."

"You barely know me."

I reached over and grabbed my glass. Guzzled the last of the champagne and put it down. Then I stared at her face. She didn't seem real.

The room swayed. Maybe because of her. More likely because of the fine champagne.

"This is the third time I've danced for you, so I know you like me."

"Okay, but why do you like me?"

A suggestive smile formed on her lips as she reached out and grabbed my shoulders. She started to rock slowly on my lap again.

"Well, you're not like most guys I dance for. You're not old. And your looks are fire. Are you American?"

"If Boston counts."

"Maybe," she said. "But you're something else too."

"I'm half Cherokee."

"So, that's where those sexy looks come from," she said and rocked a little faster. "I really like them, especially those baby blues and blond hair."

"My hair's brown."

"Close enough," she said and ran her fingers back through my hair.

"You only like me for my looks?" I said, feigning disappointment.

"Nooo," she moaned and grinded on me harder. "You're sweet too. I love how you follow my YouSEL videos. And coming here to see me. I feel desired. That *really* turns me on."

She rotated her hips, opened her lips wide and released a low groan.

"But I have a question," she said and leaned towards me.

"My name's Tom."

"A different question," she said and skimmed her cheek along mine, the smell of coconut oozing from her skin and hair.

"What is it?" I murmured.

She slipped her tongue in my ear and whispered, "Are you old enough to be here?"

I reciprocated with my tongue in her ear and whispered, "Barely. What about you?"

"Barely," she purred, brushed her cheek across my lips and nuzzled her nose against mine. "You really do make me feel special."

"I do?"

"Uh-huh. You know, like more than just a dancer."

"Okay."

"But you want to know the real reason I like you?"

"Tell me."

She started to grind hard on my lap, the warm gap between her thighs firm but supple, her legs squeezing against mine, her hands clutching my shoulders. I forgot about the fine champagne and the name game. I stopped breathing and got so erect so fast that my zipper pushed partially open.

She peered into my eyes and said, "Because I want your big hard cock inside . . ."

3

I opened my eyes. I didn't know where I was for a moment. Then I heard a distant voice calling my name. I looked down. My cell was in my hand. I lifted it to my ear.

"Peggy?" I said.

"Oh, Mr. Chisholm, what happened? I thought you hung up on me."

"No, sorry, I was just taking notes. Okay, I'll take the case."

"You will? Thank you, Mr. Chisholm. Thank you."

"I'll need an initial deposit."

"Uh, did Alyssa already pay you something?"

"She never hired me. She must have gotten my card from someone else. I'll need something to start. Can you pay?"

"Um, yes, I think so."

Money always mattered. I never had any growing up. And I didn't have any now. People lived and died for it. Even killed for it. I'd seen plenty of that. I wanted money, but I was still figuring out how to get it without fucking other people. But I had to take the case, even if she couldn't pay. I had to know if Allura Alyssa was her daughter. And if she really had been murdered.

"Alright, can you meet in the morning?" I asked.

"Uh, I was hoping we could maybe meet now. I mean, in the next hour or so? I live in Brooklyn. I know it's late, but we're both up."

"Now? Peggy, nothing's going to happen before the morning."

She had a reason. I had a feeling I wasn't going to like it.

"I know, but I'm meeting some police detectives in the morning. I told them about Tom."

I was right. I didn't like it.

"What did you tell them?"

"Um, only that I thought Alyssa might have hired you because she was afraid of a man named Tom. I just talked to them today. I mean yesterday—Monday. Did I do something wrong?"

"No. It's okay. What's your address? I'll be there as soon as I can."

She told me it and added, "It's off Flushing Avenue in Bushwick. You can buzz me from the lobby."

"Okay."

"Did you know her, Mr. Chisholm?"

I hesitated, then said, "Your daughter?"

"Yes, did you know Alyssa?"

"No."

I heard her weep softly. Then she stopped and sniffled.

"She was so beautiful," she said. "And funny. I think you would have really liked her."

I didn't know why she thought that. She didn't know me, other than every guy liked a beautiful, funny woman. Maybe the death of a beautiful, funny woman was more tragic than an ugly, funny woman. Definitely more than an ugly, boring woman. But I had never really thought about it before.

Life was ugly. That's why beauty mattered. I was still young, but I had figured that out a long time ago. Fair or not, I could never worship an ugly woman. A beautiful one—yes. I had. Once. And I would never fuck an ugly woman. Most men would. Especially if she was the only option at the time. Maybe beauty was in the eye of the guy and all that, but it had little to do with why most men fucked. Probably most women too. I had never asked. Sex had always been an escape for me. An escape from an ugly life. Sex with an ugly woman wasn't an escape.

But murder was different. You were taking away someone's daughter, sister, girlfriend, wife, mother. Beautiful or ugly—it didn't matter. It was someone else's life. Not mine to take. Not anyone else's either.

"Are you still there, Mr. Chisholm?" she said.

"Yes."

"You didn't know my daughter, but do you know anyone named Tom who might be capable of this?"

I didn't hesitate.

"No."

*P*eggy Grant wasn't anything that I expected. She wasn't that old. Forty, at most. Great body, which she flaunted with a tight white T-shirt and skinny black jeans. Tall too. Maybe five-ten. Strawberry blonde hair. Medium length. No roots. Extremely attractive, for an older woman.

And glassy blue eyes. Glassy because she was drunk. I could smell it.

But that wasn't what bothered me. She looked familiar—too familiar. The sliver of hope I had about her daughter being someone else vanished as soon as Peggy Grant opened the door.

"Mr. Chissholm?" she slurred and gave me a beguiling smile.

"It's Will. You're Peggy?"

"I am. Will? Is that short for William?"

"Just Will."

She leaned against the metal door of her apartment, her arm wrapped around the back like she was holding it up.

"You're not anything like I expected," she said. "How old are you?"

"Old enough."

I stared at her hard without moving. She became self-conscious and straightened up.

"I'm sorry, Mr. Chis—I mean, Will. I'm so rude. Please, come in."

She stepped back and opened the door wider. She swept her bangs away from her eyes, then flashed an awkward smile.

I looked at her for a second, then nodded and stepped in. I put my hand on the door to hold it open. She let go and moved farther back into the apartment. I checked behind the door, my body tensed and ready. Nothing. Just a wall, a mirror, and a crescent-shaped metal accent table. I let the door close. Turned and positioned myself to scan the apartment quickly.

The faint smell of cigarette smoke was the first thing I noticed. Menthol, maybe. I didn't see an ashtray. She smoked, but she wasn't a regular. The smell wasn't strong enough. Probably only when she drank. I knew. I grew up with smokers.

It was a two bedroom from what I could tell. Both were down a short hallway to my left. To my right was a small stylish kitchen with a table under a window. Straight ahead was the living room. A pink couch and two green and pink armchairs sat on either side of a glass coffee table, a plush green rug underneath. Hanging on the wall of a shallow nook was a flatscreen TV with a black cabinet below it that looked like a bar. No empty rocks glass with melting ice cubes.

It was neat overall. She had probably cleaned up before I showed up. And spacious, compared to my place. Compared to most New York City apartments. It was a damn nice setup. She should definitely be able to pay.

I took a couple of steps into the living room. I noticed a sleek black wrought iron bookcase with glass shelves against the wall to my right. Two large black and silver frames sat in the center of the top shelf, angled towards each other. My eyes stopped.

She stared at me. Two different profiles. Two different smiles. The same wide hazel eyes. The same full moist lips.

"Tom," she called.

I stepped towards her.

"Will," she murmured.

My pulse began to race. It was coming back . . .

"Will . . . Will . . ."

"What?" I said and turned my head.

Peggy was standing next to me, her eyes wide and still glassy.

"Are you okay?" she asked.

"Yeah."

I turned my eyes back to the two picture frames. Gazed at the two different photos of the same beautiful woman with hazel eyes. It was Alyssa from Champagne. Now, I was sure.

"That's Alyssa from two years ago," Peggy said and walked over to the photos. "On the left."

She started to tear up. I didn't say anything. I couldn't.

She turned to me and said, "I wish she had met you, Will. She would have liked you. I know you would have liked her. Everyone did. She was so beautiful . . . and funny."

I just stared at her. What was I going to say?

I'm sure we would have hit it off, Peggy. Especially if she was beautiful. And funny. I would have wanted to fuck her too. And I did.

I looked down. I felt guilty, even if the conversation was only in my head. I didn't want to be there. Everything felt like it was closing in on me. Like I was being cornered. I wanted to escape.

But I couldn't. It was too late. Not the time of day. She had my business card. I never brought them to a strip club. Allura Alyssa knew who Tom was before she even met him. I was involved in her murder somehow. I had to figure out how before I was blamed.

5

"*C*an you pay me?" I said.

Peggy looked at me and swayed slightly. She opened her lips but didn't say anything.

"I'll need money," I said.

"Um, okay," she said and hesitated again. "How much do you need to start?"

"I charge six hundred dollars a day. A hundred an hour for smaller jobs."

"Oh," she said and started to chew on her lower lip.

As soon as I said them, I knew it was a bad choice of words. But it was my standard response. When I got my license six months ago, I started out at a thousand dollars a day and two hundred an hour. After a month of cursing at nobody, I cut my rates in half and started to get some work. A few dirty jobs handled well and some good word of mouth had improved business since.

But she didn't seem offended. And it was still a sweet apartment. I figured she could pay a little extra.

I waited a few seconds. Then counted backwards from ten in my head. The alphabet was next, but that was always harder. And it was late. A voice kept telling me to get out of there before I asked for a glass of whatever she'd been drinking and tried to comfort her.

I finally said, "How much can you give me to start?"

She looked up and said, "It's just . . . I'm not working right now."

I hated this part. I studied her apartment again. Not much on the walls. Matching pretentious poster prints of some French festival in the 1930s on either side of the flatscreen TV. A Yankees pennant hung in the small hallway leading down to the bedrooms. And on the wall near the kitchen, two paint-by-number pictures. One was a log cabin in the woods surrounded by snow. The other was a frozen stream with snow covered mountains in the distance. The big strokes of a name were in the lower right corner of each, both beginning with an "A."

"Have you lived here long?" I asked.

"No. Just a few months, but . . ."

I turned my head and looked at her. There was more to the story.

"I had a good job," she continued, "at a store in Midtown. But I was laid off last month. I'm using my savings to get by."

I nodded like I cared. I glanced around again. It was too nice a place. No store I knew paid enough to afford it. She had to have more than she was letting on.

"I can give you five hundred to start," she said. "I promise to pay you whatever it costs."

A tear slipped from her eye. Then her lower lip started to quiver.

"Please, Will, someone killed my baby . . ."

She lifted her hands and covered her face. She started to sob, paused and gasped, then sobbed some more.

At twenty-five, I still didn't know how to comfort a crying woman. I only ever tried when I thought I might get laid. And the woman was hot. This time, I just stood and watched.

When I thought she was done, I said, "Why?"

She wiped some tears away and stared at me, a puzzled look on her face.

"Why what?"

"Why do you need my help to find who killed your daughter? The police are on it."

"That's not why I need your help."

"It's not? Then why?"

"I need you to find my daughter Ashley, Alyssa's twin sister. I don't think she knows about Alyssa. The police believe she might be in danger too."

I stared at her, incredulous. My mouth was half open like words were stuck in there. My eyes darted to the two picture frames angled towards each other. Two different profiles. Two different smiles. The same big hazel eyes. The same full lips. But two different beautiful women.

I closed my mouth and pressed my lips together. Narrowed my eyes and glared at Peggy. I tried to look through her glassy blue eyes to see what the hell was going on.

"Please, I have to find her," she said. "I can't lose both my babies." She started to weep.

"Stop!" I snapped.

She froze, her eyes wide and her mouth agape.

"Who gave you my name again?"

I remembered everything she had told me, but I wanted to see if she corrected me. See if she was lying. Or if she was a good liar. Because all this was too much to believe.

"I told you on the phone that I found your card in Alyssa's bag. She stayed over here last—"

"Show me the card."

"Uh, okay. I'll get it."

She wiped her cheeks and walked down the small hallway towards the bedrooms. She might have been trying to swing her hips and wiggle her ass for me, but she just looked unsteady.

"And her bag," I added.

She looked over her shoulder, brushed her bangs away, and nodded nervously. She came back quickly with a pink nylon gym bag in one hand and an ivory-white card in the other. She put the bag down at my feet and offered me the card.

"It's yours, right?" she said.

I took the card and examined it.

"CHISHOLM INVESTIGATIVE SERVICES" was printed on the front, with the words "*Former Boston Police Detective*" underneath. My full name and the rest of my contact information were there too. Thin, flimsy cardstock. The cheapest I could find. The most expensive I could afford. No question. It was one of mine.

I walked over to the two paint-by-number pictures hanging on the wall by the kitchen. I flipped the card over. "Tom" was scrolled unevenly in blue ink on the back. I looked at the first painting of the cabin in the woods. Ashley was handwritten in big, flowing letters in the lower right corner. I moved my eyes to the painting of the frozen stream. Alyssa was written in large, neat letters, also in the lower right corner.

Peggy came over and stood next to me. Her floral perfume mingled with the scent of gin. The combination smelled erotic. My peripheral vision caught the outline of her T-shirt stretched over her breasts. I felt the blood flowing, the pressure building.

I shook my head. I needed to figure out what was going on and get the hell out of there.

"Something wrong?" she asked.

"Yeah."

I examined the name on the back of my business card again. Then the signatures on the two paintings one more time. I looked at Peggy.

"Three names, three different handwritings. Two women, one man."

She gasped, put one hand to her mouth and the other on my arm.

"You think the man who killed Alyssa wrote his name on your card? But you said you don't have a client named Tom. Could it be a made-up name?"

I stepped away from her. Her questions were hitting dangerously close to home.

"I don't know who gave Alyssa my card. And I don't know who Tom is."

"Please, I need to find Ashley. I think she's in danger."

I sensed it coming before I felt it. The room started spinning. The headache—it was back. I tried to concentrate, think. But nothing made sense. I squeezed my eyes shut. I reached above my right ear and felt the scar under my hair. I heard the shot . . . the bullet . . . the pain . . . I saw Alyssa . . . on my lap . . . stroking my scar . . . moaning . . . The room slowed . . .

"Will . . . Will . . ."

I opened my eyes. Blinked several times. I saw a blurry face, light hair, blue eyes—not hazel, not Alyssa—Peggy. The headache was gone.

"Are you feeling alright?" she asked.

"Yeah. Just a headache."

"Migraine?"

"Bullet."

She gave me a quizzical look.

Then she said, "Can you help me find Ashley?"

"She's your daughter. Why don't you know where she is?"

She looked down, like she was ashamed.

"We had a falling out."

"Over what?"

"This guy I was seeing at the time. But that doesn't matter now. The only thing I care about is finding her."

"This guy, could he have killed Alyssa?"

"I don't know. Maybe. He had a mean streak. But I haven't seen him in a while."

"Is the father in the picture?"

She sighed softly and said, "No. He left when they were little."

"When was the last time you talked to Ashley?"

"Two months ago. She called to get Alyssa's new number."

"Where was she?"

"Columbus, Ohio."

"Was she living there?"

"Yes, I think so."

"You didn't ask?"

"I, I was just happy she called."

"Do you know what she was doing for work?"

"No. We didn't talk long. She was supposed to call me back, but I haven't heard from her. Now I'm afraid something's happened to her. That's why she hasn't called."

She looked like she might start crying again. I paused to give her time to gather herself.

"Did you try calling her?" I said.

"I did, but the number was disconnected. She must have switched carriers."

"Why didn't you ask Alyssa for Ashley's number?"

"I should have, but she didn't want to get in the middle of everything between us. And I thought Ashley would call back."

"Her number should be in Alyssa's cell contacts. The police probably have her phone. Ask them to look it up when you talk to them. Let me know if you get it."

"Okay, I will. Thank you."

"Is there anything else you can tell me that might help?"

"I don't know. I can't think of anything. I just need to know my baby's safe. Please, Will, can you find her?"

"I'll try. But you need to do some work before you talk to the police. Write down everyone and everything you can think of that Ashley was involved with. Anything, no matter how meaningless it seems. And every place she's lived and worked since she moved out. All her friends and family too. Include that ex-boyfriend of yours she didn't like. And her father."

"Okay, but the police said they couldn't help find Ashley because she's not really missing."

"They'll help if they think she knows who killed Alyssa. But they need something to work with. Just write it all down. I need the information too."

She nodded and said, "I'll start right away."

I knew there wasn't much chance of that. I picked up Alyssa's gym bag and slipped my card with "Tom" written on it into my pocket. I gazed at the photos of Alyssa and Ashley for a moment. Then I turned and looked into Peggy's glassy blue eyes. The urge to comfort her was gone.

"I'm leaving," I said. "Call me after you've talked to the police."

"Okay. Why are you taking Alyssa's bag and your card?"

"I need to check her bag and take a closer look at the handwriting on my card."

"But what should I tell the police in the morning?"

"Tell them I have them. They're going to want to talk to me anyway."

6

I fell asleep at four and woke up at eight. I wasn't sure I had even slept. But I wasn't tired. Everything Peggy Grant had said was racing through my head.

Dull, gray light oozed in under the window shades on the other side of the room, spilling onto the clutter covering my table. Outside, the city that never sleeps was already well into its morning routine.

I rolled onto my back and stared at the ceiling. I blinked several times to clear away the haze. The paint was ivory colored, faded and chipped, with old water stains that hinted at its age. A spider sauntered across as if it were strolling along the ground. Maybe it was, and I was upside down. That's how the world felt right now.

An uneasiness swept over me, like I'd woken for a reason. Then the sound of feet shuffling floated in from the hallway outside. I reached over and grabbed my Glock 19 off the nightstand. I aimed it sideways at the door, finger on the trigger guard while I struggled with the sheet wrapped around my legs. I finally yanked it off, sat up and shifted my aim to vertical.

Three quick, loud raps bellowed through the solid wood. The second time, I realized. The first time had woken me. I lowered my Glock and dropped my head. I let all the air out of my lungs that I'd been holding in.

Jesus, what am I doing?

I laid my Glock back down on the nightstand and swung my legs out of bed. I stood up, pulled on my jeans and searched for my T-shirt. It was hiding somewhere. I walked over to the table and grabbed a white envelope. Another knock sounded just as I unlocked the double bolt and opened the door.

Standing in the hallway with her fist paused in the middle of a knock was a thin, medium height Asian woman. Forty-something, she had on an untucked blue button-down shirt, a pair of loose-fitting black slacks, and white sneakers. Her hair was pulled back and tied with a scrunchie. A forced smile greeted me.

"Good morning, Will Chisholm," she said.

"Morning, Sally Jin," I said and offered her the envelope. "June and the rest of May that I owe."

She grabbed it and said, "No bounce this time?"

I half smiled and said, "No bounce."

She sighed. Her eyes widened and warmed.

"You don't have to pay rent today. I don't want bad check, Will. Okay?"

"I know, Sally. I got a bad check too. It won't happen again. I promise."

She nodded and smiled again.

"You late this morning. Got girl in there?"

"Late night working."

She leaned to her left and peeked into my apartment. She nodded and straightened up. Rolled her eyes down my bare chest to my jeans to my feet and back up to my face.

"Look good," she said and giggled.

I smiled and said, "Thank you, Sally. You do too."

Her face turned slightly red. She shook her head, flustered, and turned to leave. She turned back and pointed the envelope at me.

"Too many girls bad for you," she said. "One good girl all you need. Michael say hi."

Michael was her son. He had just finished his second year at MIT. I had helped him smooth over some trouble with the head of a Korean gang about a year ago. He had asked out the guy's younger sister without realizing who she was. It was my first case after I moved down from Boston. Even before I had my private investigator license. It wasn't much of a case. More muscle than investigation. But it was how I found my apartment—a studio, two floors above Jin's Dry Cleaning and Laundry on Grand Street between Chinatown and the Lower East Side. Sally and her husband owned the business and lived in the building as its supers. Sally was the boss.

"Tell him I said hi back. And tell him to stay away from girls."

She rolled her eyes and shook her head, then walked quickly to the stairs and scurried down quietly out of sight.

I shut the door, double bolted it, and took off my jeans. I spotted my T-shirt behind my old brown leather armchair and put it on. I didn't have time for a run if I was going to make my nine thirty meeting with a prospective client. A hard thirty-minute workout in my apartment would have to suffice.

I grabbed my cellphone and put on a local station to catch up on the news. Some woman with a sultry voice was saying it would be cool and cloudy for early June. Then she rattled off headlines about potential candidates for the New York Governor's race, sports scores, and various cultural events. The ongoing investigation of the heinous murder of a nightclub dancer in Manhattan was coming up after a commercial break. I wanted to listen, but I shut it off. I needed to block out everything. The way I would before all my mixed martial arts fights. It wouldn't be in an MMA cage, but I knew a battle was coming. I needed to prepare.

After I threw on workout shorts, I rattled off four hundred crunches, one hundred fifty incline push-ups, and forty pull-ups, with twenty seconds between sets. I was done in twenty-five minutes. I finished with five hard minutes on the heavy bag that I'd just hung over the weekend. The pull-up bar had gone up a month ago. A gym and an apartment in a fourteen-by-twenty-foot room. Not bad for New York City.

I was panting and my T-shirt was soaked with sweat when I took off my bag gloves. I tossed them on the bed and glanced up at the ceiling. The spider was gone. The world felt a little closer to right-side up.

In ten minutes, I showered, flossed, and brushed my teeth, then combed my hair back. It was getting long. I probably needed it cut. But no shave since I barely had to do it every other day. A blessing, I'd been told. But it made it impossible to sport the hipster look. No loss. I hated plaid.

I put on a pair of brown khakis, a maroon polo shirt, and my black leather sneakers that could pass for shoes. There was no spice in my work wardrobe. Two colors of khakis, blue jeans, and three colors of polo shirts generated nine combinations. The cold months had even less style, if that was possible.

My coffeemaker beeped, and I poured a large thermos to go. I made some wheat toast, put jam on it, and wrapped it in tin foil. I stuffed both in my black nylon backpack, then cracked a window so it wouldn't smell like a locker room later. I holstered my Glock and slid it on my belt to the back of my right hip under my polo shirt. Slipped my Ruger LCP II in a side pocket of my backpack and strapped my Ghostrike knife above my left ankle. I tossed my blue blazer on and was ready to head to the office.

Head to the office.

It sounded strange even in my head. All I needed was to kiss the wife, pet the dog, and pick up the newspaper on the way out to complete the fantasy of a life I'd never known and would probably never have.

"Fuck you," I muttered to no one.

I bounded down the two flights of stairs to the foyer. One bare, dull light bulb glowed from the ceiling. A roach tried to scurry away on the next-to-last step, but I was faster. I crushed it. He was big. Just minding his own business. He had probably just kissed his wife on his way to work. Wrong place, wrong time—for him.

My office was in a prewar building on 32nd Street, just off Lexington Avenue in Midtown. It was nine thirty-three when I opened the stairwell door to the small elevator lobby on the second floor. I turned right and walked towards a large plate glass door with block letters that read GELLER JEWELRY. As I got closer, I saw a man in a suit sitting in a cracked black leather chair against the wall to the left of the door. He looked tall and thin and uncomfortable.

I tapped on the glass door. An older man standing behind a counter examining something looked up and smiled at me. He was dressed in a white shirt and black vest, with a grayish beard, side curls and a yarmulke. He reached under the counter with his left hand. I heard a buzzing sound, pushed the glass door open, and stepped in.

"Boker Tov, Rav Geller," I said.

"Boker Or, Will," Simon Geller replied and nodded approvingly. "You've been practicing."

"Probably as far as I'll get. I have to work on my English."

"English?"

"Yeah, I have to learn it since no one speaks Boston down here."

"Ha! That's because it's a dead language. Now Brooklyn, Will, that's what you need to learn." He smiled and nodded again as if agreeing with himself. Then he tilted his head towards the man and said, "You have a client waiting."

I nodded, lifted my backpack higher on my shoulder and walked over to the man.

He stood up and said, "Mr. Chisholm?"

I stopped a long arm's length away—training and experience. Six years ago, I was two months out of the Boston Police Academy making a coffee run as the new guy when I saw a Lincoln roll through a stop sign. I pulled the car over. A stocky middle-aged man in a suit climbed out and spread his arms like he'd just been called out stealing home when he was obviously safe. A driver getting out of a vehicle after being stopped was an immediate threat—training.

I approached him cautiously, my left hand extended, signaling for him to stop moving towards me. He sighed loudly, dropped his arms, and looked up at the sky for help. I got within an arm's length of him, then caught sight of a boy in the back seat. He was shivering and crying.

My eyes darted to the man. A knife was thrusting towards my throat. I snapped a left backhand into his right forearm to redirect the blade. Then I whipped my right elbow around into his cheek, knocking him sideways. I grabbed hold of his right arm, stuck my hip into his groin, and pulled him over my side. He flipped and landed on his back—training.

In one motion, I dropped my knee down into his rib cage and drove my right elbow into his left cheek. I heard bone crack as blood splattered on my face. I hit him with two more elbows, then grabbed his ear, pulled up, and slammed the side of his head into the pavement. The knife rolled out of his hand. A small stream of blood spread out under his head and filled the pock marks in the dirty asphalt—experience.

But not from two months on the job. I learned to fight growing up in suburban Boston slums, then later in an MMA cage. In the street or in the cage, I knew once you had a guy down, you never let him get back up.

I got a commendation for saving a boy from a pervert, plus a medal for the ten stitches in my forearm. But because the guy claimed to have debilitating headaches from my beatdown, I had to take a class lecturing me on the use of excessive force. I'd always been a fast learner. That day, I learned about the screwed-up justice system and to stand an arm's length away from a man in a suit.

"Excuse me but are you Mr. Chisholm?" the man asked again.

He raised his eyebrows and tilted his head down slightly. A good three inches taller than me with a full head of gray-streaked brown hair, he looked somewhere in his fifties. Accustomed to money and respect, with a gentlemanly demanding air. Patient to a point, which I was testing.

At just under six-foot one, I wasn't tall enough to be tall and too tall to be average. But I was intimidating. Or so I'd been told. Except for my face, which was too young looking to scare anyone except kids. Or so I'd been told. He was obviously looking at my face.

"Yes, I am," I said and smiled.

"I'm Richard Morris," he said and extended his hand. "We were scheduled to meet in your office at nine thirty. The sign on your door said to check in here. I've been waiting."

I got it. He was a busy, important man who expected people he hired to be on time and professional. Late, with no espresso waiting, and a Hasidic Jewish jeweler for a receptionist was amateurish. Maybe a nonstarter.

I eyed his perfectly tailored blue pinstriped suit, white shirt, shiny pink tie, and freshly polished oxblood leather shoes. He probably had more than enough money to hire a top firm instead of a one-man outfit like mine. That meant he either wanted something done quietly that was questionably legal, or he had never done this before. Maybe both.

I grabbed his hand firmly, looked him straight in the eye, and shook his hand once.

"I'm sorry, Mr. Morris. Something urgent with another case delayed me. I would have texted you if you had given me your cell number."

"I don't rely on text messaging, Mr. Chisholm. And as I told you during our initial call, I do not want to be contacted by phone or email under any circumstances. I will get in touch with you for any updates I require."

"I remember."

Morris stared at me for a moment. His expression was a mixture of impatience and uncertainty. He glanced around the small shop, trying to appear nonchalant, as if he hired a private investigator every other day. But he was as tense as if he was hiring a hooker for the first time. He probably thought I was something of both.

"Why don't we continue in my office?" I said.

He nodded. I turned my head and thanked Simon Geller in butchered Hebrew. Morris shot me a perplexed look.

I pulled the glass door open, and Morris stepped through without looking at me. He expected people to get doors for him. He waited for me to lead the way. I turned left out of the door and walked down the hallway without looking back. I heard his smooth, long gait following me.

The hallway was painted a light gray, with cracked ridges here and there, confessing more about the building's management than its age. White panels ran the length of the ceiling, interrupted by recessed lights that revealed old stains in the worn gray industrial carpet. A single window, dark from years of dirt and soot, sat at the end of the hallway.

My office was the last door on the left, across from two unisex bathrooms. At the other end of the hallway was the office of a bail bondsman who never seemed to be in. On the other side of the elevator bank, directly across from Geller Jewelry, was Stern & Becker Fine Jewelry, a competing store specializing in gold and silver. A similar hallway ran on either side of Stern & Becker. A three-person law firm that claimed to do it all occupied one end of the hallway. On the other end was a one-man CPA office and a graphic design shop run by a pretty thirty-something black woman I sometimes exchanged stares with when we passed each other.

The place was professional enough that I thought I had gotten a steal for my three-hundred-square-foot corner office with a window looking out onto 32nd Street. That is, until I started to smell something disgusting every few days around five o'clock. It reminded me of the men's room in my precinct back in Boston on the morning after a big night out.

I figured it had to be the fat lawyer on the floor. He always hit the bathroom at the end of the day before heading out, leaving his best work behind to avert starting a stampede on the subway. But the smell continued even after he was out of commission for a few weeks getting a stomach reduction. He was innocent—of that crime.

I looked for a pattern with someone else on the floor. For one bleak week, the pretty graphic designer was a suspect. She would also stop by the bathroom at the end of the day. She'd glance into my office if the door was open and give me a smile. Life was ugly, I knew, but beauty was supposed to be a sanctuary. Then the smell disappeared after a construction project on the floor above me was completed. That's when it dawned on me that the graphic designer was trying to strike up a conversation, but I was oblivious. She lost interest before I realized she had any.

I didn't lose any sleep over it. In my business, everyone was guilty until proven innocent. That's the way I had approached being a cop and then a detective. The presumption of innocence was a luxury for people who had never had a gun pointed at them. Even a beautiful woman was guilty until proven innocent. I knew. It was a beautiful woman who put a bullet in my head.

7

I unlocked my office door, pushed it open, and flicked on the ceiling lights. The air was heavy and a little dank. It always was in the morning. I stepped in and held the door for Morris. He hesitated, then took two long strides and slid to his left to let the door close. His eyes wandered around my office. His jaw tightened every few feet of his disapproving inspection. He finished before his face could cramp up and looked at me like I should apologize.

I stared back at him with a blank expression. Then I turned my head and started mimicking his scan, pretending to look for whatever it was that offended him.

To my right, a beaten-up green leather couch slouched under a window that looked out to the side of another building. In front of the couch was a sailor's chest that doubled as a coffee table and an armory. Straight ahead was another window with a view of 32nd Street. A black swivel chair sat in front of the window and behind a gray metal desk with a computer and a pile of papers on it. Two wooden chairs hung out in front of the desk. In the corner stood a couple of four-drawer metal filing cabinets. A rectangular wooden table decorated with a printer, a flat screen TV, and a broken coffee maker was positioned against the wall on my left. Underneath was a small refrigerator for my beer and water.

I finished the tour of my office and brought my eyes back to Morris. He was staring at me, a slightly offended look on his face. He knew I was mocking him, even though I hadn't said a word. I'd made my point.

"I apologize, Mr. Chisholm. This is new to me. I can be a bit, well, judgmental. But I am aware of my tendencies." He forced a smile and added, "That's what ten years of therapy before you're twenty will do for you."

Morris seemed as genuine as a corpse. I wanted to like him, but I didn't trust people with a lot of money. Not because I didn't have any. In my experience, most people with a lot of money hadn't earned it. At least, not the way I viewed earning something. They had either been handed it or had taken it, which meant they were either spoiled or crooks. A lot were both.

Still, money came in handy. Taking on clients who didn't have money wasn't a smart business model. Unless you wanted to be a cop. I had done that once and liked it. It wasn't an option anymore. Money mattered to me now.

The good thing about my business was that people with a lot of money always seemed to have a lot of problems they wanted to pay someone else to fix. I hadn't figured out yet if the money gave them more problems or if they just looked for excuses to spend it because they had too much. I expected Morris to give me a few insights.

"Please have a seat," I said.

"Thank you," he replied.

Morris settled in the chair on the left. I laid my backpack down next to the chest, took off my blazer and placed it neatly on the arm of the couch. I pulled my notebook out of my backpack, walked around the desk, and sat in the swivel chair. I grabbed a pen, opened my notebook, and wrote the date and time at the top of a clean page. Then I looked up at Morris.

I would normally have a couple of pages of notes prepared when I met with a prospective client, but I had nothing this time. Morris had called me Friday afternoon to request a meeting on Monday—yesterday. He wanted to discuss some confidential work he needed to have done. He offered me two thousand dollars just to meet with him, even if he didn't hire me. The offer was too good to be true. I put Morris on hold while I did a quick online search. His profile looked legitimate and impressive. He even had a Wikipedia page. I jumped back on the call and asked who had referred him. He said I had been highly recommended but insisted on no questions. He added that the meeting could lead to a lucrative engagement if it went well but that his terms were nonnegotiable. I had nothing to lose. I accepted them. He said he would call back to confirm a meeting time.

A sure two grand, with the chance to make a lot more, gave me a reason to celebrate Saturday night. That would normally mean dinner and tequila at a decent restaurant. But I was craving something else. Something that I had been consuming online. Something that wasn't good for me or my wallet. Something that I wanted regardless.

I always used cash at strip clubs. Never credit cards. But I had to overdraw my checking account to have enough for what I wanted at Champagne. I estimated it would cost me about fifty bucks in overdraft fees until Morris paid me the two thousand. It was worth it so no one could track me. I couldn't imagine who would want to, but I always felt like someone was.

When Morris hadn't contacted me by yesterday afternoon, I started to worry that my tendencies would cost more than I could afford. But Morris finally called and asked to meet today instead. I was relieved enough to consider heading back to Champagne. Something had happened there Saturday night. I wanted to see if it would happen again.

But I couldn't chance it. If Morris cancelled or didn't show, I'd be overdrawn on my checking account by more than a thousand dollars. I'd have to borrow short-term from Victor again. If he tried to collect like he had the last time, someone might get killed. I didn't want to have to kill anyone because I couldn't control my tendencies. That would be on me.

Instead, I worked out for two hours. It always helped. With the headaches too. Then I made some pasta and had a few beers. When I was done, I turned on my laptop and signed into YouSEL, the pornography website that fronted as a sexy erotic lingerie retailer. That was last night, before Peggy Grant called. Before I knew my tendencies had gotten me caught up in a murder.

I stared at Morris the same way I used to stare at every victim and suspect when I was on the force in Boston—attentive but no emotion. He stared back at me, his placid brown eyes narrowing slightly, signaling the wheels were turning. He wasn't sure about me yet. I could tell.

I finally said, "Do you have the money?"

Morris straightened up and reached inside his suit jacket with his left hand. I moved my right hand under the desk nonchalantly. I kept a Glock 22 in a holster screwed to the side metal panel next to my leg. It was my old sidearm from my BPD days. I rested my palm lightly on the back strap, out of sight from Morris. He was probably reaching for an envelope, but I wasn't taking any chances. Trust wasn't one of my tendencies.

Morris sensed something and paused. He was perceptive. I was starting to like him. I nodded for him to continue. He seemed to relax and pulled out a white business envelope. He extended it towards me.

"Two thousand dollars," he said.

I grabbed the envelope with my left hand and put it on the pile of papers on the edge of my desk. I continued to stare at Morris. He held a steady gaze on me. After a few seconds, he realized I wasn't going to count it.

He cleared his throat and said, "Please excuse me. I am not quite sure how to proceed."

"This is all confidential. Just tell me what you're looking to have done."

After a brief silence, he said, "I need some work performed, and it is quite delicate."

"What do you mean by *delicate*?"

"I need to have a young man persuaded to stop dating my daughter and to never see her again. I want it done immediately and confidentially."

I took a few seconds to process what Morris had just said. I also wanted to see how he processed it. He was uncomfortable and anxious. It seemed real.

"So, delicate means you don't want your daughter to know you're involved. Is that correct?"

"Yes, that is imperative."

"Imperative? Okay, but I'm guessing *delicate* means more than just that."

Morris seemed reluctant to respond, like he didn't want to say what he knew he needed to. Words he couldn't retract. Words that would commit him. Maybe implicate him.

He took a deep breath and said, "Mr. Chisholm, I will pay you fifty thousand dollars if you accomplish what I've asked. Ten thousand dollars today to start, another ten when the young man breaks up with my daughter—or she breaks up with him—and the remainder a month later to make sure he doesn't return. I will guarantee you twenty thousand dollars even if you are not successful, assuming you have made a bona fide effort, which I will decide. Any expenses will be reimbursed."

Morris reached inside his suit jacket again, slowly this time, and pulled out another envelope. He laid it down in front of me.

"That is a cashier's check for ten thousand dollars," he said.

Offering me fifty grand for a job that should take less than a month caught me off guard. But the twenty thousand minimum almost knocked me off my chair. Then the voices in my head reminded me that no job for that kind of money was ever easy. The questions started to line up.

"That's a lot of money just to run off a boyfriend," I said.

Morris's demeanor became more intense. He leaned forward slightly.

"My daughter is at a very vulnerable time in her life. She is becoming a woman, but with that comes nature and confusion, particularly with respect to men. I do not want her to make decisions today that will irrevocably determine the course of her life. Despite my age and privilege, I am not naïve about young people and their needs. I have witnessed too many young promising lives destroyed by impulsive and reckless behavior. This boyfriend has all the markings of a young man who will drag my daughter down such a path. I have tried to discuss it with her, but I have only alienated her more. She is an only child. Her mother died three years ago. I cannot replace what her mother was to her. God knows I have tried. I must acknowledge my limitations if I want to prevent her from ruining her life. Please understand that money is not a constraint when it comes to protecting my daughter."

It was a long-winded rationalization for wanting to stop his daughter from getting pregnant by this guy. I thought about asking if he'd heard of contraception, but sarcasm would come across as insolent. He'd attribute it to my age and inexperience. Maybe cost me the job. Besides, he thought he knew about young people. For fifty grand, I'd take his word. Either way, it answered my question about the money. I was feeling better.

"I get the picture," I said. "What would my expense budget be?"

"No preset limit. Your discretion on anything in the ordinary course of your work. I will need to approve anything extraordinary."

"Would offering this guy a hundred thousand dollars to get lost be extraordinary?"

"Yes."

"Would that bust the budget?"

"No."

"What would?"

"Mr. Chisholm, you will be representing my interests while completing the task for which I hired you. While I do not want to pay more than is needed, I will pay just about anything required to persuade this young man to get out of my daughter's life."

I sat back in my chair. Something felt wrong. I reached up and touched the scar above my right ear. No sensation. It was something else. Then it registered. Morris had just said money was no object for the second time. I had been slow on the uptake. Probably because the idea of a fifty-thousand-dollar payday had numbed me for a moment. But if money was no object to Morris, was there anything he wouldn't do to get rid of this boyfriend? More precisely, was there anything he wouldn't sanction me doing to get rid of him?

"What if it will take more than money to convince this boyfriend to stay away from your daughter?"

Morris didn't respond. He pursed his lips and continued to stare at me.

"The not so delicate part of delicate," I added.

Morris nodded and said, "As I stated, I will pay whatever is required."

Morris would pay anything required, but I still wasn't sure for what. Smearing the guy to get his daughter to break it off? Roughing him up to scare him away? Killing him?

Life was ugly. That's why my profession existed. I had no problem doing the dirty things it took to be good at it. I could rationalize almost anything if it paid enough. But killing for money was a line I wouldn't cross. Maybe the only one. I hadn't been doing this long enough yet to know.

"I won't kill him for you, Mr. Morris."

Morris's eyes widened. His head started to shake vigorously.

"No, no. I am not talking about anything like that. I could not condone that."

I sat forward and said, "Then what could you condone? Exactly how far are you asking me to go to get rid of this boyfriend?"

"I mean . . ." Morris paused, then sighed quietly. "What I mean to say is that I am willing to have you pay someone for incriminating or embarrassing information on him. Or even hire another girl to show interest in him and then . . . well, I think you see."

I stared hard at Morris for a few seconds. I couldn't tell if he was just a wealthy overprotective father trying to scare a loser boyfriend away from his daughter, or if he really wanted me to kill the guy but didn't want to be on the record for it—the indelicate part that could get him indicted.

My voices told me Morris was up for anything short of killing the boyfriend. It felt like a good rationalization. For fifty thousand dollars, I could work with it.

"Okay, but if I have to get *really* delicate with this guy, it will cost you another twenty thousand."

Morris sat back, his shoulders loosening. With the terms of our deal set, he seemed to be pondering me, trying to size up who this kid was that he was entering into business with. The discussion was now about money—his world. He looked me up and down, glanced around my office and settled his eyes back on me.

"Are you always this difficult with prospective clients, Mr. Chisholm?"

I nearly smiled. He probably wanted to call me an asshole, but he never used that kind of language. Maybe not even in his thoughts. The quick look around my office was his way of suggesting I was in no position to be difficult or an asshole. He was right. But that had never stopped me before.

"Mr. Morris, if you want to pay a lot more to get one of the big, well-dressed firms to fix your problem, it's your money. I'm sure they'll take the job. But they won't get the results you want, and you'll likely lose that confidentiality you're so worried about. We both know that's why you're talking to me instead of them." I paused for effect. "None of them can do what I do. It's your money, but it's my neck. I don't make mistakes. If I seem difficult, that's why."

I sat back in my chair. Attentive but no emotion. Bluffing my balls off.

Morris continued his silent appraisal of me. Then something seemed to change. The look of a father worrying about his daughter replaced his calm calculating expression.

"I agree to your terms," he said. "But Rachel cannot know any-thing about my involvement. That is imperative."

There was that big word again. He seemed to like it. I nodded and picked up my pen.

"Let's start," I said. "First, your daughter's name is Rachel?"

"Yes. Rachel Elizabeth Townsend Morris."

"Okay, tell me who this boyfriend is, what he does, and where I can find him."

"Don't you want to know more about Rachel?"

"Eventually, but the boyfriend is the problem, not your daughter. You're hiring me to fix that problem, not your relationship with her."

Morris tensed and glared at me, his brown eyes no longer placid. It was the first hint of anger I had seen in him.

"Mr. Morris, I'm not judging anything. This is how I work. Let's start with the boyfriend's name."

"Mitchell Dugan."

"How old is he?"

"Twenty-one, I believe."

"How old is your daughter?"

"Rachel is seventeen. She's a junior at Greenwood Academy in Greenwich."

I nodded like I understood the problem—inferior, low-class muscle-head screwing his high school little girl. But I didn't. I had fucked seventeen-year-olds when I was twenty-one. They were all legal. And beautiful. I had never thought a second about their fathers.

"Is Dugan in college?"

"He supposedly attends Manhattan Community College, but he is basically a security person for a gentlemen's club called Champagne. I assume you have heard of it."

I stopped taking notes. It was my turn to tense. The air suddenly felt heavier, the walls closer. I tried to slow my mind and think. It couldn't be a coincidence. It felt like another setup. Or the same one. If Morris was part of it, I could kiss the fifty thousand dollars goodbye, along with the minimum. More questions and no answers. Just like Alyssa Grant's murder.

But I had to play along. I couldn't toss Morris out of my office if I wanted any chance of figuring out what was happening to me. It felt like a game. I needed more information to know if I had already lost.

Morris noticed my reaction and said, "I did not mean to offend you. Gentlemen's clubs—"

"You didn't"

"It seemed—"

"Don't worry about it."

I stared at Morris until he nodded.

"So, Dugan is a bouncer?" I said.

"That is correct. He is a large man, quite tall and very muscular. He may be good at his job, but he is not good for my daughter."

"I'm sure he's not."

Morris frowned in indignation.

I ignored him and tried to remember who had been at the door Saturday night at Champagne. All the bouncers had been big. But Mitchell Dugan was probably one of the white ones since his name was Irish, and he was dating a rich, white girl.

"I assume Dugan is white," I said.

"Yes, of course. He is very Irish looking with reddish-brown hair."

I froze. Saturday night at Champagne was still fuzzy, but a memory started streaming in my head. A big Irish-looking kid with tightly cut red hair was escorting Alyssa and me in an elevator up to the private floor for big spenders. I remembered wondering why a bouncer was bringing us up. It hadn't bothered me at the time. It did now.

I shook my head to stop the virtual video. I released the air I had been holding in my lungs.

This isn't a coincidence.

Morris stared at me and said, "Are you okay, Mr. Chisholm?"

"I'm fine. Does Dugan have a nickname?"

Morris thought for a moment, then said, "Rachel calls him MM on occasion. She told me it stands for Monster Mitch."

The streaming video restarted. I was sitting upstairs at Champagne, watching Alyssa stand on the toes of her three-inch stilettoes and kiss the big, Irish kid on his cheek.

She stepped back and said, "Bye MM. Give Rachel a hug for me."

Shit.

8

$\mathcal{S}$omething deep in my brain kept screaming to be heard, telling me it was a bad idea to go back to Champagne. But I had to. I didn't trust much of anything, especially coincidence. Alyssa Grant's murder, Morris and his daughter, and Champagne were all connected somehow. Right now, the connection was me.

A voice kept telling me I was being set up. The last time it was this loud, I got a bullet in my head. I took my hand off the steering wheel, reached up and felt the scar above my right ear under my hair. No headache. Just a bunch of voices arguing up there. The loudest was shouting that I had to know.

I always had to know. Ever since I was a kid, I had to answer any question that came into my head. If I didn't, it would continue to grow, like a tumor, pressing my skull from the inside out. It was more than a tendency. More than a need. It was a compulsion. Maybe even an obsession. An obsession that was taking me and all my voices back to Champagne.

But I waited a day. I needed time to think, to listen to my voices. I also wanted to see if anything came from Peggy Grant's meeting with the NYPD. I thought they might come knocking. Ask politely to speak with me. But they never showed. I never heard from Peggy Grant either. Instead, my voices had a nice long discussion about everything.

With twelve thousand dollars and an expense account, I could afford to take my Cadillac out of the garage. I kept it in a parking garage on Essex Street, a few blocks north of my apartment. I had a deal with the old Portuguese guy who ran the place. He let me keep it there without paying in exchange for a good tip whenever I took it out. I saved money. He made money. The corporation that owned the place got a little screwed. A little payback to balance the universe.

My Caddy was a black 2010 CTS-V Coupe with a hundred ninety thousand miles on it. Other than the powertrain, a few body panels, and the beige leather seats, nothing on it was original. I bought it off an old Vietnam veteran when I returned from Afghanistan. He sold it to me for a song after we shared a few war stories. It turned out to be an expensive song. The repairs cost more than the car. I did most of the work myself. But it was worth it. I put a hundred thousand miles on it in Boston.

New York was a different city. Almost no one drove themselves. If you could afford it, someone else drove you—taxi, rideshare, limo, chauffeur. If you couldn't, you took the subway or bus. It was a city where you couldn't trust anyone. But to get around, you had to trust someone. Today, I could afford not to. It felt good. I hit the gas to pass a taxi on the West Side Highway and headed up to Champagne.

A little past noon, I pulled up along the curb a block down from Champagne. I parked on the other side of the street to get a good view of the front entrance. I half expected New York's finest to be outside waiting. They wanted to talk to me about Alyssa's murder, even if they didn't know it yet.

It was quiet. No unmarked cars, no media, no yellow tape. And no customers. Just one side of a thick oak double door propped open to get some air. I turned my car off and sat there, watching and thinking and remembering.

"But you want to know the real reason I like you?" Alyssa said.

"Tell me."

She started to grind hard on my lap, the warm gap between her thighs firm but supple, her legs squeezing against mine, her hands clutching my shoulders. I forgot about the fine champagne and the name game. I stopped breathing and got so erect so fast that my zipper pushed partially open.

She peered into my eyes and said, "Because I want your big hard cock inside me . . . Ooh, Tom . . ."

She suddenly stopped and raised her pelvis off my lap. Gazed into my eyes and ran her finger along my cheek to my lips. She was panting, an eager smile on her face. I was panting, a lustful longing on my face.

"There's another room where we can be alone," she said.

I nodded.

"Don't worry, no extra charge," she said. "We can use it with special partners when we want."

I nodded.

"Let's go," she said.

Before I could nod again, she jumped off me. She slipped into her G-string and bikini top effortlessly, then strapped on her heels, turned and stood over me. Her moist full lips curled up into a mischievous smile. She reached her hand out like she was asking me to dance. I took it, lifted myself up from the couch, and grabbed my blazer.

She pulled my hand and led me towards the back where a purple velvet curtain covered the entrance to a hallway. She brushed the curtain aside, and we stepped behind it. It swished closed.

The hallway was dimly lit, about fifteen feet long and five feet wide. There was one black door in the middle of the wall on the left and two similar doors evenly spaced on the right. At the end was a door with an exit sign over it. She pulled my hand and walked quickly to the door on the left. She opened it, yanked me inside, then closed and locked it. She turned to me.

I felt very drunk but still scrutinized the room instinctively. It was probably eight feet wide by ten feet long, with mirrors covering half the wall area and the entire ceiling. The rest of the wall space was painted a deep red. In the middle of the room, a dancing pole ran from the floor to the ceiling. A long purple velvet bench sat against the wall to the right, and a dark red leather couch stood against the wall to the left. Three of the walls had lights with heart-shaped fixtures. Recessed spotlights in the ceiling shuffled between different colors, giving the room a strobe effect and making my head spin.

Alyssa brought her body up against mine. I dropped my blazer. She wrapped her arms around my neck and started kissing me aggressively. Our teeth brushed together as her tongue pushed hard inside my mouth. I put my arms around her bare back. Reached up and grabbed her hair tightly with my right hand. I swirled my tongue around hers while running my left hand down her back, squeezing her buttock, and working my fingers between her legs. Her muffled groans made me harder. I lifted her leg around my hip to reach farther under her and pushed my fingers deep inside her. She shrieked, then pulled her lips away from mine, lowered her leg and stepped back.

She grabbed my hand and said, "Come over to the couch."

We walked over and stood in front of it, kissing passionately again. She stepped back and slipped out of her G-string and top. All she had on now were her stilettos. I gazed at her. The lights and alcohol combined with her stunning body to create a hallucinogenic sensation. I barely breathed in anticipation of what would come next.

She slinked over to me and started lifting my polo shirt. I pulled it off and tossed it to the floor. She undid my belt and then my pants button. She slowly unzipped them as our tongues played with each other, our lips open and barely touching. I massaged her breasts with one hand, rubbing the moist folds of skin between her thighs with the other. She moaned loudly.

I kicked my shoes loose. She squatted down and pulled my pants off. She grabbed my penis, stroked it several times, then worked her lips around it. Everything started to go faster from there.

The room swayed with her oral stimulation. Then I lifted her from her position and swung her around onto the loveseat so that she was on her knees staring in the mirror and away from me. I dropped down, spread her legs and buttocks from behind, and started to work my tongue around her clitoris slowly, then faster as she cried for more.

Just as her body began to quiver, she rolled over to face me. She grasped the back of my head, and pulled me forward, propelling her lips onto mine, her tongue moving frantically, her hands pulling on my hair.

She pulled her lips back and said, "I want to be on top."

I sat down in the loveseat, and she climbed onto my lap. I felt lethargic from the alcohol, but I was still as hard as I could remember ever being with a woman. All her smells were erotic and intoxicating. She worked me inside of her and started to grind and bounce. She dropped onto me, and I thrust inside her. She screamed and I groaned. We started writhing in undulating rhythm. She began to tremble, and my muscles tensed like they might snap. I held my breath, then gasped for air with each plunge, over and over and over.

She cried, "Don't stop, Will!"

"Aah! I'm going to come . . ."

"Come inside me . . .

9

*U*ntil now, that night with Alyssa had been mere fragments of distorted consciousness floating in a black hole. I hadn't been that drunk since I was fifteen. Which was strange since I only recalled drinking two beers and most of a bottle of champagne. I didn't remember a headache coming on either. Maybe it had, and the alcohol had made everything worse, including the memory loss. There were still gaps I needed to fill in, but most of it had come back to me.

Alyssa knew who I was that night. I remembered now. She had called me *Will*. Someone had tipped her off. Someone who knew who I was. Probably the someone who gave her my card. It wasn't a coincidence. Murder never is.

I snapped out of my trance and focused my eyes back on Champagne. A large black bouncer in a loose-fitting gray suit, purple shirt, and black tie stepped out of the door and looked around. His head was shaved, and he had a tightly cropped moustache and beard. After turning his head in both directions, he yawned long and hard, then went back inside.

He was there to greet the *nooners*—the guys who dipped in during their lunch hour for a quick drink and whatever else they could afford. But they probably hadn't shown up since Alyssa's murder. No one wanted to risk being caught sneaking out of Champagne in the middle of the day by some reporter with a camera. The nights had probably been slow too.

I felt like a cliché sitting there scoping out Champagne—the criminal returning to the scene of the crime. I didn't have much experience with that kind of behavior, though. I was a beat cop for half my time on the force in Boston. Narcotics after that. The crimes I saw involved money and drugs. Any violence was the result of someone trying to steal one or the other from someone else. Most perps wanted to get away afterwards. Not relive the sensation. The few rapes I responded to were different, uglier.

I didn't think I was returning to the scene of my crime, but I needed to return to be sure.

Walking into Champagne and asking about Alyssa would be looking for trouble. The last thing anyone wanted was some asshole bringing up the murder that was crushing business. They wanted it to go away quickly and quietly, so that the nooners and regulars would return.

Richard Morris had given me a cover story to approach Mitchell Dugan. Rachel was close to her older cousin Jake. He lived in Boston and was a couple of years younger than me. But I looked younger than I was. According to Morris, Dugan had never met Jake. My plan was to pretend to be him and get Dugan to talk to me. I'd chat about Rachel, then work Alyssa into the conversation to shake the tree and see if anything fell out. There was a decent risk it would get contentious. My voices were screaming something about fools and angels. But I needed to know if Dugan was part of a setup.

I knew he was working because I had called Champagne and asked for him. The woman who answered thought I was another reporter trying to get information, but I convinced her I was Dugan's brother. He was Irish. He had to have siblings. Fifty percent chance of a brother. She said he'd be in at noon and hung up.

"It's twenty dollars to visit," the woman behind the glass window said.

She was Hispanic of some sort. Young and full bodied, with a Brooklyn accent. She reminded me of the girls I knew from Somerville and Revere but without the gum.

Fortunately, she wasn't the cashier from Saturday night. I remembered her. She was thin, black, and hot, with a short purple bodycon dress that showed off her perky nipples. You were supposed to think she was just a whiff of what was inside. No guy questioned the thirty-dollar cover charge after looking at her. She had spent a few extra seconds joking with me while she counted change for my fifty. Then she gave me a big smile and a wink. I was special, like the hundred guys that night before me and the hundred that would come after me. Except for the caress of her middle finger as I reached for my change through the small opening. She pulled it back slowly. Only fifty guys probably got that a night.

I gave the Brooklyn cashier a crisp new hundred-dollar bill from the two grand Morris had paid me. I inspected the booth while she made change. Two small surveillance cameras hung conspicuously from the ceiling behind her to record the customers. Another camera looked down from the ceiling just above her to make sure she didn't skim any cash. I turned my head slightly and eyed two more cameras hanging from the ceiling behind the big black bouncer who was waiting to greet me. Anyone coming into Champagne was captured on video. It was all familiar.

The cashier slid my change through the small opening in the window and gave me her best seductive smile. I shot her a quick smile back and grabbed the cash. I didn't give her a chance to stroke my hand. I turned and looked at the big black bouncer, making sure I kept the cash visible. He didn't seem to recognize me, which was good, because I didn't recognize him.

He flashed a big toothy smile and said in a deep voice, "How you doin' today, sir?"

"Good now," I said and smiled back.

His eyes wandered down to the cash in my left hand and then back up to my eyes. He was probably six foot three and at least three hundred fifty pounds.

He smiled again and said, "I got ya, bro. A little relaxation, a little lovin', then back to the grindstone. Anything I can help you with?"

I grabbed a twenty with my right hand and folded it in half twice. Then I palmed it and reached to shake the big bouncer's hand.

"I hope so," I said.

The big bouncer grabbed my hand smoothly, and I let the twenty slide into his palm.

"Thank you, sir," he said. "So, what can I help with?"

I released his hand and said, "Is Mitchell Dugan around?"

The big bouncer smiled casually and said, "You a friend?"

"I'm his girlfriend's cousin."

"You're Melissa's cousin, eh?"

"Uh, I'm Rachel's cousin. Who's Melissa?"

"Oh, right. My bad. I know Rachel. You from Jersey too?"

I smiled. This guy wasn't an idiot.

"Nah, I'm from Boston. And Rachel's from Greenwich. So, can you tell Mitchell that Rachel's cousin is here?"

He grinned, turned, and waved for me to follow him. He started walking down a short hallway into the club.

He glanced over his shoulder and said, "What's your name, bro?"

"Jake."

"Okay, Jake. Relax inside. I'll tell Mitch you're here."

At the end of the hallway, he turned left, pushed open a big swinging door, and disappeared. I turned right and wove across the floor to the far corner. I sat down at a small table with two chairs near a metal door that had a red "EXIT" sign over it. It was the same table I had sat at Saturday night when I first walked in. I remembered a sleezy host escorting me to the table as if I had made a reservation.

A buxom black waitress in a silver beaded thong and bikini top hustled over. She wasn't very tall even in three-inch heels. I didn't recognize her either. I hadn't recognized anyone yet. Maybe Champagne had a day crew and a night crew—bottom shelf, top shelf. Alyssa was probably from the private reserve.

"Hi there, handsome," the waitress said with a big smile. "What do you want to drink?"

"Sam Adams, please."

"Do you want to run a tab?"

"No, thanks."

She frowned. No big tab, no big tip.

"Would you like me to send anyone over?" she said.

I wasn't there for that, but I still thought about it for a moment. If I didn't give her an indication of interest, every girl in the place would saunter by and try to sit down.

"Yeah, but let me have a beer first, and then I'll let you know."

Her expression perked up—big tab, big tip.

"Great," she said. "I'll be right back with your beer."

She hustled off, and I took a gander at the room. I had only spent a beer's worth of time on the first floor the three times I'd been there previously. I had asked for Alyssa each time, although her dancing name was Brittany, which made me cringe. She would come over, and we would be whisked upstairs before I could finish my beer. I thought it was just great service, but now I wondered if there was more to it.

The first floor was a big square for the most part, with a two-story high ceiling that had glittery strobe lights dangling from it. An assortment of other lights filled the room with low wattage glare that reflected like the moon on the black and mirrored walls. The white tiled floor had embedded spotlights covered by flush pebbled glass. A large vagina-shaped stage with three dancing poles was positioned against the wall to my right, directly across from the entrance. It looked out over a floor of empty black square tables and chairs. They had been packed the previous times I'd been there. On the other side of the stage was an alcove with cushioned booths where customers could get more intimate dances without going upstairs to the high-rent district.

A short bar with stools ran across a wall to my left. A skinny but shapely blonde bartender in a turquoise bikini top was behind it opening a bottle of Sam Adams for the waitress. A pair of elevators interrupted the wall straight across from me. They shuttled customers to the upper floors to spend more money for longer and more realistic fantasies.

The second floor was the Bubble Room, the upper middle-class option for customers with higher expense limits. It had a balcony that overlooked the first floor.

The third floor was The Cork Room. It was exclusive, which meant anyone willing to spend a minimum of one thousand dollars, whether you could afford it or not. I'd seen plenty of working-class stiffs up there blowing their rent money. It was an addiction for some guys. For me, it was a tendency. And only because of Alyssa. That's what I told myself. Rationalizations were expensive at Champagne.

The music and lights today weren't nearly as overwhelming as last Saturday night. I was able to hear the quick, determined clicking of the waitress's heels from across the floor. She stopped at my table and bent over to set my beer down, giving me a closer view of her cleavage. She straightened up, tilted her head, and eyed me with a teasing smile.

"I think you're a brunette man," she said. "Tall, good boobs, a little bad."

My muscles tensed. I scanned the large room quickly, barely moving my head. Checked my peripheral vision and tried to sense if anything was moving near me.

Nothing.

I turned my eyes back to the waitress and glared at her like she had just screwed something up. I wanted to see how she reacted. If she became self-conscious.

Nothing.

She tossed her head the other way, rested the round bar tray on the big curve of her bare hip, and stuck out her lower lip. She lifted her eyebrows to signal she was waiting for a response.

"Don't tell me you're into blondes," she said, feigning exasperation. "I'm usually good at picking what hot guys like you want." She shook her head slowly and furrowed her brow. She was thinking hard. "No, you're definitely a brunette guy."

Without taking my eyes off her, I reached nonchalantly for the bottle of Sam Adams with my left hand. I slid my right hand partially behind me to be able to quickly grab my Glock. I nodded like I was processing her assessment, then raised the bottle to my lips and took a quick taste.

She sighed and said, "Well? That brunette over by the bar is asking about you. I guarantee you'll like her. You want me to send her over?"

She was working hard. I respected that. It wasn't going to get her anywhere. I wasn't a *nooner*. But she didn't know that. I set the bottle of Sam Adams down on the table. Before I could say something to stall her, the swinging door by the entrance opened out.

Mitchell Duggan stepped into the room, stopped, and looked around. He was bigger than I remembered. Six foot five easily and probably two hundred fifty pounds of muscle, with ten pounds of a little extra around the middle that most people wouldn't notice. He had closely cropped, reddish-brown hair. He was wearing dark slacks and shoes and a white dress shirt that stretched across his chest. It was untucked and the sleeves were rolled up like he was getting ready to clock in for his shift. He locked on the waitress and strode towards her.

She turned and started walking towards him. Her heels echoed in eerie rhythm with the music. They both paused for a moment when they reached each other. Dugan shot her an intense look followed by a quick smile. She touched his arm, then continued towards the entrance hallway.

Dugan approached me with a sense of urgency. His large shoulder muscles seemed to swing the rest of his body forward with each long step. About ten feet away, he slowed and broke into a big fake smile.

I stood up and moved out from behind the table. I gave him a big fake smile back.

He extended his right hand and said, "Jake? I'm Mitch. Rachel didn't tell me you were stopping by."

I stepped towards him and positioned my feet to be able to react to anything he might do. I had no clue if he was buying my story, but I wasn't counting on it.

I grabbed his hand. I had good sized hands. Nothing extraordinary, but I could palm a basketball easily. Dugan's hand was extra-large, even for his size. And his grip was strong. I instinctively tried to match it.

"Good to meet you, Mitch. I didn't tell Rachel because I'm only in the city for the day. I had some extra time, so I thought I'd stop by and introduce myself. She's told me so much about you."

Dugan released my hand and said, "All good, I hope."

"Yeah, all good."

"Are you going to see her before you head back to Boston?"

"Unfortunately, I don't have time. I really wanted to meet you and maybe talk a little about Rachel if you can."

"Sure, okay. Um, we should talk outside. My boss doesn't like us doing personal stuff in the club. Let's go out here."

Dugan walked to the metal door with the exit sign above it. He shoved it open easily with one hand. Sunlight and the muffled sounds of traffic poured into the room. He stepped onto a cement landing, held the door open, and jerked his head for me to follow him.

I stepped outside and blinked several times to adjust to the bright sun. The landing was about three-by-six feet with two cement steps to the left that led down to a ten-foot-wide alley. The side of a long brick building rose directly in front of me. To my right, the alley ended at the street in front of Champagne. To my left, it intersected with another alley that ran behind both buildings. Yellow crime scene tape and three emergency cones blocked the intersection.

I knew I had less than a second to prepare if anything was going to go down.

My peripheral vision caught something to my right—a shadow under the metal door that Dugan was holding open. It moved, I moved. I stepped and leapt off the landing, twisting my body in the air so that I'd be facing Dugan and whoever was behind the door when I hit the ground.

Even before I jumped, I had decided not to pull my Glock. If someone had a gun, it would have been stuck in my face by now. No one was going to shoot me and create more bad publicity that might get the place shut down. The plan was to rough me up, not kill me. I was going to play along to find out more. At least until the first swing, which would come from me.

The metal door slammed shut as I touched down on the cracked asphalt, six feet from the cement landing. I took several steps back. No one was charging me, so I stood up straight and looked at Dugan. The big black bouncer was standing behind his left shoulder. A short muscle-bound white guy with a shaved head was standing to Dugan's right. I assumed he was a bouncer too. He and the big black bouncer were only wearing T-shirts on their upper bodies. They probably expected blood and didn't want to mess up their work shirts.

Dugan jumped lithely to the ground. He was clearly an athlete. The short stocky white guy followed. The big black bouncer walked down the steps. The three of them stood shoulder-to-shoulder ten feet away from me. Dugan took a step towards me and stopped. He started to unbutton his shirt. His square jaw was clenched in anger. His blue eyes were burning.

"Don't even think about running," he said. "I'll catch you, and then I'll beat you even worse than I'm going to."

"I'm just here to talk," I said. "You're not fast enough or tough enough to play with me."

"Fuck you, asshole," the stocky white guy snapped. "He runs a four-five forty. You know what that fucking means?"

"Means your scrawny white ass is ours," the big black bouncer chimed in. "Just stay put and take your beating. Only way to minimize the pain."

I sized up the big black bouncer. Rolls of fat pressed through his white T-shirt. I looked at the short stocky white guy. He had outsized, steroid-grown muscles. I turned my eyes back to Dugan.

He undid the last button on his shirt and pulled it off like he was getting out of a wet suit. His arms and chest were thick, with the definition of muscle built naturally from repetitive weightlifting. His white T-shirt only made him look bigger.

They were all tough looking. But looking tough had nothing to do with pummeling someone unconscious, close up with your fists and elbows and legs. Being brutal and relentless until someone tapped out. Or died. Few people understood what it was like to physically beat someone into submission—what it took emotionally and psychologically.

But I never assumed anything about an opponent except that he wanted to kill me. These guys looked tough enough to try.

Still, they weren't very smart. That was a fact, not an assumption. They never thought I might have a gun. Brains mattered in street fighting, as much as anything.

"You a football player?" I said to Dugan. "Four-five is fast. If it's true."

Dugan stepped over to the cement landing and laid his shirt neatly over the edge. Then he moved back to standing just ahead of the other two bouncers.

"Fast enough to chase you down if you run," he said. "Tough enough to beat the hell out of you for what you did to Alyssa. And smart enough to give you to the cops when I'm done."

That answered just about every question I had. Dugan remembered me from Saturday night. I wasn't going to earn my fifty grand today. But they hadn't called the cops yet. They planned to soften me up a little first.

"Is this any way to greet Rachel's cousin?" I quipped.

Dugan took another step towards me. His hands were curled into fists, and his face was red.

"I've met Jake, asshole," he growled. "I don't know how you know his name or Rachel's, but you just gave me another reason to fuck you up."

Dugan flashed a look at each of the bouncers. The stocky white guy on his right moved quickly to my left. The big black bouncer on his left moved less quickly to my right.

I needed to make my move before they both got out of my peripheral vision. This wasn't the movies. No one can defend against an attacker you can't see. You might get lucky if it's just one, but not two at the same time. And definitely not with a third guy the size of a linebacker coming straight at you. They had over eight hundred pounds between them. I was one hundred ninety-five. Not great odds. Not even decent odds. But I'd had worse.

I still didn't want to flash my Glock. One of them might get stupid, and I'd have to shoot him in the knee. I'd be taken into custody. It would be all over the news. No one would talk to me after that. I'd have no chance of figuring out who killed Alyssa and how I was involved.

No Glock—yet.

To put them all down, I had to strike first *and second*. The big black bouncer was likely the slowest and easiest to take down. He'd be last. Dugan was big, strong, and fast. But he didn't move like a fighter. He telegraphed and exposed himself. No scars on his face either. He hadn't been in any real fights. He'd be second. The short stocky white guy would be first. He was lower to the ground and moved like a wrestler. His nose had been broken at least once, and he had several scars around his eyes. He'd seen his share of brawls. He was the most dangerous.

I glanced at him. He was closing the distance as he moved to get behind me and out of my line of sight. I looked back at Dugan. He was edging closer, starting to tense his muscles, preparing to attack. The big bouncer was still in my peripheral vision to my right, moving slowly.

Without a flinch of warning, I lowered my head and rushed Dugan. He startled, then came at me. Before we collided, I planted my right foot and pushed off to my left, redirecting my body and avoiding him. He flailed by me.

The stocky white guy was coming in low at my legs. I lunged by his shoulder and whipped my left fist sideways into his face, just under his nose. His head snapped back violently. A warm splatter hit my cheek. I landed behind him, grabbed him around the neck, and threw him to the ground, driving my knee into his spine. Then I spread my hand across the back of his shaved head and slammed his face into the asphalt. I heard something crack, followed by a muffled groan.

I looked up and saw Dugan shuffling towards me with his right fist raised. His legs were spread wide and even with each other. He wasn't a fighter. I jumped up to a boxing stance, bounced towards him and faked a right punch. He instinctively raised his left arm for protection. I spun my body clockwise, whipping my right leg up and around. The side of my heel hit him in his right cheek with a force that had knocked out several opponents during my MMA days. His head jerked sideways towards his left shoulder. He staggered, then buckled and fell to one knee. I wound up and hammered my fist down into his right cheek. He crumbled to the asphalt, his eyes rolling back in his head.

Out of the corner of my left eye, I saw the big black bouncer coming at me with a right-hand haymaker. I snapped my head back to avoid his punch. It grazed my chin. His legs were slow, but his hands were fast. His left fist whipped around for a one-two combination. I ducked to my right. As his fist sailed by, I wrapped my left forearm around his, and pulled it into my chest. Then I punched his elbow joint as hard as I could. He screamed and fell to his knees cradling his elbow. I immediately hit him with a hard right into the bridge of his nose and sent him sprawling.

I jumped back and turned to check on Dugan and the stocky guy. Dugan was starting to stir. Blood was flowing from a wide gash high on his right cheek. The stocky guy was still flat on his face. A small pool of blood had formed around his forehead.

Then I sensed something moving and spun my head around. I saw the big black bouncer swinging a long rusty pipe down at me.

"Motherfucker!" he screamed.

Shit.

I turned my back to absorb the strike. A sharp pain lashed across my shoulder blades. I tumbled to the ground and rolled onto my back. I whipped my left leg up and whacked his right wrist with my foot. The metal pipe flew out of his hand and landed five feet away. He hustled to pick it up, then turned back to me, his left elbow tucked into his side for support.

I snapped up from the ground into a defensive stance. My back was burning. Something warm was seeping down, soaking my shirt under my blazer. It wasn't sweat. I stepped back. I'd had enough. I reached around to my back hip and pulled out my Glock. I aimed it at the big guy's head.

"Drop it or die," I said.

"You ain't gonna shoot," he sneered.

He thought I was bluffing. I was. No need to kill anyone today. But why would he risk it?

Then I heard pounding feet echoing in the alley behind me. I crouched down and turned sideways so I could see who was coming while keeping an eye on the big guy.

A voice yelled, "Police! Drop the gun! Now!"

10

*T*he clock hand echoed in the ten-by-twelve-foot room. Hollow and monotonous. Like a lonely faucet dripping mournfully in the middle of the night.

It was a round clock, high on the wall, with black trim and a white face. Black hands and numbers. The hour hand between four and five. The minute hand between six and seven.

The room was cozy, if you liked bland and cold. It had bright fluorescent lights, cream-colored walls, beige tiles, and a rectangular gray metal table with four chairs. There was also a large one-way mirror reflecting everything in the room. And a black metal door.

My eyes settled on the mirror. I saw myself in a wrinkled polo shirt with my hair tussled and a greasy sheen on my face and arms. I'd been in a similar room more times than I could remember. Usually with my back to the mirror. Not usually with my hands cuffed to the table.

I was alone in the room but not alone. I glanced at the camera in the corner of the ceiling to my right. Then I stared at my reflection in the mirror, wondering who was watching me on the other side. I offered a smile, then looked at the clock above the door. I turned back to the mirror and raised my eyebrows to say: How much longer are you going to play this game?

My upper back was still numb from the Procaine the physician's assistant injected before sewing me up with fifteen stitches. No Obamacare to pay for it. The emergency room at the hospital was going to bill me. I'd pay, assuming I wasn't in jail.

Two uniformed officers and two detectives in suits had shown up just in time to see me pointing my Glock at the big black bouncer's head. The two officers had their handguns drawn while they shouted and sprinted towards me. They didn't care that it was three against one. Or eight hundred plus pounds versus one hundred ninety-five. Or that no one had been shot. They ordered me to drop my gun and lie face down on the ground, arms and legs spread. Then one of them told the big bouncer to drop the metal pipe and to sit on the cement landing. The other cuffed me. Extra tight to make it hurt. I was guilty.

They called an ambulance for Dugan and the stocky white guy. Dugan was half conscious, but the stocky guy was still out. I didn't think he was dead. I didn't care either way except that it would create problems. More of those, I didn't need.

The two detectives stood back while I was cuffed. Then they walked over to the big bouncer. One of them kicked me in the head as he brushed by. Natural, like he didn't realize it. Like it was an accident. It wasn't. I was guilty.

I glared up at the detective. He stared down at me and smirked. He looked Hispanic. The other one looked Italian or something close. They stopped a few feet in front of the big bouncer.

"You wanna tell us what the fuck is going on here?" the Italian detective said.

His Long Island accent hurt my ears. Hailing from outside of Boston, it probably shouldn't have bothered me so much. But no one heard their own accent. Given that my hands were cuffed and my face was rubbing against gritty asphalt, I kept my complaints to myself.

"Just a misunderstanding between that dude and one of the girls inside," the big bouncer said. "Happens all the time. All taken care of. Don't want any more problems, officers."

The Hispanic detective looked over his shoulder at Dugan and the stocky white guy.

"Doesn't look like those two will be misunderstanding much for a while," he said. "One guy did this? Did he threaten to shoot you or something?"

The big black bouncer furrowed his brow. He didn't want to share what had happened. Especially since things hadn't gone as planned. And he didn't want things to go any further. That would be bad for business, which would be bad for him, to go along with his dislocated elbow.

He tilted his head and said, "You showed up here quick. Who called you?"

"Who the fuck do you think?" the Italian detective said.

The big bouncer shook his head and said, "Don't know. Wasn't me. But like I said, just a misunderstanding. Everything's cool now."

"Yeah, right," the Italian detective said, "and we were just in the neighborhood passing by."

"Shut up, Ron," the Hispanic detective snapped.

The big bouncer gave them a skeptical look. For me, it confirmed what I had thought. No one had called to report that three guys were about to kick the crap out of me. The cops were headed there before I even showed up.

When the ambulance arrived for Dugan and the stocky white guy, the two detectives hauled me up and walked me out to the street in front of Champagne. The Italian detective went to shove me in the back of their unmarked car but realized my back was bleeding.

"This asshole's bleeding," he announced to the Hispanic detective. "We'll have to stop by the emergency room."

The Hispanic detective stuck his mouth next to my ear and said, "You get blood on my seat, I'll give you worse than you gave those boys back there."

At least the physician's assistant who stitched me up was nice. Older than me by ten years but worth eyeing while she worked. Sandy hair, brown eyes, thin lips, good shape. I was in cuffs with no shirt on, muscles tensed because of the pain. My shorts were sticky from dried blood. Not my best look. I decided not to ask for her number.

I stared at the mirror and smiled at myself and whoever was behind it.

Then the black metal door swung open.

11

*T*he two detectives entered the room and walked to the other side of the table across from me. They each pulled out a chair and sat down in unison, enough space between them to afford an unobstructed view of me to whoever was behind the mirror watching.

The Hispanic detective was on my left, a manilla folder in front of him. A nicely tailored, dark gray suit was accompanied by a white shirt and green tie. Mid-forties with thinning black hair combed to hide it, he cared about his looks. He was about five-ten, two hundred pounds. A little heavy all over but solid. He had a slick watch to go with his nasty air. No ring.

The Italian detective sat across to my right. He had on a loose-fitting, light gray blazer, powder-blue shirt, and dark blue tie. He was about my height but thicker in the middle and slimmer in the arms and shoulders. His nose had been busted a few times. Some gray in a full head of black hair. Maybe fifty, with a cheap watch and wedding band. A tough guy. Nothing more.

The Hispanic detective opened the folder and pretended to read what was inside. He raised his eyebrows a couple of times and ran his tongue across his teeth, all for effect. I'd been part of the same routine enough times to know. Then he turned his eyes up and looked at me.

"I'm Detective Gomez," he said. "This is Detective Ginelli. You're in serious trouble, Mr. Chisholm."

My instinct was to be a wise ass. Ask if there was a lesser kind of trouble I might qualify for. I hadn't been Mirandized, and it was too soon for any of the bouncers to have filed charges against me. My concealed carry license was in order, and the wound on my back justified pulling my gun. Unless they had something else, all they could do was talk at me and try to get me to talk back. But bantering with them would be a waste of time. I needed to talk to the person behind the mirror. Especially since my back was starting to ache. I wanted whatever was going to happen to get happening.

I stared at Gomez without responding. He puffed his chest out and scowled at me. His eyes were dark brown, close to black, and slightly bloodshot. They said: *I don't like you.*

His lips said, "You think this is a joke?"

I continued to stare at him without answering. He didn't like it. I was supposed to be intimidated. Just another punk for them to break. He must have skimmed over the part in the folder that said I'd been a cop.

He turned to Ginelli and said, "We got a strong silent type. Probably thinks he's a tough guy."

Ginelli nodded at Gomez, then turned and stared at me. His eyes said: *I want to fight you.*

His lips said, "Gotta be a tough guy to rape and murder four strippers."

Ginelli's grating accent didn't stop me from picking up on his remark—four strippers. He wasn't a hyperbole kind of guy. I saw Gomez cringe slightly out of the corner of my eye. Ginelli had screwed up. It was more information than they were supposed to share with me.

Before I could say anything, the door opened. Gomez and Ginelli's heads swung immediately to their right. A tall man in a sharp navy-blue pinstripe suit, white shirt, and red tie walked in holding a manila folder. He was in his mid-thirties, with an athletic build, slightly dark skin, and black wavy hair. He was a mix of something light and dark. A half-breed, like me.

He was the person behind the mirror. Or one of them. He didn't want to take the chance that Gomez and Ginelli would slip up and divulge more information. I figured he was the good cop. Good cop, bad cop, bad cop. Nice twist, but still the same game.

The good cop stood for a moment and sized me up. He gave me a look like he was sorry about how they were treating me. It wasn't his intent. He was there to help. I could trust him.

"Mr. Chisholm, I'm Inspector Jaworski," he said. "I apologize for the rough treatment. Standard for a murder investigation, as you know. Detectives Gomez and Ginelli were just following procedure until I got here. You've been a detective. You understand."

He placed the manila folder on the end of the table to my left and slid smoothly into the chair that was there. He glanced at Gomez and then focused on Ginelli.

"Ron," he said, "uncuff him, please."

Ginelli dutifully pulled a key out of his blazer pocket, reached over, and unlocked my handcuffs. A good performance. Jaworski had probably written the script. I trusted him now.

My back was aching more, and my wrists were sore from being handcuffed for four hours. I was exhausted, and my head was spinning from not having eaten or drunk anything since this morning.

"Can I go?" I said.

Jaworski smiled for a second and replied, "Sorry, not yet."

"Unless you're going to charge me for not letting those bouncers kick my teeth in, I don't see any reason why I'm still here."

"I just came from talking to those three gentlemen," Jaworski said. "In case you were worried, they'll all be okay, although a couple of them will be out of commission for a while. And no, they won't be filing any complaints against you. They all said it was just a misunderstanding."

"That's what I keep telling these fine detectives. So, I can go, right?"

Jaworski sighed and shook his head slowly. I was forcing him to do something he didn't want to do. He straightened up in his chair and looked hard at me.

"You know what this is about, Mr. Chisholm. Those bouncers wanted to kick your teeth in for the same reason we want to talk to you. You can work with us, or you can make things difficult for yourself. I can keep you here for a long time as a material witness. We're going to find out who murdered Alyssa Grant. Don't you want to help?"

It had been a long day of threats. The three bouncers, Gomez and Ginelli, and now Inspector Jaworski. I felt like I had been grappling on the mat in a cage all day waiting for the bell to signal the round was over. I was still waiting, getting angrier by the second.

"Can—I—go?" I said.

Ginelli snorted and said, "Who do you think you are, kid?"

Gomez looked at Jaworski and added, "We need to take the kiddie gloves off with this punk."

That's what I was to them—a punk. The street trash they used to smack around when they were first cutting their teeth as cops. I had grown up with the same punks. But I wasn't one of them. They didn't know anything about me. Or the cardinal rule of the streets—never pick a fight with someone you don't know.

I ignored Gomez and Ginelli and kept looking at Jaworski. They didn't like it, but they had to take it. They weren't in charge.

Jaworski continued to stare at me. He shook his head slowly again, as if he was disappointed with me. But I could tell he was holding back his anger. He glanced at Gomez and Ginelli and then looked down at the folder in front of him.

"This kid," Jaworski said as he opened the folder, "is a bona fide war hero. Served in Afghanistan. A bunch of medals. He was even recommended for the Congressional Medal of Honor." He glanced up at me with a mocking expression, then looked back down. "But it says here you were kicked out of the Army instead. Quite an about face.

Then you joined the Boston PD. Got fired for drug possession and—ooh—getting shot by a prostitute. Nice. And what's this? You were charged with manslaughter in high school? Fortunately, the charges were dropped." Jaworski sat back and stared at me. "That's a lot of violence for a young man."

I could feel the blood rushing to my head. I didn't care what he was implying about Alyssa Grant's murder. Or what any of them thought about my past. But I didn't like being reminded about what had happened with the Boston PD. That memory was too painful. Psychologically and physically. I reached up and felt the scar under my hair above my right ear. I didn't realize I was doing it until I caught Jaworski eyeing me. I slid my hand down to my neck and rubbed it like it was stiff.

Then I felt it coming on. The sensation of blood racing to my legs. The same feeling before you faint. A wave of nausea moved up from my stomach. I felt lightheaded, with ringing in my right ear. Pain spread across the back of my head.

Please, not now . . .

I fidgeted in my seat and tensed all my muscles. I closed my eyes and rotated my head. I felt my neck crack. The sensation eased. The nausea and ringing faded. Sweat dripped down my back, soaking through my polo shirt. I opened my eyes. Gomez and Ginelli were staring at me like a pair of hyenas.

I looked at Jaworski and said, "If you want my help, you need to give me more information."

"That's funny," he said. "I was going to say the same thing to you."

His smug eyes remained on me for a moment before moving to the mirror.

He looked back at me and said, "Maybe someone else can convince you to cooperate."

A second later, the black metal door opened. A woman walked in—a strikingly beautiful woman, tall and thin, with exquisite curves. Her medium length, shimmering dirty blonde hair was pulled back over her left ear. She had deep green eyes, a straight nose, and hearty lips, all encased in smooth, olive skin. A black skirt suit and open-collared white blouse hugged her body. Adorning her neck was a single string of pearls, accompanied by matching stud earrings. She held a yellow legal pad in her left hand and a blue pen in her right.

Alyssa Grant was the last woman I'd seen who was as stunning. But this woman was different—high end. The figure that drew your eye in a crowd. She had drawn my eye before.

"This is Assistant District Attorney Sorenson," Jaworski said. "I believe you know each other."

Brittany.

"Hello, Will," she said.

I couldn't talk. I hadn't seen her in almost a year. Since I was released from Boston Metropolitan Hospital, fragments of a bullet still in my head, that I blamed on her.

12

"This is Detective Gomez, and this is Detective Ginelli," Jaworski said to Brittany.

Gomez and Ginelli stood up. She ignored them and lingered looking at me. Her eyes were tentative. A shadow of a smile creased her lips, then vanished. She turned to Gomez and Ginelli.

"Detectives," she said and nodded to them.

"Good to finally meet you," Gomez said.

"So, you're the new ADA," Ginelli said. "Heard a lot—"

"Detectives," Jaworski interrupted, "we'll take it from here. Thank you."

Gomez and Ginelli stepped around Brittany to the door. Gomez opened it, stole a last look at her, and left with Ginelli in tow. Her entrance and their exit were part of the script.

When the door closed, Brittany walked to the chair Gomez had been sitting in. She took out a handkerchief and wiped the seat and back. Then she folded the handkerchief so the contaminated side couldn't touch her skin and slipped it back into her suit pocket. She sat down and started writing. When she finally looked up, her face was stoic.

She stared at me for a few seconds, coldly refamiliarizing herself. Then she glanced over her left shoulder at the one-way mirror.

She realized I was watching her and caught herself. She refocused on me.

There was someone behind the mirror she wanted to impress. It made sense. She was too inexperienced to be the lead on a murder case. I assumed she had told her boss we dated back in Boston while she was in law school. It was more than that, but she had probably minimized it. Her boss was using her to make me uncomfortable, to get me to make a mistake, since I was guilty. She was there to screw with my head. I would have done the same if I were her boss.

Jaworski watched Brittany stare at me. I could see him out of my peripheral vision. There was something in his look. He was enamored with her. I could tell. I'd walked in those shoes.

He broke the silence and said, "Mr. Chisholm needs some coaxing to tell us what he knows. Maybe you can convince him to cooperate."

She acknowledged Jaworski with a quick glance, then looked back at me.

"How are you feeling?" she said in a slightly raspy voice.

"Thirsty," I said. "And my back hurts."

She turned around and said to the mirror, "Can we get a bottle of water and a couple of Advil?"

She turned back and stared at me. My turn.

"Thanks," I said.

"You're welcome."

My turn again. She waited for me to say something. She should have known better. Getting information out of me was harder than making law review at Harvard. Her words when we first started dating. But it was now her job. She fiddled with her pen, her eyes hardening by the second.

After a long silence, she sighed quietly and said, "You need to tell us what you know about Alyssa Grant's murder."

I frowned and replied, "I'm sure you know a lot more than me. Why don't you tell me what you know first, and I'll see if I have anything to add?"

She examined me for a moment, then said calmly, "We know more than you realize, Will, but there are things we don't know that we would like your help with. It will help you too."

She surprised me a little. Except for calling me Will, no other foreplay. No effort to exploit our history together. Straight to the standard interrogation tactics: *We know what you did, but it will go easier for you if you confess.*

"So, helping you will help me," I said and paused as if I was thinking. "Okay, just tell me what you *don't* know, and I'll see if I can help."

Her jaw tightened. I was making her look bad to her boss behind the mirror. That was fine by me. I was pretty sure I looked like hell. My back throbbed, my shorts were stuck to me with dried blood, and I had already nearly passed out. I didn't care how she looked to anyone. I just wanted out of there.

She turned to Jaworski. They had a silent conversation for a few seconds. Preplanned, I assumed. Part of the show. Then she nodded to him.

He pulled something out of the folder in front of him and slid it across the table towards me. It was a photograph of Alyssa from the stomach up on an autopsy table. She was naked, her skin no longer tan. The glare of the examination lights and lack of blood flow gave her skin a bluish-white hue. There was a ragged slash down each cheek. Both breasts had three irregularly shaped lacerations across them above the nipple. The wounds were a deep dark red, almost brown. Abrasion marks circled her neck where she had been strangled. Her eyes were closed but seemed smaller than I remembered. Her lips rested together, full but no longer moist. Her hair still flowed effortlessly around her face, but it looked darker against her skin, and limp.

The essence of her physical beauty was still apparent even in the grim photo of her death before me. I thought about this private I had served with in Afghanistan. He was a philosopher, of sorts. He always insisted that there was an essence to life, apart from the physical, that could transform the soul to impossible reaches of beauty. The more bodies he saw, the more insistent he became. I always wanted to believe him. But I knew that life had a dark and violent essence too. An essence that could destroy a person's soul. I had seen it many times. I was staring at it once again—the essence of a soulless killer.

I pulled my eyes up from the photo and gazed at Brittany. She looked back at me, searching for something in my reaction. I was angry. She could tell. But she was looking for something else. I could tell. She was looking for guilt. It was there, hiding. But not the guilt she was looking for. Not the guilt of a murderer.

"Do you recognize her?" Jaworski asked.

"Yes," I said and continued to stare at Brittany.

She turned her head to Jaworski, nodded again like she had before, then looked back at me.

He pulled something else from the folder. He slid it across the table towards me the same way he had done with the picture of Alyssa. I looked down. Three photographs were spread out at different angles, partially overlapping the one of Alyssa. They showed three different young women, all on autopsy tables, all naked from the stomach up. Slashes on their faces. Lacerations on their breasts. Strangulation marks around their necks. All once beautiful. All now dead.

"You recognize them too?" Jaworski asked.

I glanced at him but didn't respond.

"Maybe these will help," he said.

He tossed several more photos across the table towards me. They were pictures of the crime scenes. The one of Alyssa stopped at the edge of the table just in front of me. I stared at it. Her naked body was stretched across the asphalt in an alley. Something black was wrapped around her neck. There were slashes across her chest and face. Yellow tape in the background.

Memories of that night with Alyssa welled up in my head. Then revulsion took over. I had seen worse crime scenes, but this felt different. I forced myself to focus on each victim—the blonde, the redhead, the black woman, and Alyssa. All young. All naked. The same wounds.

The same black lingerie around their necks. The locations were the only difference.

It was enough to confirm my suspicion. They thought I was a serial killer.

"Well?" Jaworski snapped.

Before I could say anything, the door opened. Detective Ginelli walked in and stepped over to the table. He placed a plastic bottle of water down next to Brittany. Then he opened his right hand and let two rust-colored pills slide out. They tumbled across the table, one stopping on the crime scene photo of the black woman and the other just in front of Brittany. Her head shot up. She gave Ginelli a scolding look. The kind you'd give a dog after it had done its business inside the house. He quickly slinked out of the room.

After the door closed, Brittany pushed the bottle of water towards me. I grabbed it, then reached over and picked up the two pills. I popped them in my mouth, opened the water, and chugged half the bottle. I screwed the top back on and glared at Brittany while I squeezed the bottle just shy of crushing it.

"Do you recognize any of the other three women?" she asked.

"No," I said.

"Are you sure?"

"I think so, but I can't be completely certain."

I was a good liar—very good—to other people. But not to myself. When we were together, Brittany could never tell if I was lying. But she knew I was lying now. I could tell.

Jaworski leaned over the table, stretched his arm and placed his index finger on the photograph of the blonde on the autopsy table. He tilted his head to eye me.

"Lauren Warenski," he said, then moved his finger to the redhead. "Samantha Kerry." He stretched a little farther and tapped his finger twice on the photo of the black woman. "Heather Smith." He sat back in his chair and leered at me. "Does that jog your memory?"

I looked at him and said, "I don't recognize any of those names. Who are they?"

Brittany interjected: "Lauren Warenski was twenty-four, single, attended Union Community College, and worked as a dancer at *Executive Privilege*, a gentleman's club here in Manhattan. Samantha Kerry was twenty-six, single, and danced at *The Expat Club*, another Manhattan strip club. Heather Smith was twenty-one, single, a student at Garden State University. She worked at *The Landing*, a strip club near Newark Airport. They were all raped and murdered. The wounds were post-mortem. The bodies of Lauren Warenski and Samantha Kerry were found behind the clubs they worked at. Heather Smith's body washed up in Arlington Marsh Park on Staten Island. You already seem to know about Alyssa Grant. All their murders were in the news over the past six months. I'm surprised you don't know anything about them."

I felt like I had just been punched in the windpipe. An illegal strike in MMA matches, but deadly effective in street fights. Brittany had taken off the kid gloves. Fortunately, the sensation of not being able to breathe was all psychological.

"I read about them," I said, "but they dropped out of the headlines pretty quick. There was nothing in the media about them being connected."

"So, you think they might be connected?" Jaworski said.

"Probably just a coincidence," I quipped.

"You think you're funny?"

"Never thought about it. What do you think?"

Jaworski turned to Brittany and said, "You dated this punk?"

She clenched her jaw and scowled at him. He had crossed a line and knew it. He pressed his lips together, turned his eyes back to me, and glowered in silence.

Brittany looked at me and snapped, "What do you know about YouSEL?"

First a punch to the windpipe and now one to the gut. How did she know about YouSEL? I had bought bogus credit card information from Victor to set up different accounts. He wasn't on their radar. My name never showed up anywhere in connection with the site. Nothing could be traced back to me. But I didn't believe in coincidence. They knew more than I realized. That's what Brittany had said.

"You what?" I replied.

"Y-O-U-S-E-L," she said in a monotone. "YouSEL. S-E-L stands for sexy erotic lingerie."

"And what is YouSEL?" I asked.

"It's obviously a website," she said. "It sells risqué lingerie using interactive videos. Customers pick the lingerie and watch women model it live. It has a premium membership that lets the customer pick the model and the lingerie and then watch the model strip and masturbate. Interesting business strategy. I thought you might know about it."

"Why would you think that?"

"Because all of the victims were also YouSEL models."

She set me up for that one.

"I don't know anything about YouSEL," I said. "The only victim I knew was Alyssa Grant. And I only knew her because she danced at Champagne."

"You asked for her at Champagne the night she was murdered. It was the third time you'd gone there and requested her."

My pulse quickened and my mind started racing. I thought about lawyering up and shutting the whole thing down. But I needed to know everything they knew. I had to keep the fight going a little longer.

"If you have something to ask me," I said, "then you should get to it."

"Why did you ask for Alyssa Grant?" she said.

"I liked her. I'm sure she had a lot of regulars."

"Why did you ask for her the first time? How did you get her name?"

"I went to Champagne and saw her dance on stage. I asked who she was, and they said her name was Brittany."

Brittany stiffened, paused for a moment, then said, "She also went by Brittany on YouSEL."

"Just get to your real question," I said.

Jaworski jumped in: "Alyssa Grant's co-workers said you found her on YouSEL and then stalked her at Champagne. That's what you did with the other victims too, isn't it?"

Brittany flashed a scathing look at him. He stared at her for a moment, then sat back in obvious frustration. He snorted and gestured with his hand for her to resume.

She looked back at me and said, "We know you have an account with YouSEL under an alias. That's where you first saw Alyssa Grant. Premium members can see where a model dances if she wants to advertise it. Alyssa Grant's profile indicated the nights she danced at Champagne. The same with Lauren Warenski, Samantha Kerry, and Heather Smith for their clubs. Right now, detectives are searching your office and apartment. They'll find the desktop or laptop you used to log onto YouSEL. We'll link the IP address back to the site and get your user information and search history. It will be better for you if you give us the information voluntarily."

They seemed to keep forgetting I had been a cop. Telling a suspect what you know is an interrogation technique used when all you have is a theory and no hard evidence. The aim was to scare the suspect into talking.

But they were swinging and missing. My laptop wasn't in my office or my apartment. It was in a hidden compartment in the trunk of my car. And my car was still parked a block away from Champagne. If they knew where either one was, we wouldn't be playing this game.

Brittany stared at me like an interrogation lamp, waiting for me to respond. But I didn't. I knew what they had on me now, and it wasn't much—yet. They had nothing to hold me on other than suspicion. I just had to wait until they acknowledged it.

Brittany finally blinked and said, "You haven't asked for a lawyer."

"I don't need one."

"Are you sure?"

"If you had anything, you would have Mirandized me already. And I'm innocent. The last time I checked, that still counts. Nice performance, by the way. Both of you."

"You know what happens to cocky guys in prison?" Jaworski snarled. "Especially a guy who looks like a boy?"

"They get hugs and kisses?"

He wanted to come back at me, but he glanced at Brittany and controlled himself.

He scoffed and said, "You'll get what's coming to you, Chisholm. Just a matter of time."

Everyone gets what's coming to them eventually, whether they deserve it or not. That's a fact of life. But I wanted a say in what I got. Alyssa never had that chance. Neither had the others. Murder takes away any say you have in life, whether you deserve it or not.

"Can I go?" I said to Brittany. "You're not going to charge me and keeping me here isn't going to get you anywhere."

"You took a couple of items from Peggy Grant the other night," she said. "A business card and a bag. They're evidence. We need them."

I pulled the card out of my pocket and slid it across the table to her. She picked it up and examined the back, then looked at me.

"Who is Tom?" she asked.

I shrugged and said, "Don't know."

"Are you Tom?"

"Do I look like a Tom?"

She raised her eyebrows and tilted her head as if to say I could be a *Tom*.

"The bag is in my apartment," I said. "It's pink. You should call whoever's searching my place and tell them to grab it."

"Did you take anything out of it?"

"Nothing to take. There was a change of clothes in it. That's it."

She nodded skeptically.

"Are you sure you don't have anything else you want to tell us?"

"I'm sure."

"Maybe you should look at the photos again."

That caught me off guard. I thought we were done. She had a different thought. I stared at her. A knowing look slapped me in the face.

I peered down at the photos. I looked closer this time, trying to ignore the gruesomeness. There was something there. Then silence enveloped me like I was submerged underwater. The lacerations on their faces and breasts expanded towards me. Three stars carved across the top of each breast, with slices connecting them. A half circle carved on each cheek. The same pattern and symbols on each victim. Symbols I'd seen before.

I looked up at Brittany. I tried to suppress my reaction. She sensed it anyway.

"You see something, don't you?" she said.

Jaworski hovered on my left like an animal stalking its prey. I could almost taste the faint smell of cigarette smoke on his breath.

"It's not too late to cooperate," he said. "Just tell the truth. Don't lie to us."

I stared at him for a second. His eyes were small and dark, his lips angled up to the right. I looked at Brittany, her face beautiful and blank.

"I see four murders that I had nothing to do with," I said.

She pondered me for a torturous length of time. But it was probably only ten seconds.

She finally said, "You're free to go. We'll want to talk to you again soon."

Jaworski looked shocked and confused, but he didn't say anything. I was shocked and confused, but I didn't say anything either. I just wanted to get out of there. There'd be time to figure everything out later.

As I stood up, the mirror seemed to fade out like a movie scene, showing everyone and everything in the room. I wondered who was behind it, who was using Brittany as a pawn to play with me. I glanced at her. She was writing something on her legal pad as if I was already gone.

The door opened, and a large officer stepped into the room.

Jaworski looked over his shoulder and said, "Escort Mr. Chisholm out. Make sure he gets his things at the front desk."

I walked around him and left.

13

"What are you doing to me?" she said.

"You said you want to know more about me," I said.

"I do," she said. "Getting you to talk about yourself has been harder than making law review."

"Doesn't everyone at Harvard make law review?" I said.

She brushed my hair away from my eyes.

"That's Yale," she said.

"Well, now you'll have a real achievement to brag about."

"Ha! I'm in your bed naked, begging you to fuck me while you paint symbols on me with red wine. Most guys would say *you're* the real overachiever."

I paused and peered into her deep green eyes.

"Brittany, I am going to fuck you. I promise. But if you want to know about me, this is how I need to tell you. It's supposed to be done with animal blood, but a good Pinot is better."

"I think you're making all this up to get me horny. It's working, but you better hurry, Chief Chisholm, or I'm going to come without you."

"Don't call me that. I'm not a Chief. I never will be."

"Okay."

"I'm sorry. That came out a little harsh."

"It's okay. Besides, you know I like it a little harsh."

"I do."

I finished painting a seven-pointed star in red wine on her breast, then slid my finger over to her nipple and rubbed some wine on it. It was firm, erect. I moved my mouth down and licked the wine off slowly. She moaned softly.

I straightened up, reached over to the nightstand, and dipped my fingers in the glass of wine. I brought them up to her right cheek and painted half a circle, then drew the mirror image on her left cheek. I moved my fingers to her mouth and pushed them inside. She sucked on them, licking the residual wine off with her tongue.

I pulled my fingers out slowly while I marveled at her body. There were now three red wine stars around each nipple and one in between the sensual slopes of her delicate but plentiful breasts. The two half circles on her cheeks faced each other as if part of a whole.

She slid her hands behind her knees, lifted her legs, and spread them wider. I dipped my fingers in the wine again, brought them over and held them so that the wine dripped onto her vulva. Then I lowered my head between her legs and worked my tongue along her lips and up to her clitoris, savoring the erotic mix. She tossed her head back and squealed.

I rose up and moved my pelvis closer to her opening, pressing my thighs up against her buttocks. She gripped my penis, stroking and rubbing it against her moist folds, brief smiles radiating between shallow breaths. I fought the urge to plunge inside her.

I pointed at the first star above her right nipple and said, "Each seven-pointed star represents one of the seven Cherokee clans. This star is for the Long Hair, the peacemaker clan. You will belong to this clan." I pointed to the star below her nipple. "The Blue Clan are caretakers of children." I moved to the one to the left. "The Deer Clan are the hunters."

I ran my finger down the inner slope of her right breast, up to her left breast, and circled her nipple slowly. My muscles trembled with anticipation. I pointed at the star above her nipple.

"The Bird Clan are the messengers between the Great Spirit and our people." I moved to the star below her nipple. "The Wild Potato Clan are keepers of the land." I pointed to the one to the right. "The Paint Clan are our medicine people."

I leaned forward, rested my hands on the bed, and locked my elbows. She wrapped her arms around mine and brought her knees next to my hips. I moved my lips down to hers. Our tongues danced expectantly. Then I lifted my head slightly and looked at her.

"The markings on your face represent a wreath of oak leaves. It symbolizes the sacred fire of the Cherokee. Our fire now."

"What about the star between my boobs?" she asked, breathing faster.

"That is the Wolf Clan—my clan. We are the protectors."

I maneuvered to barely penetrate her and stopped. Her body tensed, then quivered. She rotated her hips to work me farther inside her. Short bursts of air escaped through my lips.

"Now, we will be one," I said.

I slowly pushed all the way inside her. She arched her back, squeezed my arms, and screamed my name. I pulled half-way out, then thrust hard back inside her. She whipped her head to the side and screamed my name again. She let go of my arms, grabbed the sheet with one hand and the back of my hair with the other. She pulled my head down, and our lips collided in a frantic embrace. Our bodies writhed together, my pelvis smacking violently against hers again and again and again.

Our carnal delirium went on without time. I had never emersed myself so completely in a woman. It was petrifying and thrilling. Then she came, wailing loud and long before trailing off. I followed, my heart nearly bursting as I groaned her name. Then she came again. I was done, but I continued until she pleaded for me to stop.

After we had both recovered, we lay diagonally across the bed. I was on my back with Brittany half on top of me, her legs wrapped around mine. Her head rested on my chest just below my heart, still beating loudly. I caressed her back while she ran her hand lightly across my penis, kissing my stomach every now and then, suggesting she would move lower if I wanted.

She lifted her head and turned her eyes to mine.

"Was your father a Chief?" she asked.

"No. He was a warrior, like me. But he was full-blooded Cherokee."

"Did he grow up on a reservation?"

"He was born on a reservation in Oklahoma but grew up mostly in Texas. His ancestors were originally from the Carolinas, part of the tribe that today is called the Eastern Band. But most of them were removed from their homelands during the 1830s by the government. Soldiers relocated thousands of Cherokee to west of the Mississippi. Women and children and men who weren't killed were forced to leave. They marched under brutal conditions. Many died during the journey. It's known as the *Trail of Tears*. Those who settled in Oklahoma formed the band that is now called the Cherokee Nation. My father considered himself part of both tribes."

"And you?"

"I don't belong to anything."

"Don't we belong to each other now? Isn't that what your ritual was for?"

I gave her a half-smile.

"So, you did make it up just to fuck me."

"No . . . Maybe a little. I've never told a woman about my past before. It's just new for me."

"I understand," she said tenderly. "Tell me more about your parents. How did they meet?"

"They met in a bar in Norfolk, Virginia while my father was in the Navy. She was from up here. They wed a year later under Cherokee law. The mother rules the family in Cherokee culture. That's why my last name is Chisholm. It's my mother's maiden name. I'm half Cherokee, half American mutt. Mostly Scottish, but some German and Eastern European too. My mother was blonde and blue eyed."

"So, that's where you get your light brown hair and those sexy looks."

"What's so sexy about them?"

"I don't know. It's the combination, I guess. You have like a Scottish or Irish look, with something German going on. And the Cherokee, of course. I thought you might be part Asian at first. But then I saw those blue eyes. Your looks are so different. It's what I first noticed about you."

"Not my brains?"

"Maybe the brains in your pants. I'm sure *my* brains are what you first noticed, too."

"They were. I wanted my brains to get inside your brains."

She giggled. It was sexy, not silly.

"Is it okay to ask how your parents died?" she said.

"Yeah. My father was stabbed to death working as a bouncer. He—"

"Oh my god, Will. That must have been awful."

"It was. I was ten. He was my hero."

"I'm so sorry."

"I'm okay now, but thanks."

"What was he like?"

"He was big and tough and . . . I guess noble is the right word. That's how I remember him. But a knife in the back in the wrong place can kill anyone. Don't ever be a bouncer."

"Okay, I won't," she said and caressed my chest. "Was that what he did for work?"

"No, just part-time. His real job was in construction, but he was trying to make extra money to buy a house. My mother took it really hard. She died in a car crash when I was fifteen."

"That was the accident you told me about?"

I nodded. The soft glow of the streetlight outside my bedroom window reflected off her wide eyes. Even in the darkness, I could see their warm green hues reaching out to me.

"I think she really died of a broken heart when my father was killed. It seemed like that to me. She was never the same after that. Anyway, after she died, my sister and I lived with my uncle. She moved out after high school, and then I joined the Army when I got my GED."

"Why did you join the Army?"

"I got in some trouble. I knew I needed to get away and straighten my head out. The Army was the obvious choice."

"What kind of trouble?"

I stayed silent.

"You can trust me," she said.

"I know," I said and forced a smile. "I got into MMA fighting in high school—mixed martial arts. I was still angry over my father dying. It was that or drugs and gangs. It was all I could afford for sports. Anyway, I got good at it. Then after my mother died, I channeled everything into competing. I was too young to fight professionally, so I tried a lot of different types of martial arts. When I turned seventeen, I started lying about my age and got some cage fights. Then—"

"You lied about your age, and someone believed you?"

"Crazy, I know. They didn't care how young I looked as long as I had a fake birth certificate and could fight. I beat some up-and-comers and word got around that I was tough."

"So, what happened?"

"This fighter, Derek Jackson, somehow learned about my mother's death and started trash talking about her while we were grappling."

"What do you mean? What could he say about a car accident?"

"Well, the police report said she was DUI, and that's what caused the crash. I still don't believe it. But I was young and angry. He set me off, and I took it out on him."

"But wasn't it a fair fight? With umpires?"

"A referee. And yeah, it was a fair fight."

"So, what, did he sue you or something?"

"I killed him."

Brittany's face froze, her eyes wide and her lips slightly parted.

"Not on purpose," I said. "I wanted to kill him. I just didn't mean to."

She scrutinized me for a long moment. She saw my conflicted anguish. Her eyes softened. She reached up and placed the palm of her hand against my cheek. It was warm and soothing.

I lowered my eyes and said, "Yeah, so an ambitious Assistant District Attorney tried to make a manslaughter case out of it. The charges were eventually dropped, but it stopped me from graduating, so I had to get my GED."

She slid her hand from my cheek down to my heart. I felt it pounding against her tender touch.

"Then you joined the Army?"

"Yeah. No college, no training, young and stupid. Off to Afghanistan, soldier. It was like joining the French Foreign Legion. But I wasn't stupid. I became a sergeant pretty quick after showing what I could do. I was going to be sponsored for my degree. They talked to me about West Point. But then I punched an officer, and everything changed."

"Why did you do that?"

"Long story, but he got my friend killed. Anyway, that landed me a general discharge. I came back to Boston and became a cop. Made detective as soon as I finished my bachelor's at BU. And now I'm fucking the hottest girl in all of Boston. I guess I *am* an overachiever."

She glided her body on top of mine and kissed my chest lightly several times, moving up to my neck and then my ear.

"You're going to have to fuck me more than once to be a real overachiever," she murmured.

I slid my hand up her back to her hair. It was soft and smooth. I wrapped my fingers in it and pulled her head back gently. She gazed in my eyes, her lips agape in anticipation. I moved my lips to hover above hers and peered into her eyes, our lashes nearly touching.

"You know I'm going undercover tomorrow. Tonight will have to last us for a while."

"Then I guess we won't be sleeping at all."

She closed her eyes and our lips merged.

14

I never remembered my dreams. Even after I returned from Afghanistan. People told me I'd have them. That they'd be bad. I believed them because they'd been over there and back. Some had served in Iraq. A lot of them were in rough shape. So, I expected the dreams. Nightmares, really. But they never came. Or I just never remembered them.

Until last night.

It was early. A scream had startled me awake. It might have been a noise from outside that became a scream in my dream. Either way, it was gone now. My pulse raced as I stared down at my feet resting on the faded, brown-speckled carpet, my hands gripping the edge of the mattress tightly, sweat dripping down my neck.

Two dreams lingered in my head—one bad and one worse. One had nothing to do with Afghanistan. The other had something to do with it, but I wasn't sure what.

Splinters of one dream seemed stuck behind my eyes. I closed them. Velvet was lying in marshy water by the side of a dirt road wearing a white teddy, a bombed-out military Jeep nearby. Slashes on her face and body were oozing something dark. I was in my Army combat uniform looking down at her.

"Are you alright?" I asked.

"Tom, don't, I have a boyfriend," she said.

That was all I remembered. But it shook me. I had never really remembered my dreams before. The mix of Afghanistan and Velvet didn't make any sense. Maybe all nightmares were like that.

Velvet was Heather Smith, the young black woman who had danced for me at The Landing outside Newark Airport. I had liked her. She was fun to talk to. She was going to school to be a nurse. A lot of strippers said that. I had suggested meeting up after, but she had a boyfriend. She said he was older and had an important job. I didn't care, but I stopped hitting on her. She was murdered and raped that night, like the others. I probably couldn't have saved her. But I wondered.

I opened my eyes and took a deep breath. I sensed my pulse slowing.

That was the bad dream. The worse one was with Brittany, the night of lovemaking when we officially started dating. I remembered everything, probably because I had relived it so many times. It might not have even been a dream. More like a flashback.

Whether a dream or a flashback, it was a nightmare to me. The symbols carved into the victims mimicked the ritual I had performed on Brittany with red wine. Not exactly, but close. I had never told anyone about that night.

Brittany held back from calling me out on the symbols for some reason. Maybe she hadn't told Jaworski or her boss behind the mirror. But that wouldn't be smart for her career. She couldn't show any reluctance to take me down if she wanted to get ahead. Her ambition was the one thing I was confident hadn't changed.

She had told them about the symbols. I was sure of that. Why they hadn't used them to turn the heat up was gnawing at me. They probably could have arrested me, but they didn't. None of it made sense. Like all nightmares.

After I left the precinct, I had headed back to Champagne to pick up my car. It took me a couple of hours because I made sure I wasn't being followed. I kept a surveillance detector in the trunk. I used it to scan my clothes and car for any tracking devices. I didn't find any. The trip back to the garage was equally long because I took the same precautions. By the time I walked into my apartment, it was almost midnight. The place was a mess from being searched by New York's finest. I was exhausted but still took the time to scan it for any surveillance bugs. Then I collapsed on my bed.

I spent most of the past two days in bed recovering from the gash on my back and thinking. I ignored calls from Peggy Grant, Richard Morris, and my sister. I didn't listen to their messages either. I just slept, healed, and thought. As my back got better, I slept less and thought more.

YouSEL was the common thread. All the victims had modeled there. It was where I had discovered them. And where I had to begin if I was going to figure out who was setting me up. It was headquartered in Columbus, Ohio. I had researched it when I first got hooked. That happened in Columbus too.

I stood up, and a stinging pain shot through my back. It was the stretching of new scar tissue from my wound healing. The pain faded quickly. Quickly enough that I decided to try working out for the first time in three days. Then my stomach spoke to me. I remembered I hadn't eaten in almost twenty-four hours.

A long run was my plan, so nothing heavy to eat. It didn't matter since there wasn't much in my refrigerator. I slapped some strawberry jam on a slice of wheat bread, put another slice on top and downed it with half a carton of orange juice.

I threw on workout shorts, a T-shirt, and my sneakers, then stretched my legs. I had to improvise the rest of my warm-up because of the stiches. When I was done, I strapped my LCP II around my waist, grabbed my phone and keys, and opened the door.

A large black man was standing three feet away. I whipped my arm around to grab my gun but stopped . . .

Victor.

15

"You slippin', bro. Would've popped you 'fore you ever see my sweet face."

"Yeah, that's definitely not the last thing I want to see before I die," I said.

Victor half grinned.

"Guessin' you'd prefer pussy. Maybe from that hot ADA bitch harassin' my ass 'bout you. Might be worth getting popped to taste that."

Surprises were smacking me around like my first cage fight. Victor on my doorstep. Victor knowing about Brittany. Brittany knowing about Victor. And the sucker punch—her questioning him about me. My voices were screaming.

I stepped back into my apartment and grabbed the surveillance detector off my dresser. I turned it on and moved closer to Victor. He stiffened.

"Bro, you fuckin' think I'm wearin'?"

"No."

"Then what the fuck you doin'?"

"I've been wrong about a lot of people lately. I don't plan to be wrong about you."

"Okay, bro. That bitch chasing my ass, I wouldn't trust nobody neither. But I'd never wear no wire for nobody. You hear me?"

I finished scanning him. He was clean. I shut off the device and tossed it onto my bed. I closed the door and locked both bolts, then turned and looked hard at him.

"Yeah, I hear you. Now, cut the shit, Victor. You think I'm doing business with a guy who just talked to an ADA about me?"

"Whatchu think, I'm here tellin' you 'bout her after I snitch on you?"

"That's how informants work."

"You a cynical kid, Will."

"I used to be a cop, remember?"

"Ain't no excuse. Trust me or don't, you know I ain't stupid. Sharin' anythin' 'bout my clients with anybody, 'specially an ADA, ain't good for business. No coincidence she puts the heat on me the same day you text me you need somethin'. Thought you should know before you ax me for anythin'. Just good business, bro. That's why people come to me."

I thought for a few seconds while I looked Victor over. The last time I'd seen him was a few months back. He was still an inch taller than me and still a lot older. Late thirties, with a hard body and angular face. His big brown eyes were smooth, like river rocks, with wisps of green. A full head of tightly cropped curly black hair accented his dark brown skin.

He had on a black blazer, blue shirt, and brown slacks. Expensive looking but not flashy. He could have passed for a Wall Street asshole. Maybe even a lawyer. But he talked like who he was—a loan shark, sometimes pimp, and small-time racketeer. He could get just about anything you wanted at *his* price. For some reason, he didn't play in drugs. The last time I owed him money, I was late to pay. He sent a few guys to rough me up. That's when he learned I only looked like a kid. He agreed not to shoot me, and I agreed not to kill him and everyone who worked for him.

But he could help me. That's why I had texted him last night.

"What did she want?" I said.

Victor's shoulders relaxed, and his eyes brightened.

"She axed me if I sold you a fake credit card. Said she wouldn't press charges if I gave her information."

"And?"

"And I told her to press whatever charges she wants 'cause I don't know what she's talkin' 'bout. Told her don't know if I even know you. Had some tall pussy-whipped fancy-suit guy with her too. He wanted to get in my face, but she smacked him down."

"Was his name Jaworski?"

"Yeah, Inspector Jerk-off."

"Did she say how they knew about the fake credit card?"

"Nah. Probably knows I'm in that biz and guessed."

"Why would they guess I bought a fake card from you?"

"Don't know, bro. Wondered that myself."

"It's a good fucking guess."

"Didn't come from me, if that's what you sayin'."

"Guess I'll have to take your word on that."

"Told you once, told you twice, Will—I don't snitch. Don't like you 'ccusing me neither."

"Alright, don't get your Irish up. She ask about anything else?"

"Yeah. Axed about a porn site called YouSEL. High-class site. I know it but told her I don't. She was tryin' to connect you to it with the card I sold you. I didn't give her nothin'. Don't worry. That card can't be traced to you or me."

I stared at him for several seconds, my lips pressed tightly together. My back ached a little from tensing it, and a low-level anxiety simmered in my stomach.

"That it?" I said.

"She also axed if I ever went to strip clubs with you. Told her have to be real fine pussy for me to pay just to watch. Looked her up and down after. Inspector Jerk-off got pissed, but she slapped him down again."

"Is that all you said?"

95

"Also told her we don't hang out. We ain't friends."

"She believe you?"

"'bout being friends?"

"About everything."

"Couldn't tell but wouldn't count on it. Cold bitch. Hot, but cold."

"You done?"

"Talkin' 'bout her, yeah. But you texted me, remember? Said you needed something. Told you I'd be here early."

I nodded. I hadn't expected him before noon.

"Text said you'd pay good money," he continued. "If you don't trust doin' business with me, just say so, and I'm gone."

"I didn't say *good money*. I said whatever was needed."

"Same difference," he said and grinned.

I was stuck. I needed his help. He knew it. But I didn't trust him. He knew that too. He would do almost anything for money. I knew it. I had money. He smelled it.

I glanced around the hallway. It was empty. I listened. It was quiet.

I looked at Victor and said, "I'm going to Columbus."

He nodded like a priest listening to my confession.

"I'll want some things when I get there."

He acknowledged my sins again.

"I need a gun and ammo. Untraceable."

"Course."

"A car, license, and credit card too."

"Anythin' else?"

"Yeah. I need to track down a local stripper there. Goes by Lucy Lee. I don't know her real name. She worked at a club called The Big O two years ago."

"You must have money 'cause you know I won't float you for all that."

"How much?"

"Gun cost you two grand. I'll throw in the ammo. A grand a day for a car. ID and credit card cost two. Another grand for tracking down the stripper. Call it six grand upfront and a grand a day for the car after that. Plus any unexpected expenses."

"I can get that for half the price around here."

"You goin' to Columbus fuckin' Ohio, bro. Not Jersey City."

"Keep it down."

He dropped his voice and said, "I run a quality business, Will. That's why you come to me. In my business, quality is money. You know that. You got someone better, use 'em."

"You ever been to Columbus?"

"Yeah, once. Buncha farms and corn-fed mammas. Banged a sweet, tattooed bitch there. Decent restaurants. Always cloudy, though. People way too fuckin' nice too."

"That's the place. Can you get me what I want?"

"No problem."

I eyed him intensely for several seconds. Enough to provoke a sigh and an irritated look. He was confident. I believed him, but I wanted him to sweat a little.

"Sounds like you got somethin' big goin' in Columbus," he said. "Might need some help. I'm available. For a fee, of course. Could be the start of a beautiful relationship."

I think it was a line from an old movie. He was always quoting them. I ignored him.

"Seven thousand for everything," I said. "Four upfront and the other three when I return. I get the car for as long as I need."

Victor's eyes widened. He stared at me like I had just bluffed him in a poker game with a pair of deuces. Then his lips curled up.

"Done," he said. "What if you don't come back?"

"Then we both lose."

He held the grin and nodded.

"Start of a beautiful relationship," he said. "How we doin' this?"

"Put the license, credit card, and any paperwork for the gun and car in a brown envelope. Bring it to Geller Jewelry next to my office Monday before two. Ask for Simon Geller, the owner. Tell him you're looking for an engagement ring for your fiancé, Brittany. Put the envelope on the counter. He'll put a cloth mat down over it to show you some rings. There'll be another brown envelope under the mat. Look at the rings for a minute and then tell him Brittany isn't worth it. He'll grab the mat and your envelope. You take the one he leaves. It'll have your money in it. Got all that?"

"Lotta cloak and dagger, bro."

"Do I need to repeat it?"

Victor tapped his right temple several times slowly with his middle finger.

"Photographic memory, remember?"

"I forgot."

He snorted and said, "Need anythin' else?"

"No."

"Why that ADA bitch after you anyway?"

I gave him a look that said I didn't like him asking.

He ignored it and said, "It's 'bout those murdered strippers all over the news, ain't it?"

"Don't push it, Victor."

"Don't get *your* Irish up, Will. Just wanna know what I'm gettin' into."

"I'm paying you *not* to ask questions."

"Thought maybe I can help."

"Just deliver. That's all the help I want."

Victor pursed his lips and shook his head slowly.

"You hard to figure. Don't take you for no serial killer, though. Guessin' the cops and that ADA think you guilty. Gonna need help if they come after you. Just sayin'."

Victor sensed an opportunity. He wasn't going to let a handful of murders get in the way. But doing business with him was always a risk. A manageable one as long as he got his money.

We stared at each other without saying anything for a while. I was done. He seemed to want something more. Maybe a bro hug. That was never happening. He finally nodded, turned, and walked to the top of the staircase. He moved halfway down the steps, paused, and looked through the spindles at me.

"Stay alive, bro. At least 'til I get my money."

He floated down the rest of the stairs like a black ghost. He was out of sight and out of the building in a few seconds. I never heard the outside door open or close.

I dropped my head and released a long sigh.

Victor was right. I was losing my edge. Any decent muscle could have surprised me and shot me in the face when I opened my door. I reached up and felt the scar above my right ear. I had to tighten up and start watching my back better. My front too. One bullet in my head was enough.

16

I stepped out of my building and stopped in the middle of the sidewalk. Swords of sunlight cut across Grand Street as a light morning mist burnt off. The neighborhood was quiet but stirring. A typical Saturday morning. I bent down to stretch my legs and glimpse around. A dark blue sedan parked a half block away caught my eye. I wasn't sure why.

I finished stretching and took off running west. As I turned onto Essex Street to head north, I glanced at the sedan, now a couple of blocks away. It hadn't moved.

In a couple of minutes, I was sprinting along Houston Street towards the East River. My back hurt, and I was stiff. But blood soon started flowing through my body like a drug. The pain ebbed with each stride. I was high and getting higher. I kept up a near sprint for five minutes before settling into a comfortable clip.

I watched for anyone tailing me. I noticed everything. Even things that weren't there. Shadows darted at me from everywhere, grabbing me and then washing off as waves of sunlight rushed between the buildings to engulf me. I dodged people lunging at me, realizing in less than a heartbeat that they were only trying to avoid a collision. I sucked in the slightly cool, heavy New York City air rhythmically and efficiently, my lungs expanding to absorb all its energy and toxins. I was alive and in control of my immediate destiny.

My pace was fast but steady. My breathing fast but steady. My mind fast but steady. One thought consumed me—I couldn't make another mistake if I wanted to live. No online porn. No strippers. No drinking. No weaknesses. No chances.

No living until I figured out who was setting me up.

That's why I had to go to Columbus. It was where I had first learned about YouSEL, from Lucy Lee. It was where the company was headquartered and where Ashley Grant had last lived and worked. Too many roads headed there. Too many coincidences. Whoever was orchestrating all this wanted me there.

Why Columbus, I didn't know. All the murders had been in New York City. Even Velvet, who danced in Newark, had been found on Staten Island. Columbus was probably a trap. But I had to play along. I had no other leads. And I wasn't going to wait to be arrested. Whoever was behind this knew that too. Like Afghanistan, the enemy was lurking out there, faceless, waiting patiently to ambush me. I had to go and fight. There was no choice. Just like Afghanistan.

After an hour of running, I was back at my apartment building, breathing hard and soaked in sweat. I was free, for the moment, cleansed of all my emotional and psychological poisons. It wouldn't last. It never did. My real life always returned. Like the crash after a drug high.

Exercising was an addiction for me. Not a tendency. Sometimes, I needed to work out again to get back the high, so I could block out whatever pain was still there, from whatever time. When I was finally exhausted and spent, I would fall asleep. No shower, no food, no clothes. All my poisons expelled. Maybe that was why I never remembered my dreams. It was one theory.

Once I caught my breath, I scanned around again for anything suspicious. The dark blue sedan was gone. Customers were strolling in and out of Jin's Dry Cleaning and Laundry. One guy down the block and another across the street stuck out to me, but it was probably my paranoia. There were too many people ambling about now to know for sure. I decided to head upstairs to finish my workout on the heavy bag.

As I opened the building door, I heard a vehicle pull up behind me. I glanced over my shoulder and saw a white van stop next to the curb, the front tire partially on the sidewalk. It had a satellite dish and antennas on the roof, with a local news station insignia on the side. A thin middle-aged black woman in a mint green suit jumped out and rushed towards me.

I pulled my key out of the lock, stepped inside, and closed the door before she reached it. She started knocking hard on one of the windowpanes to get my attention. I turned sideways and eyed her. I realized she was a well-known local TV reporter.

"Excuse me! Excuse me!" she shouted. "I'm Brenda Cain from Metro News. Can you please let me in? I have an interview with someone in the building."

A man carrying a large camera on his shoulder appeared behind her. I shook my head, turned, and started walking towards the stairs.

"Wait!" she pleaded. "You're Mr. Chisholm, aren't you? Mr. Chisholm, I just want to get a comment on the stripper slayings. Please, just a couple of minutes? Mr.—"

Sally Jin's piercing screech suddenly silenced Brenda Cain. I paused on the second step and turned back to the door. Sally Jin came into view through the window, flailing her hands and yelling at the reporter and cameraman to leave. I smiled to myself, then bounded up the stairs two at a time. Their muffled voices evaporated by the time I got to the second floor.

At the top of the stairs, I stopped and looked up at the ceiling. I closed my eyes. Someone had leaked my name to the press. I was now a person of interest in the "stripper slayings", as they had been branded. It was probably why Brittany and Jaworski had gone easy on me about the markings on the victims. The strategy was to let the press lynch me first. Keelhaul me in the media before officially charging me. Publicly punish me to squeeze out a confession and avoid a trial.

But leaking my name meant they didn't have enough evidence for a conviction. That's why they hadn't arrested me even though they were convinced I was guilty. There was no other reason to sic the press on me. Still, playing the media game was risky for the DA's Office, especially if I was innocent. Unless that didn't matter.

I opened my eyes and saw a spider crawling above me. It could have been the same one from my apartment, wondering if I was the same guy hanging upside down. I shook my head, then stepped around the railing and headed for the next flight of stairs.

Halfway up the steps to my floor, I heard feet shuffle. I stopped, stood on my toes, and peeked through the railing spindles toward my apartment. Sunlight flooded in through the window at the end of the hallway, blinding my view. I could barely make out a figure leaning against the wall next to my apartment door.

I crouched down and reached my right hand around my back, under my shirt. I grabbed the sweaty Ruger grip and pulled it out. I moved up the next two steps slowly and quietly, crouching more with each one so that my head wasn't visible. I brought my left hand over my right for a two-handed grip, then raised the Ruger to eye level.

I stopped and watched the ceiling. After several seconds, the hallway darkened from a cloud covering the sun. I rose quickly and stuck the barrel of the Ruger between two spindles so that I had a clear shot at the figure.

The person saw me and straightened up from the wall. It was a woman, tall and thin, with shoulder-length blonde hair. She had on a pink floral camisole dress with an unbuttoned white cotton sweater. Nice cleavage and great legs. A small white purse was strapped across her body and hung on her waist. She had a cellphone in her left hand. Her right hand was empty. If she had a gun, it was small and hidden where I'd like to search.

She stared at me like a sexy blonde deer frozen with fear. The Ruger LCP II is a compact pistol. Not particularly intimidating. But even the smallest of handguns will have a paralyzing effect on most people. I lowered it to my side and climbed the rest of the steps sideways. I strode slowly towards her. She stood rigid. Her eyes moved from the Ruger to my eyes and back to the Ruger. I stopped about ten feet away. She looked back up at me.

"Talk," I said.

"I'm, I'm looking for Mr. Chisholm," she said.

"Why?"

"I need a private investigator. I mean, I want to hire one—him."

"Why?"

"Um . . . my ex-boyfriend won't leave me alone. I'm afraid. I need someone to help."

"What about the police?"

Her posture loosened. She shook her head in frustration and gave me an exasperated look.

"Are you Mr. Chisholm or not?"

"Who are you?"

"I'm Rebecca . . . Rebecca Murry."

"How old are you, Rebecca Murry?"

"Uh, twenty-one. Does that matter?"

"To hire me, you have to be twenty-one."

"Then you *are* Mr. Chisholm?"

I nodded.

"Why are you giving me such a hard time?" she said. "I want to hire you."

"I don't trust anyone who shows up at my door uninvited. It's a quirk of mine."

"I'm sorry, it's just—"

"How did you get in here?"

"Uh, I was waiting outside for you. A couple came out. I smiled, and they let me in."

"Why didn't you go to my office?"

"I . . ." She slumped her shoulders, sighed, and shook her head again. "Can we talk inside? I don't want anyone else to hear me."

I stared in her eyes. She looked down. Then she started to fidget with her phone.

"Alright," I said.

I holstered the Ruger on my back hip, unlocked the two bolts on my apartment door and pushed it open for her. She hesitated, glanced at me, then walked quickly into my apartment. I followed, closed the door softly, and locked one bolt.

She stood in the middle of the room with her back to me. Her nubile curves exuded innocence. Alarms went off in my head. Before I could say anything, she walked over to my bed and sat on it. She stared at the surveillance detector curiously, then looked up at me and smiled—an awkward flirtatious smile.

I walked across the room to my table under the double windows. I put my keys and phone down, pushed a chair aside, and turned around. I leaned against the edge of the table, crossed my arms, and stared at her.

She tried to gaze in my eyes seductively. I pressed my lips together to signal I wasn't buying. After a few seconds, she frowned. She lifted the strap of her purse over her head and dropped it on the floor. Then she took off her sweater and tossed it to the end of the bed where it clung hanging halfway over the edge. She pulled her shoulders back slightly and leaned forward to give me a full view of her cleavage. It was just as nice without the sight of my Ruger on it.

I examined her more closely. In the hallway with the window behind her, I hadn't noticed how much makeup she was wearing. It made her look older than she was. That was the point. And her three-inch white heels meant she wasn't as tall as I first thought. Tall girls always seem older. But she still had great legs, the kind that got teenage boys hard. She was adorable—for a seventeen-year-old.

My stare started to make her nervous. She bit her lower lip and looked anxiously at me. Then she picked up her cellphone from the bed and swiped the screen.

I said, "Before you call 9-1-1 and start screaming that I'm attacking you, you should know that I have a hidden camera in my apartment that's recording everything, including audio."

She paused and gawked at me. She started to say something but stopped. Her head darted around as she looked up at the corners of the ceiling in the apartment. Her bewildered eyes settled back on me.

"It's *hidden*," I said. "Maybe I should call your father. I'm sure he'll be happy to hear how his high school daughter was planning to lie to the police that I tried to assault her. Probably won't be too pleased with your outfit either, *Rachel*."

"What? My name isn't . . . I wasn't . . . I don't believe you."

She stood up quickly from the bed and shot me a defiant seventeen-year-old glare. Her eyes moved to the door. She wanted to make a run for it, but she knew the deadbolt would slow her enough for me to stop her. She looked back at me. Her eyes turned fiery, and her jaw muscles tightened under her smooth youthful cheeks.

"You raped and murdered Alyssa!" she exclaimed.

She dropped to one knee, grabbed her purse off the floor, and reached inside. Holding her phone made her clumsy, but she eventually pulled out something small and black. She stood up and pressed a button on it. A thin blade sprang out and locked into place with a click. She extended her arm towards me. Her blue eyes were wide and wild from adrenalin.

"I'm leaving," she declared, "and don't try to stop me."

I sighed and said, "You forget I'm recording this? Threatening me with a knife is assault with a deadly weapon. Switchblades are illegal, which also makes you guilty of criminal possession of a weapon in the fourth degree. How do you think all that will look on your college applications? Never mind how your father reacts when he gets the call from the DA's Office."

Panic replaced her scowl. Her eyes jumped around without focus. She started to breath fast.

"I didn't kill Alyssa," I continued. "Or any of the other women who were murdered. Just leave. I won't hurt you. I'm not going to press charges either. Or say anything to anyone, including your father. I'll erase the video too."

"Why should I believe you?"

"Honestly, no reason. Does it matter?"

"Yeah, it does."

"Why? You going to run and tell your father before I do? Make up another story?"

"It matters because you're lying. Alyssa had to know the person who killed her. She was too smart to let a stranger get that close."

"So, she trusted me, and I used that to murder her. That's what you think? If she was so smart, why would she trust me? She barely knew me."

She stayed silent, pressing her lips tightly together.

"You won't believe this," I said, "but someone's trying to frame me for murder. And they're doing a great job if you're any proof. That's the truth, whether you believe it or not. Now get out of here. If I wanted to hurt you, you couldn't stop me. I don't hurt innocent people. Especially stupid girls."

"You hurt my boyfriend."

"Mitchell Dugan? He and his buddies tried to beat the hell out of me. I was defending myself."

"You still beat him up pretty bad."

"I could have shot him, but I didn't. I got fifteen stiches in my back instead."

"I know my father hired you to scare Mitch away. It's not going to work. And once my father learns you're a rapist and murderer, he'll fire you. It doesn't matter what you say, he's not going to take any chances with my safety. I know him."

"I've never raped or murdered anyone. But you're never going to believe me, so just go. Wait, how are you getting home? I don't need something happening to you after you leave here."

"A friend drove me. He's waiting outside. If I don't call him soon, he'll call the police."

"Jesus," I said and rolled my eyes. "Did you drive, train, ride-share?"

She looked at me tentatively, then lowered the knife to her side.

"I'm parked in the garage down the street."

"Alright, go. And put that knife away."

She stared at me for a few seconds, her mouth open and her eyes wide. Then she picked up her purse, folded up the knife, and put it inside. She grabbed her sweater off the bed and walked to the door, keeping an eye on me as she unbolted it.

"Before you go," I said, "how did you know where I live?"

She opened the door halfway, turned her head and looked at me.

"I hacked my father's computer at home. He has a file on you from the police. I don't care if you tell him. That's what he gets for trying to break up Mitch and me."

"Is that why you're here? To get back at your father?"

"And you too. For Alyssa."

I shook my head and said, "What if I really am a murderer? You think getting raped and killed will get back at your father? Or me? There are easier ways to commit suicide."

"I already have a psychiatrist."

"Of course, you do."

"What does that mean?"

"It means you're rich. If you weren't, you'd have to work out your problems on your own, like most teenage girls. Just because you can afford therapy doesn't mean your problems are any worse than your gardener's daughter."

"I lost my mother, asshole. That's why I have a psychiatrist. My father makes me go."

"I lost both my parents before I was your age. I didn't have anyone to commit suicide for or a therapist to cry to. I don't know much about your old man, but he acts like he cares about you. Might be worth talking to him before you kill yourself to get his attention."

"Yeah, and say what? I miss my mom so much I want to kill myself? Or the closest thing to a sister I had was just murdered by the guy he hired to scare off the man I love? That I'm still a virgin because

Mitch won't fuck me until I'm eighteen? And I'm going to marry him as soon as he asks me? You think he wants to hear any of that?"

"Probably not. Maybe the virgin part. But I'll bet he listens."

She glared at me and swallowed the lump in her throat. Her lower lip trembled as a tear rolled down her cheek.

"You cared about Alyssa," I said, "so I'll say it again—I didn't kill her. But I'm going to figure out who did. If you know anything, tell me. It could help."

She wiped the tear away and said, "I was at Champagne with her the night she was murdered. I saw you come in just before I left. She only worked that night because you were going to be there. Even if you didn't kill her, she's dead because of you."

She hurried out to the hallway and pulled the door shut. Several light thumping sounds told me she was running. Then I heard the faint pattering of her feet descending the stairs. The sound trailed off, and everything was quiet. Except for the voices in my head.

17

$\mathcal{S}$ally Jin managed to keep Brenda Cain and a handful of other reporters out of the building for the rest of the weekend. I slinked in and
out through the back when I needed to go somewhere. But I stayed
in for the most part, just thinking, working out, and eating PB&Js.
When I woke up this morning, I was tired of thinking and PB&Js.

Columbus was beckoning. I never imagined saying that. But the
idea of going to prison for four murders I didn't commit had never crossed my mind before either. Since I still didn't have a plan,
Columbus was as good a place to start as any. And I knew someone
wanted me there.

Booking a same-day flight cost about a month's rent. I could afford it since I had another ten thousand coming from Richard Morris
even if he fired me, which I assumed he would do at the meeting he
scheduled for this afternoon.

My flight left in twelve hours. The first thing I had to do was pick
up some equipment. I was being watched, maybe listened to as well. I
didn't know how, but someone knew I was headed to Champagne last
week and tipped off the police. Someone also told them I had a YouSEL
account. That someone knew there was incriminating evidence on my
laptop too. That's what the police were looking for when they turned
my office and apartment inside out. Someone knew things about me

that only my shadow should know. If Columbus was a setup, and I figured it was, I had to have a way to watch the someone watching me.

Midtown Electronics was a hole-in-the-wall store on 40th Street just off Fifth Avenue. Paula White owned and ran it. I had been close with the head of technology for the Boston Police Department. When I came to New York to start my own gig, he put me in touch with Paula for my surveillance equipment needs. He said she had been with Mossad, the Israeli intelligence agency, in a former life. She never talked about it, and I never asked. But she was connected. That came through in our first meeting when she seemed to know more about me than my sister.

I stepped inside the store and paused to let my eyes adjust. It was dark. The lighting was dim. Paula kept it that way intentionally. I asked her about it the first time I visited. She told me it gave her a few seconds advantage if a hostile entered. Then she said I should have known that.

After my eyes adjusted, I made out Paula's figure behind the counter. Forty-something and average height, she had the physique of a long-distance runner. Her bleach blonde hair was pulled back tight in a short ponytail, accentuating sharp facial features that contrasted with soft lips. A snug navy-blue yoga outfit made her bare arms and wiry frame look surprisingly sexy. When I first met her, I wondered what she would be like in bed. She was probably twenty years older, but her intensity was erotic.

Then I got to know her a little. She was on the proverbial spectrum. Exactly where, I couldn't tell. Extremely intelligent, she had an aversion to eye contact. When she did look at you, her brilliant blue eyes were piercing. It was never longer than a second or two, and it usually meant the conversation was over.

"What do you need?" she said.

I didn't offer a smile since she was staring down at the glass counter, tapping her fingers.

"Your best button camera and ten burner phones," I said.

"The best I have is five thousand," she said without looking up.

"Okay, what's your best for under a thousand?"

"Lock the door and flip the sign."

She turned around, punched a code into a keypad on the wall, and opened the door behind her. She stepped into a backroom and closed the door.

I reached behind me and locked the door. Then I flipped the sign so it showed "Closed" to the outside. I turned back to the counter. Paula was unpacking a small box. I moved closer.

"Hearing chatter about you," she said, her eyes focused down on her task. "You in trouble?"

"What chatter?"

Her eyes darted up at me, then quickly turned down to the equipment she had unwrapped.

"Are you in trouble?" she repeated.

"A little."

"Murder isn't a little trouble."

"I can handle it."

"You want help or not?"

I thought for a moment. Given her connections, she might know something about my situation. She could even be involved. But that was just my voices reminding me that everyone was a threat. Still, I couldn't see how she could help. And I didn't want to ask. Not yet. I wasn't ready to share my secrets with her or anyone.

"I'll let you know if I do," I said.

She ignored my answer and reached over the counter. She grabbed my shirt and pulled me towards her. Her strength surprised me. A faint cigarette odor blended with the scent of soap. I realized she probably wasn't a long-distance runner after all.

She slid a small black plastic device inside my polo shirt behind the buttons. It was rectangular, with a round piece sticking straight out. She worked the round piece through the bottom buttonhole from the inside and squeezed it flush against my actual button. Then she let go of my shirt and stepped over to her computer on the counter. She plugged a flash drive into a USB port and typed something on the keyboard. She reached into my shirt and pressed something on the small rectangular piece of plastic.

When she turned her computer monitor towards me, her image appeared on the screen from my perspective. I stepped back. The image on the screen expanded to include the counter, the monitor, and the door to the backroom. I started to ask if the audio worked, but I was interrupted by my voice echoing from the computer.

"It's a hybrid," she said. "Lightweight and hard to detect. You need to carry this receiver to record." She picked up a small black plastic box from the counter. "A full charge will give you twelve hours of recording time. The rest is straightforward. Read the operating manual."

"How much?"

"Five hundred. With the ten burners, call it a thousand. No receipt, no returns."

She signaled with her hand for me to move closer to the counter. When I did, she reached over and undid the button camera from my shirt. Then she packed all the pieces into the original box, pulled out a large plastic bag, and dropped it in. She stepped into the backroom and quickly returned carrying an armful of burner phones in individually wrapped packages. She tossed them into the bag and pushed it over to me.

"Pay me when you get back," she said.

"What makes you think I'm going somewhere?"

She glanced up at me for a long moment. We were done.

I grabbed the bag and turned to leave. At the door, I stopped and turned back to her. She was staring at my feet, tapping her fingers on the counter again.

"Someone's tracking me," I said. "I don't know how. I think it might be my phone or my computer. Any recommendation for someone who knows tracking software? Someone good, who can be trusted?"

She peered at me for a second, then turned her gaze back down. She stopped tapping.

"You shouldn't trust anyone."

"I don't."

"Jon Choi."

That wasn't a name I wanted to hear. Jon Choi ran just about everything illegal in Koreatown, along with a few restaurants on the side. It was his younger sister that Michael Jin had asked out. I stopped two of Choi's goons from breaking Michael's legs. Then I negotiated with Choi to get Michael off the hook. We reached an agreement, but Choi didn't appreciate my bargaining tactics. It was my first case when I moved down to New York City. No money, but I earned some street cred.

"You know anyone else?" I said.

"Use him. If he doesn't shoot you, he'll connect you with the best for what you want."

She knew about my history with Choi. No surprise, but I wondered what else she knew. I couldn't ask. That was understood. If she knew something, she'd tell me when she wanted me to know, assuming I wasn't already dead.

I stood there a few seconds for no good reason, then turned back to the door. I unlocked it, flipped the sign back over, and walked out to a bright obnoxious Monday morning in New York City.

18

*P*eggy Grant had left two more messages on my cell over the weekend. Both said she needed to speak to me urgently. She was particularly frantic on the last one. But she hadn't sounded drunk. I texted her that I would stop by around noon. She texted back an emoji. The emoji looked drunk.

She buzzed me into her building a little after eleven. I was early to make sure there were no surprises waiting. I looked for the stairs. They were around a corner to the left of the elevator.

The building was L-shaped and six stories. I hustled up to the top floor and walked around the hallway. It had a nice new carpet and paint job. A sign for a fire escape decorated the door to the roof. It was unlocked, but I didn't go up. I found another stairwell at the other end of the hallway with a service elevator next to it. A small sitting area was laid out across from the elevator. Two upholstered chairs and a large plant looked at the building on the other side of the street.

I took the stairs down to the fifth floor and checked it out. Then I did the same for the third floor. They all had the same layout, just different mixes of neutral colors. It was a pretty swank building for an unemployed retail clerk. That bothered the voices in my head.

When Peggy opened her door, I was breathing a little fast from running up the stairs. I started breathing faster when I saw her.

She had on skinny blue jeans and a fitted white button-down blouse with the top two buttons undone. A hint of cleavage and no bra. The subtle outline of her nipples made that clear.

I didn't know anything about make-up, but hers looked perfect. She seemed five years younger. Maybe ten. Her strawberry blonde hair wrapped across her forehead like a scarf, flowing down her left cheek and stopping just above her shoulder. Her head was turned a little so that her blue eyes stared at me sideways through wisps of hair. She gave me a playful stare. Maybe a dare.

"Hi, Will," she said. "I thought you got lost. Please come in."

She stepped back and held the door open with her hand. I slid inside to the right and did a quick once-over of her apartment. Then I eyed the door and waited for her to let it close so I could look behind it. She frowned, released the door, and watched me examine the mirror and crescent-shaped table once again.

"Are you always like this?" she asked.

"Like what?"

"Like paranoid?"

I stared straight in her big blue eyes. They weren't glassy. She wasn't drunk.

"Yes," I said.

I continued to stare at her. She smiled, like we were flirting. When I didn't react, her smile faded.

"I assume you want to talk about the news," I said.

"Uh, what news? Is it about Alyssa? No one's contacted me, except Ashley. That's why I've been calling you."

"You talked to Ashley?"

"No, no. She left a message on my cell. But she's alive. What news—"

"Did you call her back?"

"No. The number was blocked. And her message said she didn't want to leave it because she was afraid whoever killed Alyssa might get it and track her down."

"So, she knows about Alyssa. Does she know who killed her?"

"She didn't say anything other than she's safe."

"What about where she's staying?"

"She didn't say that either. But she told me to leave a message with Linda at The Beer Garage in Columbus if I needed to get in touch with her. I assume it's a bar. She must live near there, don't you think?"

"Who's Linda?"

"I don't know. A friend, I guess."

"Can I listen to the message?"

"She told me to erase it so no one could listen to it. I'm sorry. I called you as soon as I got it, but when I didn't hear back for several days, I deleted it like Ashley asked."

If I had any doubt that someone wanted me in Columbus, it was gone. But I still wasn't sure if Peggy was involved or just a pawn. I didn't want to believe a mother could be part of murdering her own daughter. Especially a mother who looked like her. But the story was wrapped up too nicely, just like her.

"What news are you talking about?" she asked. "Did the police find who killed Alyssa?"

It felt like she was playing with me. I glared at her. She smiled nervously. I couldn't tell what was behind those blue eyes, but I was starting to like them. That was making *me* nervous.

"The police brought me in for questioning," I said. "The media found out about it. Now my name is being thrown around as a person of interest."

"Didn't you say they would probably want to talk to you? They don't think you had anything to do with her murder, do they?"

"Peggy, I don't have time to figure out what game you're playing. I'm going to tell you some things you should already know, but I want to make sure you do."

"I'm sorry, Will. Please don't be mad at me. I don't know—"

"Listen! Alyssa was a stripper. Not a model or an actress. She worked at Champagne, the club where her body was found. You had to have known what she did for a living."

"I—"

"I'm not done. There have been three other murders of strippers the past six months in New York City. The police think they're all connected. They think it's a serial killer. It's been all over the news. You must have heard about it."

Peggy gasped and raised her hand to her mouth.

"There's more," I said. "I was at Champagne the night Alyssa was murdered. She danced for me. That's why the police questioned me."

Her eyes widened. She stepped back and lowered her hand from her mouth. Her shoulders trembled slightly. Then she clasped her hands together and started rubbing them anxiously.

"I didn't kill Alyssa," I said.

"But . . . but you said you never met her."

"I didn't think I had until the police showed me photos."

I probably didn't need to lie about knowing Alyssa. But if Peggy was involved in setting me up, she already knew about her daughter and me. If she wasn't, I was sparing her some pain. Either way, lying would get me faster answers. That's all that mattered.

"I don't understand," she said. "How—"

"Someone's trying to make it look like I'm the killer. I don't know who or why, but I'm going to figure it out. I'll find who murdered Alyssa. But to do that, I need your help."

Peggy stared at me with her mouth slightly open, like she wanted to say something. Then her eyes darted around the apartment. They stopped at the kitchen.

"I need some water," she said, avoiding eye contact.

"Do you want me to get it?"

"No," she said and glanced uneasily at me. "I'll get it."

She walked around me, taking a wide berth. I moved away from the door to the middle of the living room so she wouldn't feel trapped. She continued to the kitchen. There was a good chance she would grab a knife and start screaming. That would be a problem. It was her apartment. I couldn't claim to have a hidden camera like I had with Rachel Morris.

When Peggy got to the sink, she opened a cabinet above the counter and took out a glass. I let go of the breath I was holding. She filled the glass with water and gulped down half of it, letting the faucet run. She refilled the glass, drank some more, and then turned off the faucet. She peered over at me.

"Would you like some water?" she asked.

"Sure."

She took out another glass and filled it. She walked towards me slowly, taking a drink from the glass in her right hand while carrying the other in her left.

"New York's finest," she said and offered me the glass.

"Thanks," I said and took it.

I drank some water, then gazed at her. She gazed back, holding her glass in front of her with both hands. I lowered mine to my side. We stood staring at each other awkwardly for several seconds. Then she looked down into her glass.

"I suspected Alyssa was still stripping," she said. "I guess I was hoping her modeling career was taking off, but I didn't want to pry. I knew she didn't want to disappoint me. She thought I wanted more for her. I guess she was right. Now, I'll never know what she could have become."

She glanced up at me. A tear slipped down her cheek. She wiped it away, sighed, and lowered her eyes again.

"Every time I see something on the news about her murder, I turn it off and grab a drink. Not water. I've been drinking a lot since I had to identify her body. I barely managed to get it together enough to call you. I guess I'm weak. I can't handle it. What do shrinks call it—denial? What mother knows how to handle seeing their dead child? But hearing from Ashley sort of snapped me out of it. It's just . . ." She looked up. "I just can't go through that again, Will."

I stared in her eyes and said, "Peggy, I didn't kill Alyssa."

"I believe you," she said tenderly.

"Thank you," I said and sighed. "Did you ever talk to the detectives?"

"Uh, yes. They came by last week. Tuesday, I think. Two men and a woman."

"Two men and a woman? Did you get their names?"

"Uh, they gave me their cards."

She walked over to the glass coffee table in front of the pink sofa. She put her water down and picked up several business cards, then turned to me.

She read the cards: "Detective Michael Gomez, Detective Ronald Ginelli, Assistant District Attorney Brittany Sorenson." She looked at me. "Do you know any of them?"

"They're the ones I talked to."

"They asked me a lot of questions."

"That's standard."

"I guess, but a lot of them were about you."

"Me?"

"Yes. They wanted to know if you were having a relationship with Alyssa. And why you came to see me. Then the woman asked if you and I were having an affair. She was kind of bitchy. Sorry, but she kept grilling me about you."

"What did you say?"

"I told the truth. There's nothing between you and me, and I don't know anything about you and Alyssa. I said I hired you to find Ashley because I'm afraid for her life. I told them about your business card with 'Tom' on the back. I also told them you took it and Alyssa's bag to try to figure out who Tom is. That's all I really remember. I wasn't feeling well that morning, so it's kind of a blur."

She had probably been hungover, but I nodded in sympathy anyway.

My eyes wandered around her apartment as I processed what she had just told me. I realized how neat and organized it was. A handful of personal memorabilia was positioned strategically for anyone to notice. Mostly pictures of Alyssa and Ashley, but a few tacky items here and there as well. Everything was well spaced. No clutter and no subtle cigarette smell. Maybe she had quit drinking *and* smoking now that she was past the shock of her daughter being murdered. It all seemed to fit, almost like it had been staged.

My eyes came back to Peggy. She was watching me. She ran her fingers through her hair to pull her bangs away from her eyes.

"I guess you don't need my help anymore now that you know Ashley is alive. But I—"

"No, Will, I still need your help. Please. I have a check for you too."

"Ashley is safe. You know how to get in touch with her. Why do you need my help?"

"I think she's still in danger. I need you to find her and convince her to come home."

"Why do you think she's in danger?"

"I got the sense from her message that she's afraid and knows who killed Alyssa. Please, Will, I can't lose another daughter."

She started to choke up but caught herself. I stared at her the same way I used to stare at suspects when I interrogated them. Her blue eyes stayed wide and pleading. If it was an act, she deserved an Academy Award.

"Alright, but I can't promise anything. Even if I do find her, she may not want to see you or talk to the police."

"I understand. Thank you, Will. Thank you."

She stepped towards me like she was going to hug me, but I moved back. She stopped and cleared her throat, then glanced towards the kitchen.

"Let me get your check," she said and started to turn away.

"Wait. Hold onto it until I see what I can do."

"But won't you need money to go to Columbus?"

"I have money if I decide to go there."

"Don't you need to go there? I mean, I think that's where she is."

"I know what I'm doing, Peggy."

"Oh, of course. Sorry. I guess you can let me know when you want the check. I want to pay you, Will. I don't want you doing it just to help me. I mean . . . you know what I mean."

"I think so."

"Thank you for everything."

"I haven't done anything yet."

"I know you'll find Ashley and bring her home."

"I'll try. I still need that information I asked you for. Did you get a chance to write it down?"

"No, I'm sorry. I should have. I'll do it today and send it as soon as I'm done."

"The sooner the better. I need to know everything about where she's lived and worked."

"Okay, I'll do it right away. I remember her talking about her apartment in the Italian Village in Columbus, if that helps. Oh, and she was working for a company there called S-E-L. I don't know what that stands for. Have you heard of it?"

A faint sense of panic crept up my legs. My head started to throb. I reached up and felt my scar. I was okay, but I needed to leave before I wasn't.

"I have to go," I said. "Send that information as soon as you can."

As I turned to leave, Peggy touched my forearm. I stopped and looked at her.

"Can I ask you something?" she said.

"Sure."

"I think you knew Alyssa better than you've said. You don't have to tell me anything. I just want to know if you liked her."

The image of Alyssa on my lap the night she was murdered flashed back to me.

"I did."

19

Richard Morris was pacing inside Geller Jewelry waiting for me. I recognized his gray-steaked brown hair and tall, lean body. He seemed anxious. Or angry. Meeting with Morris was my last stop before heading to the airport.

I still didn't know how I was going to play it. Rachel had probably already talked him into firing me. If she hadn't, the news stories suggesting I was a suspect in the stripper slayings likely sealed my fate. But I wanted the other ten thousand Morris had promised, plus expenses to pay for my Emergency Room visit. I didn't want to go back to Peggy Grant and ask for her check. Every time I saw her, I got closer to a big mistake. Right now, I couldn't afford even a little one.

Morris had called and left a message that he wanted to meet. He left his cell number, which meant I was in trouble. I had a lot of explaining to do, if he cared about explanations. But I doubted it. They were probably like pennies to him.

He was in trouble with me too. He had told me to say I was Rachel's cousin, Jake, to get Mitchell Dugan to talk to me. But Dugan had already met Jake. It played out like a setup. I wanted an explanation. Pennies meant something to me.

I knew pressing Morris too hard might cost me my ten grand. If he reneged on our deal, I'd have to go back to watching online porn and jerking off. Or worse—using my charm to try to get laid. Ten grand bought a lot of lap dances. But I had never seen a dead man with a hard on. I decided to press Morris.

Simon Geller buzzed me into his store. I shoved the door open and walked quickly towards Morris. He was wearing a gray suit, white shirt, and dark green tie that fit him like an officer's uniform. He startled when he saw me. Then his expression turned cross. He was ready to dress me down. I was sure he had done it countless times before. That's what superiors did.

But he wasn't my superior.

Simon Geller started to great me, but I said, "Not now, Simon."

I stopped three feet from Morris. My arms were tensed, and my hands were curled as if they were about to tighten into fists. I clenched my jaw and fixed my eyes on him. It felt a little dramatic.

"You tried to set me up," I snapped. "You better have an explanation."

Morris shifted his right foot back slightly like he was preparing to avoid a punch. But he didn't back away. I was impressed.

"What are you talking about?" he replied.

"You told me to say I was Rachel's cousin, Jake, to get Mitchell Dugan to talk to me."

"Yes, I did."

"Dugan knew I wasn't Jake because he's met him before. He was waiting with two other goons to work me over. I have fifteen stiches to show for it. You gave me a bullshit cover that almost got me killed. Start talking."

"Mr. Chisholm, I do not appreciate your language *or* your insinuation that I tried to get you killed. When I hired you, Mr. Dugan had never met Jake. I spoke with Jake before we met."

"I guess it was just an unlucky coincidence that they got together after you hired me."

"Most likely, unless you have another explanation."

"I might. I suppose you don't know anything about Alyssa Grant's murder either?"

"Excuse me, but you should be answering that question yourself. That is why I am here."

"Will," Simon Geller interrupted, "as intriguing as all this is, I have some customers waiting. Can you take this to your office?"

I glanced at Geller and then noticed a young couple at the door waiting to be buzzed in. They looked eager. Probably in love. They were anxious to prove it by spending stupid money on a shiny pebble for her. Fantasy—that was Geller's business. Not private investigation, strippers, or murder. Morris and I weren't supposed to be there.

I looked at Morris. He nodded.

I turned to Geller and said, "Sorry, Simon."

"Al tidag. Don't worry, Will. Oh, here, someone left this for you."

He handed me a brown envelope. A yellow sticky note was attached with "VICTOR" scribbled on it.

I walked to my office, Morris following five feet behind on my left. I unlocked the door, pushed it open, and stood to the side to let him enter.

"Please, after you," Morris said.

I stepped in, flicked on the overhead light, and tossed the brown envelope on the couch. Then I walked around my desk and faced Morris. He entered cautiously, closed the door, and moved closer. My right arm hung next to my side, ready to grab my Glock. Morris stood stiff as a board. We stared at each other like a pair of mannequins.

Morris spoke first: "I would like you to explain the media stories implicating you as a suspect in the murders of four strip dancers. One of them, Alyssa Grant, was apparently a good friend of Rachel's. She worked with Mitchell Dugan, whom you put in the hospital. Rachel seems to know that I hired you to end their relationship. She blames me for what happened to him. She also claims that you are responsible for the murder of her friend. I hired you to be discreet, Mr. Chisholm. I cannot imagine an outcome any further from that. Rachel wants me to fire you. I am giving you the opportunity to convince me otherwise."

I thought for a moment, then said, "Why?"

"What do you mean?"

"Why give me any chance to explain?"

"Are you saying you want me to fire you?"

"You're dodging my question. Any father who saw those news stories wouldn't let me near his daughter. You should have already fired me. There's a reason you haven't. What is it?"

Morris's jaw tightened and his eyes narrowed. He stared at me for a few seconds, then his eyes wandered around my office before returning to me. He took a slow deep breath, pursed his lips, and blew out. He nodded slightly as if he was having a conversation with himself.

"I have not fired you," he said, "because I don't believe you are a murderer or rapist."

"Thanks for the vote of confidence. You don't mind telling me how you know that?"

"I have no knowledge pertaining to the murders if that is what you are insinuating. However, I know the person who recommended you quite well. He saved my life. I trust him like a brother. He apparently believes in you like a son."

"My father's dead. What's this guy's name?"

"Jack McNeill."

That shut me up. Jack McNeill was my first boss when I joined the Boston Police Department. Everyone called him Sarge. He took me under his wing and taught me most of what I know about being a cop. When I was fired, he insisted on being the one to deliver the message. Tears were pouring down his ruddy cheeks when he told me.

"How do you know Jack?" I said.

"He was a sergeant under me in the Marines during the first Gulf War. Several members of the battalion I commanded owe him their lives, including me. After those stories came out last week, I spoke to him again. He was unwavering in his support. He even speculated that someone might be trying to frame you."

If Jack McNeill had really recommended me to Morris, everything made a lot more sense. Still, I couldn't shake the feeling it was all too neat, like Peggy Grant's apartment. Rachel knowing Alyssa and dating a bouncer who was at Champagne the night she was murdered was also too convenient. Morris could have hired his pick of private investigation firms to chase off Mitchell Dugan. Why me? It was too much coincidence. For once, my voices agreed.

"Okay, so you don't believe I'm a murderer or a rapist. But I'm still knee-deep in whatever's going on and sinking fast. Why expose Rachel to any of that?"

"If I thought I could shield her, I would. We would not be having this conversation. Unfortunately, she has already been exposed, and she will continue to be at risk so long as she is dating Mr. Dugan. I told you that I would do whatever it takes to protect her. That is the reason I am here. I want to retain you to guard her until the authorities find and arrest whoever murdered those young women. I will pay you ten thousand dollars a week. If her relationship with Mr. Dugan ends in the process, I will also pay you the additional thirty thousand I promised. I have a check with me for the remainder of the minimum we agreed to. If you agree to guard Rachel, I want your word that her safety will be your top priority."

I stared at him like I was thinking hard. But the truth was I didn't know what to say. It was a ridiculous offer. Maybe not for someone with Morris's money, but it was for me. I would do it for half that. Maybe a third.

"I can't guard anyone twenty-four seven," I said to not appear too eager.

"I understand," Morris said. "There will be multiple back-ups around the clock. I want you to take the lead and do anything and everything necessary to protect her."

"You obviously have enough money to hire an army to guard her. Why do you need me?"

"Mr. Chisholm, whatever I have accomplished is due in large part to my ability to assess a person's character and talent and to use both to my advantage. That is *my* talent. While Jack McNeill's endorsement carries substantial weight with me, I do not take chances with my daughter's safety. Before I approached you, I did my homework. Whatever else you are, and irrespective of your youth, you live by a code of honor. It may be unconventional, and even invisible to most people, but it clearly drives you. That is very important to me. If you say you will protect Rachel, I know you will do everything in your power to do so, including applying the unique skills you demonstrated in your handling of Mr. Dugan and his associates. You can roll your eyes, Mr. Chisholm, but those skills, and the willingness to use them, are what I believe are needed to ensure my daughter's safety. That is all I care about. Furthermore, your familiarity with the murder investigation gives you unique insight that could prove invaluable to protecting Rachel. My offer is quite generous. If it does not work for you, I would like to discuss what terms will. I hope that addresses your concerns."

"That's a long explanation for a simple question. It sounds more like a sales pitch."

"Take it how you choose, Mr. Chisholm, but I am being straight with you."

"If I had a Bitcoin for every time I've heard that."

"Payment in Bitcoin can be arranged."

"Really?"

"Or any digital currency you prefer."

"The only wallet I have is made of leather."

"I am sure you understand my point. I would like to know if we have a deal."

"Maybe. But first, did Rachel say anything else other than she wanted me fired?"

A puzzled expression crossed Morris's face.

"About you?" he asked.

"About anything."

"Well, nothing else concerning you, but she made it clear how angry she was with me. She did try to explain why, which surprised me. We have not really talked since her mother died. Some of the things she said hurt deeply, but it was better than screaming and storming away, which had become the norm. Does that answer your question?"

"It does."

"So, do we have a deal?"

"Yes. For now."

20

I dozed off intermittently on the flight from LaGuardia Airport to John Glenn Columbus International Airport. *International* was a stretch.

Columbus is a flat city of fat tattooed people. That's what I remembered from the one time I was there. Probably not fair. First impressions seldom are. But Columbus could have tried harder.

At the time, I was a detective for Boston's finest and had come to pick up a prisoner who was set to testify in a narcotics trial in exchange for a reduced sentence. The paperwork wasn't ready when I showed up, so I had to stay the night. I grabbed dinner at a downtown pub where locals hung out. They weren't all fat and tattooed. But most of them were one or the other. Then I made my way to the worst strip joint I'd ever been in. That's where I met Lucy Lee. She had tattoos. Lots of them. But she wasn't fat. She was hot and exotic. And her dances were cheap—one good thing about Columbus.

Lucy Lee was the one who turned me onto YouSEL. It was like a cheap drug instead of the expensive stuff. That was almost two years ago, the start of everything. If she was part of my setup, someone had been stalking me for a long time.

As the Embraer 175 descended through a layer of clouds, I went back over my meeting with Richard Morris. He was connected to my setup somehow. I didn't think he was part of it, but for all I knew, he

130

was the chess master controlling the game and manipulating every-thing. He had the brains and resources, but no motive that I could come up with. I couldn't think of a motive for anyone to frame me for murder. Except maybe a few women I never texted after hooking up. But they'd probably prefer to shoot me.

Morris wanted me to start guarding Rachel immediately. I lied and told him I needed a few days to visit my sister in Boston first. I knew he'd assume I was going there to verify his story with Jack McNeill. I agreed to update Morris at the end of the week. But if he was *the Master* controlling the game, he already knew everything.

The landing gear bouncing on the tarmac jostled me awake. Lights came on, flooding the cabin in a blinding glare. A woman's voice over the intercom welcomed me to beautiful Columbus. Then she told me to stay seated with my seatbelt buckled. That was going to be hard given how excited I was.

I yawned, and my ears popped. I blinked a few times, then looked out the window next to me. It was dark and late. I checked my watch: 11:05 p.m.

The parking shuttle dropped me off at the Green Lot where a black Hyundai Sonata was waiting in row 3B, compliments of Victor. The keys, an Ohio driver's license, and a credit card with the name William Chatham had been in the brown envelope I got from Simon Geller. It was the same alias and credit card Victor had sold me the last time. The picture on the license looked like me, but older. Whoever had produced it was good. Anyone examining it would assume it was a typical bad license photo.

I popped the trunk, looked under the spare tire and found a holstered SIG Sauer P365, ammo, and a concealed carry license all wrapped in a dish towel. The P365 was an older model. No bells and whistles, but a great gun. I had tested it on a practice range several times. When I got in the car, I opened the glove compartment and found a Kershaw Leek. I had everything I needed. Victor was worth the money. But I'd never tell him that.

I took I670 West to downtown Columbus. I paid cash for two nights at the same budget inn I had stayed at the last time. It was near the *Short North District*—the arts, restaurant, and shopping mecca of Columbus. The area extended up High Street, the main downtown thoroughfare, for a couple of miles, ending just before *The* Ohio State University campus. The beautiful people of the Columbus metropolitan area hung out in the Short North on weekend nights, along with an array of socialite wannabes, young professionals, rednecks, and college students. It was expensive. Too expensive for a Boston Police dick the last time I was there. Not too expensive for a private dick with an expense account now.

But it was a Monday night and late. I was tired. Tomorrow was going to be a long day, possibly dangerous. No way to know. I was in Columbus because someone wanted me there. It wasn't for a surprise birthday party.

I needed to be there too. Ashley Grant was hiding out somewhere in Columbus. I had to find her. She knew something about her sister's murder. Lucy Lee probably still lived there. My voices told me she knew something. I also wanted to see her. We had connected that night. And YouSEL was headquartered there. The common denominator for all the murdered strippers—besides me.

None of it was a coincidence. I was being manipulated. I knew that. That's why I needed sleep. I had to be fresh if I was going to get out of Columbus alive. Another thing I never imagined saying.

After checking in, I took the stairs to the second floor instead of the elevator. I eased the stairwell door open and looked both ways down the hallway. It was empty. I walked quickly along the faded green carpet, hugging the floral wallpaper on my right. I stopped just before the door to my room and lowered my backpack softly to the floor. Then I pulled out the SIG from under my polo shirt. I probably hadn't been lured to Columbus to be shot inside a hotel room, but I wasn't taking any chances.

With my left hand, I swiped the keycard above the door handle. The lock clicked. I turned the handle down slowly and pushed the door open. I listened. Nothing. I reached inside, felt for the light switch, and flicked it on. I listened again. Nothing again. I looked through the crack between the door and the hinge jamb. Nothing. I checked for a shadow below the door. Nothing. Then I peeked inside the room quickly. Nothing. I stuck my head in farther and scanned the entire room. A lot of nothing.

I picked up my backpack, stepped into the room, and swung the door closed. I laid my backpack on a chair, then crouched in front of the bed with the SIG pointed at the bathroom door. It was closed, but the light was on. My voices told me someone was in there.

A minute passed. My quad muscles started to tighten. The room was warm. A drop of sweat rolled down my neck.

Then a shadow moved across the strip of light above the threshold. The doorknob turned slowly. I exhaled quietly. The door eased open. A small head of straight medium-length bleach blonde hair poked out. Big dark brown eyes and a small, upturned nose followed. High cheekbones and red bow-shaped lips completed her face.

Lucy.

21

"*D*on't shoot, Will," she pleaded.

Lucy Lee stepped out of the bathroom with her right arm raised in defense. I recognized the multicolored sleeve tattoo covering it. A black V-neck camisole stretched across her round breasts. Implants, I remembered. Her thin bare waist showed below the camisole, exposing a similar tattoo along her right side. A pair of skinny blue jeans were painted on her shapely legs. They ended in red heeled sandals that made her taller by several inches. She could have just come from a *Vogue* fashion shoot. The shot she almost got wouldn't have been a flattering photo.

I stood up and lowered the SIG to my side. My quads relaxed.

"How did you know I'd be here?" I said.

She lowered her arm, put her hands on her hips, and sighed. Her eyes rolled up and down me like a lint brush. She cocked her head and peered at me. A tantalizing smile swept across her face.

"You still look like a boy, Will. A barely legal boy. The kind I like."

A dangerous instinct welled up inside me. An instinct that could get me killed if I followed it. But then another instinct took over. I brought the SIG up and pointed it at her.

"I won't ask again."

She raised her hands, turned her head, and cowered.

"Okay, okay. A guy came into the place I bartend last night looking for Lucy Lee. He asked if I knew her. I said I didn't. I go by Linda Lau now. That's my real name."

"Your real name is Linda?"

"Yeah. Linda Lau."

"Where do you bartend?"

"The Beer Garage. It's in the Short North. Can you please put that gun away?"

I holstered the SIG, and she lowered her hands.

"Finish telling me about the guy," I said.

"Well, he kept asking me questions. I finally just lied and told him Lucy moved away last year. I don't think he believed me, but he said if I talked to her to let her know you wanted to see her—me."

"He used my name?"

"Yeah."

"Fucking Victor," I muttered.

"Was that guy Victor?"

"Don't worry about him. You still haven't told me how you knew I'd be here. Or how you got in."

"Seriously, Will?"

She stared at me, her eyes wide and her mouth agape. I stared back blankly.

"This is the room we stayed in that night," she said. "After I danced for you at The Big O. We fooled around but nothing happened. You said it was because of a new girlfriend. We ended up just talking and falling asleep. You were gone when I woke up, so I never thanked you for the two hundred dollars. I kept the note you left. It was so sweet. You really don't remember?"

I reached up and felt the scar above my right ear.

"I don't spend a lot of time reminiscing."

"Well, I do. When it's something special, like that night. That's why I'm here. I thought you wanted to see me. You know, maybe pick up where we left off."

"How did you get in here?"

"I know the guy at the front desk. I told him you were checking in tonight and asked him to book you in this room so I could surprise you. By the way, you're late. I've been waiting almost three hours."

Her story was absurd enough to believe. I gave her a skeptical look anyway. It seemed to bother her. She shifted her stance and started to chew on her lower lip. She swept her hair from her eyes as they bounced around the room trying to avoid mine.

"You're blonde now," I said.

She looked back at me and smiled in relief.

"Yeah, you like it?"

"I do. But not your story."

Her body tensed again. She stared at me, waiting for an explanation. I just stared back, making her more nervous.

"What do you mean?" she said.

"I didn't check in as Will Chisholm. And there isn't any way you could have known what day I was coming, or if I was coming, even if you were lucky enough to guess what hotel I'd pick."

She seemed to relax.

"I knew you were flying in today and checking in as William Chatham. But it *was* a lucky guess that you'd come here. Although, I was pretty sure about that."

"How did you know any of that?"

"Brittany called and told me."

It was my turn to tense.

"Brittany Sorenson called you?"

"No, Brittany Welch. I don't know Brittany Sorenson."

Jesus.

Brittany Welch was Alyssa's dancing name. The same one she used on YouSEL. She told me she copied it from Raquel Welch, the sex symbol from the 1960's.

"You know Brittany Welch?" I said.

"Yeah, we're good friends. We both worked at YouSEL here in Columbus. You do know her real name, right?"

"Why would I?"

"She said you're like her number one follower on YouSEL. And she said you go to see her a lot at the club she dances at in New York City. I just thought you might be sort of close. Her real name is Alyssa Grant, in case you don't know."

"When did you talk to her last?"

"Uh, today, around noon. We hadn't talked since she moved back to New York. Anyway, she said you were flying in today and using the name William Chatham because of your work. She asked me to check on you as a favor. I was afraid it would be awkward, but then that guy showed up last night saying you wanted to see me. I got really excited."

"And you talked to her today?"

"That's what I said. Why all the questions, Will? I thought you'd be excited to see me too."

I took a moment to refresh my memory of her. She was over thirty but much younger looking. Her sleeve tattoo was a mix of fantastic birds and flying dragons. It extended up the side of her neck, stopping just under her soft sensual face. I knew from our one night together that a similar tattoo ran down her right side, around her lower back, and onto her left buttock. She had a new tattoo since I'd last seen her. A geometric design that looked like armor ran across her upper left arm. Her tattoos dressed her more than they marked her. There was something taboo about her. Carnal but not cheap. Provocative but still pure.

"Why are you looking at me like that?" she said.

"Sorry, Lucy—Linda. Just a lot going on."

"I can be Lucy, if that's what you want."

Anything you desire, however you desire it.

That was the opening audio of every YouSEL video. I had listened to it so many times, it sounded natural, even comforting.

"I like Linda," I said.

She smiled and moved closer.

"Listen, Will, I don't know what's going on between you and Alyssa, but you're in Columbus now. What happens here, stays here. I'm good with that if you are."

"Maybe," I said and feigned a smile.

I stepped back and rested my butt on the edge of the dresser. I unclipped the SIG and placed it next to me.

"I'm not a cop anymore," I said. "I'm a private investigator now."

"You are? Is that why you're here?"

"Yeah. I'm working for the mother of a girl who's gone missing. Columbus was the last place she lived and worked before she disappeared."

"Oh my god, Will. That's awful. Her mother must be so upset."

"She is."

Linda stepped in front of the bed and sat down on the edge of the mattress a few feet away. She leaned forward slightly and looked up, offering me an unobstructed view of her breasts. The surgeon was an artist.

"Is there anything I can do to help?" she said.

I thought about killing the moment. Telling her that Alyssa had been brutally murdered, along with three other strippers who had worked at YouSEL. That it was Ashley who had called her, not Alyssa. That I was only there because I was being framed for her murder. And that I thought she and Ashley were part of it.

I thought about killing the moment. I couldn't risk letting her seduction continue. I couldn't afford to lose control. I was an impulse away from no return.

I thought about killing the moment. But I didn't.

"Linda, it's late, and I'm tired. You might be able to help, but let's talk tomorrow after we've both gotten some sleep. Do you need a lift back to your place?"

She stood up, disappointment covering her face like too much makeup. She stepped closer so that our legs were just about touching.

"I thought I could stay here tonight. We don't have to do any-thing. Just sleep. Maybe talk a little. Like the last time. Unless you decide you want more."

I wanted more. I wanted her to spend the night, even at the risk of doing something I'd regret. I wanted the touch of her warm smooth skin against mine. I needed her exotic beauty to help me escape the violent ugliness that was engulfing me more and more each day. I needed her naked body to save me, if only for the night.

"Alright," I said.

22

*S*he screamed as I pushed inside her. Her dark eyes looked vacantly at me. Slices of blood opened on her cheeks, and her tattoos started to slither.

"Tom, don't," she said.

I gasped and jumped out of bed. I grabbed the SIG off the nightstand and pointed it at the blurry shadows in the corner. I blinked several times, then rotated the SIG around the room. I stopped at the bathroom. The door was open and the light on.

I listened . . . silence.

Sunlight leaked in around the edges of the tan window shades. The intermittent tweeting of a bird was suddenly drowned out by the noise of a truck downshifting. Its engine roared for a few seconds before trailing off as it drove away.

Silence again.

I lowered the SIG and dropped my head. I watched the bulge in my black shorts fade. Then I sat down on the side of the bed and laid the SIG back on the nightstand.

A twenty-dollar bill was sitting on top of a handwritten note next to the lamp. I picked up the note and read it:

> *Will, here's twenty dollars for letting me spend the night! I'll pay more when we finally fuck! Ha-ha! Come by The Beer Garage later—Vine and Park. I'm bartending. LL*

I remembered Linda waking early while it was still dark. She tried to arouse me by putting her hand in my shorts and stroking me. It worked. I got hard fast and woke up. I eased her hand away, then gazed in her eyes and smiled gently.

"Too complicated right now," I said.

"Okay," she replied. "So, when?"

"A few weeks. I'll let you know."

"I'll wait, but don't take too long. You might get too old for me."

Then she said she had to go home to do some things before work. As I watched her dress, I almost pulled her back to bed. But there were too many questions she needed to answer, too many holes in her story. Fucking her body and then her mind didn't seem right. I had to get some answers out of her first. What happened after that would depend.

I must have fallen back to sleep. The nightmare woke me. They were coming more frequently, after twenty-five years without them. All the previous ones had included one of the murdered strippers. But Linda wasn't dead. It probably didn't mean anything. Probably.

It was still early. Too early to check out YouSEL's headquarters or the Italian Village neighborhood where Ashley Grant last lived. I decided to go for a run to clear my head.

I threw on a pair of workout shorts and warmed up with four hundred sit-ups. My back felt a little stiff but no pain. When I finished, an outline of sweat adorned the gray carpet. I put on a black T-shirt, tightened my sneakers, and stretched my legs. I strapped the SIG Sauer around my waist and under my shirt with a running belt and holster I had brought. Then I grabbed one of the burner phones out of my backpack and took the stairs down to the parking lot. It was quiet. A handful of cars, but nothing stood out. A tough looking squirrel stopped ten yards away like it wanted to challenge me. It dove into a dumpster before I could flash the SIG.

The Columbus sun was losing its perennial battle with a cloud layer when I started running west on Chestnut Street. After a block, I turned south on 3ʳᵈ Street. Traffic was light. I passed a few people waiting for a bus. They could have been statues. A tumbleweed rolling by wouldn't have surprised me. I was a world away from New York City.

I turned west on Broad Street and quickened my pace. After crossing the Discovery Bridge, I headed south along the Scioto River. A handful of runners were out. Mostly young like me. A college-aged girl gave me a warm Midwestern smile as we passed each other. I guess even serial killers were welcomed.

It was warm and humid. I had a good sweat going, but I still wasn't breathing very hard. Columbus was flat farm country, the floor of the northern expanse of the Ohio River Valley. There was nothing that would pass for a hill. I could have been on a treadmill with a video providing a virtual sense of running along a river. Virtual because the Scioto wasn't a real river. It was more like a stream. A real body of water didn't exist within a hundred miles as far as I knew. The Scioto was as big as it got. You'd break your neck if you dove in it.

The steady pace I was running felt like meditation. But meditation always made me anxious. Speed soon took over. Then speed turned to euphoria. The nightmares and paranoia disappeared, expelled with the sweat streaming off my body. Wannabe skyscrapers flew by as I got high on perpetual motion. I wanted to run forever. If only I could.

It was a little after seven when I got back to my room. Six miles in thirty-five minutes. But it wasn't enough. I added two hundred push-ups and a hundred improvised tricep dips. It still wasn't enough for the physical release I craved. I'd have to finish in the shower.

I lingered under the hot pounding spray. My mind kept going over all the missing pieces in the puzzle of who was framing me and why. No answers came to me. No strategy either, other than playing along until the Master revealed why I was in Columbus. But there were only so many showers I could take in a day.

I got out, dressed, and grabbed the burner cell to call Victor. I dialed his number and hung up after two rings. I called again and hung up after one ring. Then I called a third time. I came up with the routine so he would know it was me and pick up my call.

"Yo bro, that's annoying. Knew it was you. You get everything?"

"So far, so good."

"Quality, bro. That's what you get from me. For a damn good price too."

"Yeah, a bargain at any price."

"You got that, bro. Beginnin' of a beautiful relationship."

"Yeah, right. Anything on Lucy Lee?"

"Yeah. Don't think she's strippin' no more. Goes by Linda Lau now. Bartends at The Beer Garage on Vine Street. Supposed to be there tonight if you wanna talk to her."

I didn't tell him his information was late or that his guy screwed up and spread my name around Columbus. I figured I might need him again before this was over.

"You find out where she lives?" I asked.

"My man says she's over by the Hollywood Casino. Been there once. Lost a couple of bands in ten minutes."

"Yeah, don't care. You have an address?"

"I'll text it."

"Okay. Anything else?"

"Yeah. What you doin', bro?"

"What do you mean?"

"You hot for this Asian stripper? Will Chisholm smitten with a Midwest ho? That gonna break a lot of ho hearts back here."

"Stick to business."

"I am, bro. My man says this girl's got a bad vibe around her. Think you might be takin' some risk. What's she to you?"

"Back off, Victor. Our relationship isn't that beautiful."

"Whoa, you zoomers are sensitive. Just lookin' out for my investment."

"Don't worry, you'll get paid. Just text that address."

"Okay, but one last thing. My man's hearing noise 'bout you. Watch your back. Or I could come out and watch it for—"

I hung up.

I took out the button camera from Paula White and hooked it on my polo shirt. Then I tested it on my laptop. It seemed to work. Exactly what I was going to record, I had no clue. But I had to be ready. My voices were telling me today was the day I'd find out why I was in Columbus. They were also saying I should have taken Victor's offer.

23

I packed up my stuff and took the stairs down to the parking lot. I wasn't coming back. If Linda could find me there, then anyone could.

My stomach was whining. The last thing I had eaten was some pretzels on the plane. I drove up High Street to an organic cafe I remembered that had good coffee. It was the only thing I could afford the last time I was there. I had an expense account now.

Three artsy types about my age were ahead of me in line. I waited ten minutes while they debated the appeal of a bean sprout and beet bowl versus some bastardization of eggs. Lunch was probably a daily existential crisis for them.

The egg and cheese biscuit, fruit smoothie, and coffee I ordered cost about the same as a semester at OSU. The girl behind the counter seemed confused when I gave her cash, but she figured it out. I sat at one of the outdoor tables under a large yellow umbrella. It was only nine o'clock but already over eighty degrees.

A middle-aged man with a rat dog plopped down at the table next to me. The dog had big bug eyes, a small smushed-in face, and a long tongue that shot out like a lizard. It kept staring at me. I thought about asking the guy to put his pet rodent away. Then I thought better about it. I didn't need more attention. Someone was already following me.

A tan Camry had been tailing me since I left the hotel. It had hung back a block until I parked across from the café. Then it drove past me and pulled over fifty yards up the street. I caught a glimpse of the driver. He was dark, with a shaved head and sunglasses. I had sensed someone following me last night on my way from the airport, but I wasn't sure. Now I was.

I ate the sandwich and drank the smoothie while pretending to read messages on my cell. The Camry didn't move. After I finished, I tossed the trash in a recycling bin and grabbed my coffee. The rat dog gave me a dirty look as I left.

The Camry was still sitting a block up the street when I climbed into the Hyundai. I wanted to see how serious this guy was about following me. I put my coffee in the cup holder, then eased into traffic behind a large white delivery truck and took an immediate right onto East 2nd Avenue. The guy was going to have to hustle to catch up with me. I saw the Camry's brake lights go on as I sped out of sight.

I rolled through a stop sign and turned right onto Summit Street heading south. There was an entrance to I670 about a mile down the road. I was headed back towards the airport. YouSEL's headquarters was located in an industrial park just south of it.

Shabby two-family houses fell away as I wove in and out of morning traffic. They reminded me of the apartment houses I grew up in. Columbus seemed to have more than its share made of brick. They were probably hangers-on from another time, now serving as way stations for college students living off campus.

As I sped through a yellow light onto the I670 entrance ramp, I glanced a bit too long in my rearview mirror. The sharp left curve surprised me. I swerved hard to avoid hitting the guardrail. My coffee cup flew out of the holder and splattered across the passenger seat and door. The Hyundai felt like it might tip over. I hit the brakes, turned back towards the guardrail, and regained control. Then I accelerated down the ramp onto the highway.

As I merged in front of an eighteen-wheeler, I spied the Camry in the passenger side mirror about a quarter mile back. It was speeding down the ramp. That answered my question—the guy was serious.

I settled into the middle lane at a steady seventy miles per hour. Slow enough for the guy to keep me in sight. Fast enough to make him work a little. He was good. I would have to work harder to lose him. No need. I wanted him in sight. I was reeling him in. But I was sure he realized it. In about ten miles, one of us was going to find out who was the fish.

The airport exit was coming up. I accelerated and cut sharply to my right just in front of a double trailer truck. The truck's horn blared like a freight train. I veered down the exit ramp, then took a hard right onto East 5th Avenue. I made it through two intersections before a red light finally stopped me. I looked in the mirror. The Camry was one intersection back.

When the light turned green, I hit the gas. The roar of jet engines suddenly overwhelmed everything. A large plane appeared to my left coming in for a landing. The plane and noise quickly disappeared behind a stretch of tall, ridged cement panels that formed a wall along the border of the airport.

I tapped the brakes and turned sharply onto Yearling Road. YouSEL was located at 100 Yearling. I coasted along, one eye in the rearview mirror, the other looking for a sign with the street number or the company's name. Empty parking lots crisscrossed with weeds ran on either side of the street. A few small industrial buildings were scattered in between, but nothing that looked like a headquarters.

A few hundred yards down on the right, a long gray two-story warehouse stood out. A large parking lot wrapped around it. Ringing the lot was a tall chain-link fence. Swaths of overgrown land buffered the property on three sides. There were no other buildings on either side of the street until it ended at an intersection. This had to be the place.

The gate to the lot was open, but there were no vehicles parked in sight. The place looked deserted. Ideal for a showdown. Or an ambush. I was tired of feeling chased. It was time to find out who was following me.

I turned into the parking lot and accelerated. Then I slammed the brakes and spun the steering wheel hard counterclockwise. The tires squealed as the rear of the Hyundai whipped around, kicking up a plume of dust. When it settled, I was facing the parking lot entrance. If the Camry followed me, it would have to come to a hard stop. I pulled out the SIG and rested it on my thigh.

I watched the intersections at either end of Yearling, my head moving back and forth like a metronome. I checked behind me every five seconds in case someone was parked out of sight.

Several minutes passed without the Camry showing. Five more minutes elapsed and still nothing. Eventually, a few cars and small trucks drove by going in opposite directions. The sound of nothing returned. The fish had gotten away.

When I was a kid, my father used to take my sister and I cod fishing off a breakwater near where we lived. I remembered my first time reeling one in. It felt big. I was thrilled. My father was grinning watching me. I wanted to show him I could do it. Then the line broke. I fought back tears. He told me that fish always come back. That the next one I caught would be the one that got away. I never caught another fish there. But fishing taught me patience.

I knew I would see the guy in the Camry again. I just had to be patient. And prepared.

24

I backed the Hyundai into a space near the entrance to the warehouse. The coffee cup was resting sideways on the passenger seat. A gulp had survived. I downed it, then tossed the empty on the floor. I waited a few more minutes to see if the Camry showed up. A couple of nondescript SUVs drove by but nothing else.

I got out and looked around. To the left of the warehouse entrance, five large windows stretched along the first floor. The second floor had three similar windows bunched together right above the entrance. The cladding appeared to be a mix of sheet metal and vinyl.

A cracked cement walkway with a few small weeds sprouting ran along the building, ending in front of the entrance. Everything grew quickly this time of year, including weeds. There should have been a lot more if the building was empty. Someone was making the effort to keep the landscaping respectable.

The entrance was a glass door. The address was painted on it in faded white letters. I was at the right location. But no company name. No indication of anything, including people. I holstered the SIG under my shirt.

The glass door opened easily. Inside was a small square foyer with a black door straight ahead. It was solid wood, with a nickel-colored lever handle. An intercom system was built into the wall to the left of the door. A small camera in the right corner of the ceiling looked down at me. The walls on either side were covered in framed individual photos of different women in lingerie—YouSEL models. I recognized a few of them. None of the murdered models were showcased.

I looked up at the camera and offered an awkward smile. Then I stepped to the door and pressed the intercom button. A buzzer sounded and the door clicked. I lifted the lever and pushed it open. I kept my right hand by my side, ready to pull the SIG.

The door opened to a large L-shaped office. A red-headed receptionist sat at a black metal table straight in front of me. Her hair was combed back tightly and tied in a complicated ponytail. A sleeveless silky white blouse accentuated her subtle breasts, while her black rim glasses gave her a naughty librarian look. Some guys got off on that fantasy. I preferred reality.

I would have spent a little longer studying her, but a large man to my left stood up from a swivel chair to make sure I knew he was there. He was thirty-something, fair skinned, and sporting a lumberjack beard that I couldn't have grown even if I had started at birth. His brown hair was slicked back on the top and shaved tightly around his ears. A white, short-sleeved button-down shirt looked a size too small on his bulging chest. His right arm had a ribbon of colorful tattoos. Both arms were popping muscles and veins.

But it was his bright white sneakers that got my attention. They were at the end of a set of long but average legs. That told me he was using something to pump up his upper body, which meant he was vulnerable from the waist down. Probably the shoulders up too.

Three large monitors sat on a desk table behind him. Two of them displayed different camera views of the inside of the warehouse. The third one had views of the outside. I quickly eyed the inside screens. They showed nothing but empty space. No one was there working. A receptionist and a security guard to watch over an empty warehouse. Something was off.

"Hi, can I help you?" the receptionist said and smiled attentively.

I glanced at the big guy to make sure he wasn't getting ready to do something. He just stood there looming, making sure I saw him. I brought my eyes back to the naughty redhead. I smiled and stepped closer.

"Yes, I hope so," I said. "I'm supposed to meet someone who works here. Her name's Ashley Grant. I might be a little early."

I didn't know what kind of reaction I would get to Ashley's name, but I knew I'd get one.

"Um, you said Ashley Grant?" the receptionist said. "Uh, we . . . there isn't anyone here with that name. Actually, no one works here anymore. I mean, I don't know any Ashley Grant. I'm sorry, but I can't help you."

She forced a smile, trying to act calm, as if her stammering didn't mean anything. But she was as nervous as a librarian who had just lost a book.

"Hmm, that's strange," I said. "She told me she worked here. Could she be at a different location? Can you check your directory?"

"Uh, no, she doesn't work here. I mean, I can't do a search for you. Company policy. Is there anything else?"

She glanced anxiously towards the big guy for help. He took a step towards me to get my attention. He wasn't nervous. Steroids give you all the confidence in the world.

"Excuse me," he said, "can I ask your name?"

I pivoted towards him and smiled.

"Sure. Bill Chatham."

"Mr. Chatham, no one named Ashley Grant works here. You must have gotten your facts mixed up. We're closing early today. I have to ask you to leave."

"You're closing now? That is early. I'm certain this is the address she gave me, but if you say she's not here, I guess she's not here."

"She's not here because she doesn't work here. Now, you need to leave."

"Of course. I'm sorry. Have a good day."

"We will."

I nodded, then smiled at the receptionist. She returned a painful smile. I turned to leave, then stopped and looked at the big guy.

"Did you know Alyssa Grant, Ashley's sister?" I asked. "She was murdered last week."

He straightened up like I had just challenged him to a fight. He puffed his chest and stepped towards me.

"You gotta go," he said.

I didn't react for a second. It felt longer. The big guy hadn't expected that. I was supposed to run away. He wasn't sure what to do. His jaw tightened as he thought about coming at me.

My instinct was to stay. But that was my fighting instinct. Not always my smartest. I had already learned more than I expected. It wasn't the time or place to make a statement. I shot him a quick smile and left.

25

*L*inda lived in the Lincoln Park West neighborhood, according to Victor's text. It was on the other side of Columbus, probably an hour's drive in midday traffic. She'd be at work by the time I got there.

I wanted to search her apartment. The story she gave me didn't add up. Victor was the only one I had told about Columbus, but she was waiting for me. Alyssa couldn't have called her, and that wasn't the hotel room from two years ago. I was a cop then. I always booked on the lowest level. First floor, corner room—that was where I had stayed that night. But we hadn't fucked. She got that right. I would have remembered that.

Everything told me I couldn't trust her. The problem was I wanted to. I didn't know why. Either way, I needed to check her place to see what I could learn. Then I'd confront her.

Her apartment was on the second floor of a two-story brick house on the corner of a quiet side street. The house looked in decent condition. Out front was a covered porch with separate doors for the first and second floors. The plot of land was narrow. A stone walkway and tall wooden fence ran along one side to a tiny backyard. A thin strip of crabgrass bordered the other side. Wooden steps in need of a paint job climbed from the sidewalk to the porch.

The neighborhood was a mix of two and three-story houses, some well maintained and others in disrepair. Small patches of grass and flowers adorned the nicer ones. Garbage and a piece of old furniture here and there littered the less aspiring ones. An assortment of economy cars and SUVs were parked on the street. Old maple trees gave the neighborhood some character. It was a community in transition, trying to improve itself. That was me once.

I sat in the Hyundai watching the house from down the block and across the street. I was working on a way to get into Linda's apartment without someone calling the police. A middle-aged woman came out of the first-floor apartment, talking on a cellphone and smoking a cigarette. She sat down on the top step of the porch. A minute later, a little girl, three or four years old, waddled out and sat down next to her.

I had a plan.

I drove to a pharmacy I had passed on the way and bought a clipboard and a pair of black rimmed reading glasses. The woman was still on the porch talking on her cell when I returned. The little girl was playing behind her. I got out of the car and made sure my SIG wasn't visible. Then I opened the trunk and grabbed my backpack.

I always carried an old Boston PD shield with me in case I needed to flash some credentials. I'd seen it done a thousand times in old TV shows. It still worked. People respected authority, even my generation. But without a uniform, I looked too young. That's what the glasses were for.

I grabbed the shield, my notebook, and a pen. I wrote a note, ripped out the page, and stuck it in my pocket. Then I clamped the notebook on the clipboard, put on the reading glasses, and walked up to the house. I climbed the first two steps and stopped.

The middle-aged woman stared at me. She was younger than I thought. Maybe thirty but worn. I flashed a polite smile.

"I gotta go, Ma," the woman said and lowered her phone.

"Ms. Lau?" I said. "Hi, I'm—"

"Oh, I'm not Linda," she said. "She's not home right now."

"Oh, I apologize. I was supposed to meet her to inspect her apartment. I'm a little late."

"Inspect her apartment? What for? Sorry, I live right below her. Is something wrong?"

I glanced down at the clipboard like I was reading something. I looked back up at the woman, took out my old shield and flashed it. Before she could examine it, I slipped it back in my pocket.

"I'm a building inspector for the city. Ms. Lau called about putting in a new electric range. I'm supposed to look at the wiring in her apartment to make sure it's up to code."

The little girl stopped jumping around and stared at me. I glanced at her and smiled. She scurried next to the woman and buried her face in her side.

"Oh, wow," the woman said. "Linda didn't tell me she was getting a new stove. Sorry, but she's gone for the day. She works late, so you probably missed her."

I sighed and shook my head in faux frustration.

"Are you the landlord, Ms. . . . ?"

"Beal. Sarah Beal. No, I'm Linda's neighbor. This is my daughter, Courtney. Say hi, Courtney."

The little girl peeked shyly at me, then stuck her head back in her mother's side.

"Very cute," I said. "She has your eyes."

The woman laughed and blushed a little.

"Well, Ms. Lau isn't going to be happy," I said. "I won't be able to come back for four weeks. We're super busy. I know she's been waiting over a month."

"I really am sorry, Mr. . . . ?"

"Bill Chatham. Bill is fine."

"I have a brother named Bill. Actually, William. But we call him— what am I saying? You don't care about my brother. Anyway, I really am sorry about this. Can't you call her?"

"I tried, but she's not picking up. By the way, my real name is William too."

She simpered and stared at me. I returned the stare. Her eyes were a pale blue, with a little spark. No ring on any finger. She probably welcomed the flirtation. It kept the spark alive.

"I really wish I could help you," she said.

"Would you possibly have a spare key? You could come in while I inspected it."

"Wait, I do, if I can find it. Linda gave me one. I'm sure she won't mind. She trusts me."

"That would be great. Thank you."

"Oh, you're welcome. I'll run inside and get it. Courtney, come with me, baby."

The woman stood up with a burst of energy. She crushed her cigarette under her sneaker and hustled inside, her daughter in tow.

I climbed the rest of the steps and walked over to the door leading to Linda's apartment. It was locked. But it was an old lock with no deadbolt. I took the Kershaw Leek out of my pocket and inserted the blade between the latch and the doorjamb. Then I hit the door hard with my shoulder and popped it open.

I stepped into a small foyer with a flight of stairs leading up to the second floor and another door. It had a deadbolt. If it was locked, I'd need the key. I turned around and bumped into Sarah Beal coming in. I grabbed her arm so she wouldn't trip.

"Oh, I'm sorry, Bill. I'm so clumsy."

"My fault. Are you alright?"

"Yes. Don't worry about me. How did you get in?"

I released her arm and smiled awkwardly. She gave me a warm smile back. Then I pulled the note out of my pocket.

"This was on the door," I said and handed it to her. "It's from Ms. Lau telling me she had to go to work and to let myself in."

"Huh, how'd I miss that? Well, here's the key anyway."

I took it and started to think of an excuse for why she shouldn't go up to Linda's apartment with me. I wouldn't be able to search it if she was there. Before I could come up with one, the little girl appeared in the doorway saying she was hungry.

"I'm sorry," Sarah Beal said, "I need to give Courtney a snack. Can you lock up when you're done and bring back the key?"

"No problem. It should only take a few minutes."

"Would you like something to eat? It's no bother."

"No, thank you. But maybe a glass of water."

"Okay, sure."

I went up to Linda's apartment, unlocked the deadbolt, and stepped inside. It was a good-sized two-bedroom. Lots of stuff but organized. The décor was modern, with large pictures of brightly colored designs throughout. In the living room, a big fish tank sat on a stand against a black painted wall. I could see a handful of large black and orange fish swimming gracefully around.

I thought there might be a roommate, but the second bedroom looked like a guest room. There were no personal items, and the bedding was generic.

Linda's bedroom was decorated in soft tones of gray and ivory. A black fan hung from the ceiling. Several large throw pillows covered the bed, with a few more on a big gray armchair in the corner. I never understood women and their pillows.

Two black picture frames sat on an ivory-colored table next to the chair. My eyes froze on a photo of Linda, Alyssa, and Ashley smiling together in a bar. It was The Big O Club where I had first met Linda. There was another woman in the background. She was older, with reddish-blonde hair—Peggy Grant.

Then something on the chair caught my eye. Something red under one of the pillows. I stepped over and lifted the pillow. A red lace, open-cup teddy lay stretched out on the cushion of the chair. A brochure from Allura Lingerie was next to it.

I dropped the pillow and stepped back. I pulled out the SIG and spun around to face the doorway. I listened for a few seconds. It was quiet. I checked the closet and under the bed, then the rest of the apartment. No one else was there. No cameras or audio devices that I could find either. I eased the apartment door open and looked down the steps. No one was coming. I peeked outside a few of the windows, but I didn't see anything suspicious.

I went back into Linda's bedroom to look at the teddy. It was the same style Alyssa had worn in the YouSEL video I had watched. I knew because that's how the videos worked. You picked out the lingerie for a model and then she stripped for you, live, with free replays. For premium subscriptions, the model would masturbate while talking to you using whatever name you gave. It felt real, like all fantasies.

An opened shipping package lay on the floor next to the chair. I picked it up and pulled out a receipt. Two teddies had been sent—one red and one black. I scoured the apartment for the black one. I couldn't find it.

Then I realized why I was in Columbus.

26

I never said goodbye to Sarah Beal. I left the key in the door and drove to downtown Columbus. I parked near the hockey stadium, four blocks from The Beer Garage. It was a little before four.

I bought an iced coffee and sat on a bench across the street from The Beer Garage. I wanted to case the place before I went in to talk to Linda. Something was going to happen there tonight. I didn't know what, but I was sure it would involve me. I reached into my shirt and turned on the button camera.

The Beer Garage occupied a rectangular cement building on the fringe of a block of bars that catered to twenty-somethings. It looked like it had originally been a repair shop. Three large garage doors facing the street were rolled up to open the place to the outside. Several industrial-sized fans hung from the ceiling. There were three bars inside—one against the back and one on either end. Each one had a collection of beer taps coming out of the wall behind it. A series of tall wooden tables were spaced across the long cement floor, with a handful of customers scattered amongst them. Outside to the left was a patio where a few people were playing cornhole. A large chalkboard next to the entrance declared that *Happy Hour* went from 4:30 pm to 5:30 pm.

I finished my coffee, stood up and stretched. My legs were a little stiff from running, but my back felt good. The heat and humidity had gotten worse. Some cumulus clouds mingled in the distance trying to decide what they wanted to do. I knew how they felt.

A short, thick Hispanic bouncer greeted me at the door and asked for ID. He glanced at me twice while he examined my license. He seemed skeptical, but there weren't enough customers inside to turn me away. He handed my license back and nodded me in.

Linda was working the bar on the left. She was rinsing glasses in a sink with her back to me when I walked over. Her black tank top stopped a few inches above a black mini skirt, exposing her tattoo-covered waist.

No one was at her bar. Weekends were the money makers. She probably made a thousand dollars in tips on Fridays and Saturdays. Hazard pay if you looked like her and had to serve a bunch of drunken men after a sporting event.

She sensed that someone was behind her and looked over her shoulder. Her eyes widened and a big smile lit up her face. She straightened up, wiped her hands on a towel, and stepped towards me.

"Hey there," she said. "What's your pleasure? Something cold? Or something hot and wet?"

"Just a Coke."

"A Coke? Really?"

"Yeah. I need to talk to you. It's important."

She stiffened.

"Okay, Will."

She grabbed a glass, scooped some ice into it, and picked up the soda gun. She filled the glass and pushed it gently towards me. Her brown eyes were wide and anxious.

I took a sip of Coke and checked to make sure no one was close enough to hear me.

"This might sound strange," I said, "but do you have a black teddy with you?"

Her eyes brightened and a suggestive smile appeared.

"You should know, you sent it to me. I can't wait to model it for you." She looked around, then turned back to me. "Or . . . it's quiet tonight. I can take a break and put it on. You can join me in the bathroom. They're singles."

"We don't have time. I need to ask you some questions, and you have to be straight with me. Your life depends on it."

She tensed and said, "You're scaring me, Will."

"Good."

"I don't understand."

"I'll explain in a second. First, who told you I was coming here?"

"I told you, Alyssa—"

"Alyssa's dead, Linda. Stop playing games with me."

She froze. Her mouth opened, as if she was about to scream, but nothing came out. She raised her hands to her cheeks. Her reaction said everything.

"How could you not know?" I asked.

"I, I've been away for a couple of weeks. I just got back on Sunday. When? How?"

"A week and a half ago. She was murdered."

"No, no, no," she whimpered and covered her eyes with her hands.

"You really didn't know?"

She shook her head and sobbed.

"What about the other murders?" I said. "Do you know about them?"

She pulled her hands away from her face and stared at me in shock. She wiped a few tears away and shook her head again.

"Four YouSEL models have been murdered," I said. "Alyssa was the most recent. They all happened in New York City. It's been all over the national news."

"I don't follow the news much," she said, choking up. "Someone told me about a YouSEL model dying earlier this year. I knew her a little. But I haven't worked there in a while. I can't believe four of them have been murdered."

She looked down, wrapped her arms around herself, and trembled slightly.

"Linda, look at me."

She lifted her head and took a deep quivering breath.

"Who told you I was coming here?"

She hesitated, then said, "Ashley."

"You spoke to Ashley?"

"No, she texted me yesterday out of the blue. I hadn't talked to her in over a year. Alyssa, her, and I used to hang out when we all worked for YouSEL. But I was closer to Alyssa."

"Ashley was a model too?"

"No, she was like a recruiter. She got me the job as a model."

"How does she know about you and me?"

"She's the one who set us up that night at The Big O. She knows I like you. That's why—"

"*She* arranged for us to meet? Why?"

"I don't know. She stopped by the club that night and said she needed to make sure this cop got special treatment. I didn't care. It was extra money. Then I met you. You know the rest."

Linda had introduced me to YouSEL, so I could see her whenever I wanted, even if only virtually. I was supposed to get hooked on the site. And I did. None of it was an accident. The Master had been setting me up for at least two years.

My head began to throb above my right ear. Flashes of light swarmed in front of me. I took several quick breaths and closed my eyes. It helped. When I opened them, Linda was staring at me, a concerned look on her face.

"Are you okay?" she said.

"Yeah. Just a headache. Why did you say Alyssa called you?"

"Ashley texted me to say that. She said you had a thing for Alyssa, and it would sound better if I said she had called me. I didn't see the harm. But why would she do that to me if she knew Alyssa was dead?"

"Can I see the texts from Ashley?"

"That's the weird thing. They disappeared. Or I accidentally deleted them. When I went to text Ashley today, I couldn't find her messages or even her number. But I'm telling you the truth, Will. She sent them, and I read them. I don't know, maybe someone hacked my phone. That happens, you know."

"Yeah, maybe. When was the last time you talked to their mother, Peggy?"

"Will, their mother died when they were teenagers. Peggy is their aunt. She took them in for a few years during high school. Alyssa hates her—hated her. Ashley doesn't like her much either."

The ceiling fan could have knocked me over. Before I could recover, Linda's eyes wandered behind me. I peered in the mirror on the wall and saw a man approaching the bar on my left. I brought my right hand down by my side near the SIG. Then I felt his body heat next to me. I turned my head slightly and saw a large man out of the corner of my eye.

Linda looked at the man, sniffled, and forced a smile.

"Can I get you something?" she asked.

"Shot of Jack and a Pabst," he said.

"Draft or bottle?"

"Bottle."

Linda poured a generous shot and pushed it towards the man. Then she stepped over to a metal cooler, grabbed a bottle of Pabst Blue Ribbon, and flicked off the cap. She set it on the bar next to the shot.

"Anything else?" she asked.

"No. Put it on Bob's tab. We're outside."

Linda stepped over to the register and rang up the drinks.

I glanced at the guy. He was in his late twenties, maybe thirty, six foot three and two hundred fifty pounds, give or take. He had a shaved head with a dark bushy mustache. His tight gray T-shirt accentuated his large biceps. He had an edge that wreaked like body odor.

He downed the shot and savored it for a moment. Then he turned his head and glared at me. I stared into my Coke, watching him with my peripheral vision.

He leaned towards me and said, "You got a problem?"

I glanced up at Linda.

She turned from the register and said, "Hey, no trouble, okay? The drinks are on me. Go enjoy them with your friends."

"He your boyfriend?" the guy sneered. "You should be with someone your own age." He turned back to me and said, "You always hide behind her pussy?"

Linda stood on her toes and waved to the Hispanic bouncer at the door.

"Jorge, can you come over here?" she shouted.

Jorge must have signaled he wasn't going to interfere because Linda raised her hands in frustration. She stared at me and shook her head in disbelief. But I knew what was happening.

I straightened up from the bar and glanced at the entrance to the patio. Three men were standing just outside the doorway with beer bottles in their hands. They were his backup. All big, all white, all the same age, all the same look. No diversity required for this job.

A waitress came in from the patio. The guy could have ordered his drinks from her if he had wanted. But he was looking for a fight. They were all looking for a fight. Not a fair fight. A fixed fight, like the old days of boxing. They still happened today, just at lower levels. It was harder to fix an MMA fight, but I'd seen a few. The fix had been in on this fight for a while. Probably before I had even landed in Columbus.

I turned and stared at the guy. I didn't tense my jaw or give any other hint of emotion. I just stared hard into his small brown eyes. It was an interrogation technique I had honed as a detective. I hadn't moved or flinched, but I knew he felt like I was crowding him, getting in his face.

"I'll meet you and your cousins outside in five minutes," I said. "Don't try to run."

The guy seemed confused for a moment, then he grinned and stepped closer. His breath smelled of chewing tobacco. A few residual drops of whiskey hung on his mustache.

"Acting tough for your girlfriend ain't gonna stop that pretty face from getting messed up. Two minutes, then I drag your ass outside. Don't *you* try to run."

The guy grabbed his beer and swaggered towards the patio. A half circle of customers had formed in anticipation of the show. No one was taking bets. I guess everyone knew about the fix.

I turned to Linda and said, "We don't have much time. You're in danger. Someone's—"

"I'm in danger? You're the one with four guys waiting to beat you up."

"Linda, listen to me. I don't have time to explain, but someone's going to try to kill you tonight. The same way Alyssa and the other three women were killed. You have to leave Columbus now. Don't go back to your apartment."

"That's crazy, Will. Why does someone want to kill me? I'll call the police—"

"Stop! You can't trust anyone. Not even the police. If you don't leave now, you'll be dead before the morning."

"I can't trust anyone?"

She bent her head and covered her mouth with her hands. Muffled sobs escaped between trembling gasps. When she was cried out, she lowered her hands and looked up at me.

"You can trust me," I said.

"Okay. But how can I just leave? Where am I supposed to go?"

"As soon as the fight starts, walk out the back, get in your car, and drive to someplace you've never been before. Leave the car there and get on a bus or a train to another place you've never been. Throw your cell away when you leave here and buy a prepaid phone. When you're someplace safe, call this number."

I grabbed a pen off the bar, took a napkin, and wrote a number on it. I handed it to her.

"It's my sister's cell. Don't tell her who you are. Just give her your new cell number. I'll get it from her and call you. Don't call or text anyone else until you hear from me. And don't use any credit or debit cards. Here's some cash."

I took two thousand dollars in fifties and hundreds out of my pocket and handed it to her.

"That's a lot of money, Will."

"Take it. When I get to the patio, you leave and don't look back."

"What happens after I get to wherever I'm going?"

"I'm working on that. When I figure out who's behind these murders, you'll be able to come back here. Until then, you just have to trust me."

She nodded. Then she stretched across the bar and cupped my face in her hands. She pulled me towards her and kissed me long and real. Her hands slid reluctantly off my cheeks as she stepped back. She smiled like she was about to jump out of a plane.

"You better fuck me when this is over," she said.

I managed a faint smile, then turned and headed for a beating.

27

*I*f there were four, there were five. Maybe even six.

This wasn't a barroom brawl. It had been planned well in advance. If you were going to make that effort, why take the chance it didn't work? Only four was a risk, especially if it was a straight-up fight. There had to be at least one more for insurance.

The fifth guy was probably hiding outside the patio doorway waiting to sucker-punch me. No guns or knives allowed. They weren't supposed to kill me or put me in the hospital. Just make a show of pummeling me so that everyone remembered I was there.

When Linda was found murdered tomorrow, the story would be that I was harassing her. Five good Samaritans stepped in to help. Witnesses would corroborate their account. But I was angry and wanted revenge. I waited until she got off work, then raped and strangled her using the teddy I had bought her. After, I carved ritualistic symbols in her body.

The media would jump on the similarity to the stripper slayings in New York City. They would highlight me as a person of interest in those murders and pump up the fight at The Beer Garage. My prints would be found in Linda's apartment. Her neighbor would be interviewed and identify me, shocked that she had met a serial killer.

That was why I was in Columbus. The only question was where I'd be arrested—here or in Manhattan. But if Linda did what I told her, I wouldn't be arrested anywhere. She'd be alive tomorrow. First, though, I had to take a Midwestern ass whooping to give her time to get away.

As I walked towards the patio, the four guys waiting for me put their beers on a table and spread out to the left. That told me the fifth guy was hiding to the right. The big goon who had challenged me stepped forward. He was the ringleader. The two guys to his right looked like farm boys. They were a little overweight but muscular. The guy on his left was my height and build, blond hair, and nasty looking. The blackjack tucked in the waist of his jeans confirmed my impression.

Five feet from the patio, I started sprinting. All four of them instinctively stepped back, thinking I was bull rushing them. As I passed through the doorway, I dove to my right, rolled, and came up into a fighting stance. A large man was lunging at me with his right fist—the fifth guy. I ducked and stepped quickly to my left. The punch sailed over my head. The guy stumbled, recovered, and turned back to me. Too late. I stepped towards him, leapt into the air, and launched a flying knee kick into his face. His head snapped back, and he crumbled to the cement.

A flash of lightning lit up the patio as I landed, followed by a loud boom of thunder. Large raindrops started to pelt everything. I glanced down at the hunk of muscle. His eyes were rolled up towards his forehead, blood covering his face and beard, a splinter of bone protruding from his cheek. It was the security guard from YouSEL.

I had to keep the fight going for another five minutes to give Linda time to get away. Only one round in an MMA fight, but an eternity in a street fight.

The other four seemed stunned for a moment. Before any of them could react, I ran at the ringleader with my head lowered like I was going to tackle him. He braced himself and raised his arms to slam his fists into the back of my head. Just as I was about to ram him, I swung my right arm in a windmill motion and hammered his left arm down, exposing his head. Then I spun counterclockwise and whipped my left elbow around, smashing it into his ear. Blood spat out, and he fell to the ground, taking one of the farm boys down with him. My forward momentum carried me out of striking distance of the other two.

The farm boy started to haul himself up but made the mistake of lowering his eyes. I took two quick steps towards him and kicked him hard in the windpipe. He tumbled onto his back and grasped his throat. His eyes bulged as he struggled to breathe, his trachea likely ruptured.

The rain was falling harder. A crowd had gathered inside the doorway to stay dry and watch the fight. That's when I noticed a black guy standing twenty feet away, expressionless, getting soaked. He looked like the driver of the Camry that had been following me earlier—a sixth guy. Probably the real leader.

The nasty guy and the remaining farm boy spread out on either side of me and started to ease closer. The nasty guy took out the blackjack. My eyes darted back and forth between them. They looked at each other, then me, then each other again. They were working out their timing.

The nasty guy nodded, and the farm boy came at me. I stepped towards him and faked a punch. He flinched. I turned quickly and ran at the nasty guy, surprising him. I lifted my right leg and drove my foot into his chest. He stumbled back, swinging the blackjack wildly in defense.

I heard the farm boy behind me and ducked, avoiding his punch. I spun to his left and hit him with a right-left combination in his ribs. He groaned and buckled at his side. I slammed my foot into his knee, hyperextending it. He screamed, and I snapped a left uppercut under his chin. His head jerked up, blood spilling from his mouth. His muscles suddenly went limp, and he collapsed.

Then I saw something coming towards me from the left . . .

Aargh!

I fell to the ground and felt a thick warm liquid seep down the left side of my face. I rolled onto my back and saw a blurry image standing in front of me. It took me a second to register that I'd been hit with the blackjack.

I instinctively raised my legs in a defensive position. My vision cleared enough to see the nasty guy five feet away holding the black-jack. He stepped back. He'd seen what I could do with my legs. I scrambled to my feet.

My vision started to blur again. Columbus was spinning. I thought about pulling out the SIG, but I could barely see. Running wasn't an option either. I had to buy time and hope my vision recovered.

A blurry figure moved towards me. I put my arms up like a boxer to protect my head and ribs. I started to bob and weave. If I could grab him, I could get him in a chokehold and put him out. The blur moved closer. It was now or never. I started to lunge, but someone hit my shoulder and spun me around. I lost sight of the blur.

I waited for the blackjack to strike as a cacophony of sirens grew in the thumping rain. Then a strong hand clenched my left tricep. Before I could react, another grabbed my forearm. A blur appeared to my left. I started to pull away—

"Chisholm, I'm Victor's cousin," the blur said. "We have to go."

28

"*W*here am I?" I asked.

"My apartment," Victor's cousin replied. "You faded in and out getting here. Surprised you didn't completely pass out. You got a nice bump. It stopped bleeding. You might have a slight concussion."

I was slumped back on a leather couch holding a plastic bag of ice against the left side of my head. A towel was draped over my shoulders, and my clothes were still wet. But I could see.

Victor's cousin sat on a kitchen chair watching me intently. In his late thirties, he looked shorter and heavier than me, with a shaved head and medium dark skin.

"David Bishop, right?" I said. "The man in the Camry."

"You remembered my name *and* car. Good sign."

"Thanks for bailing me out. What happened to the guy with the blackjack?"

"He's going to have a headache himself, but he'll live. That was an impressive display back there."

"None of them should have touched me. I screwed up on the order."

"I doubt any of them think they won that fight. If they're even conscious yet. Why did they want to work you over anyway?"

I didn't know if I could trust Bishop. He was Victor's cousin, but I didn't trust him either.

"Just a bunch of rednecks looking for trouble," I said. "Probably targeted me. I don't exactly look like a member of the Aryan Nation."

"Neither do I, but I've never had five guys jump me in a bar anywhere in the Midwest. And I've lived here all my life. How about a real answer?"

"Why does it matter to you? You have a special interest for some reason?"

Bishop stared at me calmly, like he was trying to decide the best way to talk to a problem child. I'd seen the look before. Many times. But I'd seen worse. His didn't bother me.

He said, "Victor told me you don't trust anyone. Okay, this is who I am. Ex-Chicago PD. Captain when I left. Don't ask why. Long story, like yours. Except I'm a lot older. I know you worked narcotics for the Boston PD. I checked you out. Tough way to end your career. Anyway, Victor asked me to look out for you. That's what I did. That's what I'm doing. If you want me to stop, fine with me. But you got a target on your back here. Someone wants to fuck with you bad. And that bartender, Linda Lau, too. Probably why she took off with that white chic while you were playing patty-cake. But none of that matters to me unless you want my help. Your call."

"You saw Linda leave with someone?"

"Does that mean you want my help?"

"What's it going to cost?"

"No charge. Former cop to former cop. Besides, Victor's paying me."

I put the bag of ice on the table next to the couch and sat up. My head was numb from the cold, and my back felt tight.

"Alright. Tell me about the woman."

"So, I was watching you take down the first guy when I caught sight of Linda Lau running in the parking lot. She was about to get into a car when an SUV pulled up. A white woman got out, and they started talking, all animated like. Then they hugged, and Linda climbed in the SUV. They took off in a hurry."

"Did you get a plate number?"

"No. It had started raining."

"What about the make and color?"

"I couldn't see the make, but it was white."

"What about the woman?"

"She was young. I think it was this girl I saw in a few of the bars when I was tracking down Lucy Lee, aka Linda. A real looker. Tall, brunette, smoking body, and great eyes. A bit of an attitude. Now it's your turn. What's this all about?"

I gave him a long hard look. Then I scanned his apartment quickly. It was nice but not flashy. More or less what I'd expect for an ex-cop. Nothing screaming danger. My voices were quiet too. I didn't see a lot of risk in telling him why I was in Columbus. If he was involved in my setup, he already knew. If he wasn't, he might be able to help.

"I assume Victor told you what's going on."

"Yeah, the stripper slayings. I've seen the news stories too. He says you didn't kill any of them. Someone's framing you. He vouched for you. That's good enough for me."

"Victor vouched for me?"

"You wouldn't be here if he hadn't. Besides me, you're the only cop or former cop he doesn't hate."

"I'll try to remember that the next time he shakes me down."

"Ha! Okay, that's Victor. He likes you, though."

"He likes the money."

"Don't we all. But he doesn't go out of his way for many white guys. Or whatever you are. Sorry if that triggers you."

"I only care about one trigger."

"Good, since I don't have a safe space for you to cuddle."

"You're wasting your jokes. I don't identify as anyone."

"Victor said you're cynical."

"Anyway, I'm here looking into a company called YouSEL. You know it?"

"The porn site?"

"Yeah. It's supposedly headquartered here in Columbus."

"It's out by the airport. Didn't one of the victims work there?"

"All the victims worked as models for the company. Linda used to work there too. It's the common denominator. I came here to see what I could find out about it."

"And what have you found out?"

"Not much yet. I checked out the headquarters today. The building was virtually empty. They must have moved their operations. The security guard for the building was that first guy I took down. That's no coincidence."

"No. I've had some peripheral dealings with YouSEL."

"Like what?"

"Not porn. Six months ago, several clients asked me to examine their home computing networks. They had some strange stuff going on. I found a lot of malware and surveillance software on their computers and servers. For a couple of them, their cellphones too."

"Where does YouSEL come in?"

"I traced some of it to servers at YouSEL. The company stonewalled me when I tried to talk to them. Then two months later, all the clients who hired me said it was resolved and they didn't need me anymore. No explanations. That hurt the wallet."

"Who are your clients?"

"You know I can't share that."

"I mean, what types are they?"

"All types, but mostly well-off. Small businesses, wealthy families, men, women, straight, gay, old, young—anyone who can afford me. A number of them are into crypto, which is what I thought the problem was initially. Lots of bad actors in that space. When the YouSEL connection came up, I thought it might be a porn scam, but I think there was more going on. From what you said, it sounds like they've moved all the servers out. Probably never know."

"You're in cybersecurity?"

"Cybersecurity, cloud infrastructure, data encryption. Anything with a technology and security angle. I started my own consulting business here a couple of years ago. I help Victor when he really needs it, but that's not my main gig. Unlike him, I try to stay in bounds most of the time. I still have cop blood in me."

"Thanks for stepping out of bounds this time."

"No problem. You can owe me one. Never know when I'll need a favor."

"Sounds fair. So, how do you know there's a target on my back?"

"I have some friends on the force and other low places here. When I started asking around about Lucy Lee, a couple of them contacted me to warn me off. Your name came up. The problem is I'm from Chicago. I'm hard of hearing when it comes to threats."

"Don't get killed on my account. We haven't even kissed yet."

"Just watch your back. And you're welcome, asshole."

I laughed. He grinned.

"One more thing," Bishop said. "A few months ago, an independent power provider hired me to look into a problem it was having. It sells electricity to households and small businesses in the area. It was experiencing power demand surges and couldn't figure out where they were coming from. It suspected one of its customers might be tapping the grid illegally. I traced the power surges to a couple of warehouses over by the airport near YouSEL. The client paid me and said they would take it from there. I never found out if it had anything to do with YouSEL. I thought it was strange being so close, but it might have just been a coincidence."

"Lot of coincidences in Columbus."

"Sure are. By the way, who's the hot brunette that Linda drove off with?"

"Probably Ashley Grant. Her twin sister was the most recent stripper murdered. Her aunt hired me to find her because she was afraid the killer might be after her too. I don't trust her. I think she and Ashley might be complicit in the murders."

"That ain't good. That means Linda might already be dead."

"It's possible. But then Ashley would be the last person seen with her. It would implicate her, not me. I don't think that was the plan for luring me here."

"You think someone wanted you in Columbus? Why?"

"To frame me for Linda's murder. I didn't know it until today. I only knew I was being manipulated to come here. I had to go along to try to figure out who's behind all this."

"You have any suspects now?"

"Everyone's a suspect. But that's because I don't have a motive. I have no clue why someone wants to frame me."

"Sorry, I can't help with that. But if you're going to stick around, I can probably set up a few conversations with people."

"I can't. The police probably want to talk to me. I should leave before they figure out who I am."

"Okay. Anything else I can help with?"

"Some aspirin would be good. Then I'll go."

"Sure. When's your flight?"

"I'm going to drive back. The police might be looking for me at the airport."

"It's getting late. You're welcome to crash here tonight."

"Thanks, but I want to get out of Columbus as soon as I can."

"I hear that a lot," he said and grinned.

Bishop went to the bathroom and came back with some Tylenol and a glass of water. I popped a couple of tablets and chugged the water. We shook hands, and I left.

The garage where I had parked was a block from Bishop's apartment. I picked up my car and jumped on the highway. The rain had stopped. A deep-yellow full moon glowed through some residual storm clouds. Pockets of mist whisked by in the shadows of the breakdown lane. I checked the mirrors. No one was following me that I could tell.

The airport exit was coming up. My mind went back to what Bishop had said about YouSEL and power demand surges. Manhattan was a nine-hour drive. I would need a few hours of sleep at some point. I had time for a side trip.

29

I took the airport exit and headed for YouSEL. I wanted to look inside the building. My voices told me something else had been going on there besides porn.

The building was dark, and the lot was empty. But the gate was open. I pulled over a hundred yards down the road, shut off my lights, and watched. No one went in or out. An SUV, a few cars, and a small van drove by. None of them seemed to notice me.

I waited twenty minutes, then drove back and pulled into the lot. I went around to the rear of the building. A series of loading docks and overhead doors designed for freight trailers ran along the back. No cabs or trailers where in sight. Just an empty parking lot ringed by a tall chain-link fence.

A flight of cement stairs led up to a metal door next to the first loading dock. I parked in front of it, got out and looked around. The clouds had cleared. The moon soaked the lot in a soft white glow. I walked up the stairs and tried the door. It was locked.

When I first returned from Afghanistan, I worked the night shift loading trucks in a warehouse in Boston. Guys were always punching out early and leaving one or two overhead doors unlocked. Whenever the day crew discovered one of them, the night shift workers would blame the new guy—me. I figured Columbus workers weren't much better.

I was right. The third overhead door rattled open. I stepped inside, took out my cellphone, and turned on the flashlight.

The place was cavernous. It was also empty and remarkably clean. It looked broom swept. Most warehouse floors I'd seen were covered in a layer of greasy dirt. The second floor was only half the width of the first floor to allow the overhead doors to roll up. A series of posts supporting the second floor ran the length of the loading dock.

I walked around the entire floor but didn't see anything that hinted at what had been inside. A walled-off area in the right corner looked out of place. It had a metal door. I opened it. The room inside was large and empty. About fifty feet deep by seventy-five feet long. The walls were outfitted with all different kinds of electrical outlets. Several large vents came out of the ceiling. Four control panels of some kind were attached to the wall abutting the outside.

I went out and walked around to the side of the building that lined up with the room. Eight massive air conditioning compressors hugged the warehouse. Tubing and wires entered the building at various points up to the second floor. Only freezers and mainframe computers needed that kind of cooling. The room inside wasn't a freezer.

Back inside, I found the stairs to the second floor and went up to see what was there. Various sized rooms lined either side of a long hallway running the length of the floor. The first one on the left was a utility room of some sort. It had three large circuit boxes and four more control panels on the walls, but nothing else. Most of the other rooms had furniture and lighting equipment, suggesting they had been filming studios for YouSEL sessions. It looked like they hadn't seen any action in a while.

The hallway ended in a large open room. My internal compass told me I was above the reception area I had been in earlier. A few empty metal desks and tables were scattered along the walls. A handful of monitors sat in a corner, but no computers. The entire place felt like it had been deserted for some time.

My voices started to murmur. Was the receptionist and one-man security detail just for me? To create confusion, so I would return and break in? But who would care about the break-in of an empty warehouse?

Something else was supposed to happen there. Something that had been interrupted. Or stopped. I glanced around the room, shining the flashlight in all the corners. I was being watched. Probably filmed too. My voices told me.

Then they told me to leave—fast.

I took out the SIG and double-timed it down to the loading dock. I left the way I came in and pulled the overhead door closed. I drove around to the front slowly, in case someone was waiting. No one was there. In ten minutes, I was back on the highway.

It was late, but traffic was still heavy with long-haul truckers trying to avoid daytime congestion. One big rig after another raced past me as I stuck to the speed limit. After three hours, the steady convoy of trucks eased up. I was on I80 East, cruising along a dark stretch of rural Pennsylvania, the moon illuminating a flat desolate landscape that went on for miles. Now and then, an abandoned car emerged in the breakdown lane before being swallowed by the blackness behind me.

Everything from the past two days rushed through my mind, like the endless stream of white dashes on the highway before me, shimmering in my high beams before falling away in mesmerizing rhythm. Linda was supposed to be murdered in the YouSEL building tonight. Video of me breaking in would place me there. I had stopped it. Or just delayed it. I'd know soon.

The trap was elaborate and the execution methodical. The Master was patient. Someone capable of manipulating a lot of people and organizations. Someone very smart. Probably powerful too. But I still had no clue why I'd been targeted. There had to be a reason for someone to be so obsessed with persecuting me.

I ruled out the drug gangs and dealers back in Boston. They weren't that clever or subtle. Nor were any of my old collars. They were addicts, thugs, thieves, perverts, an impulsive murderer or two. Many of them were sick. None of them were powerful.

I hadn't made any real friends since moving to New York. Or fake ones, for that matter. But I hadn't made any real enemies either. Except Jon Choi. But we had a truce, of sorts. No one else in New York City knew me well enough to hate me. I didn't matter to anyone who mattered.

There were women who might want to hurt me. Women I had slept with. A few I had made love to. Some I hadn't done anything to. But I had never forced myself on a woman. A woman had to want to be with me. Her choice and her desire. Rough, submissive, fast, slow, romantic, intense. Whatever we *both* wanted in the moment. Sex was an escape for me. Not a weapon.

By most counts, I was still young. The women I had slept with were young too. Not always younger, but not old. Thirty-something at most. None of them could manipulate my world the way the Master was doing.

Except maybe Brittany. She thought that I had betrayed her, that I had slept with the woman who tried to kill me back in Boston. It would justify punishing me, in her mind. She already had, in my mind. She never came to see me in the hospital after I was shot. She stayed away. I was dead to her. So, why kill me again?

But if it was her, she would need help from someone. Someone she could manipulate. A boyfriend. Or lover. Someone in a position of authority and capable of violence—for her.

Brittany had a dark streak. Sometimes, I didn't recognize her. That was usually in bed. It was exciting. But most of the time she was radiant—a Venus—there to worship and adore. And I had.

Maybe she had changed since Boston. Maybe she was darker now, because of me. But I couldn't believe she was part of any of this. I didn't want to.

Still, there was something intensely personal about my setup. It wasn't just a sick serial killer getting off on murdering innocent

strippers and pinning it on a pathetic former cop. Whoever was behind it wanted to torture me and drive me beyond the limits of my en-
durance. Indictment, arrest, trial, conviction, and finally prison. Most
cops would prefer suicide. Maybe that was the endgame. If it was, it
was too calculated to just be revenge. There was another purpose. But
I felt like I was staring at a one-way mirror. I couldn't see the motive
or the person behind it.

30

*N*o nightmares. The first time in a week. I felt myself to make sure I wasn't dreaming.

My head hurt a little, and my mouth was dry, but I could see the different shades of white paint on the ceiling. The SIG was on the nightstand, with the Kershaw Leek next to it. A few birds were complaining outside. I was alive and awake in a motel just outside Lewisburg, Pennsylvania.

It was a little after eight in the morning. Sunlight was crawling in through the blinds and under the door. If it was still Wednesday, I'd been asleep for four hours.

Because it would hurt, I did twenty minutes of sit-ups and push-ups, then ten minutes of running in place. I had a decent sweat going when I stepped into the narrow fiberglass tub for a quick shower. The plastic curtain was streaked with grime. I wasn't sure if I would be any cleaner when I was done. But at least the water was hot.

After I checked out, I texted Victor for instructions on where to leave the car. Then I stopped for some breakfast at a diner overlooking the Susquehanna River. I ordered two eggs over easy, bacon, home fries, toast, and a stack of pancakes, along with coffee and juice to wash it all down. A perky brunette waitress took my order and delivered the food.

"You look familiar," she said and poured me more coffee. "Do you go to Bucknell?"

I'd heard of it. It was the rich white kid college nearby. She looked like a student. Maybe not so rich since she was waiting on me. She assumed I was a student too. I was too diverse to be a local. Waiting on me would probably meet her community service requirement. I didn't care. I liked her voice. It felt like warm syrup dripping over me.

"No," I said. "I just graduated from Penn State."

Lying on a half-empty stomach went down like burnt coffee. But getting my degree at night from Boston University was a story she probably didn't want to hear, even with a 4.0 GPA.

"Oh, you've graduated. Wow, I thought you were like my age. I mean, you're only a couple of years older. I'm a rising junior. Anyway, congrats. Do you work around here?"

She was trying hard. Maybe she liked my looks. They were different, I'd been told. Better than half-breed, which I'd also been told. It was usually one or the other. But no woman had ever told me how smart I looked. Or mature. Or rich. Or white. I figured she was bored.

"Just passing through," I said.

"Oh, okay. Well, if you need anything else, just holler."

She left to wait on a table of four. I heard her over my shoulder chatting it up with them. I guess I wasn't special. Maybe she'd break down crying later.

I attacked my food. The burst of energy cleared my head. I started making a mental list of things I had to do. The first was to check in with my sister.

I finished eating and texted her: "Amy, it's Will."

Since it was a burner phone, she wouldn't recognize the number. But she would know it was me. We had a system. Always the same message, but three different versions determined by the day of the month. She would respond with the number of anyone who had called for me. The digits of the number were varied depending on the day as well. A question mark meant there were no messages. Any breach of the protocol sent her into hiding at an agreed upon location until I showed up. It had never happened.

Amy was three years older than me and a nurse in Boston. She had two cellphones—one for her personal use and a burner phone that I used as an emergency contact for people trying to reach me. I sent her a new burner phone every six months.

I had arranged the system with her while I was working narcotics in Boston. Informants wanted a way to reach me without being traced, and my superiors sometimes needed to contact me when I was undercover. Even Brittany used it on occasion while we were dating if she hadn't heard from me in a while. After I was fired, Amy and I agreed to keep the system going, just in case. But I hadn't used it in almost a year.

The busboy topped off my coffee, and I downed it quickly. I never saw the perky waitress again, but I left a good tip to ease her pain. Then I paid the bill at the register, hit the restroom, and got back on the highway.

Victor sent a text telling me where to leave the car at Teterboro Airport in New Jersey. I arrived about one and parked in a private lot. I wiped the keys, SIG, and knife, then wrapped them in a towel I stole from the motel and hid the bundle under the spare tire in the trunk. I tossed the ammo in a trash can and put the parking ticket in the glove compartment. I held onto the credit card and ID.

I caught a shuttle to the airport, then took a taxi to the garage where I kept my Caddy. My Glock, Ruger, and Ghostrike were in the hidden compartment in the trunk. I grabbed them and headed back to my apartment.

Two blocks before I got to my building, I crossed to the other side of the street and started looking for anyone looking for me. I walked fifty yards past the entrance, then turned around. There were plenty of people roaming the sidewalks, but no one stood out. I thought about hanging back for a while and surveilling the neighborhood, but I was falling asleep on my feet. If the NYPD wanted to arrest me, they were going to have to wake me up.

When I opened the door to the foyer, a roach scurried in front of me. I let it go and lumbered up the two flights of stairs to my floor. My backpack felt like an anvil. I got to my apartment and eyed the seal around the doorjamb. The sliver of wood I'd put there was gone. I looked down. A soft yellow glow oozed from the gap under the door. It was the lamp by my bed. Someone had been inside. Maybe someone still was.

I stepped away from the door and crouched up against the wall. I lowered my backpack to the floor and pulled out my Glock. A shadow crossed the gap from inside. Then the creak of a door opening floated up the staircase from the floor below. I listened. Light footsteps hurried up the stairs. I swung around so my back was against the wall. I held my Glock close to my chest, pointed forward. My eyes darted back and forth between the stairs and my apartment door.

"Will Chisholm, that you?" a hushed voice asked.

Sally Jin.

I stood up, exhaled, and lowered my Glock next to my leg. I glanced at the glow under my door. The shadow was gone. I turned my head back towards the stairs and saw Sally peeking through the spindles of the railing.

"What you doing?" she asked.

"Did you let someone in my apartment?"

"I angry at you. Reporters keep showing up. Ask everyone questions. Police search your apartment. You don't explain. Everyone in building upset. I upset. Too much, Will."

"Sally, is someone in my apartment?" I said firmly.

"Girlfriend waiting. I let her in."

"Girlfriend?"

"She nice. Pretty. She say you in trouble. You in trouble?"

"Thank you, Sally. I'm sorry about everything. Michael okay?"

I knew that would shut her up. She looked down and shook her head in disapproval.

"You take advantage because you help Michael. Not fair." She looked up. "What I do with you? Maybe girlfriend talk sense to you."

She turned and shuffled down the steps out of sight. A few seconds later, I heard the faint sound of a door closing.

I moved in front of my apartment door, grabbed the knob with my left hand and turned it. Then I pushed the door open, stepped inside, and lined up the sights of my Glock on the woman sitting on the edge of my bed.

Her eyes widened. She straightened up, her white sleeveless blouse stretching across her chest. She placed her hands on the mattress and uncrossed her legs, her tight blue skirt pulling up to the top of her sleek thighs. The corners of her lips turned up in a hint of a smile.

"I'd prefer to be spanked," she said.

31

"*A*re you *trying* to scare me?" Brittany asked.

I took an extra moment, then lowered my Glock and holstered it. I grabbed my backpack and tossed it on the floor to the left, next to my leather armchair. I closed the door and kept my back to Brittany while I thought. After a few seconds, I turned and faced her.

"How is your back?" she said in a slightly raspy voice.

"Fine."

"That's good. So, in case your super mentions it, I told her that I *used* to be your girlfriend. I don't think she understood me."

"You told her I was in trouble."

"Oh, you already talked to her. Yes, I did. I wanted her to let me in. I didn't know how long I'd have to wait. She seems to care about you."

The dull lamplight reflected off her dirty blond hair and smooth olive skin. Her green eyes appeared to glow. She reminded me of a painting I'd seen on a field trip in high school. A half-naked woman lay on a bed with a sheet covering her other half—the view from her suitor's eye. The image had stayed with me. Now, I remembered why.

"What are you doing here?" I said.

My hostility registered. Brittany moved her hands to her thighs and pressed her knees together. Her eyes turned cold, like green marble. It was disquieting. I didn't know how she did it.

"You *are* in trouble, Will. I'm here to help, if you'll let me."

"You mean the way you helped at the station last week? You told those assholes everything you know about me. You put on a show for whoever was watching behind the mirror. Here's an idea. Try *not* helping me."

"The person watching both of us was my boss. You know, the New York County District Attorney. And yes, I had to be tough to show—"

"Frank Crosby, the Manhattan DA? Why the hell was he there?"

"Besides the fact that there's a serial killer on the loose, one of the victims was the niece of the New York State Speaker of the Assembly, Ted Smith."

Shit.

Ted Smith was African American. His niece had to be Heather Smith—Velvet. The rape and murder of four strippers by a serial killer was sensational enough. But have one of them be the black niece of a powerful New York politician and you have all the ingredients for a blockbuster story that could make or break the DA's career. A perfect setup to lynch an ex-cop.

"Ted Smith is running for governor," Brittany added. "There are rumors that Crosby will announce soon too. He's not going to take any chances on such a high-profile case. I had to be extra tough to show him I wouldn't go easy on you, despite our history. He would have pulled me off the case otherwise."

"I'm sure he's convinced."

She looked at me in mocking disbelief.

"Did I hurt you? The impenetrable Will Chisholm actually feels pain?"

"You still haven't told me why you're here."

She pressed her lips together and shook her head in frustration.

"Fine. You need to come in for more questioning. There's new evidence."

"What new evidence?"

"You have to come in to find out."

"Since when does the DA's Office ask suspects to come in? Why not have your detective boyfriend Jaworski come get me?"

"He's an Inspector, and he's not my boyfriend."

It was too quick of a denial.

"If you say so."

Brittany shook her head again and sighed.

"I convinced Crosby to let me talk to you before he sent Jaworski to bring you in. It will be better if you come in voluntarily. You can avoid the media circus too. It can help you, Will."

"Yeah, it can help me. And it can help your career. And it can help Crosby appear to have the case under control so he can announce his candidacy. It can help everyone, except maybe the press. But they'll get fed eventually. Maybe another anonymous leak. You've convinced me. I'll swing by tomorrow. Thanks."

Brittany stood up and glared at me. Her eyes were molten green now.

"Fine. Be an asshole. You've never let me help you before. Why start now?"

She grabbed her suit jacket and headed for the door, but I was in her way. She stopped and stared defiantly at me. I gazed in her eyes for a moment, then looked down.

"Do you believe I'm innocent?"

"You've never been innocent, Will. But I don't want you to be guilty. You need to come in tomorrow, or it will be out of my hands."

I stepped to my right to let her by. She walked around me and opened the door. A soft click told me she was gone.

Then a text came across the burner cell from Amy. It said: "?"

32

*H*er shoulders were bare and sensual, her hair soft and flowing. I brushed it away and reached over her head to wrap the necklace around her throat. I tried to clasp it, but it wouldn't reach. I pulled tighter. She screamed . . .

I started to fall . . .

Aargh!

I shot up and grabbed my elbow. A sharp pain pulsated through my arm. I grimaced, then looked around. My elbow had hit the nightstand. I flexed my forearm and fingers. The pain faded.

The angle of the sun outside told me it was morning. I was still dressed but no shoes or socks. The lamp was on, and the clock-radio displayed 7:39 a.m. I had been sleeping almost twelve hours.

I swung my feet to the floor, sat up and sighed. The necklace from my dream was stuck in my head. The one I'd given Brittany on our one-year anniversary, just before everything went to hell. I had it custom made. Seven seven-pointed gold-plated stars hanging from a copper necklace. One for each of the seven Cherokee clans, with the name engraved in each. The necklace was designed to look like the wreath of oak leaves on the Cherokee Nation flag. Oxidation was supposed to eventually turn the copper green, like the color of a wreath. I never saw how it turned out.

The photos of the victims came back to me. I saw the symbols carved on their faces and breasts. I thought the killer was mimicking the ritual I had performed on Brittany the first time we made love. I assumed she had told someone about it, and the killer had learned of it while stalking me. But the pattern of the symbols carved into the victims was different from my ritual. It was more like the necklace. And a symbol was missing.

I grabbed the burner cell and texted Victor: "Need info."

Thirty seconds later, he texted back: "Bro how u do that?"

"Do what?"

"Always interrupt me in the middle of important biz."

"Give her my apologies."

"What u need?"

"Personal cell/home address for Brittany Sorenson, the ADA u talked to."

"Can't get it yourself?"

"Need it asap."

"Ok back in 5."

Ten minutes later, Victor texted me Brittany's information and added: "Need any help?"

"No. Finish your biz."

"Finished 2x already u want help?"

"No."

"Don't need help don't want help cynical kid."

I didn't respond.

I washed up and threw on blue jeans and a black polo shirt. Standard for a Thursday. I brewed some coffee and made some toast with butter and jam. I sat at my table and downed the toast while I looked out the window onto Grand Street. The city was sunny and busy. No surveillance or reporters that I could see. I drank my coffee slowly and planned.

The end game was nearing. The NYPD and DA's Office were going to start squeezing me hard. Brittany's visit last night was a harbinger.

Four strippers had been brutally raped and murdered. One of them was the niece of the New York State Speaker of the Assembly. The gubernatorial race was on the horizon. Political fortunes were at stake. Too much pressure. They had to deliver someone. Unless I did something, that someone would be me.

They probably had the DNA results from Alyssa's body by now. That was why they wanted to question me. I had come inside Alyssa the night she was murdered. I was drunk, but I remembered. Not that I could have forgotten.

It was enough to indict me. But they would need more for a conviction. That's why they wanted me to come in. So they could convince me to confess. Make it easier on myself. And them. Brittany would shepherd me through the process—literally—until the slaughter.

There were two times in the octagon when I almost tapped out. The first was at the beginning of my career, but I recovered and won. The second was just before I killed Derek Jackson. I was under the weather, and he had me in a choke hold. Then he said the wrong thing to me.

Maybe I had already lost whatever game the Master was playing with me. Maybe I was as good as dead. But I would never tap out. I'd fight for as long as I had left. One long fight, until you die—that's what life is. Twenty-five or eighty-five. When didn't scare me. What mattered was dying on my terms. My father hadn't.

I grabbed the burner cell and texted Brittany: "It's Will. I'll come in but I want to talk to u alone first. Meet at 10 am. Pick a place near your apartment. I'll come in with u after."

Most private sector lawyers started their day at nine thirty. Government lawyers showed up at ten. Knowing Brittany, she was in the office by nine. But she probably hadn't left her apartment yet. She would read my text and immediately contact her boss, District Attorney Crosby. She'd convince him again to let her meet me and bring me in. Her ambition made her predictable.

Crosby would probably send a plain clothes police escort to protect Brittany and ensure that I accompanied her back to the precinct.

That's why I was going to intercept her at her apartment. I needed to question her alone before she questioned me in front of a jury of her peers. I didn't plan to stick around either. If they had the DNA results for Alyssa, they would arrest me as soon as they saw me. I couldn't afford to spend the next several days being arraigned for murder. Whatever time I had left, I needed to spend figuring out how to prove my innocence.

Twenty minutes after I sent my text, Brittany responded: "Ok. Meet at coffee shop on NW corner of 10th Ave & 17th St. See u at 10."

The taxi dropped me off at the corner of 16th Street and Eighth Avenue just after nine. Brittany's apartment building was on the south side of 19th Street in Chelsea, near where it intersected Ninth Avenue. Traffic went one way from east to west. I planned to approach her building from the east in case an unmarked police car was sitting outside. If I was spotted, it would be hard to chase me driving backwards on a narrow street.

I stopped at a hipster café and bought a cup of coffee to look like I was just out for a morning walk. I strolled casually up Eighth Avenue until I got to 19th Street, crossed to the north side and turned left. I stopped under a young maple tree. Brittany's building was half a block away.

I sipped my coffee and perused the area. The neighborhood was a mixture of postwar walk-ups and larger 1970s and '80s apartment buildings. A handful of small trees were scattered along the cracked cement sidewalks. A multitude of cars, SUVs, and other small commercial vehicles lined both sides of the street.

A man and a woman were mulling around on the sidewalk across from Brittany's building. Plainclothes officers, I was pretty sure. One of the cars parked on the street looked unmarked. There were probably several plainclothes officers and a car staking out the coffee shop too. It was a large contingent just to watch Brittany and I chat. Something was up.

At nine twenty-five, I texted Brittany: "Will be there in 5. Come now."

A minute later, the man and the woman started sprinting in the direction of the coffee shop. The unmarked car pulled out, sped through a yellow light, and took a sharp left onto Ninth Avenue. Then a medium height black guy in a faded loose-fitting Knicks T-shirt stepped out from behind a tree ten yards from me. He was looking at a cellphone. A handgun bulged under his shirt on his right hip. I stepped behind the maple tree so he wouldn't see me. He typed something on the phone, slipped it into his pocket, and started jogging towards Brittany's building. I watched him turn onto Ninth Avenue and disappear.

Now I knew. I was going to be arrested, and they weren't taking any chances. No intimate conversation with Brittany over a cup of coffee. No cozy taxi ride with her to the precinct. Something had changed. But my plan was still the same.

A text came through from Brittany: "Leaving my apartment. Be there shortly."

She was five minutes away from the coffee shop. If she was still in her apartment, I had a few minutes to get to the lobby of her building to intercept her. I crossed to the south side of the street and started jogging, my coffee in my left hand. There was a chance a plainclothes officer had hung back to accompany Brittany, but I had to risk it. More than one would be a problem.

Twenty yards from Brittany's building, I slowed to a fast walk. I saw a woman pushing a double stroller up a ramp leading to the entrance. That was my opportunity to get inside. I started to hustle towards her when someone jumped out from an SUV parked on the street to my right.

In a fraction of a second, I registered that it was a woman—long white T-shirt, jeans, baseball hat, smallish, no gun drawn.

"Police!" she yelled. "Get—"

I stopped on a dime and flung my left arm around, squeezing my coffee cup to force the lid off. The coffee hit her in the face as she reached under her T-shirt for her gun. She turned her head instinctively. I stepped towards her, whipped my right arm in a backhand motion, and hit her with a hammer fist blow across the bridge of her nose. Her head snapped back, and blood exploded from her right nostril. She collapsed onto a strip of grass along the edge of the sidewalk next to the SUV. Her gun never cleared its holster.

My goal was to stun and then disarm her. But two seconds wasn't enough time to calibrate and execute a precision strike. Besides, she made me waste a good cup of coffee.

I shut the SUV door and dragged her over to a street sign. I leaned her up against the post to make it appear as if she was resting. I felt her pulse. It was strong. I used the bottom of her shirt to wipe the blood from her nose and mouth. Then I stuck it up each nostril to stop the bleeding. She started to come around. I lifted each eyelid. Her pupils were barely dilated. Tough woman. She probably had a broken nose. Maybe a concussion. She'd live and get a medal.

I grabbed her handcuffs, pulled her arms behind her, and cuffed her wrists around the post. I took the bullets out of her SIG Sauer and tossed them away. Then I laid the SIG on her lap and covered it with her baseball cap. I checked the time—9:36 a.m.

The woman with the double stroller was now standing outside the building entrance struggling to open a heavy glass door. She hadn't seen my takedown. I ran over, grabbed the door handle, and pulled it open for her.

"Thank you so much," the woman said and smiled.

"My pleasure," I replied and returned her smile.

She pushed the stroller inside and prepared to open a second glass door to the lobby. A young woman on the other side of the door pulled it open for her. She pushed the stroller inside, thanked the woman and headed for the elevator.

I stepped inside the foyer and let the outside door close behind me. I walked up to the woman holding the inside door open. She had on a beige skirt suit with a powder blue button-down blouse. A single strand of pearls circled her neck. Her hair was tied back in a loose ponytail with a blue satin scrunchie. Black sunglasses framed her exquisite face, projecting a provocative and unapproachable aura.

I grabbed the woman's right wrist with my left hand and pulled her towards me.

Brittany startled and looked up. Surprise turned to recognition turned to anger. Her eyes darted out to the street. Her reaction told me she saw her bodyguard cuffed to a signpost. She tried to pull her wrist free. I squeezed tighter. She grimaced and stopped resisting.

"I'll scream," she said.

"And I'll knock out those pristine white teeth if you do."

"No, you won't."

She was defiant, challenging me. Like the game we would play before sex. Before it got rough. But only as rough as she wanted. It was her game, not mine.

This was a different game. A deadly one. I needed to make her understand that.

"I raped and murdered four strippers. Then I carved ritualistic symbols in their bodies. You must believe that since you were setting me up to be arrested. If I killed those women, why won't I kill you? What do I have to lose?"

I was close enough to see Brittany's eyes through her sunglasses. They were tentative, no longer defiant. She knew what I said was true—if I was the murderer.

33

"What do you want?" Brittany said.

"Is there a basement in this building?" I asked and glanced around.

She hesitated. She was figuring out the scenarios of what might happen if I got her alone. That answered my question. I reached around her waist with my right hand and pulled her into me. I started walking towards the elevators holding her tight against my side. Her smell brought back memories.

"You know I have a gun," I said. "If I want you dead, nothing can stop me. Answer my questions, and you'll be fine. Which elevator?"

She stared at me and pursed her lips. After a couple of seconds, she looked forward.

"The far one," she said. "It goes to the parking garage."

A young couple followed us onto the elevator. They pressed the button for the first parking level. I hit the button for the second level. After they got off, I loosened my hold on Brittany. Once her arms were free, she tried to shove me away in a symbolic act of resistance. I didn't move. She stumbled sideways into the elevator wall.

"Asshole," she muttered.

I gave a slight nod.

When the elevator door opened, I grabbed her elbow and directed her around the corner to the stairwell entrance. A bright exit sign lit up the area around the metal door. I pushed her gently against the cement wall, took her sunglasses off and handed them to her. She glared at me, cold and captivating.

"Give me your cell," I said.

She reached into her suit jacket, pulled out her cellphone and handed it to me. I touched the screen. No bars—no reception two levels down. I assumed it had a tracer, but that would take longer to deactivate. I powered it down and handed it back to her.

"Your friends will be swarming this place in five minutes, so answer my questions and no games."

She pressed her lips together.

"What did you do with the necklace I gave you?"

Her eyes widened before she caught herself. She thought for a moment, then exhaled as if resigning herself to answer the question.

"The detectives working the case have it," she said.

"You kept it?"

"No."

"I don't understand."

"It's a long story."

"You have two minutes."

She took a deep breath, then looked at me in a way I had never seen before.

"I left it in a guy's apartment. After I slept with him."

The flush I felt was like blood pouring out of my gut from a knife wound. I'd been stabbed before. This was worse.

I grabbed her neck with my left hand, straightened my arm and forced her against the wall.

"I said no games. You have ten seconds to tell me how they got it."

"Let go of me," she demanded, then reached up and grabbed my wrist.

Two weeks ago, I would have obeyed. She was relying on that. But nothing was the same now. I had to show her that. I squeezed her neck tighter. Her eyes widened. She struggled to breath. Then she lowered her hands and focused her eyes on mine, daring me to continue. Her eyes started to glass over.

I released her neck and stepped back. She coughed and bent her head towards the ground, nearly gagging. She straightened up, massaged her neck, and glared at me.

"You really want to know?" she said, her voice hoarse. "Okay, fine. After it was plastered all over the Boston news that you were shot by that whore you were fucking and shooting up with, I slept with a guy that night."

"You . . . you just went out and found a guy to fuck while I was in a coma?"

"He was a paralegal at the firm I interned at. I had a permanent offer to work there, remember? Until they rescinded it without any explanation. But I know it was because of you."

"So, what, you called him and said my boyfriend's about to die, let's fuck?"

"Yeah, *I'm* the whore. That's how you want to spin it." She brushed a tear from her cheek like it had no place being there. "I hadn't heard from you since my graduation. I didn't know where you were or if you were even alive. Like every other time you went undercover. Then your sister called and said you were in the hospital. I was getting ready to go there when the news came across the TV about the whole incident. I called Sarge, and he gave me the details. Did you think I wouldn't find out what really happened?"

"I don't know what Sarge told you, but you should have given me a chance to explain."

"You really think I would have believed anything you said? Do you think I was that naïve?"

"You're right. Why would you have believed me? Just tell me why you left the necklace in the guy's apartment."

"He knew who you were. When he saw the news, he called me. I knew he had a crush on me. I went to his place, and we got drunk. I always wore the necklace. He wanted to know what the stars stood for.

I told him they stood for lies. I ripped it off and threw it in the garbage. Then we fucked. I remember cursing you every time he pushed inside me."

My neck and back broke out in sweat. I felt nauseous. It wasn't a headache coming on. It was the mix of anger, pain, fear, and despair exploding in my stomach, like a burst appendix.

"Not what you wanted to hear?" she said. "Now you know how it feels."

My head was swirling. I swallowed a couple of times to get some moisture in my mouth.

"How did the NYPD get the necklace?" I said.

She turned her head and wiped more tears away. After a few seconds, she looked back at me.

"I gave it to them. After I saw pictures of the first two victims."

"You said you threw it away."

"I did. Someone returned it to me in the mail. It must have been someone in Sean's family."

"Sean is the paralegal? Why—"

"He *was* a paralegal."

"Fine—*was*. And what is he now?"

"He's dead. He committed suicide a month after we slept together. He had his own issues. He was in rehab and relapsed."

"I'm sorry."

"No, you're not. And if you think I blame myself, I don't. I blame you."

"Okay, I'm guilty of that too. How did Sean's family get the necklace if you threw it away?"

She sighed, then said, "Sean must have taken it out of the garbage. He probably thought I would still want it. He was considerate like that. Someone in his family must have found it in his apartment. I don't know how they knew it belonged to me."

"So, you don't know who mailed it to you?"

"No. There was no return address."

"Did you ask them?"

"No. I didn't care."

"When did you get it back?"

"I don't know, sometime in January."

"Before the first murder?"

"Yes. Lauren Warenski was killed in February, but you know that."

"Not because I did it."

"Whatever."

"Did you show the necklace to anyone before you turned it over to the police?"

"Why does that matter?"

"It matters. Did you?"

She thought for a few seconds, then looked at me. I could tell she didn't want to answer.

"Who did you show it to?" I said.

"Inspector Jaworski."

"Before or after the first murder?"

"What are you suggesting?"

"Before or after?"

"After. But it was before I even knew anything about the case."

"Before you knew about Lauren Warenski's murder?"

"Yes."

"So, you weren't talking about the case when you showed it to Jaworski. That means you were talking about me. Why else would you show it to him? You wouldn't be carrying it around with you, so you must have shown it to him in your apartment. There's no reason to be talking about me in your apartment with Jaworski unless you're seeing him. Are you?"

"My personal life is none of your business. You gave up that privilege when you decided to fuck that prostitute."

"I didn't fuck her. And she wasn't a prostitute. She was hired by the Estratega cartel to kill me. I was meeting her for a drug deal, but it turned out to be a hit. I tried to tell you that, but you never returned any of my calls or texts or emails. Nothing! The only drugs I ever did were what I had to. I was undercover. You knew that. I was in the goddamn hospital with a bullet in my head, but you never came to see me! Why?"

I was trembling. My right ear was ringing like a landmine had just exploded near me. I had never felt so overwhelmed, even when my father died. But that was a different love.

Brittany's lips were quivering. Tears streamed down from both eyes. She started to say something, then paused. When she finally spoke, her voice was weak.

"You were both naked in bed when they found you. Sarge said she was a local prostitute. And the drugs—the amount of fentanyl in your body could have killed ten people. The doctors said it might have saved your life after you were shot. You're lucky to be alive. He told me there were bank accounts too. You were only fired—"

"Stop! Sarge told you what?"

"He said they found bank accounts in your name with more money than you had ever made. The prostitute, the drugs, the money—he couldn't explain it. But he refused to believe you were dirty. The only reason you weren't charged was because the retiring Commissioner didn't want a scandal tainting his last year. You were lucky. Again."

"I don't believe you."

"Ask Sarge yourself. He's retired on Cape Cod. But I didn't just take his word. I had someone review your case with the task force unit you worked for and the regional DEA office. I had to be sure before I took on this investigation. *Everyone* said it was unlikely that the Estratega cartel put a contract out on you. You may have shut down their Northeast operation, but they would never risk killing a cop. They consider themselves businessmen. They're patient, in it for the long run. And they were right. They're back up and running, and you're . . . a murder suspect. What did you really accomplish, other than destroying your life? And almost mine."

She wiped the tears from her cheeks and glanced at the ceiling. Then she turned her eyes back to me. She was ready for more. I had hurt her once. She wasn't going to let me do it again.

But time wasn't on my side. I hadn't shown up at the coffee shop. Neither had Brittany. By now, all the cops who had raced over there were on their way back to find her.

"I don't have time to argue," I said. "I need to know if all seven stars were still on the necklace when you got it back."

"Why?"

"How many stares were there?"

"Alright, six. The middle one was missing. I remember it broke off when I pulled it from my neck. Ironic. That star represented the Wolf Clan—you."

"You remember?"

"How could I forget? The Wolf Clan are the protectors. But you never protected me."

I felt like I had been punched in the heart. But it was the truth. She could tell I knew it. Her eyes softened.

"What are you going to do now?" she asked. "I can help you, but you need to turn yourself in and hire a lawyer. The Columbus PD wants to question you too. You can't run from everyone. Even you aren't that fast."

"You can tell the Columbus PD those rednecks jumped me. I have a witness."

Brittany gave me a perplexed look.

"I know you got in a fight there," she said, "but that's not why they want to talk to you. It's about a murder."

My mind went immediately to Linda.

"What murder?"

"David Bishop, the man who broke up your fight. He was found outside his apartment building with his head smashed in. You were the last person seen with him."

The air seemed to suck out of the parking garage. Blood rushed from my head. I stepped back to keep my balance.

Brittany noticed and said, "Was he a friend?"

I shook my head, than asked, "Did you ever tell anyone about the first time we slept together?"

"What does that—"

"Just tell me, Brittany."

"One person."

"Who?"

"Sean. That night."

"How much did you tell him?"

"I told him about your Cherokee ritual with the wine, if that's what you're asking. I was hurt. And drunk."

"No one else?"

"You think I just share the most intimate moments of my life with anyone, anytime?"

She looked away and shook her head. The faint wail of sirens floated into the garage. Her eyes shot back to me.

"I hear them," I said. "I know you recognized the markings on the victims. But there were only six stars on each one. The middle one was missing. And I think the slashes on their cheeks were supposed to mimic the wreath of oak leaves I painted on you."

"What's your point?"

"The markings on their chests were like the necklace, not the stars I painted in wine on you that night. But the markings on their cheeks were like the ones I painted on you. Sean must have shared what you told him with someone before he died. How else would the killer know to carve those markings on the victims' faces?"

"You could have performed the same ritual on another woman. Or maybe you are—"

"That was the only time I ever did it. You were the only woman. And I'm not the killer. Except for the markings on their faces, everything matches the necklace that was returned to you. But I never saw it after you got it back, so how could I know about the missing star? Did you even pick up on that?"

"I could barely look at the photos. They reminded me of that night. Of us. Of you. But I recognized the markings—the stars *and* the wreath. I don't remember every detail, but they were the same as the ones from that night."

"I remember every detail from that night."

"Is that what this is about, Will? Is that why you—"

"I didn't murder those women. The killer copied the necklace with the missing star and somehow knew about our first night together. That's what you should be focused on. Not me. But if you want me to be guilty, I guess there's no reason to question anything."

"If you're innocent, Will, why are we here? Why don't you just come in to be questioned?"

"Because it's another setup. Just like today. Like this whole fucking nightmare. I'm being framed. I don't know why, but I know it has something to do with you. I'm sure of that now. For all I know, you're part of it."

"Don't use me to rationalize your paranoid delusions. I'm doing my job. If you want to prove you're innocent, get a lawyer and work with me. I can't help if you won't cooperate."

"If I have to prove I'm innocent, then I'm already guilty. No lawyer is going to fix that."

Brittany sighed and said, "You need to turn yourself in. It will only get worse if you don't."

"If I come in, it will be on my terms."

"Will, please—"

"Brittany, stop trying to convince me to confess. Why were you put on this case? Ask yourself that. No matter how good you think you are, you're too junior to be the lead on such a high-profile murder investigation. What about today? I was going to be arrested, right? I'm guessing the media was there waiting. Four murdered strippers. One of them the niece of a powerful politician. A governor's race to boot.

Huge pressure to show progress. And who comes through? Brittany Sorenson, a rising star in the DA's Office. You're barely a year out of law school. You haven't earned anything. Why you?"

"You tell me. You're the one who sees a conspiracy in everything. Even my help."

I glared at her as the sirens grew louder. I needed to leave, but I wanted to stay.

"I have to go before your boyfriend shows up. Whoever wanted you on this case knows something about the murders. Worry about that."

34

I left Brittany standing by the stairwell door and hustled up to the first level of the parking garage. I had seen an exit door at the far end when the couple got off the elevator. I sprinted to it. The sirens were loud and pulsating now.

The door opened to a narrow walkway behind Brittany's apartment building. I followed it to an alley that ran south between two yellow brick buildings. I took it down to 18th Street, crossed to the other side, and walked quickly towards Eighth Avenue. Just before the intersection, I turned down another alley and started running.

After ten minutes of skulking through alleys, I came out on 14th Street near Seventh Avenue. I took a right. The sidewalk was crowded. I ran in spurts for several minutes until I reached the entrance to the High Line, an elevated walking park along the west side. I climbed the stairs and headed for Midtown, walking at a steady pace to avoid any attention. But my mind was racing.

Going back to my apartment wasn't an option. The NYPD would probably wait a day or two before blasting out to the media that there was a warrant for my arrest. But this weekend was the start of summer. Everyone would be distracted. I wouldn't be in the spotlight until Monday. That gave me four days to figure out who had spent the past two years framing me for murder. Not enough time, but I wasn't going to tap out.

At 30th Street, I exited the High Line and headed for 40th and Fifth. Paula White was standing outside her store puffing on an e-cigarette when I walked up to her. She was dressed to kill—literally. Whisps of bleach blonde hair escaped from the sides of a camouflage baseball cap pulled down to her eyebrows. A black tank top stretched across her wiry torso, with fatigue pants and army boots completing the ensemble.

Her eyes moved from watching people to staring at my feet. She took the e-cigarette out of her mouth and slipped it into her back pocket. Then she turned and glided towards the door of her store. She paused and eyed me out of her peripheral vision.

"You need help with your video?" she asked.

"Yeah."

She stepped inside, held the door open, and motioned with her head for me to come in. Her eyes stayed focused down. I obeyed, then moved a few feet away from her. I was hot and sweaty. I figured she had no desire to sense or smell me. If she did, she'd let me know.

She locked the door and flipped the sign over to display "CLOSED" to the outside. Then she walked around the counter, touched something under it, and pushed the backroom door open. A few seconds later, she returned with a large laptop and laid it down on the counter. She attached two cables and extended her left hand towards me.

I gave her the flash drive. She inserted it into the laptop and grabbed a mouse. She clicked it several times, typed something, muttered to herself, and then spun the laptop so I could see the screen as well.

"It was encrypted," she said. "Use the menu to navigate. The password is your Social with a question mark at the end."

"How do you know—"

She silenced me with a quick glance. Then she turned her gaze down and started tapping the counter rapidly with her right fingers.

I had videotaped different parts of my day in Columbus. I fast forwarded until just before I walked into The Beer Garage. I wanted to see if I had captured Linda leaving. I had a theory. Actually, more like a guess.

Most of the footage before I entered the bar showed people mingling on the patio. I had manipulated my torso to allow the camera to get a complete view of the surroundings. The result was lots of point-of-view jouncing, like a porn video. I went back a couple of times to make sure I hadn't missed anything. Nothing jumped out at me.

The footage inside the bar was easier to examine. The place had been relatively empty. None of the handful of customers standing around drinking seemed suspicious. Linda looked like I remembered. The camera caught me eying her ass for a few seconds. Nothing else until the big guy came in to pick a fight.

Once I got out to the patio, the video was a turbulent mess as the fight started. There was a pause in the chaos just after I kicked the third redneck in the throat. The camera captured a second or two of a dark blue sedan parked on the opposite side of the street. The rain obscured the picture, but the plates looked orange. I went back to the beginning. The same car was parked there when I entered the bar, but the license plate was blocked. Someone was in the driver's seat.

I asked Paula if she could enhance the frame. She stuck her head around to look at the screen, grabbed the mouse and clicked it a few times. The image expanded, but the glare obscured any details. Maybe it was my paranoia, but the driver's body outline reminded me of Detective Gomez. I had a knack for remembering guys who kicked me in the head.

I fast-forwarded to the fight. Just as I charged the nasty guy with the blackjack, the camera captured two figures in the distance next to a white SUV. I paused and expanded the image. The rain made it hard to discern anything, but I was certain one of them was Linda.

The next ten seconds were jostling images of the fourth guy going down after I hit him with an uppercut. Then another five or so seconds of cement and rain after I was knocked to the ground by the black-jack. When the camera stabilized, I was standing again, the nasty guy ten feet away. Linda and the other woman were in the background. I paused, zoomed in, and went one frame at a time. The other woman looked like Alyssa. It had to be Ashley. She and Linda were having an animated discussion, then they hugged. The camera angle changed, and they went out of view. A second of footage followed that captured the dark blue sedan driving away. Then David Bishop hustling me to his car. Nothing significant after that.

I scrolled back to Linda and Ashley and replayed their interaction several times. It was a warm, emotional exchange. Linda seemed relieved. No duress. Something was off. My guess was now a legitimate theory.

"I'm done," I said and straightened up.

Paula pulled out the flash drive and handed it to me. She unplugged the laptop and carried it to the backroom. When she returned, I moved back from the counter to give her space.

"What else?" she said, gazing down.

"Do you know much about crypto mining?"

"Why do you want to know?"

"When I was in Columbus, I found a warehouse that seemed to be outfitted for crypto mining. It was supposed to be the headquarters of a company I'm looking into, but it was deserted. I saw a similar setup once back in Boston with actual mainframe computers. The company in Columbus is into porn. Maybe something bigger. I'm trying to figure out the connection."

"The connection to you?"

"Yes."

"Same trouble as before?"

"Yes."

"Involves those murdered strippers?"

I nodded. She nodded back even though she was still looking down.

"What's the name of the company?" she said.

"YouSEL. Y-O-U-S-E-L."

She shot me a hard look, then lowered her eyes and started tapping on the counter again. I could tell she recognized the name. She opened a drawer under the counter, grabbed a cellphone, and slid it across the glass to me.

"It's untraceable," she said. "I'll text you when I have information."

"Thank you. Do you know about the company?"

"A little. Lots of rumors. You should leave and don't come back."

"I can't do that."

"I know. I'll find out what I can. Talk to Jon Choi. He knows crypto. I know your history with him but get over it. The trouble you're in is worse. He'll have information. It could help."

I didn't respond. I grabbed the burner cell and turned to leave.

"Will," she said.

I looked back at her.

She stepped around the counter and walked over to the door. She unlocked it and flipped the sign back over. Then she glanced up at me with more emotion than I had ever seen from her. It still wasn't much. And it didn't last. She looked back down.

"Stay alive," she said and opened the door.

I half smiled and left.

35

*V*ictor walked into the diner and was greeted with nods from guys at several different tables. It was the place to be in Harlem for Friday morning breakfast. He scanned around looking for me. I was in the back at a small table drinking a cup of coffee. A rotund waiter blocked me from Victor's view. I could see him in the mirror on the wall behind the counter.

An attractive older waitress walked up to Victor, hugged him, and planted a kiss on his cheek. He said something in response. She smiled sympathetically, then motioned her head in my direction. The rotund waiter moved out of the way, and Victor saw me.

He wove through the floor of tables towards me. A well-tailored black suit, white shirt, and blue paisley tie stood out amongst the casually dressed customers. His black shoes were spit-shined. I had never seen him clean shaven before. He looked like he had just come from a funeral.

My back was to the wall. Victor grabbed the chair across from me and moved it to the side of the table so his back wouldn't be facing the crowd. He sat down and gave me a somber stare.

"You know 'bout David?" he asked.

"Yeah. I'm sorry. I didn't have anything to do with it. In case I need to say that."

"I know you didn't."

"Anything I can do?"

"Yeah. Give me the motherfucker's name who beat his face so bad cops had to ID him from his prints."

"I don't have a name, but I have a good idea who did it."

Victor stared at me for a second, then leaned forward and folded his arms on the table.

"I know you ain't got no name. You ain't here to give me no condolences neither. This is Harlem. You stick out like me at a country club. NYPD lookin' for you. Risky you even bein' here. Wanna show respect? Don't bullshit me."

A lecture from Victor wasn't what I wanted for breakfast. But learning that his cousin had been beaten to death probably wasn't sitting well with him either. I kept my tongue and took it.

He turned and nodded to the waitress who greeted him. She strolled over in no hurry.

"Hey sugar, what do you need?" she said.

"Coffee and a glass of milk, babe," he said.

"Black, right?"

"Black and bold."

She laughed briefly and put her hand on his shoulder. Then she looked at me.

"More coffee, please," I said. "Thank you."

"Such manners. Guess there's hope for young people yet."

After she left, Victor sat back in his chair, looked at me and snorted.

"I know you here for my help, Will. Just tell me what you want."

I leaned forward and said, "You do anything with crypto?"

He nodded and said, "A little. Why you axing?"

"I came across something in Columbus that I think involves crypto."

"Have somethin' to do with who killed David?"

"Probably."

The waitress returned with a glass of milk and a pot of coffee. She poured Victor a cup and refilled mine.

"Thank you," I said.

"My pleasure," she replied and looked at Victor. "Anything else, sugar?"

"Good for now, babe."

She left, and Victor chugged the glass of milk. Then he took a big gulp of coffee and studied me for a moment.

"Crypto's popular with some of my customers," he said. "Mostly guys your age. Think they're cool playing in it. Lose their shirt every other week. Supposed to be another kind of money. How do you have bread in your pocket and lose it without ever takin' it out? Dollar is a dollar every day. But they wanna use it, so I arrange transactions with the shit. I get paid in crypto, but I convert it to cash. Figure you know that already. You really wanna talk to someone else, right?"

"Yeah. I need a meeting with Jon Choi. Can you set it up?"

"That's a tough one, bro. Haven't talked to Choi in a while. We stay out of each other's territory. Like a détente thing."

"Can you do it or not?"

"Doin' it ain't the point."

"What do you want?"

"Want in."

"In on what?"

"You a wanted man, Will. There's a material witness warrant out on you. Heard you beat up a girl cop too. Trouble for anyone seen with you, never mind helpin' you."

"Thanks. I didn't know any of that."

"Always a wise-ass."

"How much do you want?"

"Don't care 'bout money."

"Then what do you want in on?"

"David called me after you left his place. Said he talked to some of his contacts. Said your shit was bigger than he realized. Told me to watch out."

"Did he give any specifics?"

"No. Said he was working on it. Said to give you a heads-up too."

"Thanks for telling me. He was a good guy. You were close?"

"Why I got this suit on. Show of respect. He wasn't my real cousin. He was my stepmother's nephew. She's a cunt. But David and me were like brothers. He lived with me, my mom, and my kid brother when we was teenagers. Same age as me. Neither of us was good. But he was better. Surprised the shit out of everyone when he became a cop. We could count on each other."

"I'm sorry, Victor, whether you believe it or not. What do you want from me?"

"David was killed 'cause he helped you out of that jam in Columbus. I want in on finding who's settin' you up. I figure one of them did it. Gonna kill the motherfucker."

"I don't think you want anything to do with my problems."

"Don't give a shit about your problems. Someone gotta pay for killing David. That's the only problem I care about. It's not just personal. Business too. Can't let no one kill family. We can work together or separate. You want a meeting with Choi, that's what it cost you."

He was betting I didn't have another option. It was a safe bet. Choi and I weren't texting buddies. Or any kind of buddies. Bringing Victor in was a risk, but I didn't have much to lose.

"Okay, but Choi probably still wants to kill me. Any meeting needs to be someplace public. How quickly can you set it up?"

"Don't know 'til I try. Choi don't forget someone putting a gun to his head. But he owes me. Should know pretty quick."

I nodded, then slid an envelope under a paper napkin over to him. He casually pulled it towards the edge of the table and let the envelope drop in his lap.

"The rest of what I owe you for Columbus," I said. "I threw in an extra five thousand as a bonus for David's help. No disrespect intended."

"Money never disrespect me. He has a kid in Chicago. I'll make sure he gets it."

We sat looking at each other in silence for a while, trading sips of coffee. I thought about ordering some breakfast, but I had already been there too long.

"I gotta go," I said. "Five good for the coffee?"

"My turf, my treat. Where you hangin'?"

"Rather not say."

"Got a couple of places you can crash if you want."

"I'm good."

"Don't need help. Don't want help. Hard way to live, bro. Easy way to die."

"Don't need any advice on how to live *or* die," I said, then stood up.

Victor shook his head and said, "You real jaded, Will. Remind me of my kid brother."

"Yeah, well, I'm not."

"I know. He's dead."

I paused and looked at Victor. He looked back at me and took a slow sip of coffee.

"How?" I asked.

"Shot."

"By who?"

"Me."

36

On the third day, the first roach appeared. I saw it sprint across the laminate countertop of the kitchenette in my hotel room when I opened the door. Then it took a header into the crevice between the electric cooktop and the counter. It was a sign. I needed to find another refuge.

The hotel was in Queens, a few miles from LaGuardia Airport. I'd been hiding out there since confronting Brittany. I had just returned from grabbing some breakfast.

Despite the intruder, the day looked promising. Victor had come through. I was meeting Jon Choi at noon in the same restaurant where he had promised to kill me if he ever caught me in Koreatown again. He wasn't prone to hyperbole. I'd be prepared.

After I checked out, the day got better. Paula White sent me a text on the burner cell she'd given me. She had information. I had two hours until my meeting with Choi. Plenty of time to stop by her store. I jumped in a taxi and headed for Times Square.

There was a man inside talking to Paula when I arrived. He looked about my height, middle-aged and thin, with black hair. His clothes were dark and form fitting. The small bulge on his right hip under his blazer said he was packing. I stayed outside pretending to read messages on my cell while I watched through the window.

Paula was staring down at the counter, tapping her fingers. She shook her head, said something, and glanced up at the man for a second. He nodded, turned, and walked to the door. He donned a pair of dark sunglasses, stepped outside, and looked at me. I pretended to be nobody. He seemed to agree. He walked over to a black Suburban and climbed in the front passenger seat. It drove off to a couple of horn blasts from annoyed taxi drivers.

I stepped into the store and took a moment to let my eyes adjust.

"Lock the door and flip the sign," Paula said without looking up.

I did what I was told, then walked slowly to the counter. I laid my backpack on the floor and waited.

Paula was leaning on the counter with her forearms stretched across the glass. Her bleached blonde hair hung loose, enveloping most of her face. Two black straps from an athletic bra traveled down from her wiry shoulders and disappeared behind the collar of a thin green short-sleeved sweatshirt.

"You know that man?" she asked.

"No."

She straightened up and rested her hands on the lip of the counter.

"It's the second time he's come in to talk to me. The first time, he told me he represented interests that are involved in the company I was inquiring about. He said he was happy to answer any questions I had. This time, he asked me to stop asking questions about the company. He said it was a request, not a threat. He knew things about me that are hard to find out."

"You want me to go?"

She gazed up at me. Her eyes looked like blue ice crystals. She turned them back down, drew half of a deep breath and released it quietly.

"Erie Enterprises is the holding company that owns YouSEL," she said. "There are dozens of companies in between. It has a complicated corporate structure, probably to hide the true ownership. It's private, so information is hard to get. I haven't figured out who's behind it yet.

YouSEL started as an online lingerie retailer but quickly took off as an interactive porn site selling lingerie. Several other businesses sprang from it. Some are just shell companies. YouSEL is highly profitable. More than its business model would suggest. That's what my contacts have confirmed so far."

"Did they find anything they couldn't confirm?"

She nodded, then said, "There's a long list of wealthy and powerful people who have been associated with YouSEL. Rumors of escort and prostitution services when it first started. Blackmail too. Probably how it greased the wheels to grow its business with limited scrutiny, especially internationally. But now it's on FinCEN's radar."

"What's FinCEN?"

Paula glanced up at me like I was an idiot, then looked back down.

"Financial Crimes Enforcement Network," she said. "It's the bureau at the Treasury Department responsible for money laundering. There's speculation YouSEL is a front for a crypto mining venture. It supposedly started in Ohio, then moved to China, got forced out there, and now seems to have disappeared. FinCEN suspects it might be part of an international money laundering effort, but nothing has panned out with its investigation. There's been behind-the-scenes pressure from well-connected people to tamp down its scrutiny. None of this is confirmed."

"I'm not sure what to do with all that information."

"Don't do anything."

"What do you mean?"

"I told you already—leave. Hide until this is over and whoever is after you gives up."

"What if they never give up?"

"Then never come back. Never surface. Someone very smart, powerful, and sadistic wants you to suffer before he or she kills you. I don't think that's a battle you can win. But you have a chance to survive if you disappear."

"That's ironic."

"Why?"

"My father used to tell me how my ancestors decided the white man's armies were too powerful to fight, so they tried to live off the land peacefully. When that land was taken, rather than fight, they tried to live a peaceful life on the new, smaller land that was granted to them. By the time the white man came and forced them off that land too, my ancestors had forgotten how to fight and were removed to reservations. He told me you can never really live unless you are willing to fight, even if that means dying in battle. Now, you tell me I should leave so I can survive, like my ancestors did. I can hear my father's voice telling me that wouldn't be living."

Paula was silent for several seconds. She continued to stare at the counter.

"It is ironic," she said, "but you're alive today because someone chose to survive rather than fight and die. That's also ironic. You want to be a warrior. You want to honor your father. I understand. But if you are going to fight, you need to be brutal, starting with Jon Choi. I know you're meeting with him today. He has information that can help you. He'll stonewall. Don't let him. Your ex-girlfriend, the ADA, she knows more than she's telling too. Before this is over, you will likely have to kill someone."

"Killing isn't a problem. It's who. How do you know so much?"

She peered up at me. It wasn't a question I was allowed to ask.

I nodded my understanding, then said, "Is there anything else you can tell me?"

"No."

I stared at her staring at the counter. Then I picked up my backpack and walked to the door.

"Why do you masturbate watching YouSEL?" she asked.

I stopped but didn't turn around.

Paula could barely look you in the eye, but her questions were as direct as a knife in your eye. She had obviously managed to hack into my YouSEL account. She saw the videos and assumed I jerked off watching them. It was a safe assumption. I didn't know where this was going, but I wasn't embarrassed. It was my life.

"It's easier than fucking," I said, my back still to her.

"Do you like it more than fucking?"

"No."

"You can probably fuck most women you want. Why spend so much time on YouSEL?"

"You're overestimating my abilities."

"I'm not."

"You really want to know?"

"Yes."

"I fuck to escape. I've escaped with a lot of women, but only one has ever made me feel alive at the same time. With YouSEL, I can convince myself I'm alive, even if it's just an escape."

I waited for another question, but there was only silence. Not even the tapping of her fingers.

"Anything else?" I said.

"I can't help you anymore."

"Is that the deal you made with that man?"

"Yes."

I unlocked the door and left.

37

*A*t noon, I walked into Seoul Brothers, a Korean barbeque restaurant on 30th Street and Sixth Avenue in Midtown. It was dark and half filled with a mix of tourists and local Korean customers. A dozen or so square black tables with a gas-fired grill in the center populated the floor. The smell of various spices and sauces mingled with the low murmur of conversation, interrupted now and then by the searing of food just tossed on a grill.

Jon Choi was sitting alone at a table in the back corner. He was thin and tall, with a crop of black hair flowing from either side of a middle part, covering both temples down to his eyebrows. Thirty-something, his five o'clock shadow never seemed to get past the morning, making him look only a little older than me. He was wearing a white button-down shirt under a gray plaid blazer. Black rimmed glasses accentuated his Asian hipster look. I remembered he liked to project intelligence. It was probably a product of his culture and being a Hunter College dropout. I had never gotten past his ruthlessness to figure out how smart he really was.

As my eyes adjusted, I noticed four of Choi's goons standing at attention against the two walls that met at the corner behind him. Each of them had on a poor fitting dark blazer, white shirt, jeans, and red sneakers. A holster was partially visible at the waist inside of each blazer. Not very subtle. A message in case I was feeling rambunctious. Like the last time we met.

I walked over to Choi. No swagger. No fear.

"Will Chisholm," Choi said, "have a seat. You won't be staying long. Don't worry, I didn't call the cops. They aren't welcome here anymore than you."

I pulled out a chair and sat at an angle facing him, five feet away. His men were ten feet behind him. No one was behind me. I could see anyone approaching from the rest of the floor with my peripheral vision. Choi flashed a smile, then grabbed a clear bottle filled with a milky liquid and poured two half glasses.

"I think you're old enough to drink," he said.

I didn't respond. Choi slid a glass towards me. He raised his in toast.

"It's Makgeolli," he said. "Traditional Korean rice wine. To your health, so long as it doesn't interfere with mine."

He took a gulp, savored it in his mouth for a moment, then swallowed. He lifted his chin to signal it was my turn. I reached over to the table and picked up the glass. I brought it to my lips and sniffed. It had a faint smell of alcohol. I sipped it. It was sweet and tangy. I downed it quickly. It was interesting. I couldn't imagine getting drunk on it.

I looked at Choi and feigned a smile. He tilted his head and returned a similar smile.

"You like it?" he asked.

"No."

"It's an acquired taste. Doesn't matter. We are done. You can go."

I stiffened slightly. Choi noticed. I put the empty glass on the table and sat up straight, like I was preparing to make a move. I wasn't, but it signaled to Choi that I was thinking about it.

"Every man behind me is ready to shoot you if you even twitch," he said.

"You forget about my nervous tic?"

"Always a wiseass. Just get up slow—"

"Cut the shit, Jon. I can kill you before any of your men clear their guns. You know that, but I'm sitting here. That means you're not worried. Besides, shooting up your own restaurant isn't exactly good for business. Can we stop the games? You know why I'm here."

He eyed me indifferently for a second, then snorted.

"Yes, I do. Do you remember the last time we met here? You wanted my help then too. You asked me to let you convince Michael Jin to end his relationship with Christine. You knew the price of a non-Korean dating my little sister. You gambled that I would let you intercede and spare her from seeing him hurt. You tried to play me. I could have killed you then. Out of respect, I told you not to interfere in my business. But then . . . then you put a gun to my head."

Choi stared at me, waiting for me to acknowledge my transgression.

"I asked you to let Michael walk away without hurting him," I said. "You wouldn't listen."

Choi nodded slowly, then said, "I never forget insults to my honor. I told you I'd kill you if I ever saw you in Koreatown again. It won't be today because Victor called in a favor. But we are even now. There are a hundred thousand people in Koreatown. The chance of getting shivved in the liver while you're walking in a crowd is higher than you might think. You already know how easy it is to get shot in the head."

"Thanks for the warning. Now, let's talk about why I'm here. Paula White said you could help. I'll owe you. You know that's worth something."

Choi recognized Paula's name. I could see it in his eyes. He straightened up and sighed as if struggling with what to do with me. He adjusted his glasses for effect. It was all a show to make me sweat. I tried to look worried.

"Christine is the reason I didn't kill you the last time," Choi said. "You probably didn't realize that. She credits you for me letting her date Michael."

"Michael and Christine are dating?"

Choi widened his eyes in surprise.

"Interesting," he said. "Michael is keeping secrets, even from you."

"Not that it matters, but why the change of heart? I was sure you didn't have one."

"You can be funny, Chisholm. But there was no heart involved. Michael came back after that stunt you pulled and said I'd have to kill him to keep him away from Christine. He has balls. I thought about cutting them off. I didn't. A business decision. His skills have been useful. MIT's teaching him something. And Christine's happy. For now."

"I'm happy for them."

"Don't be too happy. She'll dump him one day. I'll make sure of that. Or he won't have a dick *or* balls. She won't like him so much after that."

I stayed silent. Choi continued to stare at me like he was conflict-ed. I had to endure the performance. Then the corners of his mouth turned up slightly.

"So, you'll owe me if I help you. That could be worth something. Of course, you know what will happen if you go back on your word."

It wasn't a question. I nodded. He nodded.

"Okay," Choi said. "What do you want?"

"I need information on a company named YouSEL. Mainly its crypto effort. It operates an online porn site too. You've probably heard of it. I need to know who runs and controls the company, how it makes money, who are its big customers—anything and everything you can find out about its operations. But the crypto business is the priority."

Choi looked uncomfortable. I had clearly touched a nerve.

"Didn't Victor give you a heads up?" I said.

"He said it was about those stripper murders. I've seen the news stories. I wouldn't take you for a pervert, but I guess everyone has a dark side. Victor says you're innocent, but he's not exactly a righteous man himself."

"I didn't realize I was in the presence of a saint."

"Do you want to confess to me?"

Choi was stonewalling, like Paula warned.

"Nothing to confess," I said. "I'm looking into the murders. One of the victims worked at YouSEL. I know it's expanded into crypto mining recently. I think it might be related. You supposedly have a lot of connections with crypto miners operating under the radar. I've heard you're a player on the darknet too. I assume that's for your less than legitimate businesses. Crypto is a popular way to pay for that activity. You would know if YouSEL is involved in any of it."

"You sure this isn't about your secret fetishes, Chisholm? Either way, my businesses are all legal. Sorry, I can't help you."

"You're giving me the runaround, Jon. You afraid of something?"

Choi's eyes widened in false indignation.

"Enough of this," he said. "Come back in a week. I might have some information then."

"I don't have a week. Whatever you know, I need to know now."

Choi leaned towards me and said, "I don't give a fuck what you need. No one comes into my home and demands anything. You want my help, I say how it goes down. Come back in a week or don't ever come back. That's my last warning to you."

I never understood warnings, especially last ones. When I fought in the octagon, I never warned my opponent I was going to spin and kick him in the head. Or jump and break his face with my knee. I wasn't going to warn Choi now either.

I shifted my weight on the chair, leaned forward slightly, and slid my feet below my knees. Then I exploded towards Choi while pulling out my Glock. Before he could flinch, I grabbed him by the throat with my left hand and shoved the muzzle into the underpart of his chin.

Choi's eyes bulged as he gazed into mine, now six inches away. He tried to say something, but my grip on his throat caused him to wheeze instead. He reached to pull my hand from his throat. I shook my head. He stopped.

His men rushed towards us, guns drawn but pointed down. If any of them raised a barrel, things would get messy fast. One twitch of my finger would blow a tunnel from under Choi's chin through the roof of his skull. They realized that.

"Tell them to go outside so we can talk," I said.

Choi raised his hand. His men stopped. I loosened my grip on his throat. He coughed, then shouted something in Korean. They hesitated. He shouted the same command again but louder. They holstered their guns and hurried outside.

Once they left the restaurant, I released Choi's throat. I grabbed the chair I had been sitting in and positioned it so I could watch the door and Choi at the same time. Then I sat down and rested my Glock on my thigh.

Choi took a deep breath, sat back in his chair, and massaged his throat. He glared at me in silent defiance. He knew I'd be packing when I came in, but he assumed I was there to plead for his help, not coerce it out of him. He relished his intellectual image, but that's all it was. A smart guy wouldn't have been so arrogant. He had miscalculated with me for the second time.

I took a quick look at the customers still in the restaurant. They were all Korean. The tourists had hustled out at the first sign of trouble. The staff was going about business with their heads down, pretending that nothing was happening. They had been through this before. But the roles were reversed. It still didn't matter to them. They were survivors.

I wasn't sure how much time I had before more muscle showed up to bail out Choi. I looked at him. He was watching me calmly.

"Now you know I'm desperate," I said. "I figure I have ten minutes before someone comes in here to kill me. You have five minutes to tell me everything you know about YouSEL."

Choi remained silent. I lifted my Glock and pointed it at his groin, sideways for effect. If I had to, I'd graze him in the thigh to get him to talk. If he still refused, I'd leave without learning anything. I wasn't going to kill him. But he didn't know that.

Choi nodded his head slowly. I didn't know what it meant. I waited.

"You're twenty-five, Chisholm," he said. "A half-breed. Parents dead. Served in Afghanistan. Lots of medals. Now, you are a disgraced former Boston Police detective with a weakness for strippers. I learned all about you after the first time you put a gun to my head. I always get to know the person I am going to kill. That is how I honor the life I take. You are still alive only because Christine talked me out of killing you. She is the only thing more important than my honor. Now, you not only insult my honor again, but you demand that I put my business at risk for you. You should kill me. Then my men will kill you. We should both die today."

We stared at each other for a while. I didn't believe any of his talk about honor. He would double-cross his mother if he had to. I was pretty sure he was more worried about looking weak to his men. He didn't want some ambitious punk getting the idea that he was vulnerable. But I didn't need to call him out on it. I didn't need to make a bad situation worse—for me.

"You're a smart guy, Jon. Does it make any sense for both of us to die today? I need information. Without it, I'm dead. I have nothing to lose. But you do. We can both lose today, or we can both walk away with something."

"There is nothing you can offer to compensate me for the risk of helping you."

"What about Christine?"

Choi's body tensed. His jaw clenched, and his eyes narrowed.

"What about her?"

"What happens to her if I spread it around that you gave me damaging information on the people behind YouSEL and their activities?

228

True or not, once it's out there, you'll be on the hook. Whoever these people are, you clearly think they're dangerous. Maybe they go after you, but maybe they go after Christine too. You know them. You want to take that risk?"

Choi's eyes froze on me like two search lights on an escaped convict. He was trying to figure out if I was bluffing and calculating his options if I wasn't.

"I tell you, I don't tell you. Same risk either way. Like I said, we should both die today."

"Maybe, but I'm betting I can escape from here and stay alive long enough to put a target on Christine. If you're that afraid of these people, you know they don't take chances with potential leaks. I can kill you now if you want, but the last thing you'll think about will be how *you* killed Christine."

Choi's lips tightened. He continued to examine me, searching for a tell that would betray my hand, trying to decide if he should call my bluff. After a long silence, he snorted and shook his head in frustration.

"How does helping you help me?"

"I'll protect Christine. You can call on me whenever she's threatened or needs help. She'll be safer than anything you can do alone."

"First you threaten to put her life at risk, then you offer to protect her from that risk in exchange for information. That's an old school racket you're trying to push. It won't work on me. Christine was safe before you walked in here. She'll be safer when your body is carried out."

"As long as she's Jon Choi's sister, her life's at risk. That's on you. But if I don't get the information I need, I have nothing to lose. I die, she dies. I live, she lives. Your choice."

"What's to stop you from coming back to that well whenever you want something?"

"Besides my word, I know you'll kill me the next time I come to you for anything. You might not even wait. But I have to take that risk. I'm dead if I don't."

"And if you're killed? How will you protect Christine then?"

"Someone's going to die in this. We both know that. I'm your best bet to make sure it's not Christine. I need your answer now, Jon. Whoever's coming to help you will be here any minute. Things will get out of control then."

Choi reached into his blazer pocket slowly and pulled out his cellphone. He typed something, then put his phone down on the table. He looked up at me.

"We have time," he said.

"Okay. What's your answer?"

"First, I want your word you'll do whatever it takes to keep Christine safe, whether I am alive or not."

"You have it."

"Second, you will owe me one job of my choosing, regardless of what it is."

I knew what Choi was capable of. It would be a steep price when the time came. I didn't like the terms, but it was die now or die later. Later gave me a chance.

"No murder," I said.

"I don't need you for that."

"Okay."

"Third—"

"No third. That's all you get."

Choi stared at me. Then a wry smile appeared, and he nodded.

"Start talking," I said.

Choi reached over and grabbed the bottle of Makgeolli. He poured a full glass, then took a long drink. He put the glass down and composed himself.

"I don't do any direct business with YouSEL. I've tried to get in with them, but it's a very secretive organization. I've interacted with parts of its operations, but most of what I know is from others who have worked inside the company. There have been attempts to hack into its network, but they must have people in Israel working for them because no one's been able to break through."

"Have *you* tried?"

"Let's just say if I had, I'd be frustrated, but I'd keep trying."

"Go on."

"There are three main businesses that I know of. The online porn and retail sites, strip clubs and nightclubs, and crypto mining. There's a small security business that shows up now and then too, but—"

"Security business? What's that?"

"Maybe security isn't the right description. It's really hired muscle. Protection and intimidation. Can't screw with them. Officially, they work as heads of security for the clubs that YouSEL has interests in. They've forced some start-up porn sites to shut down. A number of strip clubs too. There's also rumors of them pressuring smaller crypto players to sell their operations. I know one baller programmer who was beaten up so bad that he left the crypto biz. And then there's the blackmail whispers. Those are all over the darknet, with the names of some big politicians and business execs attached."

"Do these security guys do murder?"

"I've never heard about them being involved in any killings, but people might be too scared to talk."

"Or dead."

Choi raised his eyebrows.

"What about drugs?" I asked.

"Nothing there either. I'm not surprised. Drugs are the fastest way to get on the wrong side of politicians, business execs, and the Feds. Can't go there if you want to limit scrutiny of your own shit. Been there, done that. Porn's better. You should know. Acceptable so long as you stay away from kids. Always a fine line, though. I've never heard of YouSEL crossing it."

"Any money laundering?"

"That's the brass ring. Finance and tech, layered over every legitimate and illegitimate business in the world. Making money by cleaning money. As simple and pure a money-making machine as there is. Every part of YouSEL is positioned to exploit it, including its crypto biz."

"How big a player is YouSEL?"

"Can't tell. That's where the company is really opaque. If the people running it are smart, they're in it big time. But no one talks about YouSEL and money laundering. That tells me they're probably a big player."

"Do you know who runs the company and the different businesses?"

"Tough to get that info. You can bet the listed names of top executives aren't the ones in charge. I never hear anything about the real generals. Not even anything about the lieutenants on the ground. It's like they're invisible. Either they're all hiding in one place, or they're all walled off and don't even know each other. The only name I hear tossed around is for the unofficial head of security."

"Who's that?"

"A dirty cop here in the city. I've had a couple of run-ins with him myself. Someone bigger is behind him, but I haven't figured out who that is."

"What's his name?"

"People call him El Capitán."

"What's his real name?"

"Detective Michael Gomez."

38

*A*fter I slipped out the back of Seoul Brothers, I found a no-name boarding house on the outskirts of Queens. I picked up some Chinese food and spent the evening processing the new information I'd uncovered. Learning about Detective Gomez triggered something. A picture of the game was starting to form in my head, along with a plan.

One night turned into two turned into three. By the third morning, I decided my flophouse vacation was over. My name was showing up in news stories about the lack of progress in the stripper slayings. I was surprised I hadn't been highlighted more. Either way, I had to get going on my plan, even if it was closer to an outline.

The clock radio next to the bed said it was 7:06 a.m. I got up, walked over to the window, and peeked out. A deluge of rain blurred the view. I could see traffic racing by, smashing through puddles and propelling sheets of water onto the sidewalk. Dark billowing clouds hovered, all worked up and ready to explode. A crack of lightning and low growl of thunder seemed to be telling me to go back to bed. I did a quick workout instead.

As it turned out, there wasn't much point to showering before I abandoned the lovely resort. By the time I hailed a taxi, the rain had soaked me through. It was a long ride to Manhattan to pick up my car, but I was still wet when the taxi dropped me off.

The old Portuguese guy was working in the parking garage. I knocked on the plexiglass window of the cashier booth, then slipped him a twenty to lift the gate when I came out. He gave me a sly, yellow-toothed smile and grabbed the money. I kept an anytime ticket in my wallet in case he was off duty. But he seemed to live there.

I stood in the garage stairwell for a while and surveilled the level where I had parked. Nothing suspicious jumped out at me. I walked over to my car, unlocked it, and slipped quietly inside. I took off my wet running jacket and T-shirt, then grabbed a lightweight Henley out of my backpack and put it on.

A little before one, I took Exit 3 on 195 to Greenwich, Connecticut. Maybe the wealthiest town in America. It's a cesspool of old money, new money, Wall Streeters, hedge fund managers, doctors, lawyers, and all flavors of white-collar criminals who had yet to be caught.

I drove by several affordable housing complexes that looked built for millionaires before I reached the rarefied neighborhood where Greenwood Academy was located. It was the exclusive all-girls high school that Rachel Morris attended. If you had to ask what it cost, you shouldn't apply.

According to Richard Morris, Rachel had recently stopped using the family chauffeur to bring her home from school. He said Mitchell Dugan was picking her up most days. It was the last day of the school year. I was betting Dugan would be there to give her a ride. He drove a black Chevy Blazer. It would be easy to flag in the throngs of foreign luxury cars and SUVs. I needed to speak to both of them.

I was early. Another hour before school let out. I cruised around to scope out the neighborhood. The smell of money was pungent. Nothing that I would ever get used to. Then I drove downtown, grabbed a coffee, and strolled around. The rain had stopped. The sun burst intermittently between the gray clouds being hurried along by a strong breeze.

I drove back to the school and pulled over fifty yards down from the entrance. A steady stream of one-hundred-thousand-dollar SUVs carrying teenage girls not yet old enough to drive flowed from the parking lot. In between, older students zipped out in sports cars and Jeep Wranglers probably given to them for their birthdays.

Twenty yards on the other side of the entrance, a black BMW SUV caught my attention. It was an X5 High Security model, with an antenna setup that looked capable of secure communication and surveillance. It could have been there for any of the girls. But my voices told me it was the security service hired by Richard Morris.

After fifteen minutes, a black Chevy Blazer with New York tags pulled up just short of the school entrance. I was sure it was Dugan. Then a thin, medium height girl walked quickly out of a side gate and headed for the passenger door. Her head was lowered, covered by the hood of an oversized maroon windbreaker, strands of blonde hair dangling down. The maroon and black pleated skirt of her uniform barely showed below the jacket. She climbed into the passenger seat. The Blazer signaled and eased into the slow-moving traffic. The BMW waited until it passed and then pulled out three vehicles behind.

I hung back until both SUVs cleared the school traffic. Then I did a U-turn and caught up to the BMW. After a half mile, the Blazer turned south towards downtown. The BMW did the same. I followed, maintaining a casual distance. If the driver of the BMW was worth anything, I had already been made. There was no need to pretend we weren't all going to the same place.

Once downtown, the BMW pulled into a diagonal parking space in front of an Italian coffee shop. The Blazer was already parked two spaces to the right. I pulled into an empty space next to the BMW on the left. Rachel and Dugan were already in the coffee shop. I watched Rachel sit down at a small table against a brick wall. Dugan was at the counter ordering.

I stepped out of my Caddy, walked around the rear, and came up next to the driver's side of the BMW. I stopped just short of the door. My right hand was behind me, under my shirt and resting on the back strap of my Glock.

The driver's window rolled down.

"Will Chisholm?" a woman's voice said.

"You are?" I replied.

A dark-haired woman wearing a New York Mets baseball cap stuck her head partially out the window to look at me. She could have used a day in the sun. Then the rear window next to me rolled down, giving me a view of a muscular black man in the front passenger seat. His head was turned to me. He had a crew cut and was wearing sunglasses and a green polo shirt.

"We're Brinson Services," the man said. "Mr. Morris hired us. Told us to identify ourselves to you when we crossed paths. Here is Mr. Morris to confirm."

The man held out a cellphone towards me with a prerecorded video of Richard Morris.

"Mr. Chisholm," Morris said, "these people are with Brinson Services. I hired it to provide security for Rachel, as we discussed. You will receive a confirmation text as proof in a moment. It should match the one that appears following this video. Thank you."

A four-digit number flashed on the screen as soon as the video ended.

"Did you receive the text?" the man said and pulled the cell back.

I had shut off my cell and stored it in the compartment under the passenger seat cushion in my Caddy. I was pretty sure it was being tracked somehow. The same for my laptop. I still needed to have both looked at by someone I could trust, but I hadn't found that someone yet.

"Yeah, I heard it ping," I said.

"Do you want to check that the numbers match?" the man asked.

"I'll trust you."

"Okay. Our instructions are to monitor and follow Ms. Morris. Try not to be noticed but go wherever she goes. We were told to follow your direction."

"Have they made you yet?"

"Not that they've indicated. It's been a week. Guess they're in love. What's the plan?"

"My plan is to go in and talk to her and Dugan. You two keep doing what you're doing."

"Are you sure that's wise?"

"No, but I'm not old enough to be wise."

I walked into the coffee shop and made my way over to Rachel. I sat down in the chair opposite her. Her head was down reading texts on her cell. She looked up. Her big blue eyes peered through the blonde bangs spilling out from under the hood of her windbreaker. They widened when she recognized me. Then her mouth opened slightly.

"Hello, Rachel," I said.

She didn't respond. Her eyes whipped towards Dugan, then back to me.

I caught Dugan out of my peripheral vision coming towards us. I turned my head to see him clearly. He was carrying two plastic cups of iced coffee, with a brown bag pressed under his left arm against his ribs. The bag looked like it held a couple of muffins. He was concentrating and didn't notice me until he was a few feet away.

Dugan stopped just before the table. He stared at me, confused. His jaw clenched when he recognized me. His eyes shot towards Rachel to ask what was going on. Her look told him she didn't know. She nodded to signal she was okay.

I grabbed an empty chair and slid it over to Dugan. He moved next to Rachel and placed the iced coffees on the table. He took the bag from under his arm and dropped it next to the coffees. He widened his stance and shifted his weight to the balls of his feet. Like he had in the alley behind Champagne before I took him down. He started to curl his fingers into fists.

"I'm just here to talk," I said. "To both of you."

"What if we don't want to talk?" Dugan said. "I hear the police—"

"Mitch, it's alright," Rachel said. "Let's give him a chance."

Dugan looked at her. Their eyes talked for a long moment. He turned and stared hard at me, then sat down slowly. He laid his right arm on the table to display his bulging bicep. He subtly placed his left hand on Rachel's thigh under the table. She moved her hand to grasp his. He took a deep breath and released it. She had soothed the beast.

"I didn't murder Alyssa," I said. "Or the other women."

"Yeah, yeah," Dugan replied. "Rachel told me everything you said. Don't expect me to believe you."

"I don't. Not without proof. But to prove it, I have to figure out who *did* kill Alyssa. I need both of your help for that."

"The only help you'll get—"

"Mitch," Rachel interrupted, "we need to hear him out. I want to do whatever we can to find Alyssa's killer. Please?"

Dugan looked at her and said, "What if he's the killer?"

"I don't think he is," she said and glanced at me.

Dugan sighed quietly. His expression softened. He nodded, then turned to me.

"Okay, go ahead," he said.

"I know you were both at Champagne the night Alyssa was murdered. I need each of you to tell me everyone you saw and when they were there. Whatever you can remember." I looked at Dugan and said, "You should start since you probably saw most of the people there that night."

Dugan pursed his lips. His eyes flicked quickly to Rachel before coming back to me.

"I don't want Rachel's name brought up in any of this. Otherwise, we're done talking. Do you understand?"

I nodded. But I was lying. Nothing was going to get in the way of figuring out who was framing me. If Rachel had to be exposed, so be it. I wasn't going to sacrifice myself to protect anyone's image.

"So, Alyssa and her sister, Ashley, were there when I punched in," Dugan said. "They were there when I left with Rachel too. That was shortly after eleven. Something was going on between them earlier.

It seemed like an argument, but I'm not sure. Besides them, Steve, James, and Easy were on that night. They're doormen. Easy is the black guy who got the better of you."

"The metal pipe got the better of me. But continue."

"Anyway, all the regular bartenders and dancers were on that night from what I remember. It's a long list. I'd have to think a little and write their names down. Oh, and Terry was there too. He's the short bald guy you knocked out. You did a job on him. He hasn't been around since that day. Let me think—"

"What's Terry's last name?"

"Zezulin. I think he's Russian."

"And what does he do?"

"He's in charge of security for Champagne. All the doormen report to him. He's also responsible for surveillance, but that's another issue."

"What do you mean?"

"I can't talk about it."

"Mitch," Rachel said, "you need to tell him everything. You already quit. There's nothing they can do to you now."

"You quit Champagne?" I said.

"Yeah, yesterday. I'm going to do construction while I finish school. But talking about Champagne can be dangerous. Not for me. I'm not afraid of those assholes. But they might try something with Rachel. I don't know, but I don't trust any of the people who run that place. I don't want to take any chances since I can't be with her all the time."

"Don't worry about me," Rachel said. "I'm tougher than you think. We need to do everything we can to figure out who killed Alyssa. That's what's important."

Dugan looked tenderly at her. He wasn't convinced.

"I'll make sure Rachel's safe," I said. "You've already seen what I can do. Besides, her father's paying me now to look out for her."

"What do you mean?" Rachel said. "Isn't he paying you to try and break us up?"

"Not anymore. Now, he just wants me to make sure you stay safe until Alyssa's murder is solved. Not that he would mind the two of you breaking up, but whatever you said to him made an impression. You should keep talking to him."

She choked up a little, then looked at Dugan and smiled tentatively. She turned back to me and nodded.

I looked at Dugan and said, "Can you tell me about surveillance at Champagne?"

Dugan thought for a moment. He glanced briefly at Rachel, then looked at me.

"So, after you put Terry out of commission, they asked me to fill in managing surveillance for him. It was only one day. They never asked me again. I'm majoring in computer science. I know something about the equipment and software Champagne uses. I can tell you they're doing more than just monitoring the cashiers and entryways. They're videotaping sessions in the private rooms on The Cork Room floor. I never saw who or what they recorded, but I can guess. That's just one of the reasons I quit."

"What are the others?" I asked.

"Champagne started advertising that it would accept different cryptocurrencies as payment. It never took off. No one ever paid with crypto. But I overheard Terry on his cell talking about all the crypto they were pulling in. Then one night, I was closing after a shift, and a couple of cars showed up in the alley where you and I fought. I knew they were unmarked police cars. Something was going on. When I asked Terry about it, he told me to mind my business if I wanted to stay healthy. The next day, he asked me if I was interested in learning more about the other businesses Champagne has. I said I didn't have time. That's when he really started to be an asshole to me. It was obvious he wanted me out of there, but they were short staffed. I knew it was only a matter of time before they fired me, though."

"Anything else?" I said.

Dugan looked at Rachel.

"Tell him everything," she said. "I'll be okay."

He turned back to me and said, "We met when Rachel was auditioning at Champagne. I asked her out. Alyssa took Rachel under her wing during the process. Just before she was going to be hired, Alyssa told me she was only seventeen."

He glanced at Rachel. A coy smile crossed her face. He grinned, then came back to me.

"Anyway," he continued, "I used her age to stop her from being hired. But then Terry and his boss tried to press me to get her to audition again. I couldn't believe it. I—"

"Who's Terry's boss?" I asked.

"This NYPD cop who moonlights as a security consultant. Terry calls him El Capitán. His real name is Gomez. I think he's actually a detective. But he acts like the boss, not a consultant. He approached me a little over a month ago and said management was interested in Rachel joining the team. I wanted to tell him to fuck off, but he's a cop. So, I told him she was underaged. Asshole asked when she would be eighteen. I said I would check. That's when I really decided to quit. Alyssa was murdered three weeks later. I stuck around to see what would happen. I have some good friends there. But I finally had to get away from the place."

"Did Alyssa have much to do with Terry or Gomez?"

"I never saw them really interact. And she never said anything to me about them. But I know Ashley works with both of them. I've seen her talking to Terry a lot. And the night the two unmarked cars showed up, I saw her out there with Gomez. I think she's part of the management team. But I don't really know what she does."

"Did you see Ashley with Terry the night Alyssa was murdered?"

"No, but I did see her out back with Gomez."

"Gomez was there?"

"Yeah. When Rachel and I were leaving, I saw Ashley talking to someone in a car in the alley. Rachel wasn't supposed to be there, so I was taking her out the back way. Anyway, it was the same blue unmarked car I'd seen Gomez driving before. The front and back windows were rolled down. Ashley was talking back and forth to both. Just as we turned down the street behind the club, I saw Gomez step out of the driver's side of the car. I don't think any of them saw us. I can tell you Ashley looked stressed, but I couldn't hear what they were saying."

I looked at Rachel and asked, "Did you see or hear anything?"

"No. I was trying not to be seen. I wasn't supposed to be there."

"Why *were* you there?"

"Alyssa asked me to stop by."

"Why?"

"She wanted to tell me something."

"What was that?"

"She told me to stay away from Champagne. That it was getting dangerous. She said the company that owned Champagne was trying to get my father involved as an investor. She told me to tell him to stay away too. I didn't know what she was talking about. But then you showed up, and she said she had to go. I guess she was waiting for you."

"You said that before. I never told anyone I was going to Champagne. And I'm the one who requested Alyssa. Why would she be waiting for me?"

"That's not what she told me. She said she hadn't danced all night because she was waiting for a special customer to show up. She pointed you out when you came in. Then Terry pulled her over by the elevator to talk. She looked upset after."

I thought for a moment. How could anyone have known I was going to Champagne that night? I didn't even know until just a few hours before.

"Have either of you heard from Ashley or know where she is?" I asked.

They looked at each other for a second, then at me.

"We're not sure," Rachel said.

"What do you mean?"

"I got a strange text yesterday. I didn't recognize the number, and when I tried to respond, my text wouldn't go through. I called the number, but it was out of service."

"What did the text say?"

Rachel picked up her cell, touched the screen, and scrolled down. She showed me the message.

The text read: "You & Mitch are in danger. Don't go to the police. Get away and hide. A."

"Who is A?" I asked.

"Alyssa," Rachel replied. "But that can't be. It has to be Ashley. She must sign her texts the same way. They *are* twins. I mean, they were."

39

I followed Rachel and Dugan back to her house. I owed Richard Morris an update. I hadn't communicated with him since our last meeting a week ago. More important to me, I needed information from him.

Rachel lived with her father on a gated five-acre estate in the middle of Greenwich, surrounded by other obsessively manicured estates. Fields of money cordoned off from common creatures longing to graze. A foreign and forbidden world for everyone but the one-percenters.

The security team followed me and parked just outside the gate. I heard the woman on the intercom ask Rachel about the old car behind Dugan's Blazer. Rachel referred to my Caddy as an antique. I didn't hear what she called me. Then the gates unlocked and slid open smoothly.

We drove in and around a large grass circle bordered by ornate multi-colored flowers. Dugan parked in front of a stately bleached brick mansion with all kinds of shrubs and small trees running along the foundation. I parked behind him. The place looked like the cover of some magazine I had never read or even opened. That was the extent of my architectural expertise.

Everything about the estate looked impressive. But fake. Like plastic displays. I guess that's what multitudes of zeros bought you—lots of natural stuff made up to appear artificial. Maybe that's what you did to let everyone know you had too much money. I didn't get it. That's probably why it wasn't my problem.

Dugan got out of the Blazer and opened the door for Rachel. They kissed goodbye for a long time. Their love was real. Like all love at their ages. In twenty-five years, I'd loved once. It was why I was being framed. I was certain. Love kills. I wanted to warn them. But it was their lives. Everyone needs to love and die for themselves.

Dugan climbed back in the Blazer and drove off. He knew he wasn't welcomed. I didn't know if I would be either.

Richard Morris greeted us at the door in a light gray suit, white shirt, and mint green tie. He gave me a cold nod of acknowledgement, then placed his hands on Rachel's shoulders. He leaned over and kissed her on the top of her head.

"How was the last day of your junior year?" Morris said. "You are a rising senior now."

"Uneventful, until Mr. Chisholm interrupted my coffee with Mitch." Rachel frowned sardonically and shook her head as if to admonish her father. "And no, I didn't break up with him. I think you should fire Mr. Chisholm. He's not very persuasive. I'm going to change. I don't want to watch a grown man cry. Especially such a cute one."

She spun playfully towards me and blew a kiss. She winked, waved, and headed into the house. She stopped in the doorway and looked at her father.

"By the way," she said, "Mitch likes those people keeping an eye on me. Thanks."

She flittered off and disappeared inside. I was certain I didn't want to be Morris. Not for all the zeros in the world.

Morris composed himself, then looked at me sternly. Playtime was over.

"I am not fond of surprise visits, Mr. Chisholm. I was expecting an update from you by now. That was our agreement. I am aware there is an outstanding material witness warrant for you in New York, but that should not have stopped you from communicating with me. I told you that Rachel's safety must be your top priority."

"It is," I said, lying as convincingly as I could. "But I have to be alive and out of jail to keep her alive. I apologize for not communicating until now, but even being here is a risk for me."

Morris scrutinized me for a moment, then nodded. More to himself, it seemed.

"You are a good liar," he said, "particularly for a young man. It is not necessary. I have no delusions about your motivation. Rachel's safety will be your top priority so long as it doesn't conflict with proving your innocence. I know that. Right now, both of our priorities are in alignment. However, I expect you to inform me immediately when you believe they no longer are. That will be the measure of your character. I believe I know who you are, as well as who you are not. There is no need to lie to me."

"Sounds like you know me better than I know myself."

"Mr. Chisholm, I am asking that you be honest with me, for Rachel's safety. That is all."

"My clients don't usually want honesty, no matter what they say. But fair enough. No lying. Unless I have to. Starting now. I need information. That's why I'm here."

Morris scrutinized me, trying to decide if I was being honest. We both had trust issues.

"Very well," he finally said. "We can continue in the study."

Morris moved aside to let me enter. I stepped into the house, then paused while he talked to a middle-aged Hispanic woman in a knee-length blue dress.

"Elliana," he said, "can you please bring a pot of coffee for two to the study? Thank you."

I followed Morris down a long hallway to the back of the house. A dark oak double door opened to a spacious sunny room. A large mahogany and marble table desk sat to the left, surrounded by built-in mahogany bookshelves. To the right, a wall of French doors and windows looked out on an expansive lawn. I could see a tennis court, pool, and small house in the distance. Two green fabric wingback chairs with a glass coffee table in between were positioned near the French doors. An imposing stone fireplace loomed straight ahead. The room was decorated in some combination of modern and antique styles. My design knowledge barely exceeded my architectural expertise.

Morris shut the doors and walked over to the sitting area. He motioned for me to take a seat. I did, and he followed. Before he could say anything, the Hispanic woman entered with a tray holding a silver coffee pot, a setup for two, and a plate of cookies. The cookies looked too fancy to eat. She laid the tray down and Morris thanked her. Then she left.

Morris poured two cups of coffee and pushed one over to me. He signaled for me to help myself to the sugar and cream. He drank his black. He picked up his cup, took a sip, and placed the cup back on the saucer. Then he sat back in his chair and examined me.

I poured a little cream in my coffee, stirred it, then took a taste. It was hot and strong and smooth. I sat back and returned Morris's gaze.

"Before you ask me anything," Morris said, "I would like the progress update you were supposed to give me three days ago."

"Alright. I should start by telling you I didn't go to Boston."

"I suspected as much."

"I went to Columbus to track down some leads on the stripper murders. Alyssa Grant's sister, Ashley, supposedly lives there. I was trying to find her. I was also looking into a company that I think is involved. That's what I want to talk to you about."

"That is fine, but do you have anything to share regarding Rachel?"

"I do. I'll get to her security in a moment. First, she and Mitchell Dugan are not having sex. They haven't even had it once. I assume that means intercourse to them. Apparently, he won't have sex with her until she's eighteen. She doesn't want to get pregnant before she finishes college. And he doesn't want to get married and have kids until he's established in a career. But she plans to marry him as soon as he asks. I think you have a few years before you have to worry. If they make it that far. A lot can happen."

"She told you all that?"

"Yes."

"Just today?"

"No. She had tracked me down last week. We talked then. I didn't tell you the last time we met because I thought you might be involved with setting me up."

"Am I to infer that you no longer believe that?"

"I'm here."

"So, you are still unsure. You will have to resolve that for yourself then. Were you able to confirm with Mr. Dugan any of what Rachel told you?"

"Most of it. If character matters to you that much, he has some. He may not be who you want Rachel to be with, but he's crazy about her. He won't do anything to hurt her. She knows what she's doing too. I don't think she's dating him to get back at you for anything."

Morris was silent, gazing down. He sipped his coffee as if an afterthought.

"You're probably aware of this," I continued, "but in case you're not, Rachel talked about suicide. It sounds like it's in the past, but you never know. She misses her mother. I'm not telling you anything you don't know, but she needs to be able to talk to you. That's in your control."

Morris stared at me, a pained look on his face.

"Anything else?" he said.

"Yeah. Rachel learned about me by hacking into your laptop. It wasn't my screwup. She must be talented. If you don't want her to know your business, you should get some better encryption software."

A faint smile seeped across Morris's lips. He nodded slightly. To himself, it seemed again. Then he turned pensive.

"What are your plans to protect her?" he said.

"That depends on how you answer my questions."

"Then proceed."

"What do you know about a company called YouSEL?"

Morris's eyes widened briefly, then his brow furrowed.

"May I ask why you want to know?"

"YouSEL is an online lingerie and porn website. All the murder victims worked as models for the company, in addition to stripping at clubs. For a fee, premium customers of the site can get access to what clubs the models strip at. I think YouSEL has ownership stakes in all the clubs they dance at. I think the process is really a cover for arranging prostitution services from the models. It's targeted at wealthy and influential men, for the most part. The clubs are where they meet. The customers think the sessions in the rooms are private, but they're recorded. Most likely for blackmail. I don't think the blackmail is for money. It's for something bigger."

"Such as?"

"That's what I'm trying to figure out. Influence. Maybe politics. Money laundering is a possibility too. Ultimately, it's either about money or power or both."

"Why are you asking me about YouSEL?"

"Rachel met with Alyssa Grant at Champagne the night she was murdered. Alyssa warned her to stay away from the place. She also said you were being solicited to invest in the company that owns it. I assume that's YouSEL. Alyssa told Rachel to warn you not to get involved."

"Rachel never conveyed that message to me."

"Her friend was raped and murdered. Then she found out her father was trying to break up her relationship. Might have slipped her mind."

Morris pursed his lips and frowned.

"I assume you want to know about my dealings with YouSEL," he said.

"For starters."

Morris put his coffee down on the table and straightened up in his chair. He gazed out the French doors, nodded to himself, then turned back to me.

"I will spare you asking the question. I have used the services of several YouSEL models in the past. I have four apartments in Manhattan. I arranged for them to meet me at different ones. Their visits were never recorded. I take exceptional precautions. I do not want this to be shared with Rachel. I am not ashamed of my actions, but I do not want to add to the emotional burden she is already carrying."

"I'm not one to judge."

"Your opinion of me is immaterial."

"But you seem to want me to know that."

Morris sighed and said, "Your next question is whether I am being blackmailed."

I nodded.

"The answer is no. At least, not yet. One of my companies has developed a proprietary trade clearing and custody platform for digital currencies. It employs artificial intelligence to integrate blockchain technology and traditional securities trade clearing. It is more secure and powerful than current crypto exchanges. I'm sorry. That is probably more than you care to know. The process and software are currently under review for patent. Representatives of a company affiliated with YouSEL approached me three months ago and proposed a joint venture with its crypto mining unit. I was skeptical but decided to perform some due diligence before responding. I recently decided not to pursue the venture. I have yet to communicate that to the company. That is the extent of my relationship with YouSEL. Now, I need to know if you believe Rachel is in danger from these people?"

"Alyssa Grant thought so. Now she's dead."

"What could her murder have to do with my business dealings?"

"I don't know, but there's a connection. Too many touchpoints. Too many coincidences."

"That brings me back to my original question. How do you plan to protect Rachel?"

"I told you I can't guard her twenty-four seven. Now that school is out, the best thing you can do is send her someplace where she'll be safe. You have the resources to do that. I recommend you go with her. If YouSEL *is* involved, that should come out when the murderer is caught."

"I have no intention of fleeing my home. However, your recommendation for Rachel is probably the wisest move to keep her safe. Assuming she cooperates, that is, which I am doubtful of. Still, I can send her away for the summer, but she will have to return for school. I believe it is time to speak to the police."

"That would not be smart."

"Please explain yourself."

"I think someone in the NYPD is involved in the murders."

"That is very troubling. Why do you think that?"

"It's a long story. I'd prefer not to get into it right now."

"Do you have the same concern about the local police?"

"My concern is their competence. And they would coordinate with the NYPD."

"What about the FBI? Are they an option?"

"Eventually, maybe. But they don't have any jurisdiction right now."

"Jack McNeill provided a contact in the NYPD when I first talked to him about hiring someone. I spoke to him. He seemed trustworthy. He may be able to help us and keep it confidential. I do not know how this can end without involving the authorities. You will have to speak to them eventually as well."

"Don't worry about me. When did you talk to this contact?"

"I spoke to him when I was first researching your background. He did not know you, but he said he had heard positive things. I spoke to him again when the news broke that you were a person of interest in the stripper murders. He would not share anything with me at the time, but he said to call him whenever I wanted."

"What's his name?"

"Inspector Benjamin Jaworski."

40

*M*ichael Jin was sitting at a small table upstairs in the back corner of the Korean deli. The same Korean deli where I would buy him lunch while I tried to get him out of his bind with Jon Choi over dating his sister. The same table where we would sit and eat salads with chicken while he talked about how he had never met a girl like Christine. The same table where he cried when I told him he had to stop seeing her.

Today, he was sitting in the chair with its back to the wall. The one I used to sit in. Two salads in plastic containers were on the table, along with two bottles of water. He was waiting for Christine.

Michael had just finished his second year at MIT. Sally told me he had a summer internship with a big bank, but it hadn't started yet. I needed him to look at my laptop and cellphone. But my apartment was being monitored by plainclothes police. I couldn't approach him until he was far enough away to safely show myself. That's why I had followed him to the deli. I knew he would spend as much time with Christine as he could, every day, starting with lunch.

Michael looked like he had grown another inch and filled out some more. I had gotten him into working out last summer. He was still a little gangling, but not bad looking for a complete nerd. He had an intellect and work ethic that would give him his choice of careers. His only problem was that he was no longer a Chinese immigrant. He was American now. The last time we talked, I could see expectations and privilege seeping into his attitude. That was inevitable. Unless life beat it out of you before you could dream. That was my story, not his.

I pulled out the chair across from Michael, sat down and laid my backpack on the floor next to me. Michael looked up from his cellphone. His mouth opened immediately, and his eyes widened. He smiled, then seemed to doubt that response. His expression changed to looking like he had just been caught jerking off in the bathroom.

"How's Christine?" I asked.

"Christine . . . uh . . . okay, you obviously know about us. My mom and pop don't know. My sister doesn't either. Please don't say anything to them. Christine will be here any minute. You probably already know that, right?"

"Don't worry, Michael, your secret's safe with me. I want to hear about everything going on with you, but I can't right now. You know I'm in trouble. I didn't kill any of those—"

"Will, I know you'd never do something like that. Just tell me what I can do to help."

"Thanks. I need you to look at my laptop and cellphone. Check both of them for surveillance software and anything else that shouldn't be there. I think I'm being tracked. Maybe watched too. It's probably been going on for a while. If you find something, I need you to try to identify the source. But I need it done by tomorrow. I know that's short notice."

"I'll get it done, even if I have to stay up all night. My internship starts tomorrow, but the first day is just orientation. I don't think it will matter if I fall asleep during an HR lecture. Unless I snore. But I don't think I snore."

I nodded like I cared. Then I pulled my laptop and cellphone out of my backpack and slid them across the table. He gave them a once-over and frowned.

"I can get you a real good price if you want to upgrade either of these."

I shot him an impatient look.

"Sorry," he said. "Um, how should I contact you? Since I'll have your phone."

"I'll text you from another cell."

He nodded, then his eyes fixed on something behind me.

"I assume that's Christine," I said. "I'm gone. Thanks again. I owe you."

He looked at me and said, "No problem, Will. You've done more for me than I can ever pay back."

I shot him a smile. Then I grabbed my backpack, turned quickly and headed for the stairs. A tall, thin Asian girl broke out in a big grin as she passed me. If it was Christine, she had matured a lot. I glanced behind me and saw her walking towards Michael. He stood up, happiness smeared all over his face. They were in another world. I think I was there once, with Brittany. But it might have been a dream.

41

*P*eggy Grant had been lying to me from the beginning. Since her tearful performance on that first call. I didn't know if she was a pawn in the Master's game or the queen. But she was one of the pieces. It was time to confront her. The next step in my evolving plan. She was going to tell me everything she knew, even if I had to force it out of her.

She had left several voice messages over the past week looking for an update on my search for Ashley. Her last one was today, just before I turned my phone over to Michael. She said Ashley had called and wanted to talk to me. I knew she was lying. But it gave me the excuse I needed to see her. I texted that I would stop by near the end of the day. She responded with the same drunken emoji.

After I left the deli, I drove to Peggy's apartment and parked two blocks away. I was two hours early, intentionally. I slinked around her neighborhood a few times looking for cops, uniformed or otherwise. Or anyone else watching her building. No one jumped out at me.

I was still uneasy. And my voices were whispering. A trap could be waiting. But nothing was going to change if I didn't risk it. The status quo would eventually kill me, one way or another.

I texted Peggy from my burner cell that I was downstairs. She seemed surprised. A good sign. She buzzed me in. I took the stairs up to her floor. I opened the door from the stairwell and stepped softly into the carpeted hallway. I sensed something and paused. I listened. Silence. It could have been a faint smell. I wasn't sure.

I guided the stairwell door closed so it wouldn't make a sound. Then I walked cautiously to where the hallway turned to Peggy's apartment. I stopped and listened again. Silence again. I poked my head around the corner. A heavy older woman in a light green casual dress was waiting for the elevator. A rat dog on a leash panted next to her. It had a scruffy face and squinty eyes. A big tongue licked the scrub around its mouth. It stared at me.

The elevator pinged and the door opened. The rat dog whimpered at me as the woman dragged it onto the elevator. The door closed, and I stepped around the corner. Something still didn't feel right. It was probably the rat dog. I didn't understand the appeal.

I walked quickly to Peggy's door. It opened just as I knocked. My eyes widened before I could stop them. Peggy stood there smiling, dressed to get me killed.

A black wrap sleeveless dress spilled over her body and down her curves, stopping just above the middle of her thighs. The plunging neckline competed for attention. Her strawberry blonde hair was styled with long playful curls, while the three-inch heels put her blue eyes almost level with mine. They dazzled against her tanned skin. I thought I was back at Champagne.

"Will, hi!" she said.

"Hi," I said as natural as I could fake.

"Come in," she said and slid to the side. "You look good."

I didn't. Unless a wrinkled black polo shirt, old blue blazer, and brown khakis were a fetching combination to her. I needed a haircut and hadn't shaved in four days, even if it only looked like one. And I was a little pale from hiding out in hotel rooms with the shades drawn for the past week.

I stepped inside and moved to my right. She closed the door and mockingly gestured for me to look behind it. The same wall, mirror, and crescent-shaped table stared at me.

"See, no one hiding," she said. "You're safe with me."

I didn't feel safe. Not with the way she was dressed. I had to remind myself why I was there.

"I'm getting a glass of water," she said. "Do you want one?"

"Sure."

I watched her strut to the kitchen out of the corner of my eye. I managed not to gawk. Then I did a once-over of her place. It looked the same, except the faint cigarette smell was back. Menthol for sure. But no ashtray anywhere. No indication she smoked at all. She hid her tendencies well. Unlike me.

She strolled back from the kitchen, sipping water from a glass in her left hand. She offered me the one she was holding in her right. It had a wedge of lemon in it. I glanced at her glass. It had a lemon too. I took the glass, raised it to my lips, and drank some water. It was cold and a little tart. It tasted good. My mouth was dry. Probably from trying not to gape at her.

I gulped down some more water, then asked, "Going somewhere?"

"Oh, you mean, the way I'm dressed?"

"Yeah."

"It's one of my girlfriend's birthdays. A few of us are meeting for drinks to celebrate. I haven't gone anywhere in a while, so I thought I'd dress up a little. What do you think?"

She turned and modeled her profile. Then she cocked her head slightly and gave me a coy smile. I took another long drink of water.

"You seem to be in a good mood," I said and stared at her.

"I guess so," she said, her voice trailing up.

"You said Ashley called. Did she happen to tell you who killed Alyssa?"

Her body stiffened, then her eyes widened, and her face turned pale.

"I'm . . . I'm sorry. I should have . . . It's just . . . I've been a wreck since Alyssa was killed. I'm not sleeping . . ."

She lowered her head and took a deep breath. Her voice quavered like she might cry. She stopped and was silent for a few seconds. Then she looked up and brushed a curl from her face.

"Yes, Ashley did call yesterday," she said. "She wants to talk to you in person. I guess she's here in the city now. She wouldn't tell me where. She said she knows who killed Alyssa. I was going to tell the detectives today when they stopped by, but I thought it was better to talk to you first."

"Who stopped by?"

"Detective Gomez and Detective Ginelli."

"When?"

"Uh, about nine thirty this morning."

"What did they want?"

"They wanted to know if I had talked to you recently. I told them you came by a week ago, but I hadn't heard from you since. They had some sort of warrant for you. They talked like they thought you killed Alyssa. I said I didn't believe that. Maybe you can get Ashley to tell them who did it."

A vague sensation spread across the back of my head. But it wasn't another headache. It was different. I finished the rest of my water, then closed my eyes and stretched my neck. When I opened them, Peggy was staring at me.

"Is something wrong, Will?"

"No. No. Did Ashley say . . . did she say how to reach her?"

"She gave me a number for you to call."

Peggy stepped closer. Her floral perfume enveloped me. She reached her hand up to my face. It seemed in slow motion. She caressed my cheek. I just watched.

"You sure you're okay?" she asked.

Her words echoed. The lights seemed to flicker in the kitchen. I turned my head and gazed at them. My eyes wandered back to the living room. I heard my voices, distant, telling me something was wrong.

I looked at Peggy. She was sitting on the couch next to me, saying something. Her hand was on my thigh. I sensed myself smiling.

Bursts of light . . . moaning . . . screaming . . . blood . . . cigarette smell . . . spinning . . . falling . . .

42

*T*he rat dog was barking in the dark.

Where am I?

"Will . . . Will . . . wake up," a voice murmured.

A soft hand slapped my face.

I can't see.

The soft hand hit me harder. I grabbed it with my left hand, pulled it across my chest and twisted it. I reached up with my right hand and felt hair. I grabbed it and pulled down.

"Will, stop! You're hurting me!" the voice cried.

The ringing in my right ear overwhelmed the plea. I tried to open my eyes. My lids felt stuck. I forced them open. They scraped across my eyes, revealing only depthless gray. I blinked. Light seeped in. I blinked again. More light appeared. The outline of a body took shape. Then a head and hair. My eyes started to water. The ringing eased.

"Will, let go!" the person shouted.

It was a woman's voice. She tried to push away from me, but I held onto her. I opened my eyes wider. Light flooded in. I saw her hovering above me, my hand holding her wrist, the ceiling above her. Her dark hair was draped in front of her face, wrapped around my fist.

Alyssa . . . No . . . Ashley . . .

Tears were streaming out of my eyes. I blinked rapidly. Her face blurred, then came back into focus. I released her hair and wrist.

Ashley pushed off my chest and stood up. She stepped back and looked down at me. Her yellow blouse and blue jeans were stained with blood. She picked up a Yankees baseball cap off the floor and put it on.

"We have to get out of here," she said, her voice steady but urgent.

I lifted my right hand to brush my hair from my eyes. It was covered in blood. My chest too. I tried to sense if I was shot or cut, but there was no pain. I felt a rug under my legs and lifted my right knee. I didn't have any pants on.

The rat dog barked again, high pitched and muffled. It came from next door. I remembered I was in Peggy's apartment.

My body felt heavy, like I was in mud. I turned my head to the left. Ashley was hurrying around, wiping the furniture with a dishtowel, and grabbing things. She came over to me, kneeled and placed a pile of clothes next to my head. She stared soberly at me.

"Will, you have to get dressed. *Now!* The police will be coming. If you don't get moving, I'm leaving without you."

Her warning sparked something. I lifted my head. The haze cleared a little. I forced myself to sit up. I gazed down at my body. Streaks of half-dried blood ran across my chest and down my right side. I was naked, but it didn't fully register. I closed my eyes and tried to remember.

Bursts of light exploded behind my eyelids. Brief images appeared and vanished before I could process them. I remembered kissing Peggy. And her kissing me. Then a gruesome image flashed for a moment. I opened my eyes and whipped my head to the right.

Peggy was on the floor, naked, staring at the ceiling, her mouth open. Her legs and arms were stretched out, slightly bent. What looked like a black teddy was wrapped around her neck. Blood oozed from cuts across her breasts and face.

"*Run!*" my voices yelled.

I staggered to my feet, spun around and nearly fell back down. Blinding sunlight hit me from the kitchen window. Out of the glare, a figure walked quickly towards me, holding a gun. I squinted—Ashley.

"I think this is yours," she said.

She handed me my Glock, still holstered. I took it, stared at her, then glanced over my shoulder at Peggy's body. The coffee table was tipped on its side and leaning against the black cabinet. On the rug were two glasses and a half empty bottle of vodka.

"She's dead," Ashley said.

I turned back to her and nodded weakly, still in a daze. It slowly hit me that I was standing there naked, holding a gun, covered in blood. Panic shot through my body.

"Move it, Will!" Ashley snapped.

I stepped back and shook my head violently. I looked down, saw my clothes and hustled them on. My socks and sneakers were by the couch. I threw them on, then my blazer. I stuffed my Glock in the pocket and looked up.

Ashley was standing at the door, gripping the knob with the dishtowel, her eyes fixed on me. The ringing in my ear returned. Then I realized it was a siren. A second one joined in. They grew.

"My knife," I said and looked around, disoriented.

"It's in your pocket," Ashley said.

I found it as I stumbled towards her. She opened the door. I stopped at the threshold and peered out both ways. Then I stepped into the hallway and turned right.

"Other way," Ashley said. "We'll take the service elevator."

She closed the door and wiped the knob with the towel. I watched curiously. Everything was processing slowly. It took me a second to understand she didn't want any fresh fingerprints in the apartment. They could implicate her.

As the elevator door closed, a faint yelp from the rat dog floated in. I remembered I didn't like rat dogs. We rode down in silence. The elevator stopped and opened to a dimly lit cement basement. I stepped off, a little unsteady. Ashley wiped the buttons and jumped out.

"Follow me," she said and started jogging towards a metal door in the far corner.

I managed to stay close to her, lurching to my left a couple of times. The door opened to a narrow alley behind the building, next to a fire escape. She turned left and started running down the alley. I struggled to keep up. The wailing of sirens was getting closer.

We passed behind another apartment building, then Ashley turned right. She climbed over a small metal fence. I fell over it. We turned into a narrow space between two commercial buildings. I had to shuffle sideways to get through. Trash, beer cans, and broken bottles littered the ground, with a used syringe here and there.

We came out on a side street populated with brick warehouses. Ashley turned right and walked briskly down the street with me trailing behind. She handed me the towel to wipe the blood off my hands. I did my best, but most of it had dried. I dumped the towel in a trash can.

Ashley took a fob out of her pocket and pointed it ahead. A beep came from a cobalt blue Honda parked by the curb ten feet away. She got in the driver's side. I tumbled into the passenger's seat. The car started smoothly. She pulled out and headed away from the sirens. Five minutes later, we were crawling along on a main street in heavy traffic.

"Where are we going?" I asked.

"I have a hotel room on the Upper East Side," she answered without looking at me. "You can recover there. Then we'll talk."

My wheels started to grind slowly. I could almost hear them. If I had killed Peggy, Ashley should be scared. But she wasn't. Maybe she had killed her. Then why save me? The wheels got stuck.

"I didn't kill your mother," I said.

"I know," she said, her eyes focused straight ahead.

"You do?"

"Peggy wasn't my mother."

"Right . . . she's your aunt. I didn't kill her either."

"You sure?" she said and glanced at me.

My eyes widened and my mouth opened. I realized my reaction with a delay. I shook my head to clear the fog and tried to remember. Pieces were coming back.

"I'm pretty sure," I said. "Do you know something?"

"Just what I saw."

"What did you see?"

"You were there, remember?"

"No. I only remember Peggy's body. It looked like she was killed the same way as Alyssa. And the others. I didn't kill them either. But I can't remember what happened to Peggy."

"I believe you."

"That I can't remember?"

"That you didn't kill Peggy. Or my sister. Or any of them."

"You do?"

"Yeah."

"Did you kill them?"

"You think you'd be here if I did?"

"I'm not sure why I'm here."

"No, I didn't kill them."

"Do you know who did?"

She stopped at a red light. She turned and scrutinized me. Then her eyes moved back to the light.

"I have an idea," she said.

"Who?"

"El Capitán."

43

"El Capitán?" I said. "I think he kicked me in the head."

Ashley looked at me skeptically. Then a horn blared behind us. She muttered something, turned her eyes forward, and took off through the intersection.

"No more questions," she said. "Rest and clear your head."

She thought I wasn't making sense. I couldn't argue with her. I shut up. It took the entire hour drive for me to begin forming coherent questions in my mind.

The hotel was on 56th Street and First Avenue. Ashley parked a block away. It was one of those new boutique hotels for hipster travelers. No real front desk or concierge. Digital everything. No one to ask us about the blood on our hands and clothes. Perfect for a pair of serial killers.

The room was small, dark, and modern. It barely fit a queen bed, chair, and nightstand. Two feet separated the bed from the wall where a flat screen TV hung. A bottle of brown liquid sat on the nightstand, a paper bag and three bottles of water behind it. The bathroom was bigger than I expected, probably because it included the closet and some shelves in lieu of a dresser.

"Sit down, Will," Ashley said. "I'm going to take a quick shower to wash this blood off."

I made my way to the chair. It was squeezed in the corner next to the window. I took off my blazer and sat down. Ashley handed me a bottle of water, then went into the bathroom and shut the door. I heard the lock click. I stared at the bottle suspiciously. I checked the cap. It hadn't been opened. I twisted it off and gulped down the entire bottle.

Ten minutes later, Ashley came out, her hair wet and dangling down. She had changed into skinny black jeans and a short white workout T-shirt with a lightning bolt across the front. She climbed onto the middle of the bed, crossed her legs, and looked at me. I wasn't particularly into feet, but hers did something for me. I knew I had recovered.

"Okay if I take a Marine shower?" I asked.

"I'll be here."

Her eyes followed me as I walked to the bathroom. I stopped to let them play with mine. They brought back memories. Memories of Alyssa. I looked down, then stepped into the bathroom and closed the door.

I took off my clothes and turned on the cold water in the sink. I used a small bottle of soap to clean off the blood and wash the rest of my body. I dried myself with a hand towel, then grabbed a small tube of toothpaste on the sink and squeezed some into my mouth. I brushed it around with my finger, gargled with some water and spit it out. I put my clothes back on, wet my hands, and ran my fingers through my hair.

When I came out of the bathroom, Ashley was sitting at the head of the bed against the pillows. Two plastic cups half filled with a brown liquid were on the nightstand next to her. I looked at the bottle. It was Woodford Reserve. She picked up the two cups and offered me the one in her left hand. I hesitated, then took it.

I moved over to the window and looked outside. It was dark now. A narrow space separated the hotel from the building next door. No one could see inside the room. I lowered the blinds anyway, turned around and leaned on the sill.

Ashley raised her cup in a toasting gesture, then took a drink. She savored it for a second before swallowing. I reciprocated the gesture and downed a good gulp. It burnt my throat. I wasn't a bourbon fan. Beer and tequila were my poisons. And the occasional bottle of champagne under the right circumstances. That hadn't gone so well the last time.

"Were you in the Marines?" she asked.

"No, Army. Why?"

"You said you were taking a Marine shower."

"It's an expression. You wash your entire body from the sink. My father taught me it. Today, it means throwing a bunch of deodorant and body spray on. Same idea, basically."

"Got it. Was your father in the Marines?"

"No, Navy. But his father was."

"Where is your father now?"

"Dead."

"Sorry. What about your mother?"

"Dead."

"Sorry again. I guess we're the same."

She said it matter-of-factly. Like the casual icebreaker before slinking over and sitting on a guy's lap at Champagne. I had to remind myself that she was Ashley, not Alyssa.

"I guess we are," I said. "Except my sister is alive."

"And mine is dead," she said, then gulped down some more bourbon.

Another matter-of-fact fact. She wasn't distraught or looking for sympathy or offering it. Just the facts of what had been a hard life to date.

"I should probably thank you for saving me," I said.

"Probably. But I didn't do it for you."

"I didn't think so. So, why did you?"

"I want to find who murdered my sister."

"And . . ."

"And I think you can help."

"How am I supposed to do that?"

She took a long drink of bourbon, then said, "I thought you'd be either dead or in jail by now. But you're here. And you figured out Peggy was helping set you up. You're smart, but the people who killed my sister are smart too. They knew you'd go there. They killed Peggy because of you. You know that, right?"

"I do now. But I'm surprised they killed her."

"They didn't care about killing my sister. Why would they care about killing Peggy?"

"Because she was working with them. And she didn't fit the profile of the other victims. But you're obviously right. I'm sorry for your loss."

"If you're talking about Peggy, don't be. She deserved it. I know she had something to do with my sister's murder. But whoever killed her is really after you. That's what I don't get. Why not just kill you? Sorry. But it's like someone wants to torture you instead."

"You're telling me."

"Who wants to punish you like that?"

"I don't know. I thought you might be able to tell me."

"If I knew, we wouldn't be here. That's why I want your help."

"Then I guess you never called Peggy and told her you know who killed Alyssa?"

"Is that how she lured you to her apartment? No, I never called her. I haven't talked to her in weeks. If she knew where I was, I'd be the one dead."

"If that's what you think, what were you doing at her apartment?"

"I've been watching her place on and off since my sister was murdered. I wanted to see who visited her. I'm positive she was involved. There's a utility closet in the store across the street with a window that looks right at the entrance. I snuck in there to watch who went in and out. I saw you go in today. About an hour later, two guys came out. I hadn't seen them go in. They walked around the corner and disappeared. One of them looked like the guy who's in charge of security for Champagne and a bunch of other clubs. Everyone calls him El Capitán. He's this asshole cop named Gomez. I didn't recognize the other guy. Anyway, when you didn't come out, I started to think something had happened. I even thought you might be fucking Peggy. But I decided that was too risky, even for you. Sorry, no offense."

"None taken. Go on."

"Well, about twenty minutes after the two guys left, a tall guy came out talking on his cell. Something about him was off. I thought he might be a cop, but he had a fancy suit on. Then a car pulled up, and he got in and drove away."

"What kind of car?"

"A dark blue one. Not an SUV. I think it was a Buick. After he left, I decided to check on you. I had a bad feeling. I was right."

"How did you get in?"

"Same way we left. I've done it before. Maintenance leaves the basement door open all the time. Peggy's apartment was unlocked when I got there."

"The guy who left with Gomez, what did he look like?"

"He was younger, maybe thirty. About your height and build, with blond hair."

"Blond hair. Okay. And what about the tall guy who got in the car?"

"All I really saw was dark hair. I couldn't see his face because he was talking on his cell."

I gazed down at the laminate wood floor while I thought. I sipped some bourbon and tried to connect everything in my head. I closed my eyes. That night with Alyssa came back to me. Everything we did streamed through my mind. Then the crime scene photos appeared. I forced myself to look at them, until images of Peggy seeped in.

I opened my eyes. Ashley was studying me. I stared back at her— her eyes, her face, her body. She was a vision of Alyssa. I downed a gulp of bourbon. It burnt.

"You still haven't told me how I'm going to help you find Alyssa's killer," I said.

She drank the last of her bourbon and wiped her mouth. She put the plastic cup on the nightstand and bounced up on her knees. Her entire body was suddenly energized.

"So, if we work together," she said, "we can both get what we want. We should be able to figure out who killed my sister pretty quick. I have some ideas. When we do, I'll kill whoever did it. You just make sure I don't get killed too. After, I'll tell the police everything I know. It should be enough to prove you're innocent."

"Really? Okay, but why don't *you* tell *me* everything you know first? Then I'll have a better chance of figuring out who murdered your sister, along with who's trying to frame me."

My response froze her on the bed. She looked like a mannequin in a trendy store, her T-shirt clinging on her breasts, her flat stomach peeking out from below. She eyed me suspiciously.

"Alright," she said tentatively, "what do you want to know?"

"For starters, how about why you're pretending to be Ashley?"

44

A sly grin crept across her face. Then she tilted her head and pursed her lips.

I took a sip of bourbon. Not too fast. Not too slow. I was learning.

"How did you know?" Alyssa said.

"I guessed. You just confirmed it."

"But how did you know to guess?"

"A bunch of little things."

She sat down on the bed and slid over to the side near me. She put her feet on the floor, reached over and poured herself some more bourbon. She faced me and took a slow drink.

"What little things?" she asked.

"Okay. I caught you on video picking up Linda in the parking lot behind The Beer Garage. You two are friends. She thought you were dead. She wouldn't have reacted like she did if you had been Ashley. She probably wouldn't have gotten in your SUV either."

"You videotaped us? Wow. Is that it?"

"No. The way you talked about Gomez wasn't what I expected from Ashley. I know she worked with him. You talked like you barely knew him. But then you were very familiar with me. I never met Ashley, so that was another giveaway. And you never said your own name. You always used *my sister* instead of Alyssa."

"Ha, you really were guessing."

"There were other tells, but one thing in particular."

"What's that?"

"The crime scene photos of Ashley. I saw them when I was questioned by the police."

Alyssa stiffened. She lowered her cup of bourbon and rested it on her thigh.

"And?" she said.

I hesitated.

"Just tell me," she said.

"I know you're completely shaven. But I could see in the photo that Ashley wasn't."

Her expression relaxed. She looked down. A melancholy smile formed on her lips. She took another slow drink of bourbon, then looked up at me.

"Ashley kept some hair in a heart shape. She thought it was sexy. I'm surprised you remember what I look like there."

"I might have been drunk, but I remember."

"You were probably more drugged than drunk."

"Drugged? You drugged me that night?"

"*I* didn't. But I know someone put something in your champagne. A roofie of some kind. Maybe the same stuff Peggy slipped you today. Although she must have given you a way bigger dose based on how out of it you were."

"*Shit.* That explains some things."

"You've been in someone's sights there for a while."

"What do you mean?"

"So, before you came into Champagne the first time, Terry—he's the head bouncer—and Gomez pulled me aside. They said a young guy who followed me on YouSEL would be coming in and to really turn it on for him. That was you. They wanted to make sure you left thinking I liked you, so you would keep following me and come back."

"Did they say why?"

"I asked. Gomez told me to keep my mouth shut and do what I was told. He was such an asshole. I went and talked to Ashley about it. She said I had to stop asking questions. That I would be paid really good money if I did what they wanted. I knew it had to be important for Ashley not to stand up for me. She always had my back. But she was corporate, and I was just a dancer. I never wanted her job. She was always stressed. Anyway, I did what I was told. It was easy. You were cute, and I started getting paid a lot more."

"Unbelievable," I muttered. "Okay, tell me what happened that night. You were the one who was supposed to be killed, right?"

"Yeah. So, at the start of my shift, Terry comes and tells me El Capitán wants to talk to me out back in the alley. I went out, and Gomez was all nice to me. Then he told me you were coming in that night and *management* wanted me to have sex with you."

"What?"

"Sorry to burst your bubble, Will. That's what the roofie was for. To loosen you up so you'd be more willing to fuck me."

"They thought I needed a roofie for that?"

"I'll take that as a compliment. We were videotaped too, in case you didn't realize."

"I figured as much. So, who is *management*?"

"I don't really know. It's the way all the higher-ups talk about the real higher-ups. None of us worker bees know who they are. The whole company is like a secret society. Ashley knew something, but she would never talk to me about it."

"And they just tell you to have sex with customers and you do it?"

"It's not as crazy as it sounds. I'd done it a few times before. Each time was videotaped. I assume for blackmail, or something like that. It was always older businessmen, though. And I made them use condoms. But this time, Gomez said management wanted me to let you come inside me. He said you were clean. I knew that was bullshit. How could he know? But then he told me I'd be paid a fifty-thousand-dollar bonus."

"Fifty thousand?"

"Yeah. When Gomez first said it, I was like, I'll do it for half that. I didn't say that to him. But then I started to get suspicious. It was too much money. I wanted to talk to Ashley, so I said I had to think about it. He got pissed at me."

"Did Ashley convince you to go through with it?"

"I didn't end up talking to her until later, after you left. When you showed up, Terry grabbed me and said if I didn't do it, a friend of mine would be hurt. I knew he wasn't kidding. I've seen what his men do to people who get on the wrong side of management. Guy or girl doesn't matter."

"Was Rachel Morris the friend?"

Alyssa stiffened, a confused look on her face.

"You know Rachel?"

"Her father hired me to look out for her."

"That's too weird. I don't really believe in coincidence."

"Neither do I. Rachel told me she was at Champagne with you that night. She said you warned her off. Why?"

"Ashley gave me a heads up that management wanted to hire Rachel to be a model and dancer. They knew she would be eighteen this fall. I was supposed to help recruit her, then train her. Ashley said it was a way to get Rachel's father to cooperate on a business deal. But she didn't like using Rachel like that. She also thought Rachel was too young, which is funny because we were the same age when we started. Anyway, we agreed that I would warn Rachel not to do it and try to convince her to stay away from Champagne. That's why I asked her to stop by. I knew Mitch, her boyfriend that you beat up, was working and would make sure she got home safe."

"For the record, *he* tried to beat me up. I was defending myself."

"He probably thought he was protecting Rachel. He's a really good guy."

"I believe you. To be clear, though, you had unprotected sex with me to protect Rachel?"

"I was going to do it anyway. You're better than an old business-man. And fifty thousand dollars made it a no-brainer."

"Thanks, I think."

"Yeah, well, I never got the money."

"You didn't?"

"No. Terry told me I would get it at the end of the night. Cash, like the other times. I think that's when they were going to kill me. But I didn't stick around."

"Why?"

"After you left, Ashley showed up and pulled me outside. She said I was in danger and had to get away. She gave me her car keys and told me to go. I wasn't even dressed. I argued, but she said I was going to be murdered like the other dancers. It was going to look like you did it. That's why management wanted you to come inside me. It was all part of the plan."

"Did she tell you why they wanted to frame me?"

"She didn't have time to explain anything. The last thing she said was to stay away from your ex-girlfriend."

"Brittany?"

"Yeah, like my dancing name. She works for the police, right?"

"No, the District Attorney's Office. Did Ashley say why?"

"I didn't get a chance to ask. She made me leave right then."

"Did she know Brittany?"

"I don't know."

"Do you know her?"

"No. But Ashley wouldn't have warned me unless she thought your Brittany was dangerous."

"But how?"

"Maybe she's helping to set you up. Or maybe she's jealous of me. Maybe both. You know, kill two birds with one bullet."

"That's crazy."

"Is it?"

"Enough about her. Why didn't Ashley leave with you?"

Alyssa bowed her head. She seemed close to crying but then looked up at me.

"I tried to get her to come with me," she said. "But she insisted they wouldn't hurt her. She said the guy in charge would never let that happen. But she didn't think she could stop them from hurting me. That's why she made me leave that second. She stayed to talk to the guy. She thought she could convince him to do it another way."

"Do you know who this guy is?"

"No."

"Did Ashley say if he was behind the other murders?"

"No. I figured she'd tell me everything later. I never would have let her stay if I thought . . . but she was trying to protect me. She had my back. And now she's dead."

"Ashley's dead because of this guy, not you."

"She's still dead, and I'm not. But I'm going to kill him and who-ever else was part of it. I need to know if you're going to help."

Alyssa stared at me, her eyes cold and hard. For a moment, she reminded me of Brittany.

"First, tell me where Linda is," I said.

Alyssa's expression suddenly changed. She shook her head like she didn't understand.

"She hasn't called you?"

"No."

"That's not good. After I picked her up, we drove all night. I dropped her off at a diner outside Albany early in the morning. She said she had a friend there she could stay with until this is over. She was going to call you. Do you think she's alright?"

"I don't know. What do you think?"

Alyssa looked incredulously at me.

"You think I did something to Linda? And what, I killed my sis-ter too? If I did all that, why did I pull you out of Peggy's apartment today? Why didn't I just leave you there to be arrested? Tell me that, Will."

"Someone's been after me for the past two years. Whoever it is has put a lot of time and effort into setting me up, including recruiting people like Peggy and possibly Linda. If I'm going to help you, I need to be certain you're not helping whoever's behind all this."

"Unless you need to fuck me again to be certain, you're just going to have to trust me."

I thought about it, for a moment. I felt like an asshole, for a moment. She was pure, unadulterated sex. The only drug I had ever relied on. But using her now wasn't going to solve my real problem, no matter how much I wanted to.

"You're right," I said. "We have to trust each other."

Alyssa's body relaxed. She sighed quietly, then took a long drink of bourbon.

"Did Linda tell you anything during the drive?" I asked.

"Just what you told her. She didn't seem to know anything about Ashley or the other girls who were murdered. Besides that, she mostly talked about you. She kept saying she couldn't believe any woman would dump you for another cop."

My reaction must have been obvious.

"Does that mean something?" she asked.

"It means Linda's been talking to someone about me."

"Probably Ashley."

"Why do you say that?"

"I forgot to tell you that I switched cells with Ashley that night. She said mine was being tracked. I don't know how she knew. After she was killed, I went through her calls and saw that she talked to Linda the week before. I remembered Ashley telling me she first saw you at The Big O in Columbus. Then I realized you were the same guy Linda used to talk about when we worked at YouSEL. She was obsessed. Like I said, I don't believe in coincidence. That's why I went to Columbus. I wanted to see what Linda knew. I thought you might do the same."

"Good guess. Do you have Ashley's cell with you?"

"No. I got rid of it in Columbus. I was afraid it was being tracked too."

"Was that after you texted Linda pretending to be Ashley?"

"I never texted Linda. Before I saw her in the parking lot, I hadn't talked to her in months."

"Then Linda lied to me. Someone else must have told her I'd be in Columbus. Did she say anything else?"

"No. That was pretty much it."

I nodded, then asked, "So, why *are* you pretending to be Ashley?"

She shrugged and said, "When the news reports came out that I was murdered, I decided to play along. I thought it might help in figuring out who killed Ashley. Maybe keep me safe too."

"Do you think Peggy knew it wasn't you?"

"She definitely knew."

"Why do you say that?"

"Because she texted Ashley the next day. But the text was addressed to me. She said she knew I was alive and wanted to help. I don't know why the cops still think it was me."

"Have you ever been fingerprinted?"

"Once."

"When?"

"Five months ago, for prostitution. One of those businessmen from Champagne complained. But I wasn't charged. Ashley got them dropped. She knew someone. Does that matter?"

"If your fingerprints are on file, the police and DA's Office should know by now it wasn't you. But they haven't come out with that. And they talked to me like it was you. Why?"

"I don't know. Maybe you should ask your ex."

"Maybe I will."

Neither of us said anything for a while. There was still one more thing we needed to talk about. She knew what it was, but she was waiting for me to bring it up. I wasn't ready. We just watched each other think and sip bourbon. Until we both finished. But I still wasn't ready.

"Do you want to talk about it?" she asked.

"No."

"Don't you want to know?"

"Things are already coming back. It's just a matter of time."

"You should probably know what I saw. So you're prepared, in case you're arrested."

"Probably."

"You want me to tell you or not?"

"No. But go ahead."

"Okay. I'm just going to say it. You were passed out on top of Peggy when I walked in. I pulled you off. I couldn't find any wounds on you. Just a lot of blood. I checked Peggy. She wasn't breathing. She was pale and a little cool. You saw her body. There was some semen between her legs. I cleaned it up as much as I could, but if you came inside—"

"I did. I remember. I'm starting to remember other things, too."

"You couldn't have resisted, Will. You were too drugged up. They probably told Peggy they were going to make it look like you tried to rape her. She'd done things like that before. She didn't know she was going to be killed this time. You couldn't have stopped any of it. I've seen women who were drugged for sex. They didn't know what was happening. It's rape. I know women who've been raped. Some move on. Some never get over it. You were raped, Will. That's a fact. But you can't afford to think about it right now if you want to survive. That's a fact too."

45

"*B*ro, no guy ever been in my place," Victor said. "Only ladies. Got a pad for you four blocks from here. Wait outside. I'll be right there."

I had texted Victor asking to use one of his places for the night. I couldn't stay with Alyssa. She offered. I wanted to. I think she wanted me to. But it would have been like drinking to sober up. After what had happened with Peggy, I needed to be alone. We exchanged cell numbers and agreed to talk in the morning.

Victor brought me to a brownstone on 110th Street, just off Third Avenue in East Harlem. He handed me a set of keys to a second-floor apartment. It was a quiet night, except for the sound of traffic floating in from the FDR Drive.

"You gonna need my help, bro," Victor said.

"Probably."

"That's a fact. We got a deal, remember?"

I nodded.

"There's clothes inside should fit you."

I nodded again.

"Need anythin' else?"

I shook my head.

"Somethin' goin' on with you? Need a girl tonight? You know I can help."

"I'm good. Just tired."

He stared at me for an extra second, then turned to leave.

"What happened with your brother?" I said.

Victor stopped and peered over his shoulder at me.

"I killed him. Told you already."

"That it?"

He nodded and stared at me for an extra second again, then sauntered away.

My sleep was fitful. Flashbacks of Peggy's naked body on top of me streamed through my head all night, with clips of Alyssa and Brittany mixed in. Dark images of faceless men came in and out. Even Victor appeared for a moment. But I woke up feeling better. I wasn't sure why. Nothing had changed.

It was early, so I did a quick workout. After I showered, I picked out a white short-sleeved Henley and a pair of fancy black sweatpants from the closet and got dressed. Then I wrapped my clothes in a bundle, left the keys on the dresser, and headed out. I dumped my clothes in a trash bin on my way to the East River. When I reached it, I threw my knife as far as I could. Peggy's blood was still on it. The killer had used it to carve the symbols in her body. It made a small splash, joining thousands of other weapons in New York City's unmarked grave of evidence.

I walked back to Third Avenue and headed south. I stopped at a deli and grabbed a bagel and coffee. No one seemed to take special notice of me. When I finished, I hailed a taxi and headed to Brooklyn to pick up my car.

Two NYPD vehicles were sitting outside Peggy's apartment building. As I drove by, the radio reported on the violent murder of a woman in her Brooklyn apartment. No details had been released yet. I knew it wouldn't be long before my name was leaked to the press. But it would take a few days to perform an autopsy and identify my semen. I had a little time.

I drove back to Manhattan and parked my Caddy in the garage. Then I jumped in a taxi. I needed to talk to Brittany. I had an hour before she left for work.

The weather was already oppressive. Shards of light plunged in between dark bloated clouds tumbling across building rooftops. I cracked open the taxi window. The wind whistled in. I rolled it all the way down and let the angry air course through my hair. I closed my eyes halfway and wandered.

Peggy Grant had been murdered like the others. No question about that. But she hadn't been raped. She had forced sex on me. Had I been raped? I didn't feel like I'd been violated. I didn't feel like a victim. Another time, another place, I would have fucked her. She fucked me first, but without my consent. Did that matter to me? This couldn't be how a woman felt after being raped. Something was different.

I shook my head and opened my eyes. I noticed the driver watching me in the rearview mirror.

"You okay, man?" he said.

"Yeah."

"You know you were talking to yourself, right?"

"Yeah, sorry. Girl stuff."

"Don't get me started, man. Go to work, go home, do what they tell you, and everything be okay. Don't get on their bad side. You're young, but you know I'm right. Am I right, man?"

"You're right."

"You know it."

I gazed out the window for the rest of the ride to avoid any more conversation. I had him circle the block around Brittany's apartment building before dropping me off at 18th Street and Eighth Avenue. I did another walk around the block on foot. No one was guarding her that I could detect.

I was going to sneak into her building through the parking garage, but then some construction workers showed up. They needed to go through the front door with their equipment. They were buzzed in. I held the door for them, then walked right in like I lived there.

Only one elevator was operating. The workers had blocked off the other one. I hung out pretending to talk on my cell. A few couples went up the elevator, but I waited. Then a young dark-haired woman with no ring on her finger pressed the up button. A minute later, the elevator dinged, and the doors opened. I followed the woman onto the elevator, still pretending to be on my cell. She used her key fob to press the fifth-floor button. The doors closed, and I reached to press the button for the fifteenth floor. I stopped and started fishing around in the pockets of my sweatpants like I was looking for something.

"Damn," I muttered and looked at her. "I forgot my key fob. Sorry, do you mind?"

She hesitated. I smiled sheepishly. She nodded, then placed the fob on the sensor so I could press the button. I gave her a big fake smile as she got off the elevator.

I found Brittany's apartment three doors down from the elevators on the other side of the hallway. I paced outside her door, once again pretending to be on my cell. An older woman stepped out of her apartment and stared at me suspiciously. After a brief inspection, she concluded I was just another young person glued to my phone. She shuffled to the elevator and went down. Five minutes later, I heard a door unlock.

Brittany's eyes widened when she saw me standing in front of her. I stared calmly at her. She recovered quickly and stared calmly back. With her white pantsuit, blue blouse, and thin ivory necklace, she looked headed to the Hamptons. I couldn't remember why she had ever dated me.

She stepped back and to the side to let me in. I entered and stopped just past the door. She closed it, walked over to a thin table against the wall, and placed her leather satchel on it. She took out her cellphone and started typing a text. I stepped towards her and put my hand over her phone.

"Sorry, it can wait," I said.

She looked up and said, "I have to let my office know I'll be late."

"This won't take long."

She put her phone on the table. We gazed at each other for several seconds. Then I sensed something. A faint smell, maybe.

"I assume you're not here to turn yourself in," she said. "What do you want?"

"Do you have Alyssa Grant's fingerprints on file?"

"We didn't before she was murdered, if that's what you're asking. Why?"

"Alyssa Grant isn't dead. Her twin sister, Ashley, is the one who was murdered."

She stared at me, trying to control her reaction while she processed what I had just told her.

"And how do you know that?"

"Because I was with Alyssa yesterday."

This time, she looked like I had just thrown a drink in her face.

"There's more," I said. "Alyssa was supposed to be the one killed that night, but Ashley warned her and ended up paying the price. Whoever murdered Ashley wanted to frame me for it. Detective Gomez was one of the people telling Alyssa what to do to set me up. He moonlights as the head of security for the clubs owned by YouSEL, including Champagne. I don't know if he's the killer, or one of them, but he's involved in the murders."

I had never seen Brittany stunned before. It lasted as long as it took her to realize I might be lying. Then she shook her head like she didn't believe me.

"Where is Alyssa?" she snapped. "If she really is alive, she needs to come in. So do you. You have a material witness warrant outstanding. And I'm sure you heard about Peggy Grant's murder. It looks like the others. We want to talk to you about it. Actually, both of you now."

"I just told you an NYPD detective is involved. Why would either of us risk coming in?"

"Those are explosive allegations. No one's going to just take your word. You know that. The only way you *and* Alyssa are going to prove anything is by coming in and telling everything you know to the DA's Office. If what you claim is true, we'll protect her and you. But nothing happens unless the two of you come in and talk to us."

"What if it's bigger than just one cop?"

"What are you suggesting?"

The vague smell returned. I turned my eyes down. Then I realized what it was.

"Are you alright?" Brittany asked reluctantly.

"I'm fine," I said and looked at her. "How's your boyfriend doing?"

"Don't even try to go there. If Alyssa is alive, you need to—"

"I know he was here last night."

Brittany's eyes narrowed. I could tell she was hiding something, but she couldn't tell I was lying.

"Have you been watching my apartment?"

"I'm being framed for murder. It has something to do with you. I'll do whatever it takes to figure out who's doing this to me."

"My personal life has nothing to do with your guilt or innocence. You really are losing it, Will. You need help."

"Does the DA know you and Jaworski are having a relationship? What will he say when he learns that a crooked cop helped set me up while the lead detective and his ADA were hooking up? Not great optics for a gubernatorial candidate."

"The only way Crosby will know anything is if you turn yourself in. And if you *were* watching my apartment, you saw Ben leave last night after ten minutes. But since you're so determined to know, I ended our relationship as soon as I was put on this case. There's no conflict. It's all in your head. You're obsessed with our past. That's not going to help you. You need to come in, and you need to convince Alyssa to do the same. That's what will help."

She clenched her jaw and exhaled through her nose, like a bull getting ready to charge. I wasn't going to taunt her. I had learned what I wanted.

"I'll think about it," I said.

I stared at her for longer than I should have, then left.

46

"Hello?" Alyssa answered.

"It's Will."

"I know. I recognized the number."

"Are you still at the hotel?"

"No. On the move. I'll let you know when I land."

"Okay. I have a question."

"Ask."

"Did Peggy smoke?"

"No. She thought it was bad for a woman's skin. Why?"

"I remember smelling cigarette smoke in her apartment before I blacked out. It was faint, but I'm sure I smelled it."

"I didn't smell anything. But I was a little distracted."

"I noticed the same smell the first time I was in her apartment too. Menthol, I think. If it wasn't from her, it was someone who smoked and had just been there."

"A lot of people smoke. It could have been a friend or someone who stopped by."

"Does Gomez smoke?"

"I don't know. But I'm sure he was one of the men I saw leaving Peggy's building. Wait, I did see the tall guy light up when he came out."

"You did?"

"Yeah. Maybe it was him."

"But you didn't see his face?"

"No."

"Killing Peggy and moving me around is too much for one guy. There had to be at least two of them. Whichever one smoked was in her apartment before it went down. She knew at least one of the people who killed her."

"She had to. She was probably going to accuse you of trying to rape her. Maybe kill her too. She wouldn't do that for a stranger."

"What did she do for work? Was it anything to do with Champagne or YouSEL?"

"She used to work in a lingerie store, but she quit over a year ago. I think she had a sugar daddy. I never met him. She stripped when she was younger. I don't think she ever worked at Champagne, though. She's the one who got Ashley and me into stripping. Peggy always wanted to be an actress. The farthest she got was a few porn films. I don't remember her saying anything about YouSEL. Does that help?"

"Maybe. I don't know. I'm just thinking out loud."

"Okay. I have a question."

"Go ahead."

"What did your ex have to say?"

"How did you know I talked to Brittany?"

"I could see your wheels turning last night when I mentioned her. Was she happy to see you?"

"Yeah, thrilled."

"Did you learn anything?"

"She said your fingerprints weren't on file before your body was brought in. The NYPD must have assumed it was you because all the other victims were strippers. But that means someone in the NYPD managed to expunge your prints from their records. It might have been Gomez. But I don't think he could have done it without help. It's not easy to do."

"You told her I'm alive, didn't you?"

"Yeah. And I told her Gomez was involved in Ashley's murder. I needed to see her reaction."

"What *was* her reaction?"

"She wants both of us to come in and tell the DA everything we know. They want to question us about Peggy's murder too. She said they'll protect us."

"Ha! And you trust her?"

"I don't trust anyone. But I know these murders have something to do with her, not just me. I have to play along until someone makes a mistake."

"You mean like killing you? Or me?"

"I won't let that happen."

"I almost believe you, Will. But I'm not talking to any cops or the DA or anyone else until the asshole who killed my sister is dead. Even if it turns out to be your ex. Tell her that."

"I'm not asking you to talk to anyone. But I plan to. I'm going to turn myself in. It's risky, but I think it might force whoever's behind all this to show their hand. I'm just asking you to hang low for the next few days. If you don't hear from me, or I'm dead, disappear and never come back."

"You think I'm going to spend my life hiding? If someone had murdered your sister, would you run away? Good luck, Will."

Her voice went silent, but her words lingered. I'd heard them before.

47

I walked into the Manhattan North precinct Friday morning. Through the double doors to the bulletproof reception window. The riskiest ten steps of my life. Maybe the stupidest too. But it was time, if I wanted my life back. And I did. Even if it wasn't worth much to anyone else.

I was cuffed, roughed up a little and shoved into a small holding cell as soon as I identified myself to the officer at the window. A couple of kidney punches, one to the stomach, and several hard slaps to the head. Nothing that would leave a mark. A little payback for taking down one of their own outside Brittany's apartment building.

The chessboard was still blurry, but I could make out the pieces and players. Not all of them. Some of them would be there to inter-rogate me, to break me. One might be the Master. That was the bet. I didn't have any other leads to follow. No more ideas. And I was almost out of time. Just enough for a showdown, of sorts. Get everyone in the cage and see what happens. That was my plan. Not even half-cocked. But it was all I had.

It wasn't long before they came for me. Maybe an hour. I was brought to the same interrogation room as the last time, handcuffed to the table, and left alone. Not really. Someone was watching me behind the one-way mirror. Maybe everyone. Devising a strategy to get me to confess. Drawing straws to see who would have the first crack at me.

Twenty minutes in, the door opened. Brittany was the first to enter. I thought I was ready but seeing her felt like getting decked with the first punch. Her light gray skirt suit was clingwrap on her thin curved body. A green satin blouse hung on her breasts, matching her eyes, cold and bright against her dirty blonde hair cascading down her cheeks. I was almost ready to confess.

Inspector Jaworski trailed Brittany. No leash. He looked about the same as the last time I was there. Tall, slightly dark, and proudly GQ. It could have been the same fancy suit. But he had a heavy Millennial stubble now that accentuated his intense countenance.

One of the two large, uniformed officers who had brought me to the room followed Jaworski in. He took up position in the corner to the left of the door. A strong show of force to intimidate a guy handcuffed to a table.

Brittany and Jaworski stood across from me in silence as if following some ritual. Brittany slid a bottle of water towards me, then Jaworski reached across and uncuffed my hands. Both moves surprised me. The door opened, and their heads swiveled towards it. I turned my eyes from watching them to the man entering the room.

He was a few inches shorter and a lot older than me. At least fifty. He was lean and fit, with deeply set brown eyes and a hint of gray in a full head of dark brown hair. A thin flat scar ran from the left side of his chin to just under it. His black frame glasses were probably for reading since he took them off and laid them on the table. A dark gray suit was well tailored but not too stylish. With a white dress shirt and pale blue tie, he looked every bit the part of the Manhattan District Attorney.

Frank Crosby—I recognized him immediately.

The other large, uniformed officer who had escorted me to the room walked in behind Crosby. He stepped to the side and positioned himself in the corner to the right of the door. Except for the fact that he was black and the other one was white, they could have been twins.

Crosby sat down at the end of the table to my left. Brittany and Jaworski followed suit and sat down across from me. Crosby and Brittany both had leather-bound notebooks and opened them. Crosby pulled out a fancy pen from inside his suit jacket and wrote something down. Brittany took a generic blue pen from the spiral of her notebook and did the same. Jaworski just gave me his death stare.

I opened the bottle of water and took a long gulp. I tried to catch Brittany's eye, but she was attentively waiting for Crosby to speak. I gazed at her profile for a moment. Maybe longer. Then I turned to Crosby. He was staring at me, calm and blank, except for the right corner of his mouth, which hinted at either a wry smile or a leer. It was too subtle to tell.

"Thank you for coming in, Mr. Chisholm," Crosby started. "As a former police officer, you know that cooperation makes the process of ensuring justice better for everyone."

Everyone but me.

I stared at him and drank some more water.

"You have not been read your rights," he continued, "because you are not under arrest. You are here as a material witness. As you know, we are investigating the murders of four young women, all in a virtually identical manner, which suggests they were victims of a serial killer. We want to ask you some questions as well as request any assistance you can provide in identifying and bringing to justice the killer or killers. There has also been an additional murder that fits the profile, but certain aspects are different. We would like to discuss that case with you as well. Of course, it is your prerogative to have a lawyer present. You may request one at any time. I would like to conclude your interview today, if possible. I have instructed Inspector Jaworski to detain you for as long as the law allows until we are satisfied with your cooperation. That may seem heavy handed, but five women have now been slain. All of them had an association with you at some point in the past six months. ADA Sorenson has informed me that you have information which could be of significant help. Before we start with our questions, is there anything you would like to say or ask?"

I was more than confused. It was not the tack I had expected. This was their opportunity to go hard at me and pressure me to confess. Not ask for my help. I hadn't been Mirandized or waived my rights. Any incriminating information I might inadvertently give would be inadmissible in court. This felt like a different fight, even if it was the same cage.

I looked at Jaworski. He was still glaring at me, but he seemed a little agitated now. His lips were pressed tightly together, and his demeanor was noticeably tense.

I moved my gaze to Brittany and peered into her eyes. My pulse started to accelerate. She gazed back, cold and hard. The titillating moment passed. I turned back to Crosby.

"There is one thing before we start," I said.

"What is that?" Crosby asked.

"I was involved in an incident in Chelsea last week. A woman pulled a gun on me, and I had to subdue her. She never identified herself, but I think she may have been a police officer. I didn't stick around to find out. I'd like to know if a report was filed, and what I need to do if there was. I also want to make sure the woman is alright."

"You assaulted an NYPD officer," Jaworski snapped. "Do you—"

"We are aware of the incident," Brittany said, cutting him off. "And yes, she is a police officer. Other than a broken nose and a bruised ego, she is fine. She claims to have identified herself. In any event, no charges will likely be filed. At the moment, you don't need to do anything. Of course, your cooperation today would help in mitigating any lingering ill will."

Jaworski stared at Brittany until she acknowledged him. She offered the same gaze she had given me. He turned and glared at me with even more venom.

"You should cooperate, Chisholm," he said. "Cops have long memories. You know that."

I returned a stoic look. His dark eyes had a hint of panic. Something was going on, but I didn't know what. I turned to Crosby.

"Ask your questions," I said.

Crosby contemplated me silently with the same calm, blank look. The same something hinted from the right corner of his mouth. He put on his glasses, looked down and read some notes. Then he peered at me over the rims.

"You told ADA Sorenson that Alyssa Grant is alive," Crosby said. "You also told her that the body we found was her twin sister, Ashley Grant. Is that correct?"

"Yes."

"You claimed that Alyssa Grant was the intended target of the killer but that Ashley Grant warned her and ended up being murdered instead. Is that correct?"

"It is."

"And you asserted that the real motive for the murders was to frame you. You accused the NYPD of being complicit in that effort. Do I have all of that correct?"

Jaworski shifted slightly in his chair, his shoulders stiffening. I let my eyes wander to him for a moment, then I looked back at Crosby.

"For the most part," I said.

"And Alyssa Grant told you this herself, in person, on Wednesday?"

"Yes."

"How do you know it was her?"

"She told me."

"Could she have been lying?"

"I'm confident it was her."

"What is your confidence based on?"

"I've spent time with her previously. But you know that already."

I glanced at Brittany. She looked at me like I was a wall, painted white.

"In that case," Crosby said, "do you know where she is so that we can speak with her?"

"No, but she knows I talked to Brittany. And she knows that you want to meet with her."

Brittany tensed slightly at my use of her first name. My eyes smiled. Crosby noticed. I thought he might react, but he continued to look at me with a calm, blank expression. No hint of irritation. He was going to make a good politician.

Crosby looked at Brittany. She looked back at him with the reverence of a student to a teacher. He nodded, then her eyes turned to me.

"Were you at Peggy Grant's apartment on Wednesday?" she asked with an accusatory tone.

The pivot to Peggy threw me off. I glanced at Crosby to get a sense of whether they knew something. His expression hadn't changed. I caught Jaworski watching me with a restrained eagerness, waiting for permission to attack. I looked back at Brittany.

"Wasn't that the day she was murdered?" I said.

"Yes. Were you there?" she asked again.

"Are you asking me if I killed Peggy Grant?"

"You're avoiding the question. Were you in Peggy Grant's apartment Wednesday?"

"No. But I've been there before. She was a client. You already know that."

"Where were you on Wednesday?"

"Let's see, I did a long workout in the morning. Then I had an early lunch at a deli by myself. And then I spent the rest of the day with Alyssa."

"You're saying you were with her the entire afternoon?"

"And evening."

"Really. Will she corroborate that?"

"I'm sure she will. Whenever you talk to her, that is."

Jaworski slapped his hands on the table and leaned towards me. His warm breath hit me like a rapid dog reaching for my throat.

"You were at Peggy Grant's apartment Wednesday," he shouted. "You raped and murdered her to stop her from telling us what she knew. Then you carved those symbols in her body, just like you did to all the others. This time, we have your hair and DNA to prove it you sick—"

"Inspector Jaworski!" Brittany exclaimed.

His head whipped towards her, his mouth agape. Then his eyes shot at Crosby. He turned back to me, pressed his lips together and clasped his hands tightly. His tall frame seemed to shrink in his chair. He shook his head slowly.

Brittany took a deep controlled breath, then said, "We think Peggy Grant was raped before she was murdered. We found semen at the crime scene. Symbols were carved into her body post-mortem. They are similar to the other victims. There are some differences, though. That, along with the fact that neither Peggy Grant nor the venue fit the profile of the previous murders, raises the possibility that it was a copycat killing."

"And what about the evidence the inspector so eloquently referenced?" I said.

Jaworski's jaw clenched. His knuckles turned white as he clasped his hands even tighter. I might have enjoyed goading him on if I wasn't expecting the guillotine to drop at any moment. They had access to my DNA from my time with the Boston PD. Jaworski had just revealed that they had the results from Peggy's autopsy. It was sooner than I expected. Brittany was about to announce that the semen matched my DNA. My head was going to officially roll.

"Inspector Jaworski was premature," Brittany said. "We *have* received the serology results from Peggy Grant's autopsy, but the semen doesn't match to you. Some of the hair we found does, but your previous visits to her apartment could explain their presence."

I couldn't hide my relief or confusion. I caught Crosby watching me.

"How can that be?" Jaworski blurted, an incredulous look on his face.

He echoed my thoughts. Even if Peggy Grant had been raped by someone else, I had come inside her. I remembered. My DNA should have shown up. The results were wrong. But I didn't think it was a mistake. Something else was going on.

Jaworski glared at me as if I had just cheated him in a game. Then he regained his composure and looked at Crosby.

"Did they identify a DNA match?" he asked.

"Not yet," Crosby replied calmly. "Can we continue with Mr. Chisholm?"

Jaworski stared at Crosby for another second, then sat back in his chair. A slight smirk appeared on his lips, but it didn't seem directed at anyone.

Crosby looked at Brittany.

She turned to me and asked, "When was the last time you saw Peggy Grant?"

"Almost two weeks ago," I replied.

"Did you speak with her after that?"

"She left me a couple of voice messages, but I never talked to her. She wanted an update on my search for Ashley. I was going to stop by her apartment yesterday, but then I learned about her murder on the news."

"Did she know or suspect that Ashley had been murdered instead of Alyssa?"

"She didn't say anything to me, but Alyssa said Peggy knew."

"How did Alyssa know that?"

"She switched phones with Ashley the night she was killed. She said Peggy texted Ashley's phone the next day specifically addressing her, not Ashley."

"What did the text say?"

"According to Alyssa, Peggy said she knew she was alive and wanted to talk. But Alyssa didn't respond. She didn't trust her. She thinks Peggy was involved in Ashley's murder."

"Why does she think that?"

"I'm not sure. You'll have to ask her yourself."

"We would if we knew how to contact her."

"I'd like to help, but I don't know where she is."

"Why don't you start with where the two of you spent Wednesday together?"

"We stayed in a hotel on 56th and First. It was nice. You should check it out with your boyfriend sometime."

A scowl shot across her face.

"Do you have Alyssa's cellphone?" she snapped.

"If I did, that would suggest I killed Ashley and took it. I never even met her. You didn't find it in any of Ashley's possessions?"

"Obviously. Does Alyssa still have Ashley's cellphone?"

"She told me she got rid of it. She thought it was bugged."

"By whom?"

"By whoever murdered Ashley, Peggy, and the other three women."

"Alyssa thinks that, or you do?"

"Does it matter? The murders are all connected."

"If they are, you're the only common denominator that we've identified."

"You have DNA evidence that someone else killed Peggy. If her murder is connected to the others, which is highly probable, then it follows that I'm innocent of those as well."

"We have evidence of another man's semen at the crime scene. That doesn't mean you didn't murder her. Or help. The same goes for the other victims. What would help prove your innocence better than anything is Alyssa. That's *if* she's really alive and *if* she'll come in to talk to us. She seems to know a lot about who might be behind these murders. You still insist you have no idea where we can find her?"

"I don't know where she is. If she contacts me, I'll try to convince her to talk to you. But she doesn't trust the NYPD."

"Because of Detective Gomez?"

"Yes. Like I told you, she's convinced he tried to set her up to be murdered."

Jaworski sat up in his chair and stared at Brittany. He didn't seem to know about the accusation against Gomez. Her brow furrowed like she was confused. She clearly thought he did.

"Inspector," Crosby interjected, "can you leave us alone for a few minutes?"

Jaworski looked at Crosby like he'd just been fired. Crosby returned a steely gaze. After a few seconds, Jaworski stood and left the room without acknowledging Brittany. The door closed, leaving a tense silence behind.

I took a long drink of water to give myself time to think. Crosby had an aura of command and control about him. Like many of the senior officers I encountered in the Army. It was hard to believe he would allow my interrogation to be this sloppy. Kicking the lead investigator out of the room seemed reactive. But I was sure it wasn't. And Jaworski probably walked right into the surveillance room behind the one-way mirror after he left. What was the point? Crosby was sending signals to someone. If they were meant for me, I didn't understand them.

"Detective Gomez works for YouSEL as a security advisor," I said. "He would have to report that as outside work. It's hard to believe his boss doesn't know about his connection to Champagne. I think Inspector Jaworski and Detective Gomez both have some questions to answer."

Crosby examined me for a few seconds. He knew I was trying to stir things up, but he wasn't taking the bait.

"Assuming it was Ashley Grant who was murdered," Crosby said, "what evidence do you have that Detective Gomez was involved?"

"Mostly what Alyssa told me. But I did see Detective Gomez at Champagne the night Ashley was killed."

"Gomez was there?" Brittany said.

"Not inside. He was in the alley behind Champagne. I was coming from the men's room and saw a woman going out the back door. I thought it was Alyssa leaving, so I went to check. But it wasn't her. I realize now it was probably Ashley. Anyway, the woman walked over to an unmarked car and started talking to someone inside."

"An unmarked police car?" she repeated.

"Yeah, a blue sedan. I think it was a Buick. New York plates. I didn't notice the number."

"How did you know it was Detective Gomez?" Crosby asked.

"He got out of the driver's side when the woman walked over. There was someone in the backseat too. The window was rolled down, and she was talking to whoever it was. It looked intense. Then a bouncer came over and told me to get away from the door."

"Could you see the person in the backseat?" he asked.

"No, but you should examine the video surveillance in case Gomez and the person went inside."

"The only video surveillance Champagne has is at the entrance," Brittany said. "They probably would have gone in through the back. In any event, the surveillance system was down for maintenance that night."

"Alyssa told me there are cameras on the two floors upstairs where the big spenders hang out. She said they videotape sessions in the private rooms too. I assume for blackmail. If Gomez is running Champagne's security, he knows all about it."

Crosby looked at Brittany and asked, "Are we aware of any of this?"

"I'm not," she said, "but I need to speak to Inspector Jaworski. His men handled the search of the premises."

Crosby stared at her, calm but clearly dissatisfied with her response. Her demeanor stiffened. She knew she was being scolded.

I looked at Brittany and said, "It's too convenient that the system was down that night. You should talk to Terry Zezulin, the head bouncer there. He's in charge of surveillance and reports to Gomez."

"I know how to do my job," she shot back.

"Then why am I telling you about the additional video surveillance?"

"I'm wondering the same thing. Aren't you concerned that you were taped that night?"

Her comeback slapped me in the face. I needed to stop stirring the pot. I had lied enough to cast suspicion on Gomez and Champagne. I decided to shut up and just answer their questions.

That's what I did for the next hour as Brittany and Crosby grilled me about the first three murder victims. They knew I had been at the clubs where they danced on the nights they were murdered. Video footage and some of the other strippers confirmed it. I just lied again and said I didn't remember who danced for me. It was a standard guilty response. We all knew it.

Their questions told me they didn't have any new incriminating evidence. That bothered me. I was innocent, but they should have had enough evidence by now to convict me in any court. Maybe they did, and they were just waiting to hit me with it. But that strategy didn't make sense given the pressure they were under to arrest a suspect. It was possible that the Master was extending the game to torture me longer. But my voices were telling me something had changed. They just didn't know if that was good or bad.

When Brittany and Crosby finally finished questioning me about the first three victims, Crosby opened a folder. He took out a photograph and put it in front of me.

"Was this girl at Champagne that night?" he asked.

It was a recent photo of Rachel Morris. It looked like her school yearbook picture.

"I don't remember seeing her," I said. "She looks young to be in Champagne."

"She visited your apartment a couple of weeks ago," Crosby said.

"That's her? She looked a lot older. How old is she?"

"Seventeen," Crosby replied. "Why did she go to see you? It's not a particularly safe neighborhood."

"Good to know you're finally watching out for young women in the city."

"Please answer the question," Crosby said.

"She's the girlfriend of one of the bouncers who jumped me at Champagne. The big redhead guy. She was upset that he landed in the hospital. She asked me to lay off him. I told her I wasn't looking for trouble if he wasn't. She seemed reassured. Then she left."

"That's all she wanted?"

"What else would there be? She's too young for me if that's what you're implying."

"I'm not implying anything. But you're certain you didn't see her at Champagne?"

"I'm certain. What does she have to do with anything?"

"She's the daughter of a prominent businessman. She was spotted at Champagne that night. Before we speak to her or her father, we want to know what or whom she may be involved with."

"She's involved with one of the bouncers. That's all I know."

"Very well. Is there anything else you remember that could help us?" Crosby asked.

"Maybe one thing. I don't know if it's significant."

"We will decide that," Crosby said.

One last lie.

"Okay. Alyssa told me there was a lot of talk around Champagne about crypto. You know—Bitcoin, Ethereum. There were rumors it was being used at Champagne for money laundering. Alyssa asked her sister about it, but she didn't get an answer. She said that's when things started to go south for her. She thinks Ashley's murder is related to it."

Crosby scrutinized me once more with the same calm, blank look on his face. I felt like a corpse but still alive. After a while, he looked at Brittany. Then Brittany looked at me. They had the routine down.

"That will be all," she said. "We'll want to talk to you again soon. We'll contact you. Is the number we have on file still good?"

"Yes."

"Will you be back in your apartment? You haven't been there or your office in a while."

"I've been traveling, but I should be."

"Traveling?" she said skeptically. "Well, if you learn where Alyssa Grant is staying, please contact us immediately. If you can convince her to come in and talk with us, it will not only help our investigation, but it will help you. Do you have any questions?"

I shook my head.

"Thank you for coming in, Mr. Chisholm," Crosby said. "Officer Johnson will accompany you out."

The black twin opened the door for me. I left without looking at Brittany, Crosby, or my reflection in the one-way mirror. I had no idea what had transpired over the past four hours, other than I hadn't been indicted for murder.

48

I was sitting at the same small table upstairs in the back corner of the same Korean deli. I was drinking coffee and waiting for Michael Jin. I wasn't thinking that it had been three days since we met there. Or three days since Peggy Grant drugged me. Or three days since she did something else to me. Or three days since she was murdered. I was thinking about being stepped on.

Two weeks ago, I was the roach, scurrying around, trying not to get squished. Now, I was the spider on the ceiling. I was no longer going to be squished, but everything was upside down and backwards. Something had changed.

The place was mostly empty. What I expected for a Saturday afternoon. I could see anyone coming and going. That was why I had texted Michael to meet me there with my laptop and cellphone. He was late. I didn't mind. It gave me time to think. Not that I needed it. I'd been thinking nonstop since I left Brittany, Crosby, and the twins at the Manhattan North precinct.

Sleeping in my own bed for the first time in over a week wasn't the reprieve I had hoped. Nightmares flooded in every time I closed my eyes. When I woke up this morning, I was too tired to work out. Instead, I drank some coffee and thought. It was the theme of the day.

I took a sip of coffee and texted my sister again using the burner cell. She responded immediately with a question mark. Linda still hadn't called. If she was dead, why hadn't her body shown up? I added it to the pile of evidence that should have been there but wasn't.

Michael appeared at the top of the stairs, a backpack hanging on one shoulder. He saw me and hustled over. He sat down, a little out of breath.

"Sorry I'm late," he said. "I went the way you told me, but it took longer than I expected. I'm pretty sure no one followed me. But I barely made it past that dog out back."

"Don't worry about it. Do you want something to eat or drink?"

"No, thanks. I'm meeting Christine for a late lunch after this."

He unzipped his backpack and pulled out my laptop and cellphone. He gave a quick look around the floor, then slid them across the table towards me.

"It took so long," he said, "because they both had an unbelievable amount of spyware and other surveillance software on them. I've never seen anything like it. I had to tap into someone I know at MIT for help."

"That can't be normal."

"More like abnormal. Whoever put that software on your laptop and cell basically controlled both of them. Even when you thought they were shut down, they weren't. Your camera and audio functions were recording everything you did. And anything you typed, including texts, was being tracked. The only time you weren't being monitored was when the battery died. Given how many programs were running, I'm guessing you ran out of juice a lot."

"I did."

"Will, there was some bad stuff on both your laptop and cell. I don't mean the porn. There was some video of murders. I think they might be those strippers. If the police get their hands on them, I think you'll be in real trouble. I know you didn't kill any of those girls, but someone's trying to make it look like you videotaped murdering them.

I figured out that they were downloaded and not recorded directly. I wiped everything bad off both devices and put it on this."

Michael looked around again, then handed me a small flash drive. I took it and slipped it in my pocket.

"I'd destroy that, if I were you," he said.

"I need to look at it first. Thanks for doing this. Now get out of here. Go out the front way."

After Michael left, I waited twenty minutes, then walked downstairs and out the backway. I threw a treat to the dog chained by the door and walked around it.

When I got back to my apartment, I bolted the door, powered up my laptop, and plugged in the flash drive. I navigated to the videos. There were four of them. The first was labeled *Tom and Amber*. Amber was Lauren Warenski, the first stripper murdered. The second was *Tom and Cinni*. Cinni was Samantha Kerry, the redhead. The third was *Tom and Velvet*. Heather Smith was Velvet, the niece of the Speaker of the Assembly. The last one was *Tom and Ashley*.

I clicked on Ashley's video. It was more disturbing than I was prepared for. Only the killer's hands and arms were visible as he strangled her with a black teddy. She seemed lethargic. Like she'd been drugged. He wore surgical gloves and a long-sleeved black shirt. The blade he used after she was dead could have been a Ghostrike or a Kershaw. I had one of each. The angle of the video was from his shoulder. Probably a mounted camera of some kind. I was supposed to be alone. A disguised voice explained that Ashley had betrayed me by warning Alyssa. For that, she had to take Alyssa's place.

Every nerve and muscle in my body tensed as I watched the gruesome spectacle. I had to refrain from punching the screen. When I finished, I forced myself to watch the other three. I had seen the worst of hell in Afghanistan. Things no one should ever see. But in one way, the videos were even worse. They were soulless.

My anger started to grow. But it didn't get far. A text came across my burner cell from *Unknown*.

It read: "Mr. Chisholm, time to meet."

I stared at the text, my hand trembling slightly. Was this the Master? I tried to pull up the number, but it was blocked. I hadn't had the phone long enough for it to be spam. I thought about how to respond. There was only one option.

I texted: "When and where?"

An immediate answer: "Tonight."

I replied: "Where?"

For forty minutes, I paced around my apartment waiting for a response. Nothing came back. I finally gave up and started to plan.

There was a hint of desperation in contacting me. Whatever had changed was beginning to play out. I had to be prepared. Desperation led to mistakes. I couldn't be the one making them. I decided to improve my odds.

I texted Victor: "Can you meet?"

He responded: "Where?"

I texted: "Diner in 60."

I picked up my Caddy and drove to Harlem. I parked across from the diner and walked in fifteen minutes early. Victor was already in the back drinking coffee at the same table as last time, sitting in the chair I had been in, his back to the wall. He had a black tracksuit on with blue stripes down the arms and legs. I grabbed the chair across from him, moved it to the side, and sat down. A cup of coffee was waiting for me.

"Thanks," I said and drank some coffee.

"Told you you gonna need my help," Victor said.

"I meant thanks for the coffee."

Victor snorted, then said, "What you need?"

"I need you to be ready tonight. I think I'm meeting the person behind everything."

"You think? Bro, can't go into a sitch blind. Gotta know who you dealin' with. First rule. You were a cop. You know that."

"No choice. It's coming to a head. I have to play it out."

"Don't ax me to take a bullet for you, Will."

"Whoever's behind this gave the order to kill David. You in or not?"

He stared at me for a while, rotating his cup on the table, mimicking the gears turning in his head. Then he gulped the last of his coffee, put the cup down and pushed it away.

"Alright," he said. "What we gonna do?"

I went through the details of what I needed from him. He agreed to be on call for the rest of the day. I said I would text where to meet as soon as I knew.

When I finished, he said, "Gonna shoot without axing first. Just warning you."

"Ask first and we're probably both dead."

Victor nodded, stood up, and left. He left the tab too.

It was just past 4:00 p.m. and still plenty light out. It was too early for dinner, but I figured it would be a long night. I decided to get something to eat. I ordered some more coffee and a stack of pancakes with a side of bacon. Breakfast for supper. The same meal my father would cook up when my mother had to work the occasional night. If it was going to be my last one, it might as well be my favorite.

I was halfway through the pancakes and thinking of ordering some eggs when my burner cell rang. It was Richard Morris.

"Mr. Morris," I answered.

"Mr. Chisholm, I just got a text message claiming to be from Rachel, but it's a number I don't recognize."

"She's probably using the burner cell I gave her. What does it say?"

"It says you are going to kill her."

"What? Does it say anything else?"

"Yes. She's at Mitchell Dugan's apartment and wants me to pick her up. I called the number back, and her cellphone, but she didn't answer either one. I texted both too. What is going on, Mr. Chisholm? I think I need to call the police."

"Hold on. First, you know I would never hurt Rachel. If she really did send that text, someone made her. That someone knew you would call me. Whoever it is wants me to go there. If the police show up first and Rachel's there, I'm pretty sure she'll be killed. If she's not at Dugan's apartment, the police will just make it harder to figure out where she is. It could be a hoax, but we can't take the chance of ignoring it. Give me a little time before you call the police."

"Very well. How long should I wait?"

"First, where does Dugan live?"

"He lives in Manhattan on East 26th Street. I have the address right here."

"I need his cell too, if you have it."

"I do."

Morris recited Dugan's address and phone number. I quickly typed both into my cell.

"Alright, call Dugan," I said. "If he doesn't pick up, leave a message to call you immediately. Text him the same message. If you talk to him, tell him what's going on and to wait outside his building for me to show up. But only if you talk to him. His texts are probably being monitored. I doubt that Rachel is at his apartment, but someone might be there waiting for him or me to show up. I'm heading there now. If you don't hear from me in thirty minutes, call the NYPD and tell them what's going on. You got all that?"

"Yes."

"What happened to the security team? They were supposed to contact me if they ran into anything suspicious."

"They were in an accident on I95. Their vehicle was disabled, so they lost track of Rachel. She was with Mr. Dugan. They said they had a backup team. I don't know what happened to it."

"That's not acceptable."

"None of this is acceptable, Mr. Chisholm. I thought you could protect Rachel."

"I know you're upset, Mr. Morris, but you need to stay calm and work with me. Can you do that?"

"Yes. Do whatever it takes to save Rachel. Do you understand me?"

"If she's alive, I'll get her back."

I hung up and texted Victor.

49

*I*t took me twenty-eight minutes to get to Mitchell Dugan's apartment. I parked a block away and texted Richard Morris to wait another fifteen minutes before calling the police. Victor was waiting for me at the corner of 26th Street and Third Avenue. He was dressed in the same tracksuit but had added sunglasses and shooting gloves with both index fingertips cut off. He carried two guns—a Heckler & Koch VP9 and a M&P 9 Shield. I knew from experience.

Dugan lived on the fourth floor of a red brick, five-story building. The first floor was occupied by a doctor's office, a deli, and a small retail store of some kind. I assumed the other four floors were all apartments. Small air conditioning units protruded from random windows. A fire escape climbed the building at the far end. The entrance was smack in the middle. No doorman that I could see. And no Dugan.

I called him twice, but it went to voicemail each time. I texted him, but there was no response.

"Not good, bro," Victor said.

I nodded and said, "Whoever's in there is expecting me. I'll go through the front so I'm seen. It's an old door. I'll pop it open somehow and wedge it. Follow me in three minutes."

"Make it two. I'll walk in cool and easy. No one will know we together."

"You think?" I quipped.

I jogged across 26th Street, then strolled to the entrance of Dugan's building as if I lived there. The door was open. It had already been jimmied. I stepped into a small dark foyer with a narrow hallway that headed back about twenty feet. The building was a walk-up. The stairs started on my left. They were a half-turn design with two flights between each floor.

I took out my Glock, then quickly scaled the six flights to the fourth floor. There were two doors on either side of the hallway. To my right, a window looked out to 26th Street. On the other end, a window looked out at another fire escape. Dugan's apartment was on the right, closest to the back window.

I crept over and squatted next to his door. I grabbed the doorknob and turned it. It unlatched. I gave it a shove. The door swung open, hit something and stopped. I waited and listened. The only sound was the murmur of a ceiling light dying above me. I took out my cellphone and touched the camera button. I eased it around the doorjamb to get a view.

The door had wedged against two large legs sprawled along the floor. I couldn't see the rest of the body, but I was sure it was Dugan. I rotated my cellphone. No one else that I could see. I slipped my phone in my pocket, gripped my Glock with two hands, and squat walked inside.

It appeared to be a one bedroom. To the left was a kitchenette with a small table and chairs. A couch, armchair, and flatscreen TV occupied the space to my right. The bedroom and bathroom were on the other side of the room in an alcove. Both doors were closed.

I stood up and looked down at the body. It was Dugan. There were two bullet holes in his forehead. A pool of blood had formed underneath his head. The bullets had gone through. He was probably shot when he opened the door. He never had a chance.

I heard a noise behind me. I turned, squatted back down, and peered out to the hallway. It was Victor doing what I had just done, his VP9 pointed down at the threshold and his sunglasses dangling from his mouth. I waved him in, then signaled that we needed to check the bedroom and bathroom. He nodded.

Victor crept along the left side of the living room towards the alcove while I did the same along the right side. The bedroom and bathroom doors were opposite each other. On a silent three count, we pushed the doors open, turned into the rooms, and aimed our guns. There was no one.

I walked quickly to the apartment door and swung it closed with my elbow. Then I took a closer look at Dugan. He had been beaten badly. His face was swollen and had multiple lacerations. A few teeth were knocked in, and his right arm appeared broken. A burner cell was on the floor next to him. It was probably the one I had given Rachel. I picked it up and stuck it in my pocket.

Victor walked over and stood next to me. He gazed down at Dugan.

"Put up a fight protecting his girl," he said.

"No. Place is too neat. They shot him when he opened the door. Then they kicked the shit out of him to make it look like he had another run in with me. Probably took her away immediately in case her security detail showed up."

"*Damn.* Someone really don't like you, bro."

I felt Dugan's body temperature. Then I looked around the apartment. There were two holes in the wall by the alcove. One was near the ceiling, and the other was a foot below it. I examined them. Specks of blood were splattered around the holes. I visualized Dugan opening the door, being shot, and the bullets exiting his head and hitting the wall.

I looked at Victor and said, "Whoever shot him was short. I'm guessing a Glock 19 to make it look like I did it. Probably used a suppressor. But he's been dead for over an hour. The timeline doesn't match the text to Morris. Sloppy if you're trying to pin it on me."

"Short, sloppy—don't matter to him no more."

Then my voices started screaming. I hurried into the alcove and used my shirt to wipe our prints off the bedroom and bathroom doors. I hustled back to Victor.

"Whatchu thinkin', bro?" he said.

"I think I know where Rachel is. Let's go."

50

A blue Buick with New York plates was parked by the dumpster behind Jin's Dry Cleaning and Laundry. It looked like the car I was tossed into after I was arrested at Champagne. Like the car Mitchell Dugan saw Detective Gomez get out of the night Ashley was murdered. Like the car Alyssa saw outside Peggy's apartment the day she was murdered. Like the car that had brought Rachel Morris here to be murdered in my apartment.

Victor and I were sitting in my Caddy, parked a block away on Clinton Street. It ran perpendicular to Grand Street, past the alley behind Jin's Dry Cleaning and Laundry. We were watching a short muscular man with a shaved head smoking a cigarette and leaning against the wall by the back entrance to my building.

The guy was Terry Zezulin, the head bouncer I had taken down in the alley behind Champagne. I figured he had shot Dugan. Dugan knew him and probably opened the door to greet him. Now, he was the lookout. He was probably supposed to be inside, but he needed a smoke. Gomez was in my apartment preparing to kill Rachel. If she wasn't already dead. I would be shot as soon as I walked in. Gomez would call it in. His story would be he killed me before I could kill him, but he was too late to save Rachel.

"Bro, there a store around here?" Victor asked. "I need a bottle and a paper bag. You got anythin' help me look like a bum?"

I stared at him and raised my eyebrows. He stared back at me blankly. Maybe no one had ever mocked him before.

"There's a store around the corner on Grand Street," I said. "Just past my building. I have a Boston Bruins cap and a black hoody in the trunk that should work."

"Anythin' Boston make me look like a real bum."

I popped the trunk. Victor got out and grabbed the cap and hoody. After he closed the trunk, I could see he had taken off his jacket, revealing a white compression T-shirt pronouncing he was a workout fanatic. He strode towards Grand Street carrying the cap and hoody against his left side to hide the bulge from his VP9. Then he crossed the street at the corner and disappeared.

Five minutes later, Victor came staggering down Clinton Street on the same side as Jin's Dry Cleaning and Laundry. He was wearing the cap and hoody and carrying something in a paper bag. He headed for the alley, looking like a bona fide New York City homeless drunk.

He turned into the alley, stumbled past Zezulin, and stopped at the dumpster. He pretended to relieve himself. Zezulin eyed him suspiciously, then flicked his cigarette to the ground and pulled himself away from the wall. Victor turned around and wobbled towards him. Zezulin shouted something, but I couldn't hear it because of the traffic and distance.

Then Victor lurched forward, grabbed Zezulin before he could react, and shoved him up against the wall. Zezulin raised his hands halfway, a passive gesture of resistance to the VP9 that I assumed Victor was pressing against his stomach. I could see them talking, Victor smiling menacingly as he looked down into Zezulin's eyes eight inches away. After a minute, Victor grabbed Zezulin by his collar and walked him behind the dumpster out of sight. Even with the traffic and distance, I heard the two pops. Twenty seconds later,

Victor stepped out, looked towards me, and gestured with his head for me to come over.

I got out and casually crossed the street. I walked up to the alley and over to the dumpster where Victor was standing. I looked behind it. Zezulin's body lay crumpled under two cardboard boxes. A trickle of blood flowed down the crevices of the worn asphalt to within a few inches of Victor's shoes. Like a finger pointing at the killer. I looked at Victor.

He shrugged and said, "I axed first."

"What did he say?"

"Gomez in your apartment with the girl. Just him. Been there twenty minutes. Knock two times quick, three times slow. He'll let you in. Offered me fifty grand to pop you. Didn't say please. I used his gun. Glock 19, like you said."

"Let me see it."

Victor pulled the Glock from behind him. I took it by the grip to put my prints on it, released the magazine and tossed it in the dumpster. I cleared the round from the chamber, then dropped the gun next to Zezulin.

"I'll claim self-defense," I said, then looked at Victor. "I'm going up. You in?"

"Don't need to ax. One of these mofos killed David."

"There might be someone else inside besides Gomez. Zezulin could have lied."

"Gotta kill 'em all. Only way to be sure."

"Okay. If Rachel is alive, protect her at all costs. Something happens to me, get her back to her father. I want Gomez alive to question him. But if he starts shooting, do what you have to."

We walked over to the back door. I stopped and picked up Zezulin's cigarette butt. Smelled it. It wasn't menthol. Victor gave me a *WTF* look. I shook my head that it was nothing.

The door was unlocked. I pulled out my Glock. Victor pulled out his VP9. We slipped inside and headed to the stairs. Then the front door opened, and someone stepped into the foyer. Sunlight flooded in. I squinted and made out a figure carrying a backpack and looking at a cellphone. It was Michael. I lowered my Glock and hurried towards him.

The door closed, and Michael looked up from his cellphone. He saw me and started to smile. Then his eyes widened as he caught sight of Victor.

"It's okay," I said. "Go into the shop, lock all the doors, and stay with your parents until the police come. They're on the way. Go."

Michael nodded and slid by us. He opened the side door to Jin's and went in. I heard the door lock, then Sally Jin's high-pitched voice yelling something in Chinese.

"No cops comin', bro," Victor said.

"Someone will call once the shooting starts."

In ten seconds, we were both squatting against the wall in the hallway on either side of my apartment door. Victor was on the right. I was on the left, nearest to the doorknob. I stood up, reached over, and knocked two quick times, then three times slowly. I crouched back down.

Someone cursed inside. The sound of the floor creaking floated from under the door. Then the top deadbolt unlocked, and the door-knob turned. I stepped away from the wall and positioned myself in front of the door. It eased open. I charged forward and rammed it with my left shoulder.

The door smashed into Gomez and propelled him back into my apartment. He banged into a chair and stumbled over it, catching himself by bracing his left hand against the wall. My momentum car-ried me into the room. I jumped to my left and aimed my Glock at Gomez's chest. Victor rushed in behind, slid to his right and pointed his VP9 at Gomez.

Gomez reached for his gun on his right hip, then stopped. His eyes locked on mine. He glanced at Victor, then looked back at me. He knew he was dead if he continued. He wasn't a stupid man. Or a brave one. He steadied himself and stood up straight.

"Shoot him," Victor said.

I couldn't tell if he was asking me or telling me.

I signaled for Gomez to raise his hands. He lifted them up to his shoulders, palms out. Sweat stains showed under the sleeves of his gray button-down shirt.

I saw a figure out of the corner of my eye. It was Rachel. She was lying face down on my bed, her wrists, feet, and mouth taped. She turned her face to me. Her eyes were wide and petrified. A black teddy was wrapped loosely around her neck. She was naked.

"Shut the door," I said.

Victor swung the door closed without taking his aim off Gomez. Then he moved carefully to Gomez's side and stopped. He reached around Gomez and pulled his gun from its holster. Victor stuck it inside the back waist of his pants. He took a step back and straightened his left arm so the VP9 was a foot from Gomez's temple. Gomez's eyes danced back and forth between me and the barrel of the VP9.

"Tape his wrists and sit him down," I said.

"Shoot him," Victor said.

This time, it was a command.

"Tape his wrists and sit him down," I repeated.

Victor shook his head and holstered his VP9. He grabbed a roll of duct tape that was on my nightstand and taped Gomez's wrists behind his back. He picked up the chair Gomez had knocked over and pushed him into it.

"Give me the hoody," I said.

Victor took it off and tossed it to me. He pulled his VP9 back out, and I holstered my Glock. I walked over to Rachel and covered her with the hoody. I gently pulled the tape from her mouth. She gasped. Tears ran down her cheeks. I pulled my jackknife out and carefully cut the tape off her wrists and feet.

"You want to take it from here?" I asked softly.

Rachel nodded, then swung her legs around to the side of the bed facing the bathroom and away from me. She sat up and untied the

teddy from around her neck. She put the hoody on. It covered everything down to the middle of her thighs. Then she grabbed the teddy
and rolled it into a ball. She stood up, turned, and glared at Gomez.
Her jaw tightened. She wound up and threw the teddy at him. It hit
him in the side of the head. He snarled something in Spanish.

She stared at me. Her eyes blinked rapidly, and her lower lip started to quiver.

"Is Mitch dead?" she whimpered.

"Yes. You're not. That's how he would have wanted it."

She nodded, then started sobbing. I gathered her clothes from the
floor and put them on the bed in front of her.

"Get dressed," I said. "You have to leave right now. Victor will take
you home."

Rachel stepped quickly into the bathroom. She was dressed and
ready in two minutes. She still wore the hoody when she came out,
her arms lost in the sleeves and wrapped tightly around her body. Her
blonde hair was disheveled, and her eyes were puffy. But there was life
in them.

I gave Victor my car keys, and he gave me Gomez's gun. It was a
SIG Sauer P226. Standard NYPD issue. I stuffed it inside the back
waist of my jeans.

Victor walked to the door. Rachel followed close behind. He eased
it open and poked his head out, holding his VP9 against his chest. He
glanced back at me and nodded. Rachel looked at me. Her eyes were
moist, and her lips were pressed tightly together.

"Shoot him," she said.

51

I grabbed Gomez by his shirt collar and pulled him out of the chair. I stood him up against my heavy bag, facing me, then stepped back. He looked nervous, but his eyes were defiant. He didn't believe I would shoot him.

"I'm going to ask you some questions," I said. "If you don't answer or I think you're lying or I just don't like your answers, I will shoot you in the face."

Gomez scoffed and said, "You kill me, and thirty-five thousand cops will be after you. You'll never see the inside of a prison. Why risk that if you can get paid and get out of this alive? I can give you at least a million. And I'll guarantee no one comes after you. No charges, no revenge. You just go away and stay away. Work with me, Chisholm. We'll both make out good."

"Who are you working for?" I said.

He stared at me defiantly and didn't answer.

"Why am I being framed?"

No answer.

"Is Jaworski working with you?"

No answer.

"Is Brittany Sorenson working with you?"

No answer.

I stepped over to him, pointed my Glock in his face, and reached around his head. I grabbed his hair and yanked it down. His head snapped back, forcing his mouth partly open. I stuck the muzzle of my Glock in it. His eyes bulged.

"Did you kill Lauren Warenski?"

He tried to say something, but it came out garbled. Then he shook his head.

"Did you kill Samantha Kerry?"

He shook his head.

"Did you kill Heather Smith?"

He shook his head again.

"Did you kill Ashley Grant?

He hesitated, then shook his head.

"Did you kill Peggy Grant?"

He shook his head one more time.

I pulled the Glock out of his mouth and released his hair. I stepped back quickly and lowered the Glock to my side. Gomez bent over and gagged like his lung might come up. He cleared his throat, then spit on the carpet to his right. He straightened up and looked at me. His eyes were still defiant but less so.

"Did you rape any of those women?" I said.

"They wouldn't complain if I had," he sneered.

I took a deep breath through my nose.

"Where is Linda Lau?"

Gomez smirked and shook his head slowly. Like I didn't get it.

I took another step back, raised my Glock and shot him between the eyes. A brief smack sounded as the bullet embedded in the heavy bag. Gomez collapsed to the floor. Blood started to soak the carpet around his head. The heavy bag swayed slowly back and forth like a light breeze had stirred it. A large, irregular hole gaped near the top.

I had five minutes.

I kneeled next to Gomez and cut the tape off his wrists. I pulled his SIG from the back of my jeans and put it in his right hand. Then I lifted his hand with the SIG, maneuvered his index finger, and fired a bullet into the door molding where it wouldn't go through to the hallway. I cleaned the residual glue from the tape on his wrists, wiped my prints off the SIG, and placed it next to him. I took out the flash drive with the murder videos and cleaned my prints off. Then I rubbed it across Gomez's fingers and slipped it in his pocket.

Gomez shot at me when I opened the door. I fired back in self-defense. Rachel would corroborate my story once I told her it. The flash drive would implicate Gomez in all the murders except Peggy Grant's. Michael Jin didn't see anything. That's what he would say if questioned. And Victor was never there. I didn't call the police because Gomez was a Detective. I didn't know who to trust. I left with Rachel in case anyone else showed up. Someone did—Terry Zezulin, the dead guy by the dumpster. We fought, and I killed him with his own gun. That was my story—if I ever got to tell it.

I cracked open my door and listened. It was eerily quiet. Like the entire building was holding its breath. Someone had called the police by now. Sally Jin was going to be furious. It was probably time to move on anyway. Maybe I could find a nice six-by-eight-foot studio upstate.

I stepped into the hallway, my right arm flush along my side, holding my Glock. I shut the door, then hurried down the stairs and out the back. I turned right onto Clinton Street and started walking like a guy who hadn't just shot an NYPD Detective in the face. There were no sirens yet. I kept walking.

The streets were starting to show some life ahead of the Saturday night chaos to come. Long shadows from tall, quiet skyscrapers blanketed nearly everything. It was still warm and humid.

I stopped at a coffee shop, bought an iced coffee, and made my way up to the second floor. I sat at a window table and looked out on the slowly growing hordes of people and traffic. Before I had taken a sip, a text buzzed on my burner cell. It was from *Unknown*.

It read: "10 pm W19th St."

I stared at the message in consternation. That was Brittany's street.

I texted: "Address?"

After ten minutes, there was no reply. I waited another twenty, then called Brittany's cell. Someone answered but immediately hung up. I tried again. It rang until it went into voicemail. I left a message telling her to call me immediately. Then I texted her.

It was a few minutes past eight. The coffee shop had closed. A worker started sweeping up around me. I took the hint and left.

Brittany's apartment was four miles away. I figured I'd catch the subway to West 14th and walk up to her street from there. There wasn't much else I could do until the Master told me where to meet. Except maybe think. But my head hurt from doing so much of that already.

A text came through from Victor: "Dropped off Rachel heading back whats the plan?"

I texted: "Meet at W19th and 8th at 9:30 pm. No plan yet."

Victor replied: "You gonna owe me."

52

*I*t was just past dusk. Brightly lit windows scaled the neighborhood high-rises in disciplined columns, a random dark window interrupting the order. The warm Saturday night had brought out swarms of two-legged beasts to trespass on the feeding grounds of the multi-legged creatures who normally scavenged the streets at this time.

I was standing on the north side of 19ᵗʰ Street, a block from Brittany's apartment, trying to figure out where I was supposed to meet the Master, assuming it was the Master who had texted me. Her building was the only place that made sense. She was wrapped up in everything as much as I was. Maybe more. I was there because of her. I was sure of that. It was a trap. I was sure of that too.

Across the street, a dark figure walked casually along the sidewalk. It stopped and turned to face me. The outfit looked familiar. It was Victor. He lifted his chin to acknowledge me. I did the same, then crossed over.

"Got a plan yet?" he asked.

"Sort of. Meeting's at ten. I think it will be in Brittany Sorenson's apartment building."

"The ADA bitch?"

"Yeah. Her building's the tall one down the street."

"I know. Got the address for you, remember? Didn't you used to bang her?"

"How do you know that?"

"I do homework too. Where in the building?"

"Probably the roof. I'm waiting for a text to tell me."

"Why the roof? No easy escape. Don't seem smart."

"I know, but the lobby makes no sense unless you want everyone to see you. Garage doesn't make sense either. Can't tell who's coming or going. Her apartment is too small and only has one way in or out. Plus, the neighbors would hear any gunshots. Unless she's being held hostage there. But whoever's behind this could have done that anytime. Why now and why play this game? Someone wants a showdown. It has to be the roof."

"You thinking this is 'bout her?"

"Yeah, unless I'm missing something."

"You call her?"

"I tried. Someone picked up and then hung up. I called back but it went to voicemail. Texted her too but no response."

"Could be somethin'. Could be nothin'. You scope out the roof?"

"Looked it up online. There's a deck with furniture and grills. It closes at ten, which fits the timeline of the meeting. It's three floors above her apartment. Not ideal, but it works for an ambush if you have support."

"What if she the one ambushing you?"

"She's not a murderer."

"Gonna bet your life on that?"

"No choice."

"Bullshit, bro. Walk away. Wait for this motherfucker to make a mistake."

"Can't. I killed a cop. It's out of control now. I have to end it. Or die trying."

"Can't die, bro. You owe me. Owe me more after today."

I rolled my eyes.

"We just gonna wait here?" he said.

"No. I expect to get a text right before ten telling me where to meet. That gives us twenty-five minutes. I want to check out Brittany's apartment. I'll sneak in through the garage and find a way up to her floor. If she's there and safe, I'll make up something. If she's not there, I'll head to the roof and figure it out on the way."

"That your plan?"

"I'm open to suggestions."

"I say we go straight through the front door and up to her place. Shoot anyone get in our way. Why you shakin' your head? You axed. Then what you want me doin' while you sneakin' 'round like a pussy?"

"Funny you should ask. I want you to walk through the front door and get to Brittany's apartment without bringing attention to yourself. You know, like shooting someone."

"How you want me to do that?"

"Figure it out. Pretend to be a delivery guy or something."

"You labeling me, bro. Why don't I just go with you?"

"I need you to wait and check for any backup. Then come up."

Victor shook his head, mocking me. He took out his cell and called someone.

"Girl who works for me lives there," he said before a woman picked up. "Hey babe, it's Vic. . . . You too, babe. . . . I'm outside your building. . . ."

Victor gestured for me to go. I turned and headed for Brittany's building.

Sneaking into the garage proved easy. I hid behind a large garbage bin and waited for a car to leave. After five minutes, the automatic door opened, and a car pulled out. Before the door closed, I dove underneath and was in. There were no surveillance cameras that I could see.

The building was thirty years old. The security system looked ten years old. Nothing too sophisticated. You needed a fob to open any door in a stairwell except probably the one to the lobby. I waited for someone to come down the stairs to the garage and then pretended like I had just gotten there. Once I was in the lobby, I looked around. It was empty except for the doorman.

I had to decide between climbing the stairs or talking my way up the elevator again. I opted for the stairs. They went all the way to the roof. Two flights per floor, plus an extra two for the lobby. Thirty flights up to Brittany's apartment. No cameras. I planned to pound on the door to her floor until someone opened it. Once you were past the lobby, most residents assumed you lived there.

I took the stairs two at a time for the first five floors, then slowed down. The stairwell wasn't air-conditioned. It felt like a hundred degrees. By the time I reached the fifteenth floor, I had a nice sweat going. The door to the floor was unlocked. My voices started chirping.

I took out my Glock and pulled the door ajar. I propped it open with my left foot and listened. The faint high-pitched buzzing of the hallway lights was all I heard. I used my cell camera to surveil the hallway. No one was there. I stepped out of the stairwell and turned right. I checked the floor again, then lowered my Glock to my side. Brittany's apartment was down on the left. I walked casually along the hallway and stopped just before her door.

My cell buzzed with a text from Victor: "2 guys in lobby brother doorman & white guy w blond hair."

I texted: "Nasty white guy, 30ish, my height?"

Victor replied: "Y."

I texted: "Bad guy. Watch out. I'm outside the apartment."

Victor replied: "Waiting for my girl to come get me."

Then I sensed something—a cigarette smell, menthol, barely perceptible. I moved closer to the door. The smell was a little stronger. I heard a cough inside the apartment. A man clearing his throat. Someone walking. Water running for a moment. Silence.

I squatted next to the door. I reached over with my left hand and turned the knob slowly. I felt it unlatch. The door started to glide open from its own weight. I let go of the knob and moved in front of the doorway. Then I launched forward, shoving the door open with my left hand while I extended the Glock with my right.

An explosive crack came from inside just as a splintering noise sounded behind me. I dove forward and fired at a figure rushing from the kitchen. I heard a shriek. Two successive loud cracks followed, then two thumps in the wall above my head. I landed hard on the floor and saw a man stumbling to the right of my Glock sight. I nudged my aim and fired twice. The first shot hit him. The second got a bookshelf as he fell forward. His gun discharged into the rug. I kept my Glock sighted on him.

The man lay slumped over a wide green armchair, his gun on the rug in front of him. His right hand dangled down, blood dripping from his fingers. He started to slide off the chair, gained momentum and landed on the rug with a thud. He rolled over to his back. I recognized him—Detective Ginelli.

I got up, keeping my aim on him. My first shot must have hit him in the side since his shirt and blazer were covered in blood there. My second one had hit him in the throat. Blood was bubbling from the entrance wound. It had probably severed the carotid artery. If he wasn't dead, he would be soon. I walked over and kicked his gun away just in case. I'd seen stranger things out of dead men.

Then I rushed to the bedroom. The door was closed. I peeked in the bathroom across the hall. It was empty. I squatted to the side of the bedroom door and raised my Glock. I turned the knob and pushed the door open. It swung back and hit the wall. I peeked in. It was empty too. I checked the closet. Nothing.

I hustled back to the apartment door, closed and locked it. Then I walked into the living area and looked around. A half-filled glass of water sat on the kitchen counter with a pill bottle next to it. A few sofa pillows were strewn on the floor around the coffee table. In the dining area, a chair was tipped over and another had been pulled several feet out from the table.

My eyes stopped. On the floor between the two chairs lay a pair of blue jeans, a Harvard Law School T-shirt, a white lace bra, matching panties, and a pair of blue leather flats. It looked like Brittany had changed into another outfit right there.

Then my cell buzzed. A text from *Unknown*: "Roof."

I immediately texted Victor: "Meeting's on the roof."

I ran to the door, unlocked it, and stepped out to the hallway. Several people were looking cautiously from their doorways to see what was going on. They saw me with my Glock and ducked back inside. The sound of doors locking followed. I sprinted to the stairwell, pushed the door open, and took the eight flights of stairs up two steps at a time.

When I got to the top landing, there were two metal doors perpendicular to each other. One said "ROOF-DECK," and the other said "NO EXIT." Pieces of torn yellow caution tape hung from the walls on either side of the "ROOF-DECK" door. A pile of the tape lay next to it with a crumpled paper sign on top that read "Closed For Renovation." Someone had used the door recently.

I decided to take the "NO EXIT" door. I figured it went directly out to the roof. I brought my Glock up to my chest and pushed the handle down. I eased the door open a few inches. The wind whooshed in, along with the faint sound of muffled voices. I opened the door farther and peeked outside. The cement casing of the elevator shaft blocked any view of the deck. I stepped gently onto the gravel covering, then crept over to the shaft wall.

It was a dark night with no moon. There were no clouds to reflect the city lights either. The shadows were pitch black. I was in them. No one could see me. I slinked around the first corner of the elevator shaft and hurried to the next one. I knelt, took out my cellphone, and turned on the camera. I stuck it around the corner just above the rooftop.

The deck was twenty feet away, illuminated by several spotlights above the entrance to the elevator foyer. Composite planks the color of teak covered half the rooftop, stretching from the foyer to the far corner of the building. Large rectangular flower boxes ran along the inside perimeter of the deck. A three-foot-high barrier and railing, with laminated glass panels anchored on top, bordered the outside perimeter along the edges of the roof. It was a safety measure so that no one fell or jumped. All the furniture and grills were pushed near the foyer for the renovation. A few pieces of equipment were next to them. I could make out two people in the far corner of the deck by the edge of the roof.

Then I heard a scream.

I slipped my cell in my pocket and stepped around the corner, my arms extended, holding my Glock with a two-handed grip. The two people looked like they were on the railing. I started walking faster. Then panic surged through me.

I could see Brittany kneeling on the railing, wearing a black teddy and holding frantically to a glass panel with both hands. Inspector Jaworski was standing on the railing behind her, trying to pry her hands from the panel. She was crying, her hair tossed wildly in front of her face.

"*Stop!*" I shouted and started running.

I sprinted to the edge of the deck and jumped over a flower box. I landed in stride and continued running. Fifteen feet from Brittany, I slid and took aim at Jaworski's chest.

Just as I came to a stop, he yanked Brittany up by her waist, forcing her hands from the glass panel. He spun her body towards me to shield himself. He almost lost his balance but recovered. He wrapped his left arm around her neck and twisted her right arm behind her back to control her.

I still had a shot, but not a good one. The impact would likely knock Jaworski off the roof, taking Brittany with him.

She looked dazed and was having trouble standing. She had probably been drugged with whatever was in the pill bottle I saw in her apartment.

Jaworski's feet were spread wide on top of the railing, his hamstrings pressed against the top of a glass panel for stability. He held Brittany tightly. His eyes peeked out from behind her head as strands of her hair flapped across his face. Their bodies wavered in the warm night breeze, two hundred feet above 19th Street.

Then I noticed a necklace on Brittany—the one I had given her. All the stars were attached now, including the one she had said was lost.

It was going to be a suicide, I realized. Brittany was distraught after learning that her ex-boyfriend was behind the stripper murders—murders motivated by my obsession with her. She wanted to end the killings by ending her life. The black teddy and necklace were symbols of my perversion that had driven her to jump to her death.

That was Jaworski's plan. I was certain. But the theatrics were over the top. Why not overdose in her apartment? Why jump off her roof? There was a reason. Right now, it didn't matter.

"Put the gun down, Chisholm," Jaworski shouted, "or Brittany dies."

"She dies, you die," I yelled over the noise floating up from 19th Street.

"Maybe, but you're going down too," Jaworski shouted. "Every cop in the city is looking for you, Chisholm. The pervert who murdered and raped a seventeen-year-old girl and killed her boyfriend. You're taking the fall for those, not me. I'm not being double-crossed again."

The warm breeze suddenly died. The city sounds retreated into the darkness, leaving a heavy quiet hanging over the roof. I could hear Brittany whimpering now, her eyes frightened and wandering. Then she saw me.

"Will," she murmured.

I rose to a standing position. I stared at Jaworski, aiming my Glock at the small part of his face showing behind Brittany's head.

"Aren't you wondering why I'm here?" I said. "I'm supposed to be dead."

"It doesn't change anything," he said. "You kill me, you kill Brittany too. I'll die a hero trying to save her, and you'll die in prison. Is that what you want?"

"Try again. Rachel Morris is alive. Gomez, Ginelli, and Zezulin are all dead. No posthumous medals for you."

Jaworski's eyes widened in disbelief. They swept across the roof in desperation. He had no intention of dying a hero. Or dying at all. But he needed a new plan, another way out. He was calculating. I could see it. He looked over the edge of the roof. Then he slid his face around to Brittany's cheek and kissed her. He nestled his chin tenderly in her hair for a moment.

He peered back at me and said, "We can all walk away from this alive. I have money—millions. Half of it's yours. You'll get it. I'll make sure. I know I'm screwed if you don't. Just let me leave. But Brittany comes with me. I'll let her go downstairs. I care for her as much as you do. I just didn't know she was taken. I learned that too late. What do you say, Chisholm? You're a smart kid. No one dies. Everyone gets another chance. It's the only way to save her."

"Only one problem," I said.

"What's that?"

"I don't trust you."

"Ha! That's right, you have trust issues. She told me all about them."

A wail of sirens grew in the distance. Jaworski glanced in their direction. Then his eyes darted back to me.

"I'm not going to prison," he exclaimed.

"Then come down. You can leave. I won't shoot. You have my word. But Brittany stays."

Jaworski shook his head and scoffed.

"This whole setup is *un-fucking-believable*. You were supposed to take the fall. Not me. I should have seen it coming. Maybe if I had your trust issues, I would have. Well, I'm not going to make it easy for anyone. Decide Chisholm. Let me leave with Brittany or kill her."

He tightened his arm around her neck. She gasped. Their bodies wavered, like they might tumble over the glass panel at any moment. I had to get them down from the railing before I could risk taking a shot.

Where are you, Victor?

"Alright," I said and started to lower my Glock.

Then I felt the tingling sensation above my right ear. A pounding pain began to pulsate up the side of my head. Flashes of light burst in front of my eyes, and blood rushed to my legs. I heard shouting, but the ringing in my right ear drowned it out.

God, no . . .

I took several quick breaths and shook my head. The ringing faded, and my vision cleared. I looked back up at Brittany and Jaworski.

"Shoot him!" Jaworski yelled.

Someone's behind me!

I dropped to the deck just as two sharp cracks exploded to my right, followed by another louder one behind me. I rolled to my left, trying to sense if I'd been hit.

No pain. No warm moist feeling of blood.

I continued my roll and came up on one knee, pointing my Glock in the direction of the foyer. A man's body was slumped on the deck twenty feet away, blood flowing from his temple and coloring his blond hair red.

I whipped my Glock to my left. Victor was standing in front of the elevator shaft, his arms extended, holding his VP9. Then I heard Brittany scream my name.

I spun back to her. Jaworski was swinging a gun around her body towards me. Two startling cracks sounded in succession—one from behind me, then one from in front.

Jaworski's right shoulder jerked back, and his arm dropped. I snapped my head over my left shoulder . . .

Alyssa!

She was standing in front of the stacked furniture, the muzzle of a gun pointed up towards Jaworski. I whipped my eyes to him. He was falling backwards over the glass panel, almost in slow motion, pulling Brittany with him.

I jumped up and bolted towards the railing. A searing pain ran up my left side. I pushed off with my right foot and lunged for Brittany. My shoulder hit the glass panel hard as I wrapped my left arm around her bare thighs. I squeezed them tight against my chest, stopping her from toppling all the way over. But her upper body continued to fall. Her back slammed into the other side of the glass panel, reverberating through to me.

She was much heavier than I expected. Her legs started to slip through my arm. I quickly holstered my Glock, then shimmied to the top of the panel. I reached over and grabbed hold of her left arm. I hooked the toes of my sneakers under the inside lip of the railing to stop from being pulled over myself. Something warm seeped across my stomach.

Brittany was sobbing in between desperate gasps for air. Her head, hair, and torso were dangling upside down, twenty stories of nothing between her and the sidewalk. Jaworski was clinging onto her from behind, his left arm wrapped across her sternum under her exposed breasts. His right heel was caught on the top of a glass panel, stopping him from plunging off the roof.

The weight of Jaworski clinging to Brittany was too much for me. Brittany's legs slowly slid through my grasp. As I squeezed tighter, I began to be pulled over with her.

I let go of her arm, reached down and tried to wrench Jaworski's forearm from under her breasts. He lifted his head, and our eyes locked. Then he raised his blood-soaked right arm. His gun was still in his hand.

I released his forearm, reached back and grabbed my Glock. I swung my arm down, aimed to the right of Brittany's face, and squeezed the trigger. Jaworski's head snapped back, and his arm slid from under Brittany's breasts. The weight of his limp body pulled his heel off the glass panel. He dropped straight down, gaining speed before hitting the pavement with a distant thud. A scream rose from somewhere on 19th Street.

I holstered my Glock and reached my arm around the back of Brittany's waist. She was lighter now, but I was hanging too far over to pull her up. My left side was burning.

Then my right toe slipped from the lip of the railing. I lurched partially over the glass panel and stopped. I glanced back to see if anyone was there to help—no one.

I raced through my options. There was only one. I had to let her go. If I did it right, I could swing down, grab the edge of the railing, and wrap my legs around her before she dropped. I would just have to do one pullup with an extra one hundred fifteen pounds between my legs. It sounded crazy, even in the moment.

Then someone grabbed my legs and lifted them from the railing. I started to fall . . .

Alyssa!

I stopped. Two strong hands squeezed my ankles and started dragging me back. I glanced over my shoulder and saw Victor. He was puffing and pulling hard to get my knees over the top of the glass panel. I held Brittany tightly. Her eyes opened and stared at me briefly before closing again.

Once I had enough leverage, I pulled Brittany back over the glass panel. I lifted her in my arms, turned, and dropped to the deck. I looked around. Alyssa was gone. I turned to Victor. He was panting, a smug grin on his face.

"You owe me big, bro," he said.

53

*T*he room felt cozier without my hands cuffed to the table. A cup of weak coffee and a bottle of water were touches of charm that had been missing during my first two sessions there. Even the one-way mirror seemed to be more part of the décor than surveillance. All the place needed was my music to feel like my home away from home.

It had been five days since I stopped Jaworski from killing Brittany. I was finishing up my second meeting with her and District Attorney Crosby following the incident, answering the same questions for the third time. The media had eaten up the bad cop corruption and murder scandal like chum to sharks. But the food was now down to scraps. Without the prospects of a sensational trial, the feeding frenzy was fading. News outlets were segueing to the burgeoning political battle for the Governor of New York.

The election was more than a year away, but Frank Crosby's name was front and center in the latest headlines. Not only because the stripper slayings had presumably been solved, but also because Speaker of the Assembly Ted Smith had publicly accused him of turning a blind eye to corruption in the NYPD. Smith had invoked his murdered niece in the first salvo of an expected contentious gubernatorial race between the two likely candidates. I cared because the election would drive Crosby's agenda, especially on crime. Since

I still hadn't been officially cleared of anything, his agenda mattered to me.

Crosby sat at the end of the table to my left. Navy-blue suit, white shirt, and blue paisley tie. Brittany was straight across from me. Royal blue skirt suit and white button-down blouse, open at the collar, with a thin silver necklace. Her demeanor during the session had been all business, mirroring Crosby. But her eyes had been soft, maybe warm.

Crosby put his pen inside his suit jacket and closed his notebook. He took off his reading glasses, placed them on the table, and looked at Brittany. He gave her a quick smile of acknowledgement, then turned and stared at me sternly.

"ADA Sorenson will wrap up," he said. "We will contact you if we need more of your time. Please inform my office if you plan to leave the state for any extended period."

The moment begged for a wise-ass remark, but I resisted. I wasn't out of trouble yet. Maybe not even close. I didn't know.

"Can I assume no charges are coming my way?" I said.

Crosby's dark eyes peered at me like an animal from its lair. They narrowed slightly.

"That is the third time you've asked me that question. I have advised you to be patient. Now, I will be blunt. You should not assume anything regarding potential future charges. The only indisputable facts we have are five murdered women, three dead NYPD personnel, and three other dead men, one of whom was a completely innocent young man. While we know that Inspector Jaworski's DNA was found in the bodies of Ashley and Peggy Grant, we do not have definitive proof that he either murdered or raped those women. Or, for that matter, that he had anything to do with the murder and rape of the other three women. The fact that he is dead, along with two detectives who could have shed light on these heinous crimes, is problematic for our investigation. The circumstantial evidence clearly casts a guilty shadow over those three, but it is not lost on this office that it also deflects guilt away from other possible perpetrators. It will be difficult to conclude anything with certainty. That, however, is our job. We will take the time needed to ensure justice for the victims."

"Excuse me, but you seem to be forgetting that those upstanding NYPD detectives and their friends tried to kill ADA Sorenson and Rachel Morris. And Gomez had videos of the murders being committed. He worked for Jaworski. They *are* guilty. I'm not. What you can prove about them is your problem. But you have more than enough evidence to exonerate me. I'd like to know when I'm going to get some justice."

Crosby glared at me for a moment, then gazed down at his notebook. He pursed his lips as if trying to temper his reaction. After a few seconds, he looked up.

"Mr. Chisholm, you admitted to killing three members of the NYPD and Mr. Zezulin. *Even if* your actions were all in self-defense, these are not everyday incidents that get processed with routine paperwork. There have been loud cries for further investigation. While some of them may be politically motivated, I nevertheless intend to pursue the people's wishes, as well as the evidence, wherever it leads. That being said, your cooperation has been very helpful, and your efforts to assist ADA Sorenson when she was in danger are truly appreciated. This office thanks you. I'm sorry, but I cannot share anything more with you until our investigation is completed. Unfortunately, you will have to continue to be patient."

Crosby rose from his chair and picked up his glasses and notebook. He turned and walked out of the room, but the tension lingered like cigarette smoke.

I peered at Brittany. She was staring at the middle of the table, her face a montage of emotions—a look I hadn't seen since we were together. Her hair was pulled back behind her ears, and her lips were slightly parted. I was feeling something I thought had died in a hospital in Boston.

She sensed my gaze. It made her self-conscious. She pressed her lips together and looked up with a sober expression.

"He's right," she said. "This is going to be a mess for a while. We still need to find and interview Alyssa Grant. Linda Lau too, based on what you've told us. Ben did likely rape and murder Ashley and Peggy Grant, but we don't have anything firm yet to tie him or the others to the first three murders, especially since the killer appears to have used a condom. That doesn't match the way Ashley and Peggy Grant were raped. As for YouSEL, the money we found in the detectives' bank accounts and homes points to organized criminal activity, but there is no connection to the company. Its lawyers pretend to be cooperating, but they keep putting us off. We don't have any leverage since it isn't implicated in anything. Even Richard Morris and his daughter are being less than forthcoming. You *are* going to have to be patient, Will. I'm sorry."

"So, I'm supposed to just cool my heels in a virtual cell while the DA's Office sorts through paperwork and Crosby runs for governor? How many years will that take?"

"I don't expect you to be charged with anything. I know Crosby. The law comes first. He isn't very political. And he hasn't even announced his candidacy yet."

"Seriously, Brittany? Crosby and Smith won't hesitate to use this case and sacrifice me in the process if it will help their chances of getting elected."

"Politics aside, the process takes time. Even longer when the case is this complicated. You know that better than me. What you *can* do is help us fill in the missing details."

"You're talking about Alyssa again?"

"Yes."

"How many times do I have to tell you I wasn't working with her? I don't know how she got on the roof. But she must have been watching your building. She probably recognized Jaworski when he went in."

"But why was she watching *my* building? You know something, Will."

I stared at her hard to signal my anger. I was half acting. I knew I had to give her more to shape the story I wanted them to believe. But I had to make it seem like she was pulling it out of me.

"Alright," I finally said. "The night Ashley was murdered, she warned Alyssa to stay away from you."

"From me? Why?"

"Alyssa never found out. But it made her think you had something to do with Ashley's murder, either directly or through someone you knew. Turns out she was right. We're probably both alive because she was on that roof."

"I'm alive because of you. For all I know, she intended to kill me with Ben."

"I don't believe that. She shot him, not you."

"It was dark. Is she that good of a shot? You can believe whatever you want, but we won't know anything until she's sitting where you are."

"I don't have all the answers. She clearly didn't tell me everything. I have a theory, but you probably won't like it."

"We're way past that, so go ahead."

I knew the session was being recorded, maybe monitored too. There was still evidence out there that pointed to my guilt. Why it hadn't shown up yet was a mystery. Before it did, I wanted to plant some seeds to influence their thinking. I needed to guide them through the maze towards the Master and away from me. Even if the Master was already dead.

"I think Ashley was having an affair with Jaworski," I said.

"What?" Brittany said and shook her head in exasperation.

"I said you wouldn't like it but hear me out. Ashley was part of my setup from the start. She was the one who arranged for Linda Lau to come on to me in Columbus two years ago. And she knew about the scheme to have Alyssa give me attention at Champagne so that I could be set up later. She probably knew a lot about what Jaworski, Champagne, and YouSEL were involved in too. That's how she found out that Alyssa was going to be murdered and that I was going to be framed for it. She warned Alyssa, but she didn't think her own life was in danger. She told Alyssa the guy behind everything would never hurt her. That's why she stayed that night after making Alyssa go. But why would she think she was safe unless she had a special relationship with the killer? And you just said Jaworski was the killer. Ashley and Alyssa were twins. They were close. Alyssa must have known about Ashley and Jaworski. She suspected he killed her. When she saw him go into your building, she followed him. She hid until she had the opportunity and shot him."

Brittany looked at me skeptically, then gazed down and shook her head slowly. She tapped her fingers rhythmically on the table. She was quiet for a long time as her tapping echoed in the room. Then she stopped tapping and looked at me.

"Where does Peggy Grant fit into your theory?"

"So, Jaworski murdered Ashley because he still needed a victim to set me up. He also wanted to punish her for warning Alyssa. He knew people would assume it was Alyssa since she was a stripper like the other victims. Alyssa's fingerprints should have been on file with the NYPD, but he found a way to delete them so no one would know the body wasn't hers. Jaworski still needed to kill Alyssa to cover his tracks. He got Peggy to hire me to find Ashley, but it was really a ploy to flush out Alyssa. When she was found dead, I'd be the obvious suspect. But Jaworski must have thought the case against me was unraveling. He needed another victim. That's why he killed Peggy, even though she didn't fit the profile. She told him I was going to stop by that day, so he timed it for when I was supposed to show up. He was going to make it look like he caught me in the act of murdering her and killed me. But I never made it because I was with Alyssa. That screwed up his plan since he had already killed Peggy. It's probably why he was so sloppy in making her murder look like the others."

"I don't know, there are a lot of holes in your theory," she said, then sighed quietly. "It does tie some things together, though. And it could explain why Ben went after Rachel Morris and me. He panicked when he learned the evidence in Peggy's murder didn't implicate you. Still, there's no real proof. But why didn't you share your theory with us earlier?"

"You never asked me what I thought, only what I knew. And like you said, there's no real proof. But I'm confident that's how it went down. Or close."

"Well, if you're so confident about that theory, who do you think shot Stefan Schuler, the other man killed on the roof?"

"Clever, but you know I didn't see it. I was trying to stop you from going off the roof."

"I know, but you must have a theory."

I pursed my lips for a moment, then said, "Alyssa is the obvious choice. But again, I didn't see it."

"That's what we thought at first. But we only found one spent casing where you said she was standing. She would have fired at least three shots if she killed Schuler too. And his entry wounds were on the right side of his head and chest. She was positioned on his left. Someone else had to be on the roof. What about your friend, Victor Bennett?"

"I told you he's not my friend. If he was there, it wasn't to help me. But I thought you said someone saw him getting on the elevator with a woman? Did you talk to her?"

"Yes. She claims she doesn't know him. He told her he forgot his key fob and asked her to press the twelfth floor for him. That button is right below the fifteenth-floor button where I live. She said she might have pressed the wrong one."

"You don't believe her?"

"No, but I can't prove anything. It seems all the security cameras were down."

"Just like at Champagne. That must have been Jaworski."

"Maybe."

"Did the bullet from Jaworski match the ones you pulled out of Schuler?"

"We don't know. The bullet that struck Ben went through his shoulder and off the roof somewhere. We may never find it."

"All I know is Schuler was one of the guys who jumped me at the bar in Columbus. There's a good chance he murdered David Bishop too. I'm not sad he's dead."

Brittany stared at me without saying anything. Her eyes were now different shades of green, as if manifesting her conflicted feelings for me.

After a long silence, she said, "How is your side?"

"It's fine. The bullet only grazed me. How are you doing?"

"Still recovering. But you know me, I'm resilient. I'll get past it. Thanks to you."

"Thanks to me?"

"You saved my life, Will. No words are enough to thank you. But you've helped me in other ways too. I'm stronger. I realize that now. It's getting me through this. I want you to know that. I just . . . I don't have anything else for you right now. I don't know if I ever will. I'm sorry. I don't want to hurt you."

We hadn't even kissed, and I was already getting the brush off. I guess it was better than another bullet in my head. I nodded and feigned an understanding smile.

"Anything else?" I said.

"Just that your investigator's license has been reinstated. I wanted to make sure you knew that. You can have your life back now."

"Yeah. Whatever that's worth."

She hesitated, then said, "When our investigation is completed, I'll return the necklace to you."

"If that's what you want. Where did you find the missing star?"

"I didn't. It must have been attached to the necklace when Ben put it on me. I was too out of it from the sleeping pills to notice. I don't even remember putting on the teddy."

"How did he get the star? I thought you said it was lost."

"I thought it was. But it was the original. I could tell from the engraving. I have no idea how he got hold of it. Maybe from Sean's family. It's weird. I guess we'll never know."

"What was Sean's last name?"

Brittany gave me an admonishing look.

"I don't want you trying to ask his family a bunch of questions," she said. "They've been through enough. Let us finish the investigation. It's over as far as you're concerned. Let it go."

"If it was over, I would let it go. But it's not. You don't really believe Jaworski did all this? The murders, framing me, recruiting Gomez, Ginelli, and whoever else? He wasn't expecting me to show up on the roof. He wasn't prepared. Neither were Gomez and Ginelli. I was led to them by someone texting me. I surprised all of them. They were trying to set me up while they were being set up. Jaworski realized that at the end. That's why he panicked. But he wasn't smart enough to see it coming. He admitted that on the roof. He couldn't have orchestrated any of this, never mind all of it."

"What texts, Will? You said they disappeared from your cell. How does that happen?"

"I don't know. It was a burner phone. But it must be possible because it happened."

"Okay, say there were texts. It wasn't the headaches or the trauma from everything you've been through. Who sent them? Who's behind all this? Wait, what about Alyssa Grant? Oh, that's right, it can't be *her*. But she *is* the logical suspect if everything you're saying is true."

"She could have shot me, but she shot Jaworski instead. Her sister was murdered by—"

"Ashley was murdered by Ben. What if he was in it with Alyssa, and she killed him to protect herself from being discovered. Everything she told you could be lies. Did you ever think about that, Will?"

"Maybe she was involved in the beginning, but I don't believe she was ever after you or me. Either way, it doesn't explain the other murders or why I was being framed. What's the motive? There has to be one. Someone else is behind all this."

"Will, I know when . . ."

"When what? Just say it, Brittany."

"Okay. I know you fucked her, and it's affecting your judgement."

344

"And how do you know that?"

"Because I know when you've fucked a woman. I've always known."

"You mean like you know I fucked the woman who shot me? But I didn't. You just convinced yourself that I did. Like you're doing now."

"You were shot in the head, Will. You were in a coma. Do you even remember?"

"I remember, Brittany. We were *one*. Do *you* remember? You were the only woman I fucked when we were together. The only woman I wanted to. It's called making love."

We sat in silence for a while. Me staring down at her delicate but firm hands. Her looking off to my left. She brushed something from her cheek. I pretended not to notice.

When it felt like it had been long enough, I took a deep breath and looked at her. She took the cue and looked at me. She offered a forgiving smile. I didn't want to accept it. I wasn't guilty. But I didn't want to fight with her anymore. I returned the smile.

"Sean Hall," she said. "That was his name."

"Thank you."

I stood up and turned to leave.

"Will," she said.

I looked back at her.

"I'm sorry," she said.

"For what?"

"For not visiting you in the hospital."

"It's in the past."

She nodded.

I left.

54

*A*lyssa sat on my lap, her legs straddling and squeezing my hips, grinding against me, making me harder with every glide. She felt hot and moist. Her arms were wrapped around my neck, her hands clawing and pulling my hair. Her tongue played inside my mouth. I pushed back with mine, our lips pressing frantically against each other. Her breasts rolled up and down my chest, her firm nipples dragging and catching on my skin. Her moans grew louder. She pulled her lips from mine and took a deep breath.

"I want you inside me," she exclaimed.

She slid her pelvis forward on my penis, writhing until I caught on her. She squealed, then groaned as her hips rotated to ease me inside her. I thrust up, and she released a shrill cry. I stayed deep inside her for an extra second. Then she lifted off me, inhaled, and dropped down on my lap, driving me harder into her. She screamed. I gasped and pulled out, then pushed back inside her as far as I could. She shrieked.

We started to move in rhythm—her lifting her pelvis, me pulling out, her dropping onto me, me thrusting inside her—both of us panting and grunting wildly.

I grabbed the back of her hair and pulled down, forcing her head back and her breasts up. I gripped her nipple with my teeth and ran my tongue over it as she bounced on me. She moaned desperately. I released her hair. She pressed her forehead against mine.

"Don't stop!" she cried. "Harder . . . Harder!"

I gasped and heaved, groaning louder and louder. I was about to come . . .

"Strangle me, Tom," she said calmly.

I looked at her. She was on top of me now, choking me with a black teddy . . .

Peggy!

A loud crash exploded in my ears. My eyes shot open. I scrambled to my knees. I felt a gun against my leg and grabbed it. My eyes scoured the room. My arm and Glock followed. I was panting, my heart pounding.

Where am I?

I blinked several times and looked around again. Sunlight was knifing in between the curtains of the windows in front of me. I was in a bed, in a room . . . in the hotel I had checked into. I remembered now.

I lowered my Glock, exhaled and dropped my chin to my chest. Then I saw my laptop lying on the floor. It had fallen off the bed—the crashing sound that woke me.

I picked it up and flipped it over. It was on the YouSEL site. Alyssa was frozen on the screen, modeling a black teddy, her lips in the process of saying something.

My cellphone buzzed. I grabbed it off the nightstand.

A text from *Unknown*: "We're not done, Mr. Chisholm."

www.ingramcontent.com/pod-product-compliance
Lightning Source LLC
Chambersburg PA
CBHW031428240626

47154CB00001B/254

9798987815816